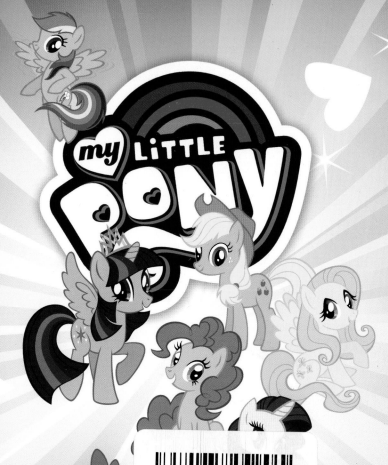

my LiTTLE PONY

The Crystalling

Special thanks to Meghan McCarthy, Eliza Hart,
Ed Lane, Beth Artale, and Michael Kelly.

ISBN: 978-1-68405-307-0
21 20 19 18   1 2 3 4

Greg Goldstein, President & Publisher
John Barber, Editor-in-Chief
Robbie Robbins, EVP/Sr. Art Director
Cara Morrison, Chief Financial Officer
Matthew Ruzicka, Chief Accounting Officer
Anita Frazier, SVP of Sales and Marketing
David Hedgecock, Associate Publisher
Jerry Bennington, VP of New Product Development
Lorelei Bunjes, VP of Digital Services
Justin Eisinger, Editorial Director, Graphic Novels & Collections
Eric Moss, Sr. Director, Licensing & Business Development

Ted Adams, IDW Founder

Licensed By:

www.IDWPUBLISHING.com

The Crystalling

Story by
Josh Haber

Adaptation by
Justin Eisinger

Edits by
Alonzo Simon

Lettering and Design by
Gilberto Lazcano

Production Assistance by
Amauri Osorio

MEET THE PONIES

Twilight Sparkle

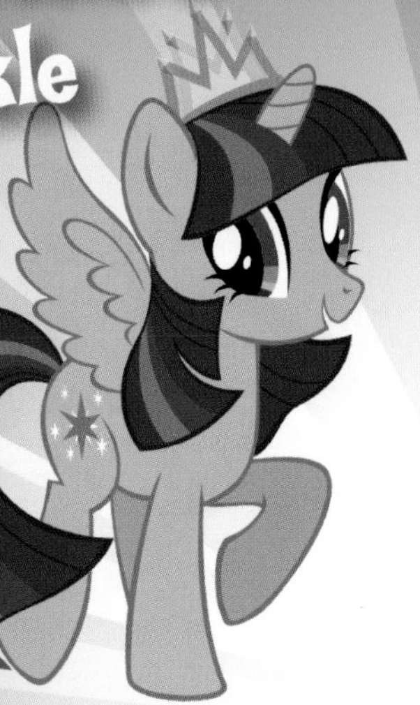

TWILIGHT SPARKLE TRIES TO FIND THE ANSWER TO EVERY QUESTION! WHETHER STUDYING A BOOK OR SPENDING TIME WITH PONY FRIENDS, SHE ALWAYS LEARNS SOMETHING NEW!

Spike

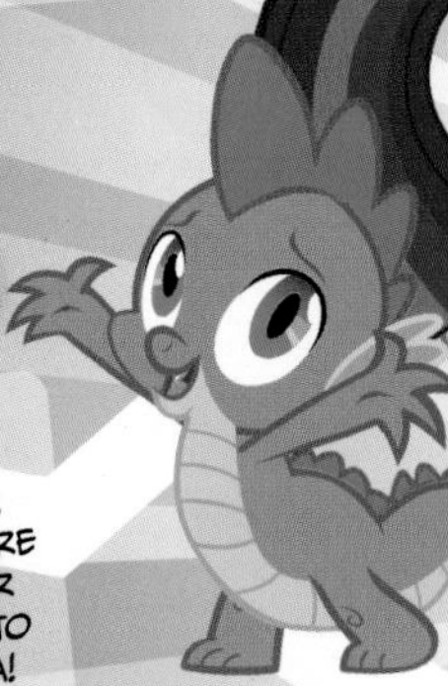

SPIKE IS TWILIGHT SPARKLE'S BEST FRIEND AND NUMBER ONE ASSISTANT. HIS FIRE BREATH CAN DELIVER SCROLLS DIRECTLY TO PRINCESS CELESTIA!

Applejack

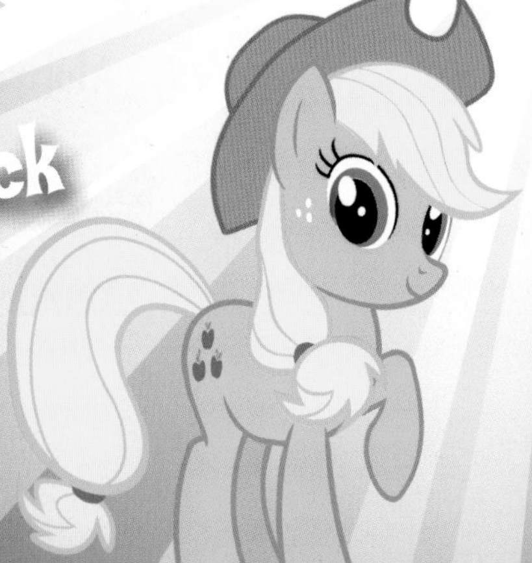

APPLEJACK IS HONEST, FRIENDLY, AND SWEET TO THE CORE! SHE LOVES TO BE OUTSIDE, AND HER PONY FRIENDS KNOW THEY CAN ALWAYS COUNT ON HER.

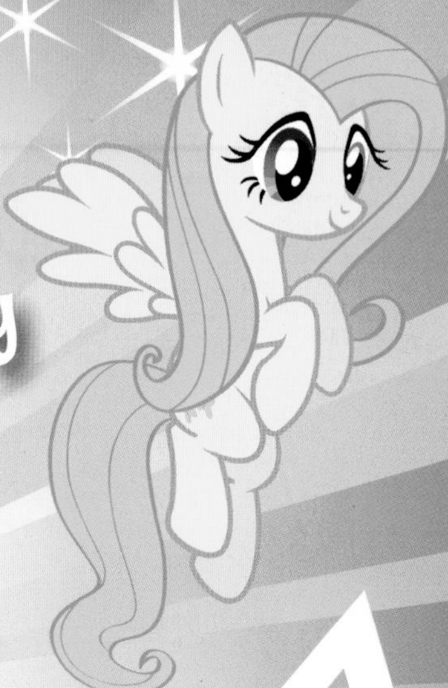

Fluttershy

FLUTTERSHY IS A KIND AND GENTLE PONY WITH A BIG HEART. SHE LIKES TO TAKE CARE OF OTHERS, ESPECIALLY HER LITTLE ANIMAL FRIENDS.

Rarity

RARITY KNOWS HOW TO ADD SPARKLE TO ANY OUTFIT! SHE LOVES TO GIVE HER PONY FRIENDS ADVICE ON THE LATEST PONY FASHIONS AND HAIRSTYLES.

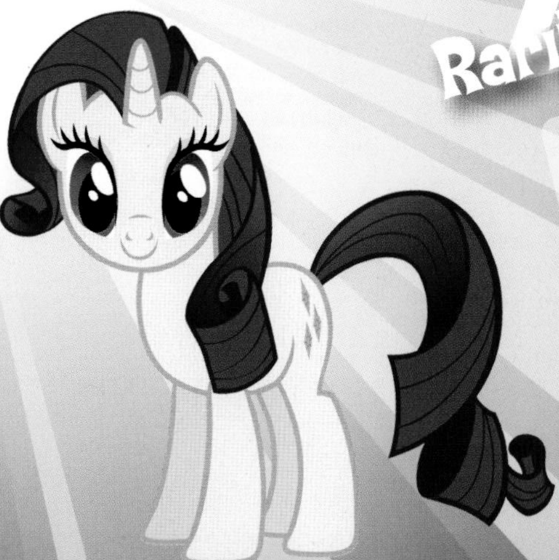

Pinkie Pie

PINKIE PIE KEEPS HER PONY FRIENDS LAUGHING AND SMILING ALL DAY! CHEERFUL AND PLAYFUL, SHE ALWAYS LOOKS ON THE BRIGHT SIDE.

Rainbow Dash

RAINBOW DASH LOVES TO FLY AS FAST AS SHE CAN! SHE IS ALWAYS READY TO PLAY A GAME, GO ON AN ADVENTURE, OR HELP OUT ONE OF HER PONY FRIENDS.

Princess Celestia

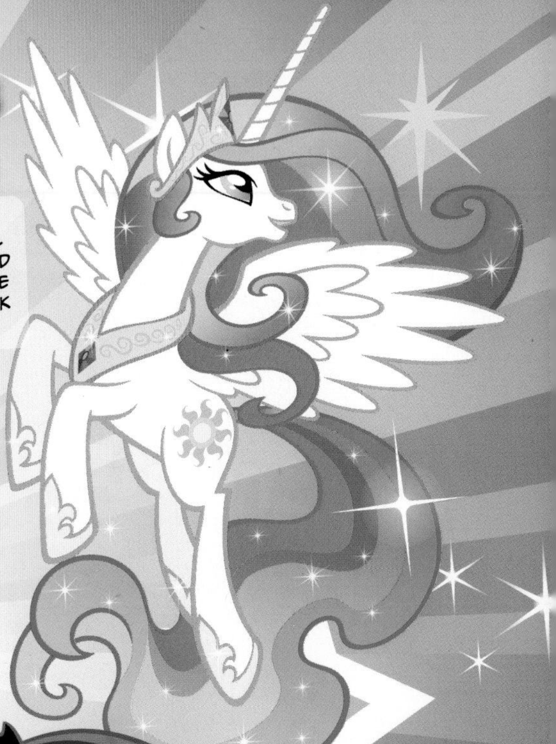

PRINCESS CELESTIA IS A MAGICAL AND BEAUTIFUL PONY WHO RULES THE LAND OF EQUESTRIA. ALL OF THE PONIES IN PONYVILLE LOOK UP TO HER!

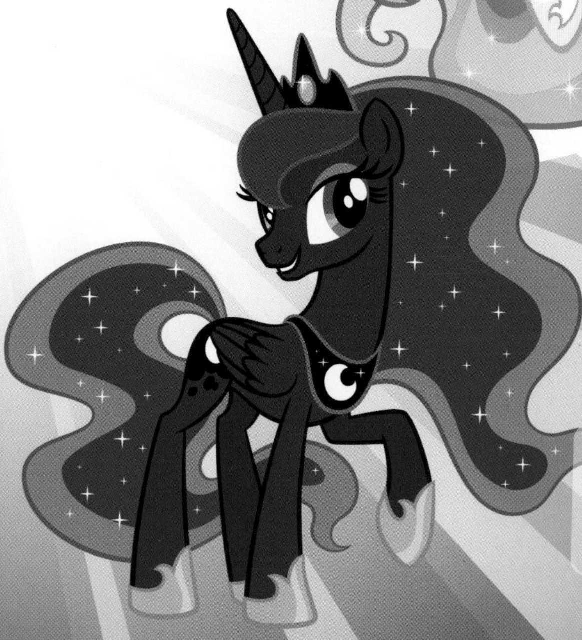

Princess Luna

ONCE CALLED NIGHTMARE MOON, A VILLAIN IMPRISONED ON THE LUNAR SURFACE, LUNA NOW RULES EQUESTRIA ALONGSIDE HER SISTER, PRINCESS CELESTIA.

The Crystalling

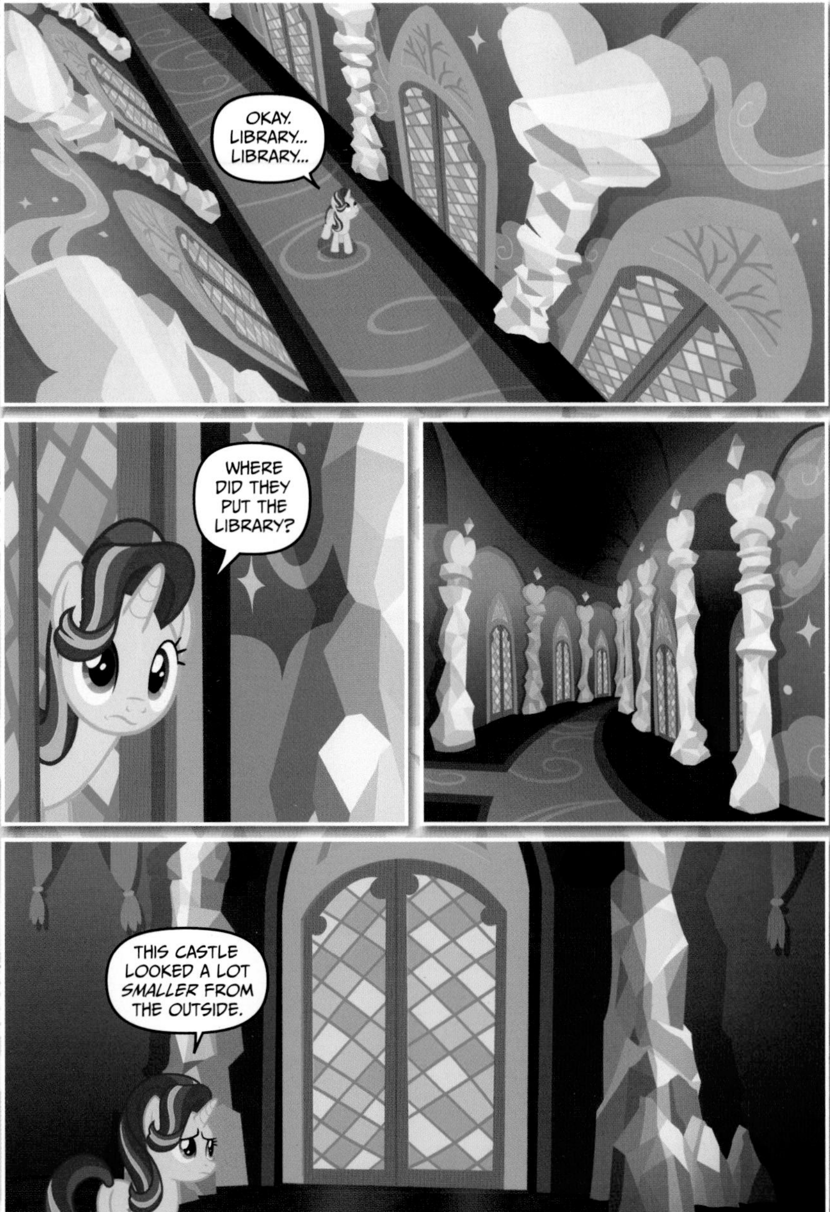
OKAY. LIBRARY... LIBRARY...
WHERE DID THEY PUT THE LIBRARY?
THIS CASTLE LOOKED A LOT *SMALLER* FROM THE OUTSIDE.

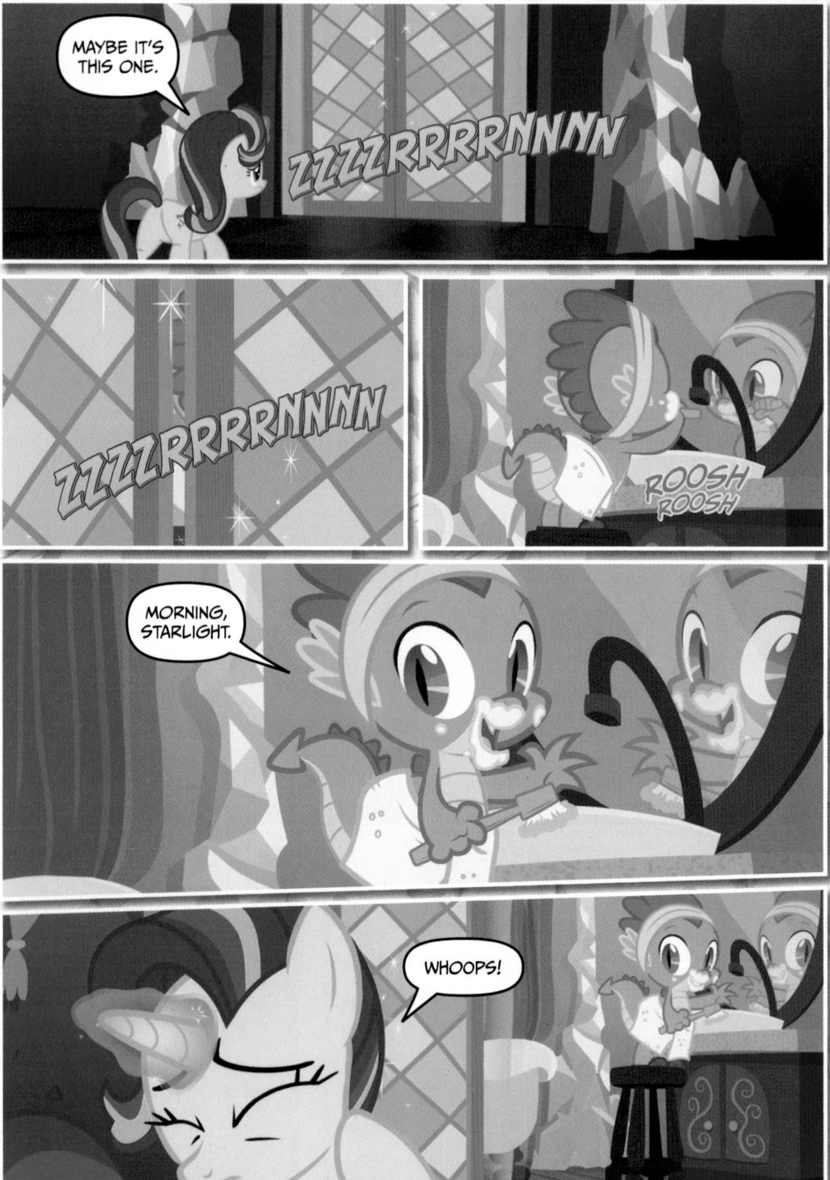
MAYBE IT'S THIS ONE.
ZZZZRRRRRNNNN
ZZZZRRRRRNNNN
ROOSH ROOSH
MORNING, STARLIGHT.
WHOOPS!

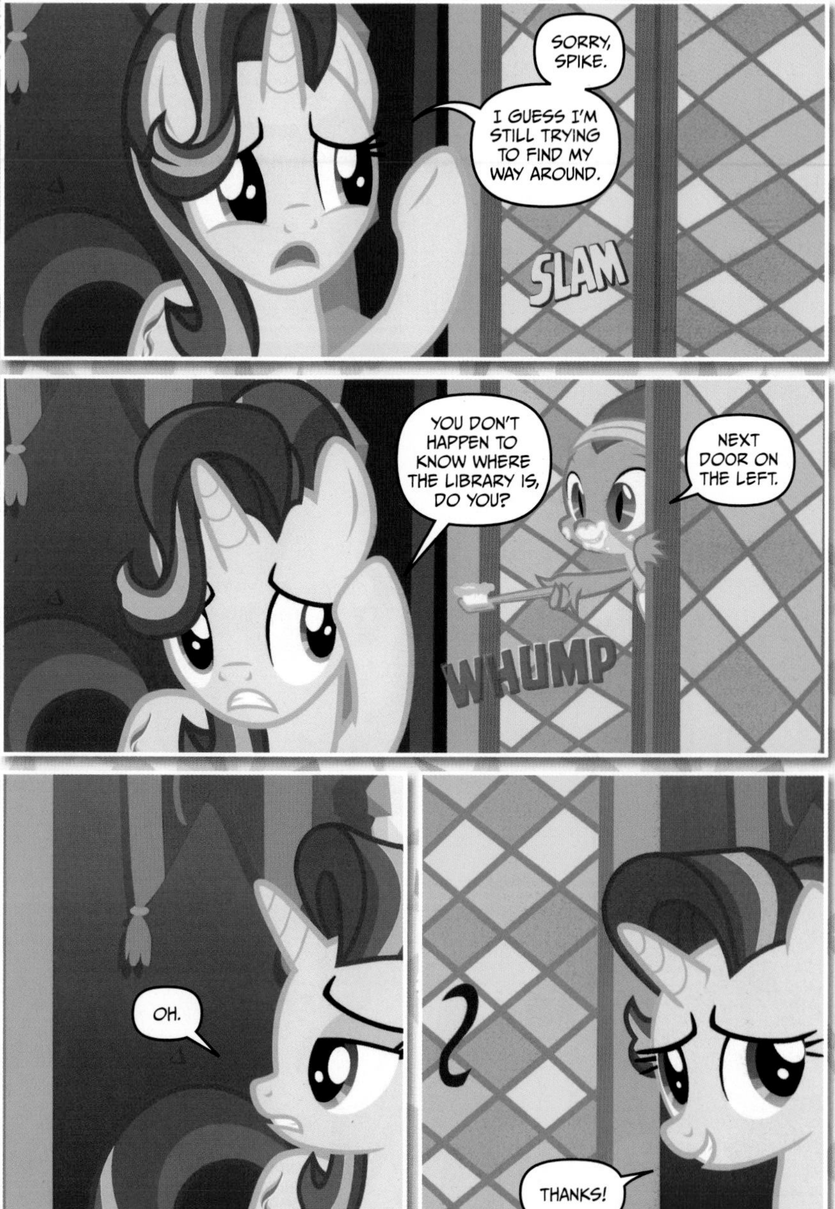
SORRY, SPIKE.
I GUESS I'M STILL TRYING TO FIND MY WAY AROUND.
SLAM
YOU DON'T HAPPEN TO KNOW WHERE THE LIBRARY IS, DO YOU?
NEXT DOOR ON THE LEFT.
WHUMP
OH.
THANKS!

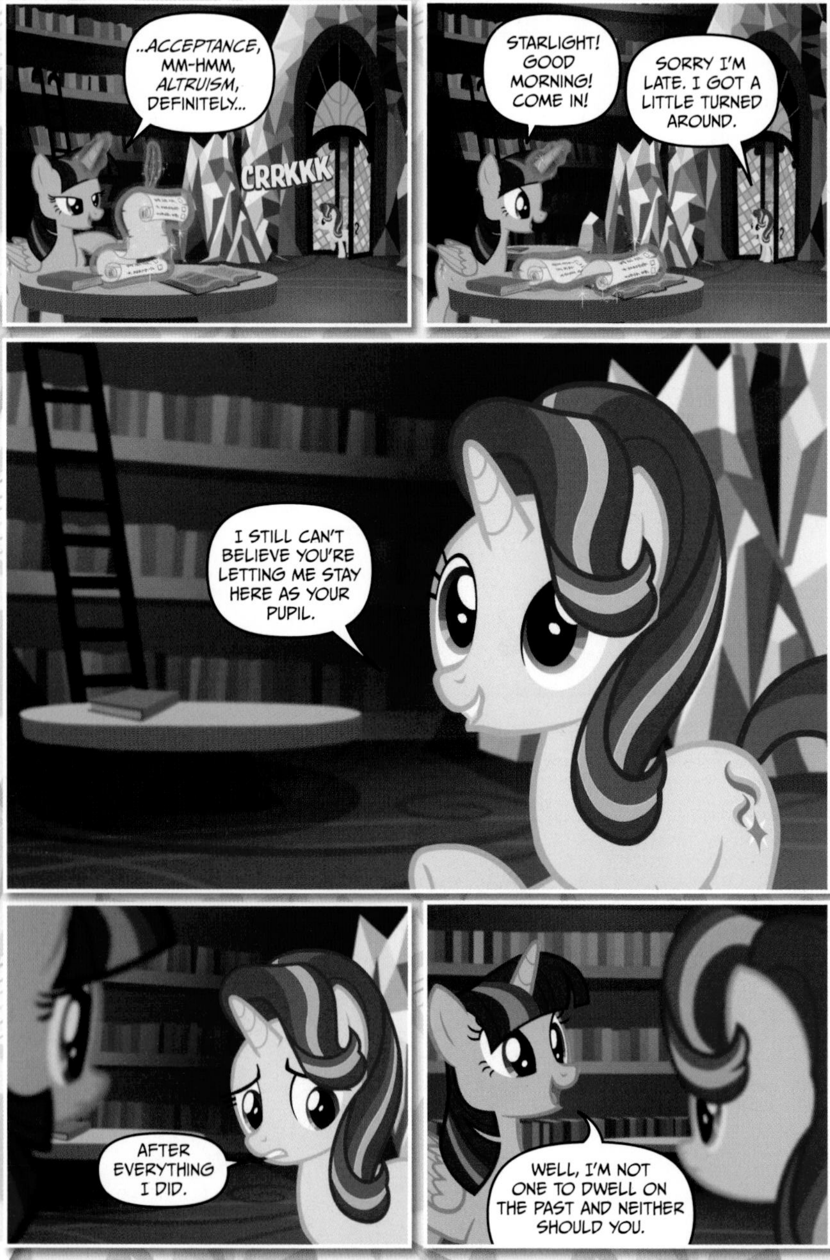
...ACCEPTANCE, MM-HMM, ALTRUISM, DEFINITELY...
CRRKKK
STARLIGHT! GOOD MORNING! COME IN!
SORRY I'M LATE. I GOT A LITTLE TURNED AROUND.
I STILL CAN'T BELIEVE YOU'RE LETTING ME STAY HERE AS YOUR PUPIL.
AFTER EVERYTHING I DID.
WELL, I'M NOT ONE TO DWELL ON THE PAST AND NEITHER SHOULD YOU.

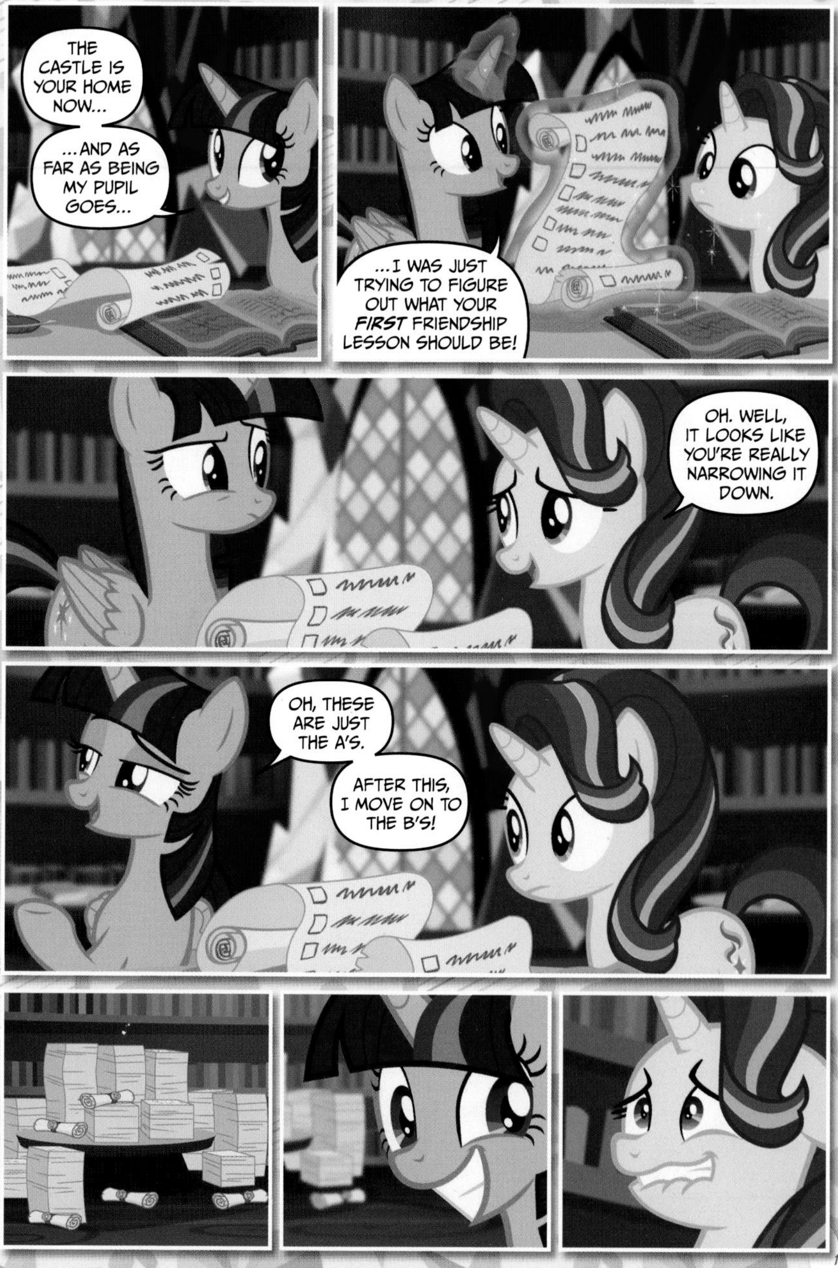
THE CASTLE IS YOUR HOME NOW...
...AND AS FAR AS BEING MY PUPIL GOES...
...I WAS JUST TRYING TO FIGURE OUT WHAT YOUR FIRST FRIENDSHIP LESSON SHOULD BE!
OH. WELL, IT LOOKS LIKE YOU'RE REALLY NARROWING IT DOWN.
OH, THESE ARE JUST THE A'S.
AFTER THIS, I MOVE ON TO THE B'S!

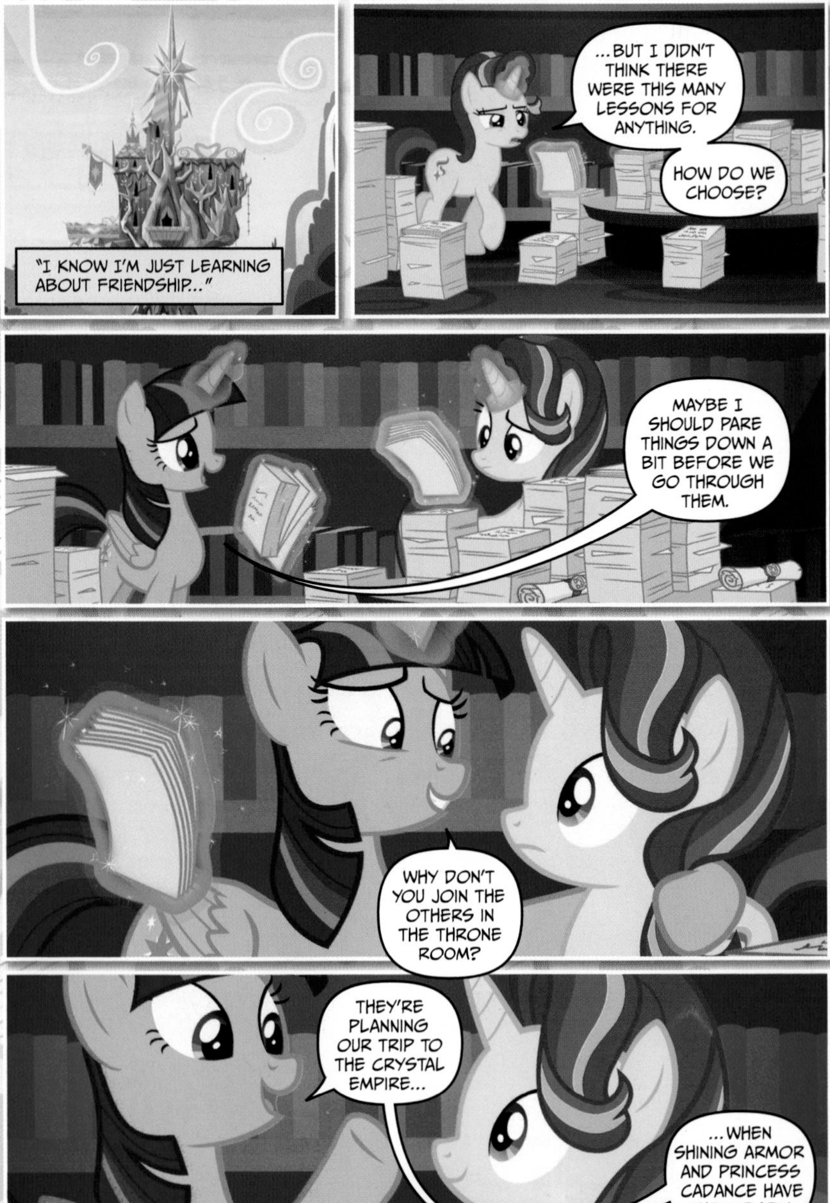
"I KNOW I'M JUST LEARNING ABOUT FRIENDSHIP..."
...BUT I DIDN'T THINK THERE WERE THIS MANY LESSONS FOR ANYTHING.
HOW DO WE CHOOSE?
MAYBE I SHOULD PARE THINGS DOWN A BIT BEFORE WE GO THROUGH THEM.
WHY DON'T YOU JOIN THE OTHERS IN THE THRONE ROOM?
THEY'RE PLANNING OUR TRIP TO THE CRYSTAL EMPIRE...
...WHEN SHINING ARMOR AND PRINCESS CADANCE HAVE THEIR *BABY*.

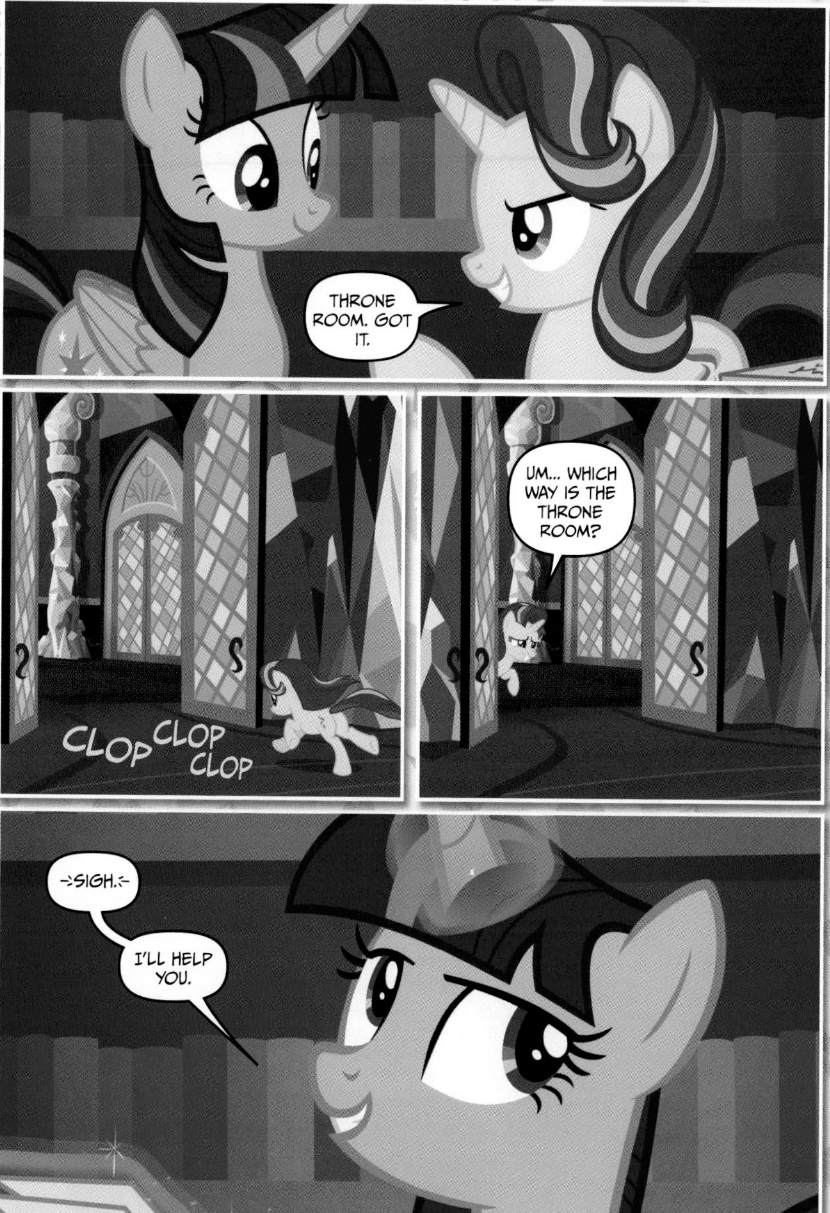
THRONE ROOM. GOT IT.
CLOP CLOP CLOP
UM... WHICH WAY IS THE THRONE ROOM?
-SIGH.-
I'LL HELP YOU.

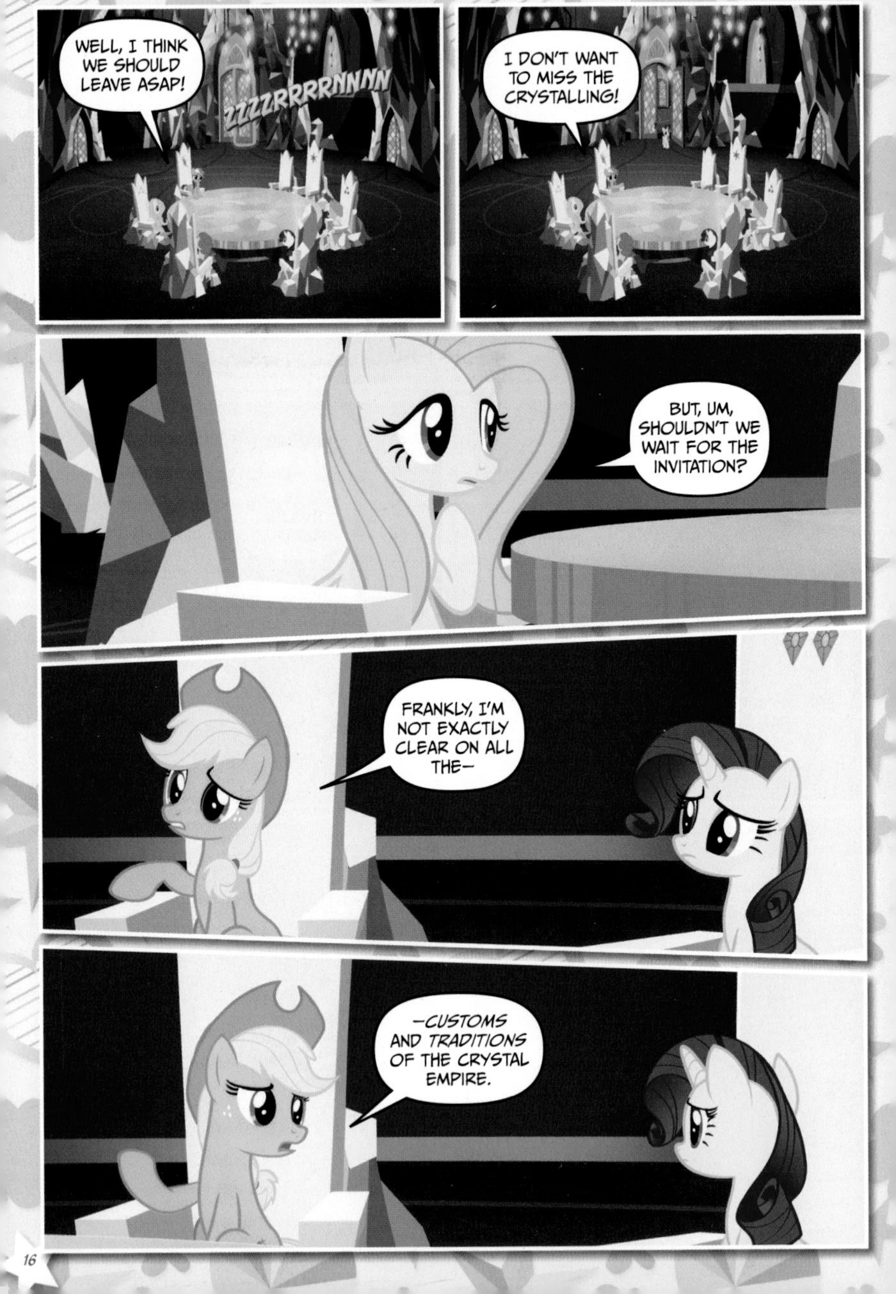
WELL, I THINK WE SHOULD LEAVE ASAP!
ZZZZRRRRNNNN
I DON'T WANT TO MISS THE CRYSTALLING!
BUT, UM, SHOULDN'T WE WAIT FOR THE INVITATION?
FRANKLY, I'M NOT EXACTLY CLEAR ON ALL THE–
–*CUSTOMS* AND *TRADITIONS* OF THE CRYSTAL EMPIRE.

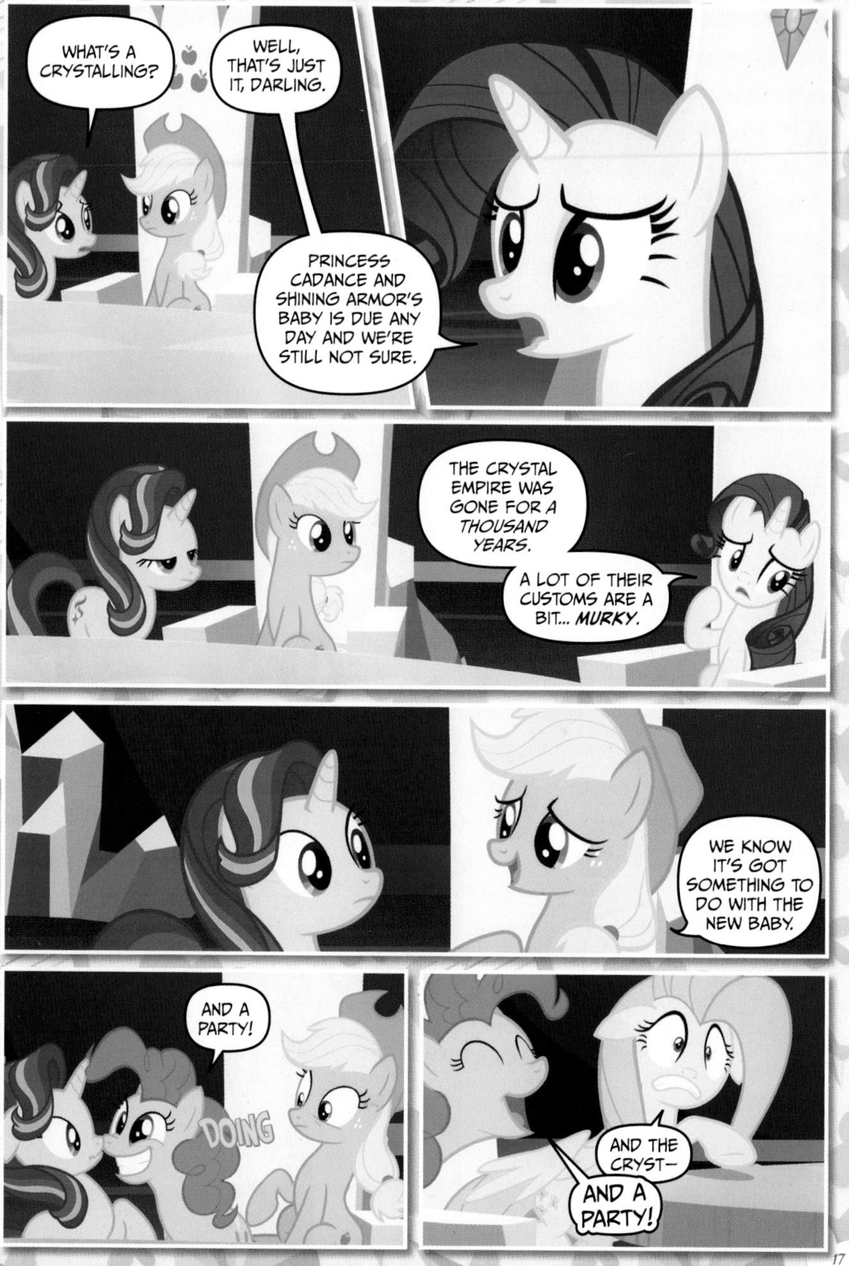
WHAT'S A CRYSTALLING?
WELL, THAT'S JUST IT, DARLING.
PRINCESS CADANCE AND SHINING ARMOR'S BABY IS DUE ANY DAY AND WE'RE STILL NOT SURE.
THE CRYSTAL EMPIRE WAS GONE FOR A *THOUSAND* YEARS.
A LOT OF THEIR CUSTOMS ARE A BIT... ***MURKY***.
WE KNOW IT'S GOT SOMETHING TO DO WITH THE NEW BABY.
AND A PARTY!
DOING
AND THE CRYST—
AND A PARTY!

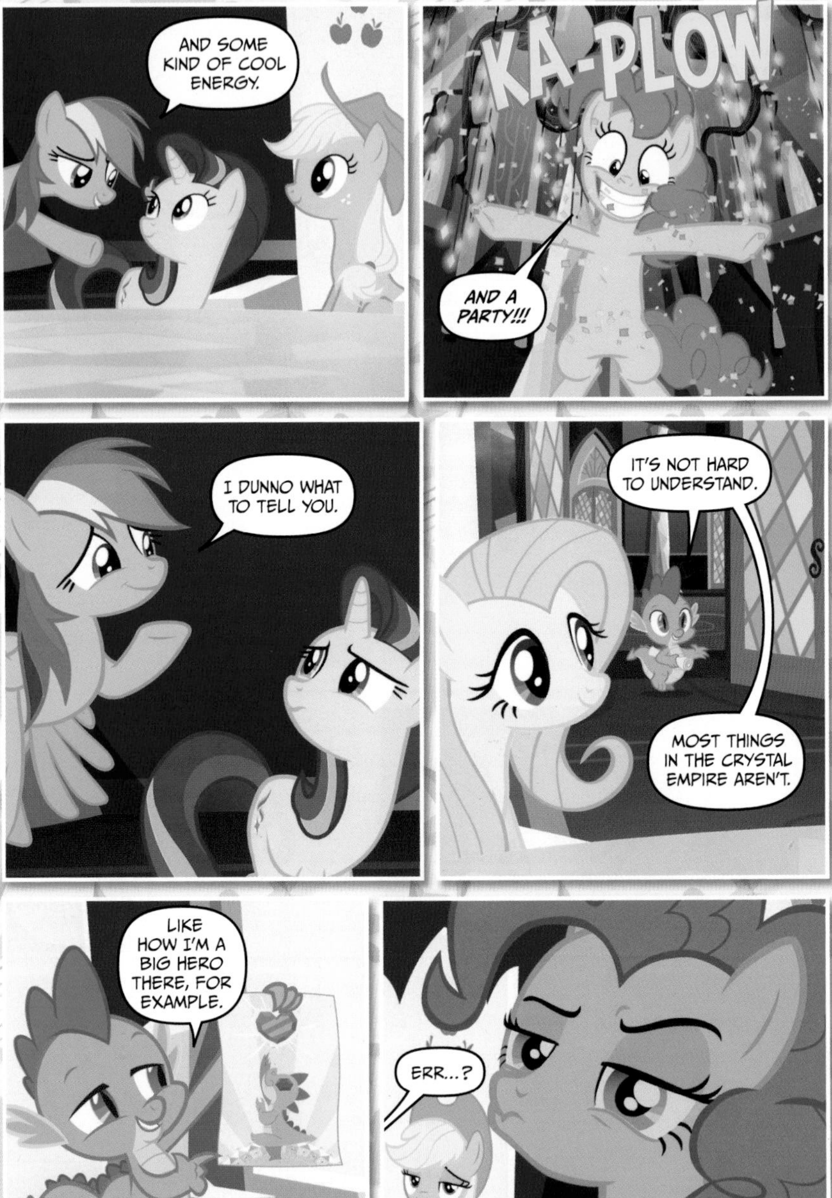
AND SOME KIND OF COOL ENERGY.
KA-PLOW
AND A PARTY!!!
I DUNNO WHAT TO TELL YOU.
IT'S NOT HARD TO UNDERSTAND.
MOST THINGS IN THE CRYSTAL EMPIRE AREN'T.
LIKE HOW I'M A BIG HERO THERE, FOR EXAMPLE.
ERR...?

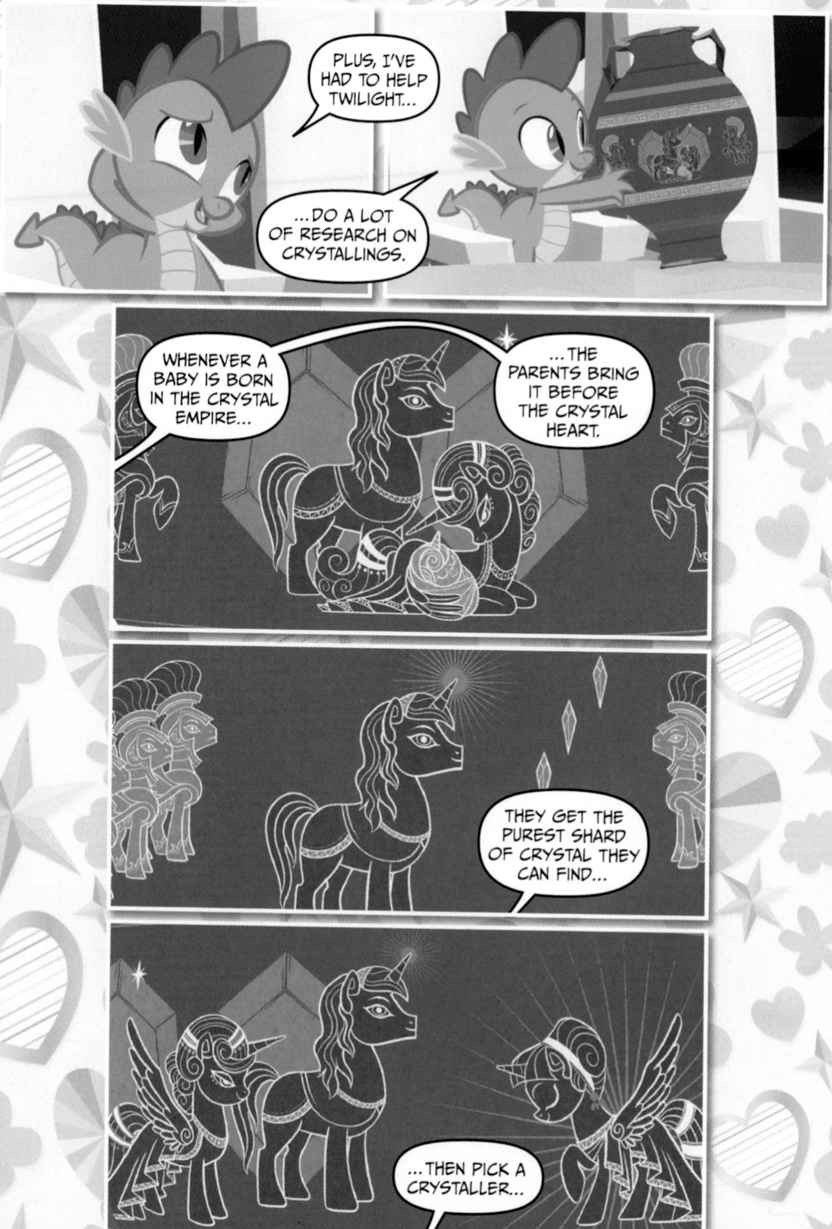
PLUS, I'VE HAD TO HELP TWILIGHT...
...DO A LOT OF RESEARCH ON CRYSTALLINGS.
WHENEVER A BABY IS BORN IN THE CRYSTAL EMPIRE...
...THE PARENTS BRING IT BEFORE THE CRYSTAL HEART.
THEY GET THE PUREST SHARD OF CRYSTAL THEY CAN FIND...
...THEN PICK A CRYSTALLER...

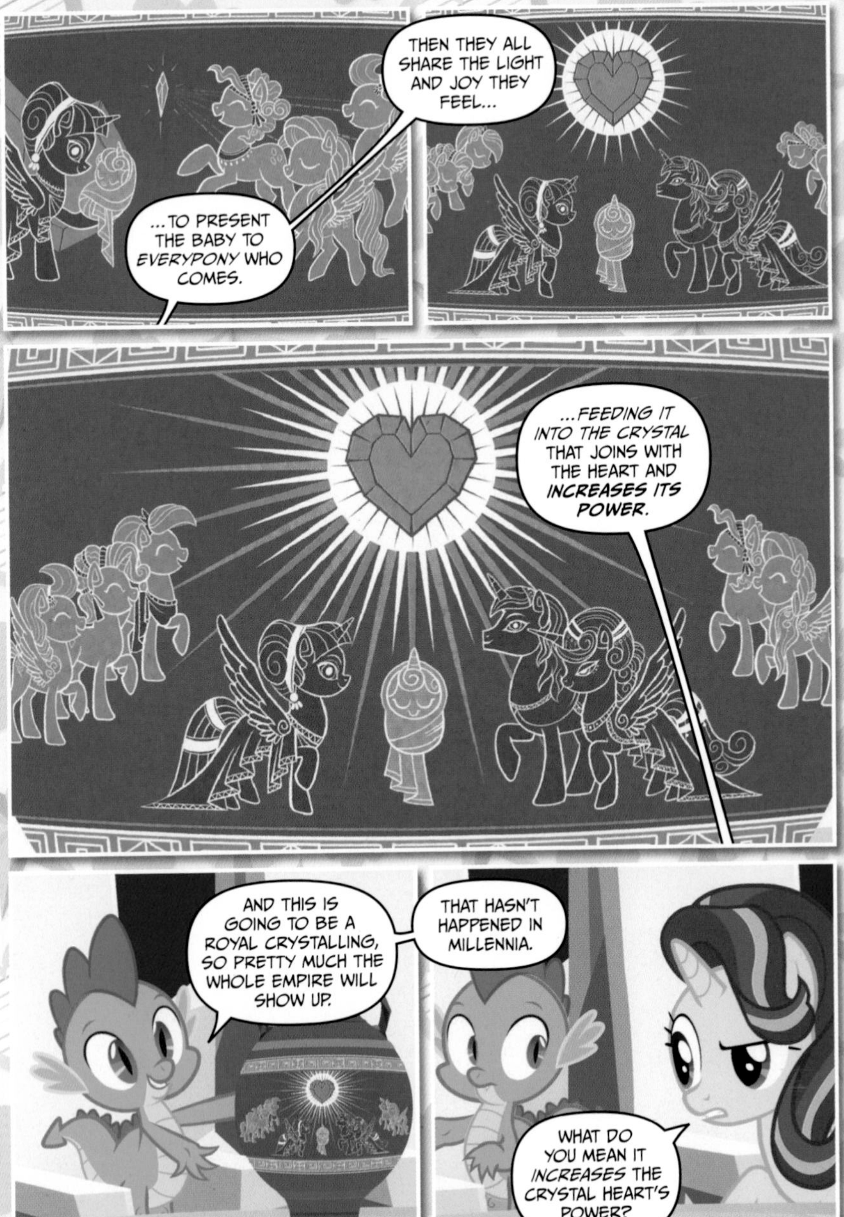
...TO PRESENT THE BABY TO EVERYPONY WHO COMES.
THEN THEY ALL SHARE THE LIGHT AND JOY THEY FEEL...
...FEEDING IT INTO THE CRYSTAL THAT JOINS WITH THE HEART AND INCREASES ITS POWER.
AND THIS IS GOING TO BE A ROYAL CRYSTALLING, SO PRETTY MUCH THE WHOLE EMPIRE WILL SHOW UP.
THAT HASN'T HAPPENED IN MILLENNIA.
WHAT DO YOU MEAN IT INCREASES THE CRYSTAL HEART'S POWER?

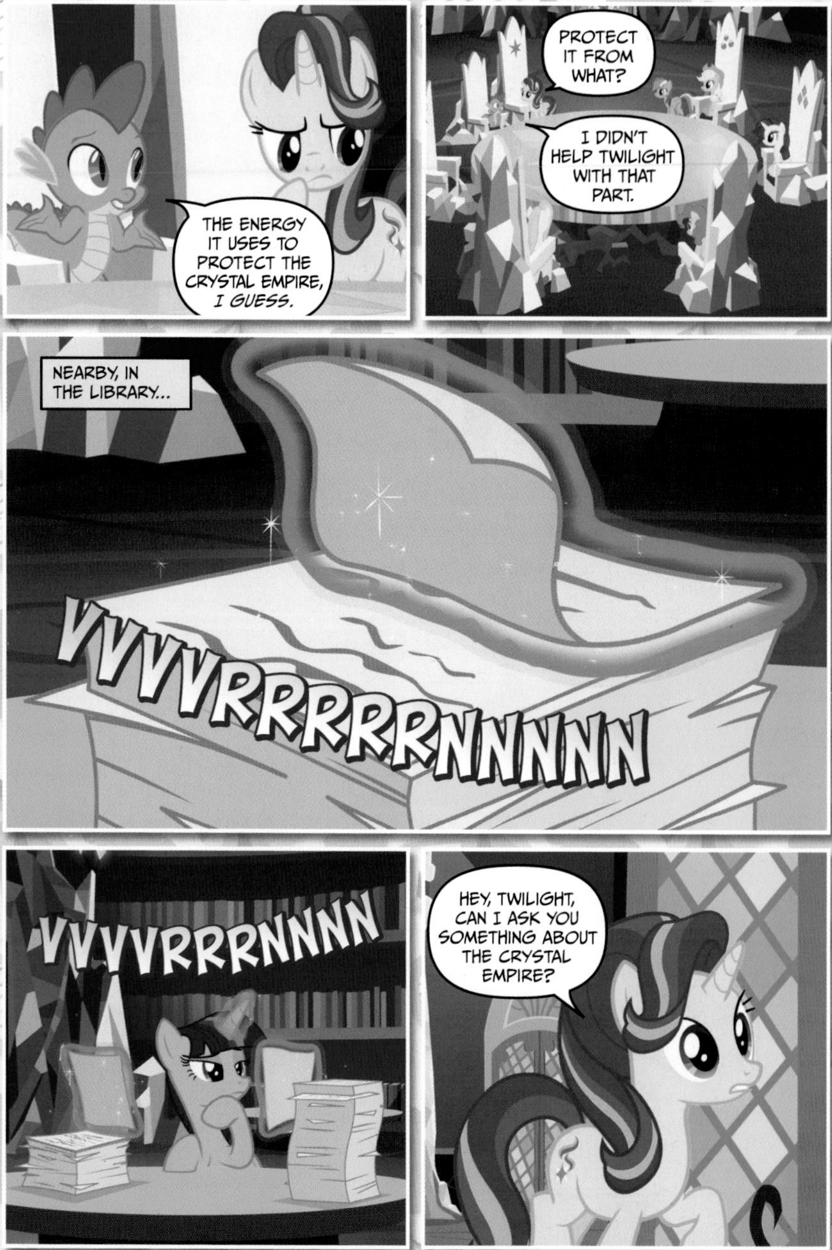
THE ENERGY IT USES TO PROTECT THE CRYSTAL EMPIRE, I GUESS.
PROTECT IT FROM WHAT?
I DIDN'T HELP TWILIGHT WITH THAT PART.
NEARBY, IN THE LIBRARY...
VVVVRRRRRRNNNNNN
VVVVRRRNNNNN
HEY, TWILIGHT, CAN I ASK YOU SOMETHING ABOUT THE CRYSTAL EMPIRE?

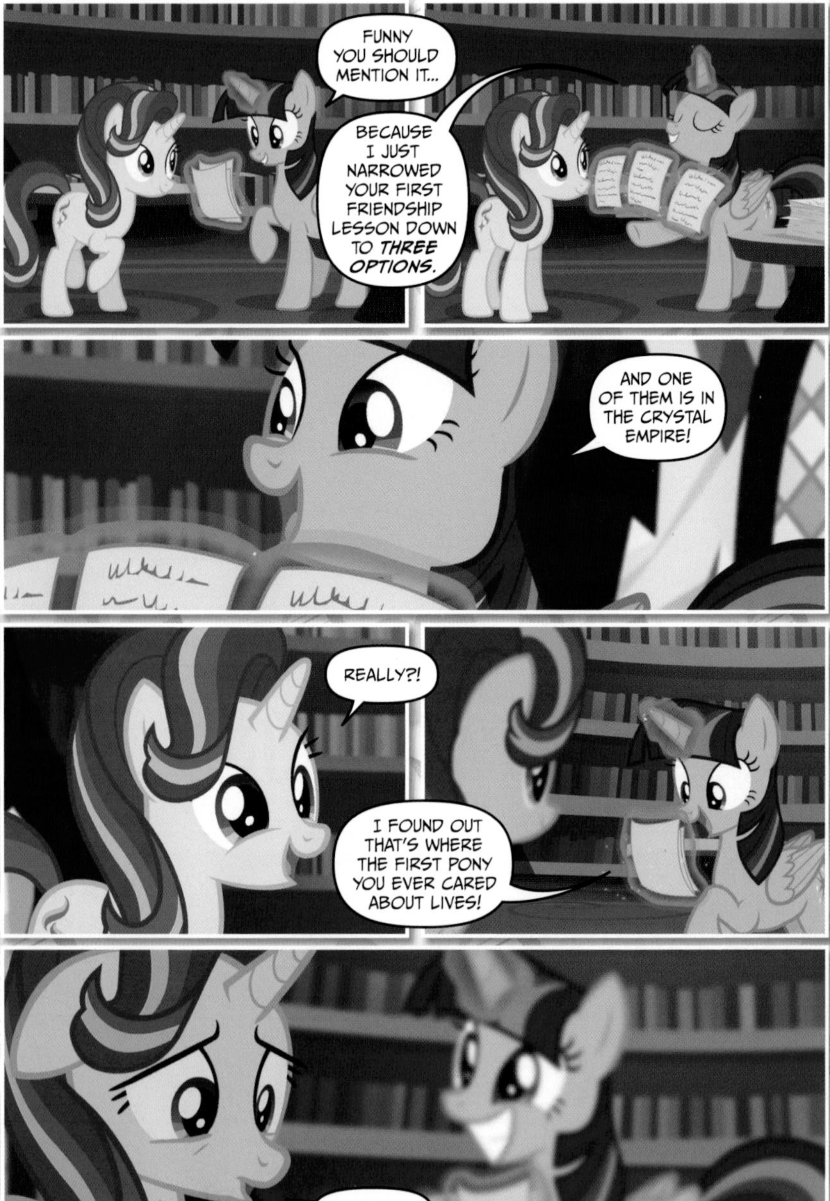
FUNNY YOU SHOULD MENTION IT...
BECAUSE I JUST NARROWED YOUR FIRST FRIENDSHIP LESSON DOWN TO *THREE OPTIONS.*
AND ONE OF THEM IS IN THE CRYSTAL EMPIRE!
REALLY?!
I FOUND OUT THAT'S WHERE THE FIRST PONY YOU EVER CARED ABOUT LIVES!
SUNBURST?

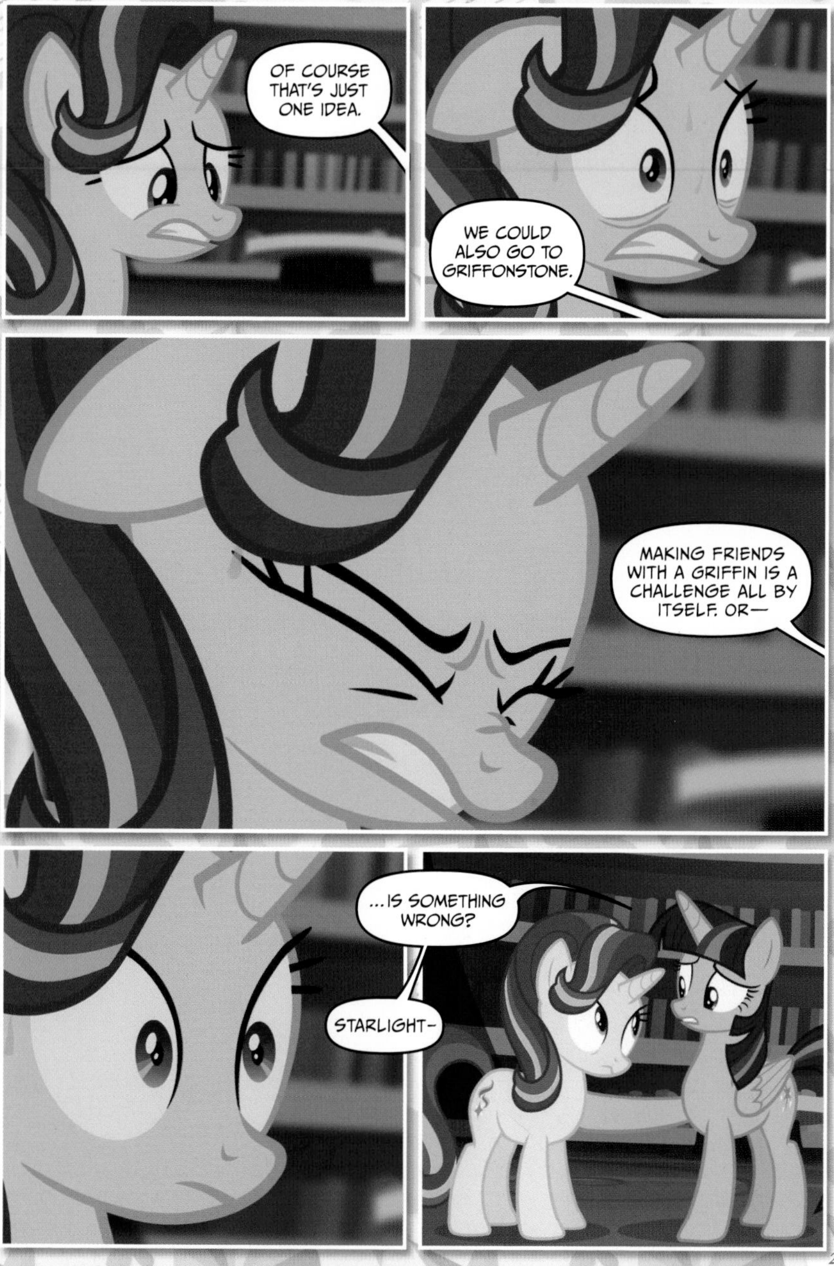
OF COURSE THAT'S JUST ONE IDEA.
WE COULD ALSO GO TO GRIFFONSTONE.
MAKING FRIENDS WITH A GRIFFIN IS A CHALLENGE ALL BY ITSELF. OR—
STARLIGHT-
...IS SOMETHING WRONG?

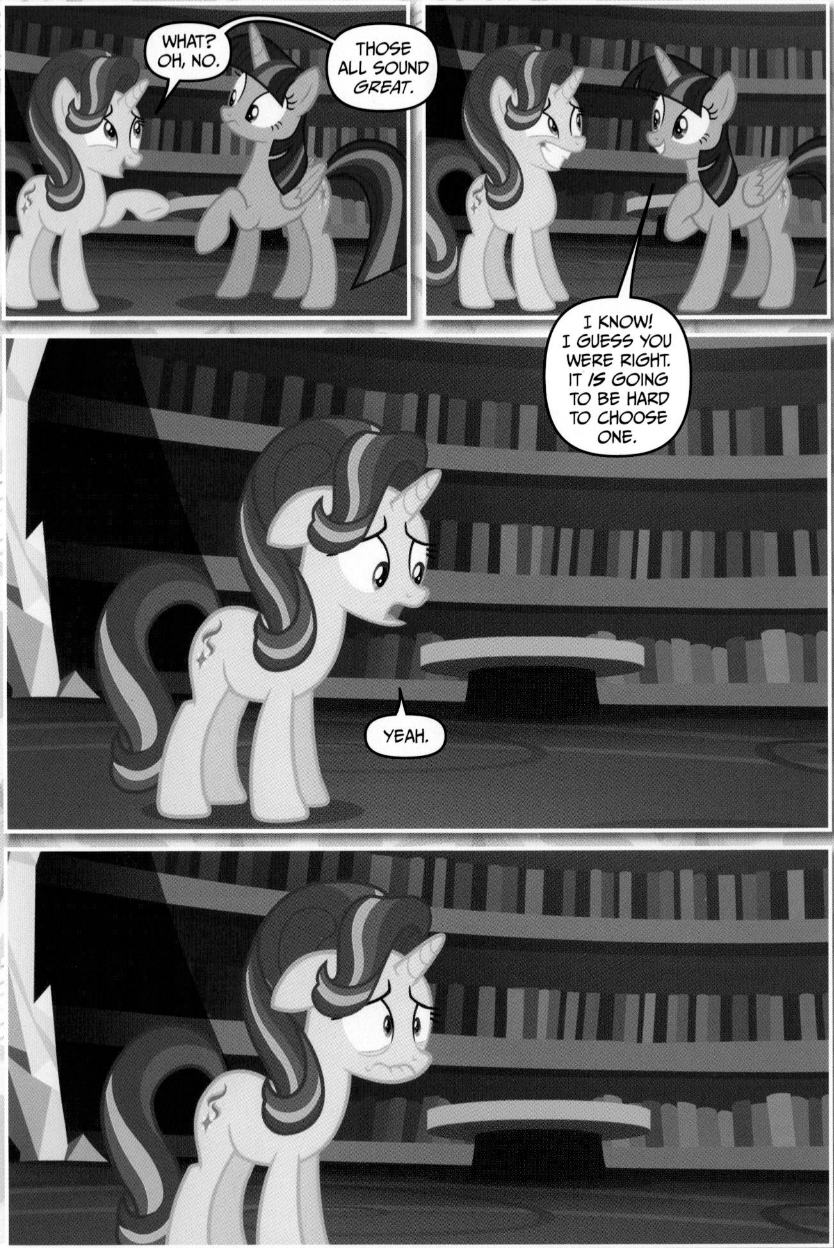
WHAT? OH, NO.
THOSE ALL SOUND GREAT.
I KNOW! I GUESS YOU WERE RIGHT. IT IS GOING TO BE HARD TO CHOOSE ONE.
YEAH.

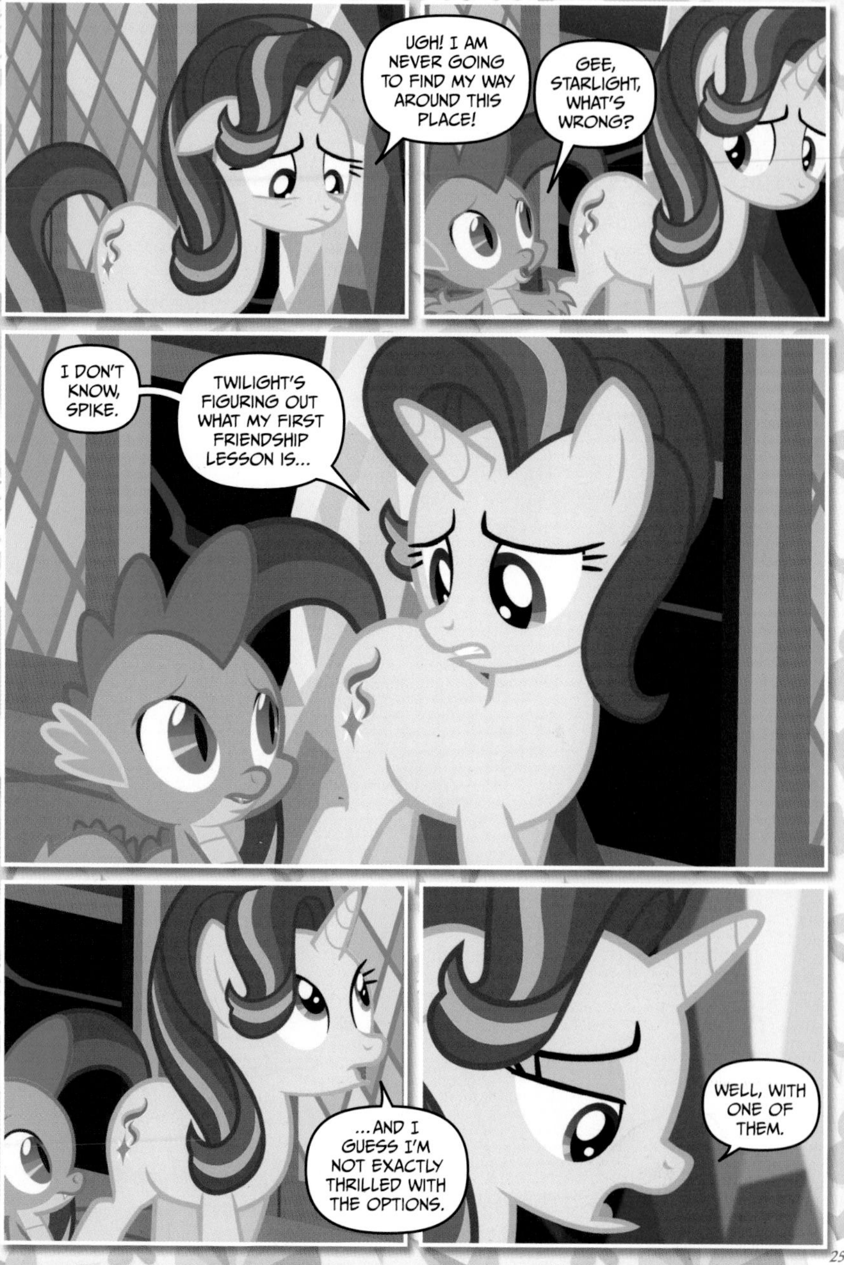
UGH! I AM NEVER GOING TO FIND MY WAY AROUND THIS PLACE!
GEE, STARLIGHT, WHAT'S WRONG?
I DON'T KNOW, SPIKE.
TWILIGHT'S FIGURING OUT WHAT MY FIRST FRIENDSHIP LESSON IS...
...AND I GUESS I'M NOT EXACTLY THRILLED WITH THE OPTIONS.
WELL, WITH ONE OF THEM.

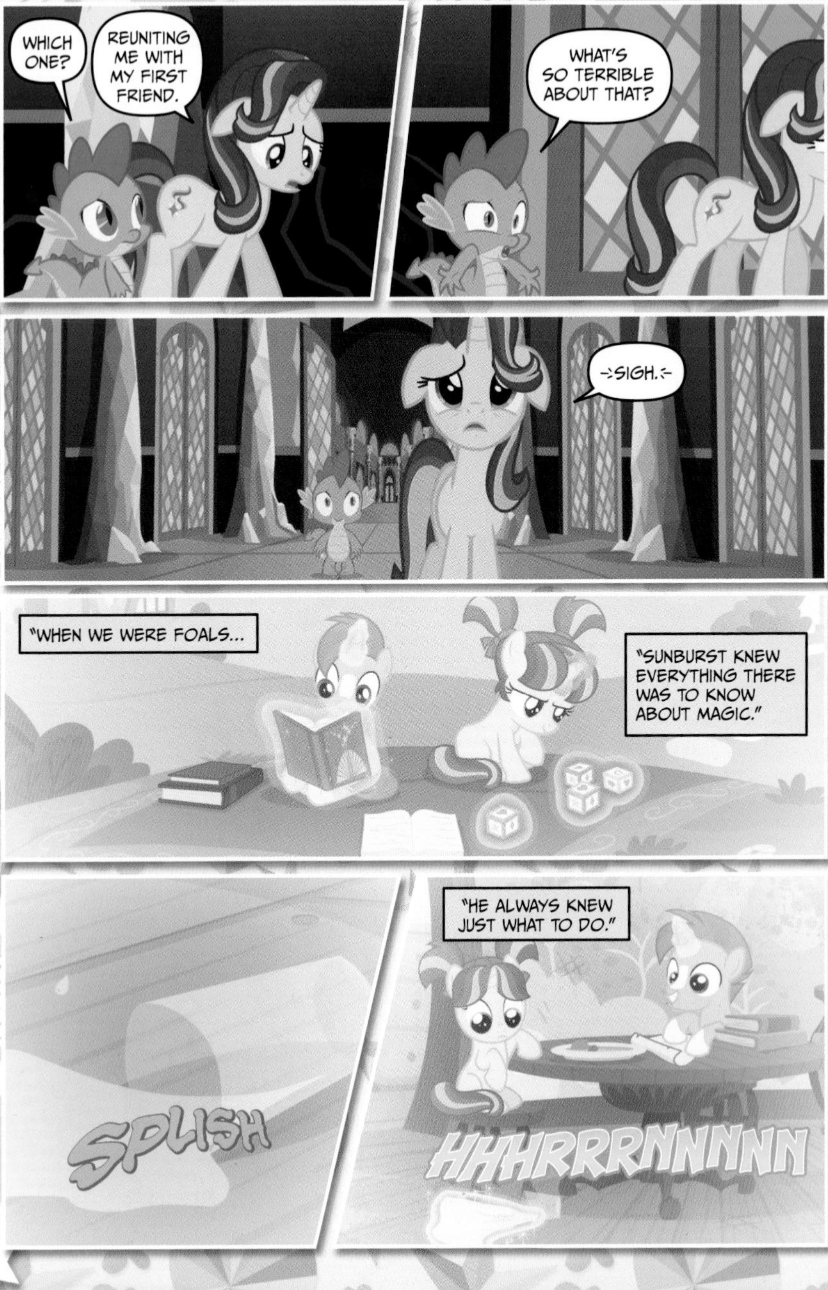

WHICH ONE?
REUNITING ME WITH MY FIRST FRIEND.
WHAT'S SO TERRIBLE ABOUT THAT?
-SIGH.-
"WHEN WE WERE FOALS...
"SUNBURST KNEW EVERYTHING THERE WAS TO KNOW ABOUT MAGIC."
SPLISH
"HE ALWAYS KNEW JUST WHAT TO DO."
HHHRRRNNNNN

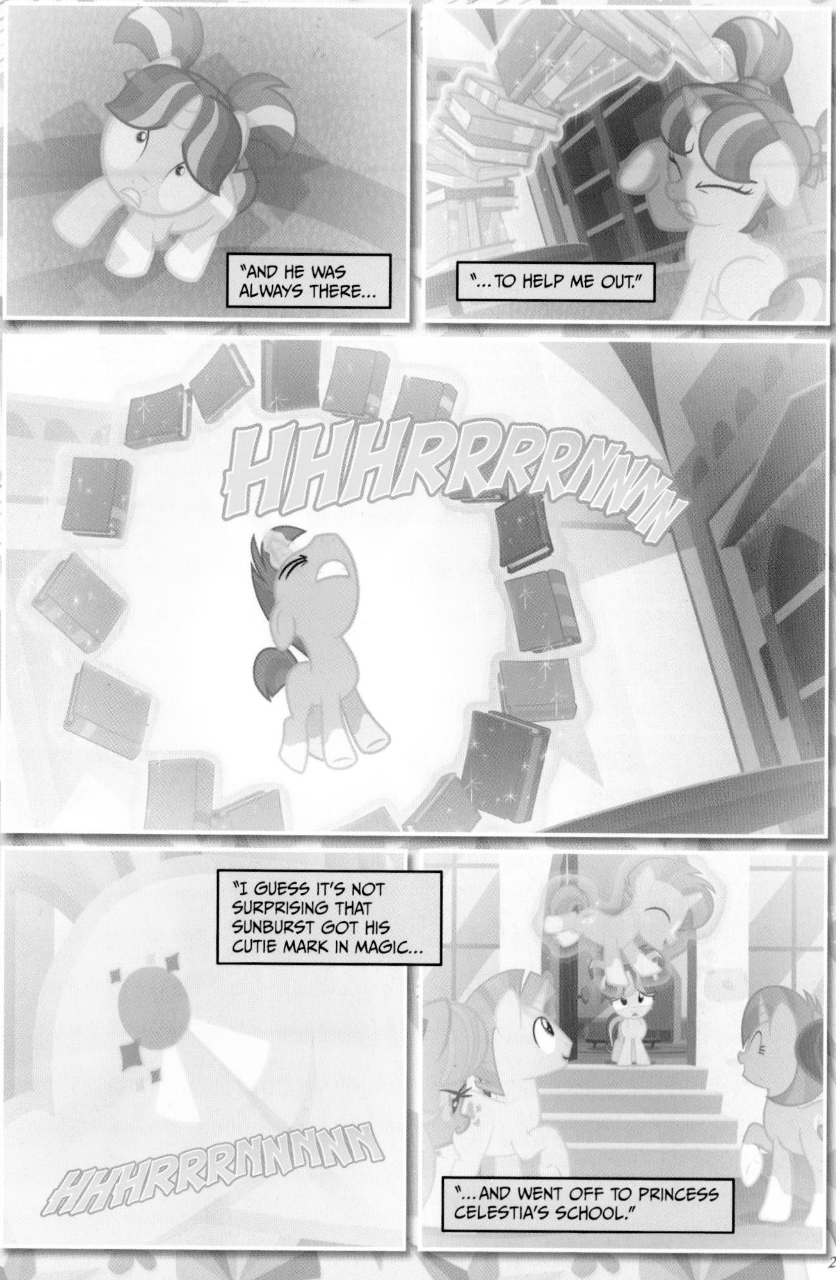
"AND HE WAS ALWAYS THERE...
"...TO HELP ME OUT."
HHHRRRRNNNN
"I GUESS IT'S NOT SURPRISING THAT SUNBURST GOT HIS CUTIE MARK IN MAGIC...
HHHRRRNNNNNN
"...AND WENT OFF TO PRINCESS CELESTIA'S SCHOOL."

"BUT WHEN HE LEFT..."

YOU BLAMED CUTIE MARKS AND *STRIPPED* A WHOLE VILLAGE OF THEIRS...

...AND WHEN TWILIGHT AND THE OTHERS STOPPED YOU...

...YOU WENT *BACK IN TIME* AND ALMOST *DESTROYED* EQUESTRIA.

POOOOOOF

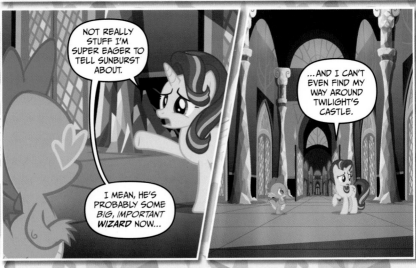

NOT REALLY STUFF I'M SUPER EAGER TO TELL SUNBURST ABOUT.

I MEAN, HE'S PROBABLY SOME *BIG, IMPORTANT WIZARD* NOW...

...AND I CAN'T EVEN FIND MY WAY AROUND TWILIGHT'S CASTLE.

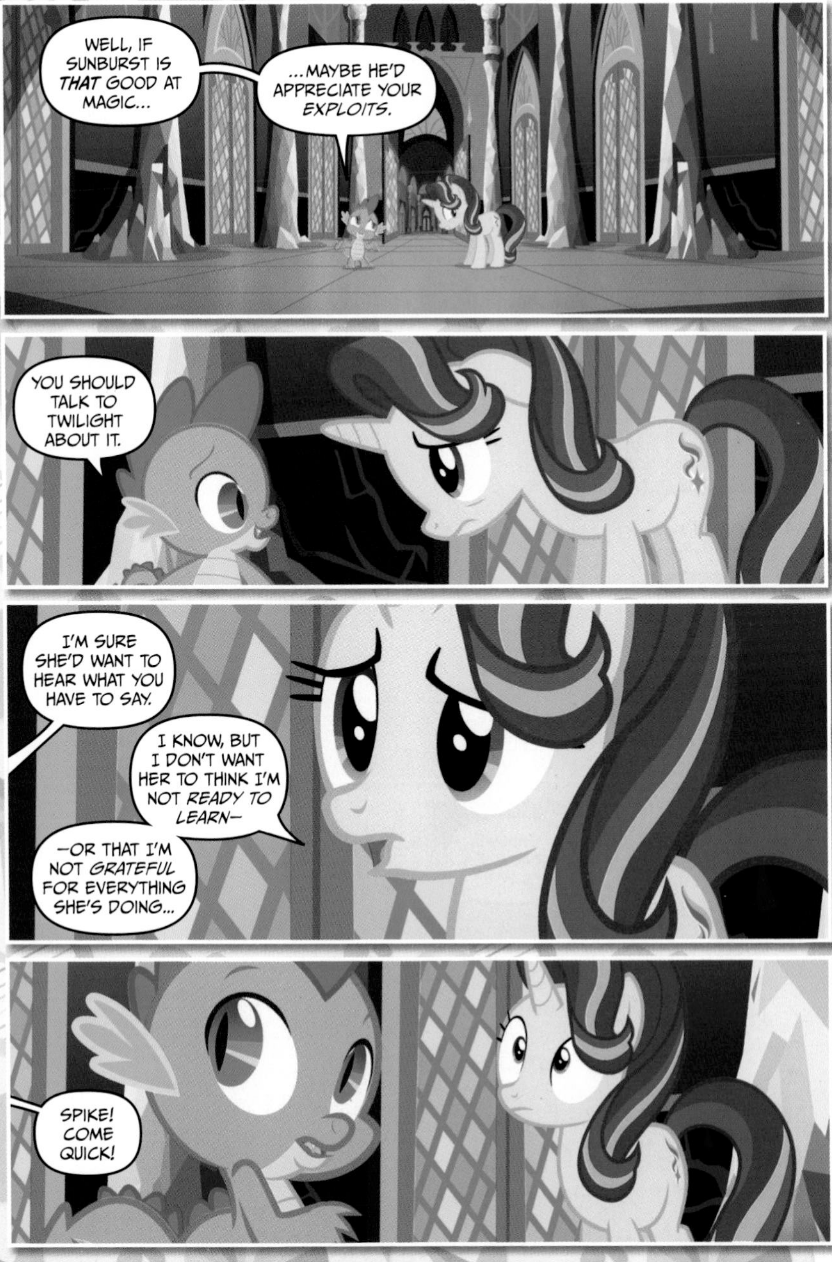
WELL, IF SUNBURST IS *THAT* GOOD AT MAGIC...
...MAYBE HE'D APPRECIATE YOUR *EXPLOITS*.
YOU SHOULD TALK TO TWILIGHT ABOUT IT.
I'M SURE SHE'D WANT TO HEAR WHAT YOU HAVE TO SAY.
I KNOW, BUT I DON'T WANT HER TO THINK I'M NOT *READY TO LEARN*—
—OR THAT I'M NOT *GRATEFUL* FOR EVERYTHING SHE'S DOING...
SPIKE! COME QUICK!

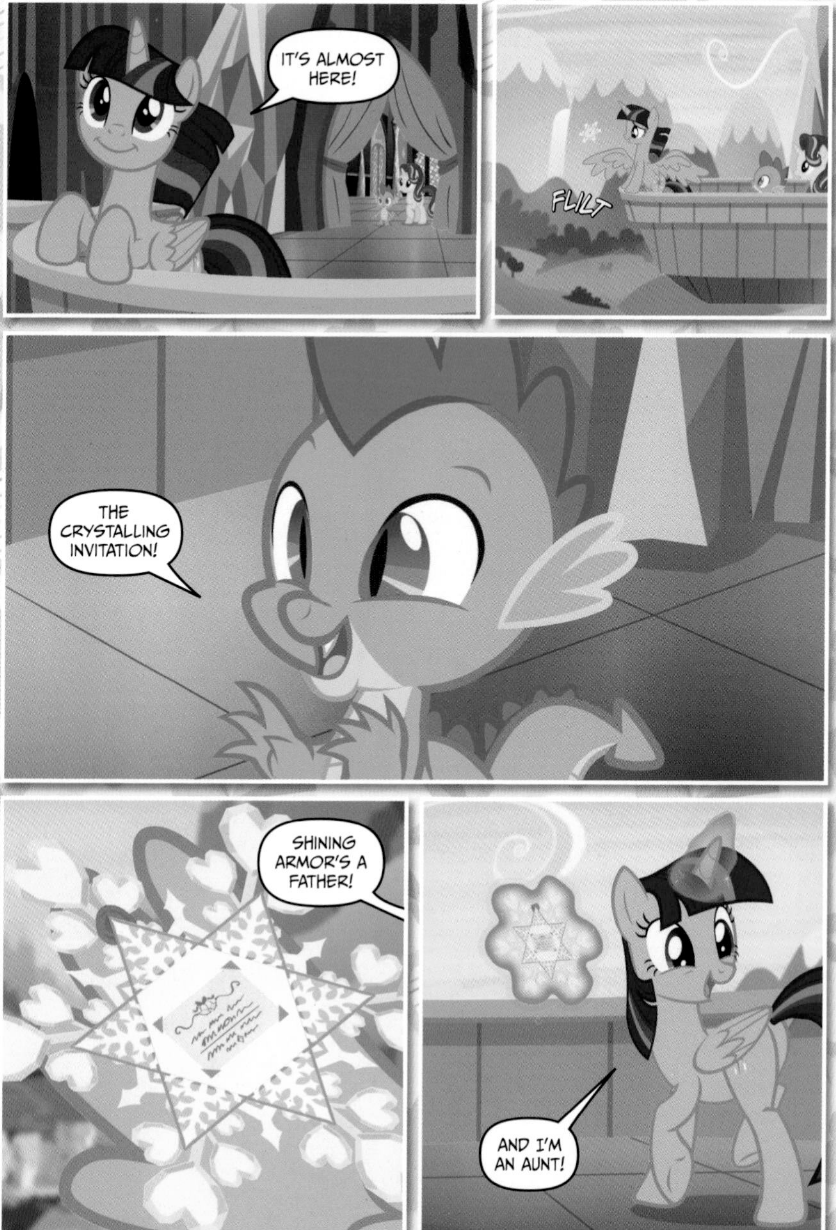
IT'S ALMOST HERE!
FLILT
THE CRYSTALLING INVITATION!
SHINING ARMOR'S A FATHER!
AND I'M AN AUNT!

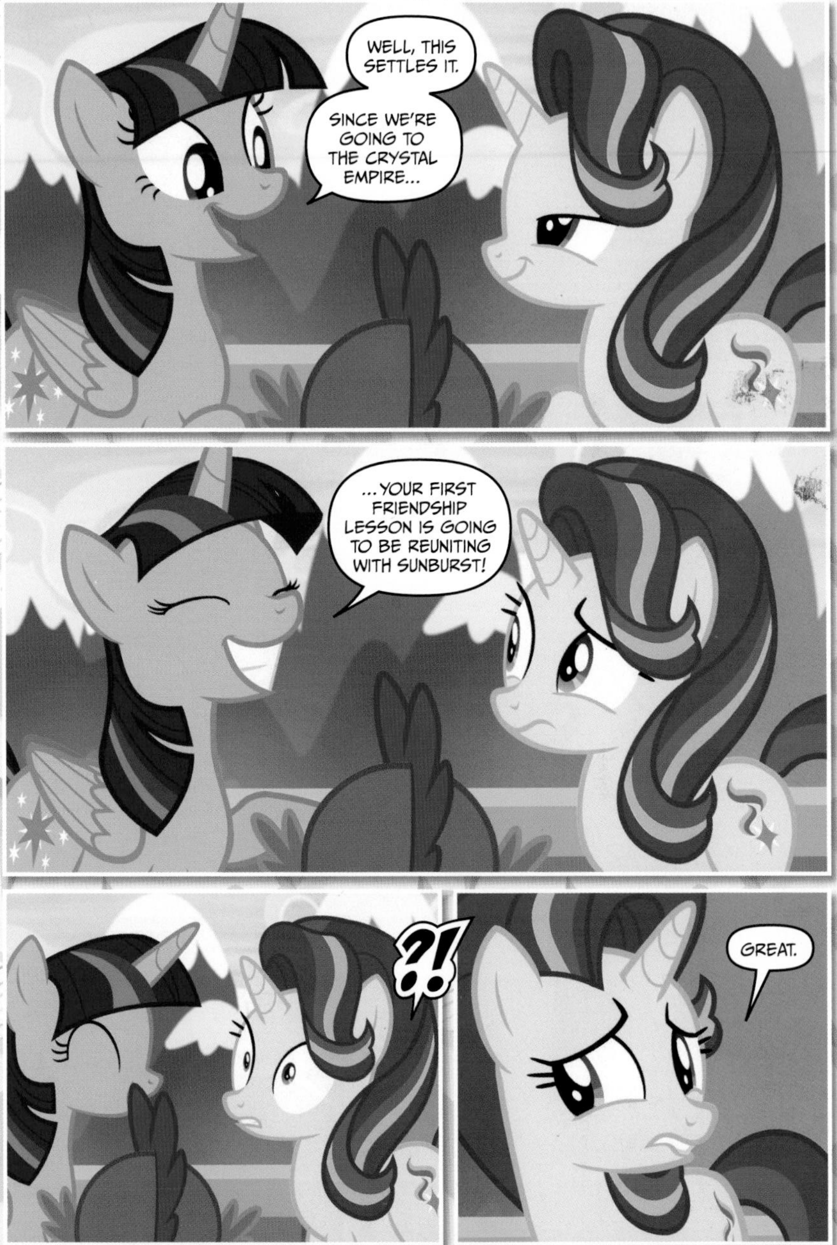
WELL, THIS SETTLES IT.
SINCE WE'RE GOING TO THE CRYSTAL EMPIRE...
...YOUR FIRST FRIENDSHIP LESSON IS GOING TO BE REUNITING WITH SUNBURST!
?!
GREAT.

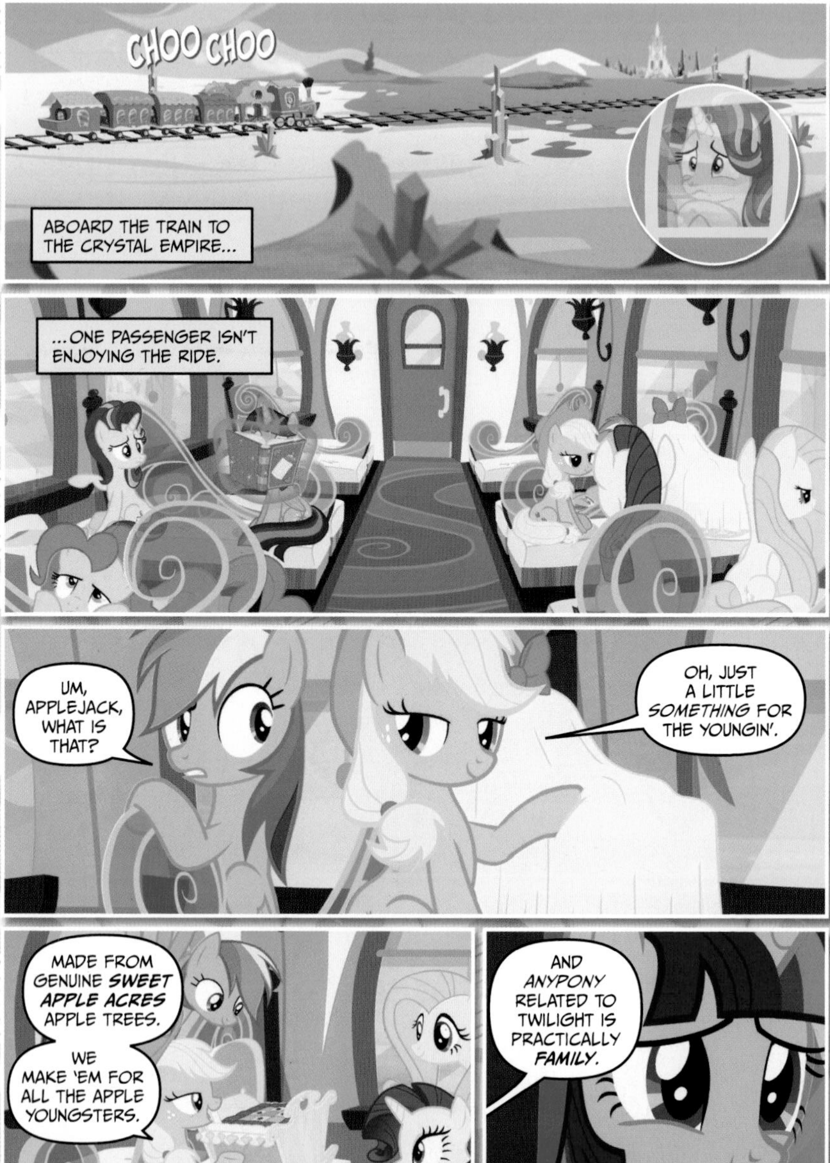
CHOO CHOO
ABOARD THE TRAIN TO THE CRYSTAL EMPIRE...
...ONE PASSENGER ISN'T ENJOYING THE RIDE.
UM, APPLEJACK, WHAT IS THAT?
OH, JUST A LITTLE *SOMETHING* FOR THE YOUNGIN'.
MADE FROM GENUINE ***SWEET APPLE ACRES*** APPLE TREES.
WE MAKE 'EM FOR ALL THE APPLE YOUNGSTERS.
AND *ANYPONY* RELATED TO TWILIGHT IS PRACTICALLY ***FAMILY***.

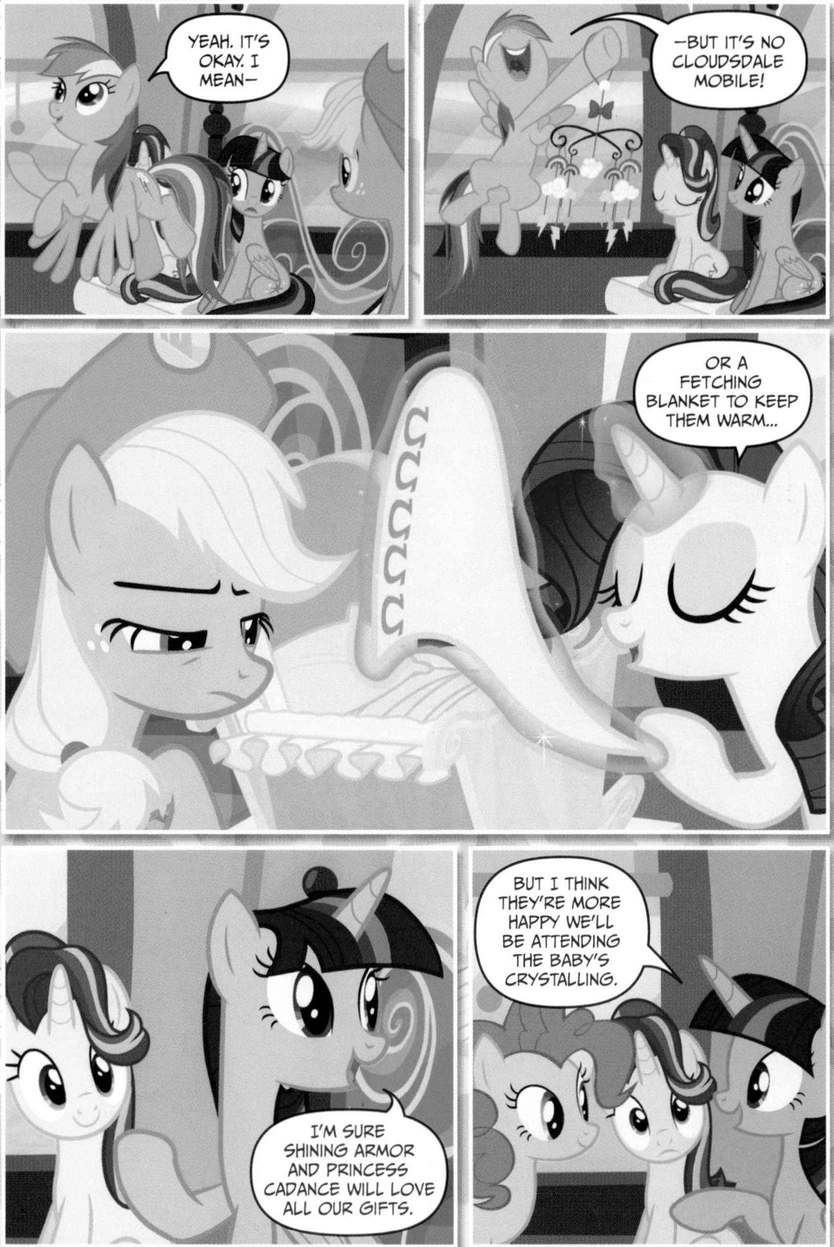
YEAH. IT'S OKAY. I MEAN—
—BUT IT'S NO CLOUDSDALE MOBILE!
OR A FETCHING BLANKET TO KEEP THEM WARM...
I'M SURE SHINING ARMOR AND PRINCESS CADANCE WILL LOVE ALL OUR GIFTS.
BUT I THINK THEY'RE MORE HAPPY WE'LL BE ATTENDING THE BABY'S CRYSTALLING.

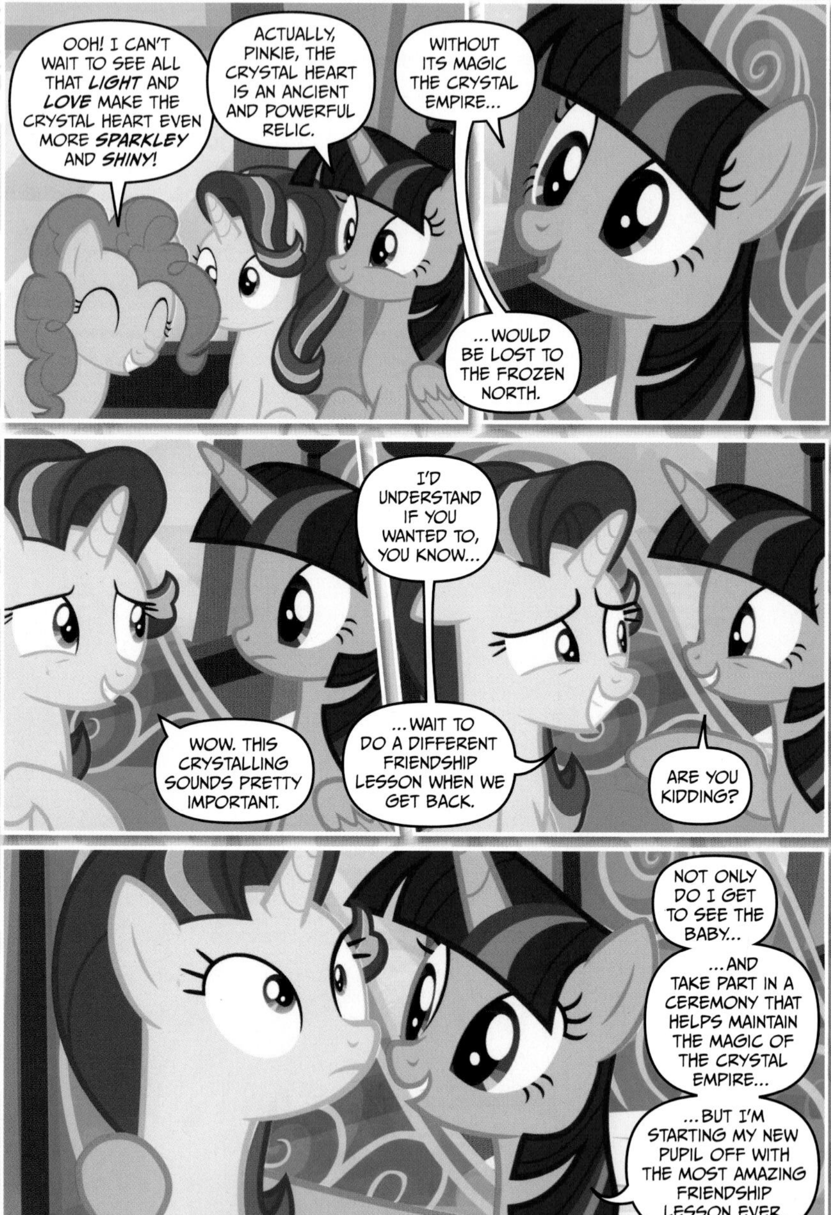

OOH! I CAN'T WAIT TO SEE ALL THAT *LIGHT* AND *LOVE* MAKE THE CRYSTAL HEART EVEN MORE *SPARKLEY* AND *SHINY*!
ACTUALLY, PINKIE, THE CRYSTAL HEART IS AN ANCIENT AND POWERFUL RELIC.
WITHOUT ITS MAGIC THE CRYSTAL EMPIRE...
...WOULD BE LOST TO THE FROZEN NORTH.
WOW. THIS CRYSTALLING SOUNDS PRETTY IMPORTANT.
I'D UNDERSTAND IF YOU WANTED TO, YOU KNOW...
...WAIT TO DO A DIFFERENT FRIENDSHIP LESSON WHEN WE GET BACK.
ARE YOU KIDDING?
NOT ONLY DO I GET TO SEE THE BABY...
...AND TAKE PART IN A CEREMONY THAT HELPS MAINTAIN THE MAGIC OF THE CRYSTAL EMPIRE...
...BUT I'M STARTING MY NEW PUPIL OFF WITH THE MOST AMAZING FRIENDSHIP LESSON EVER.

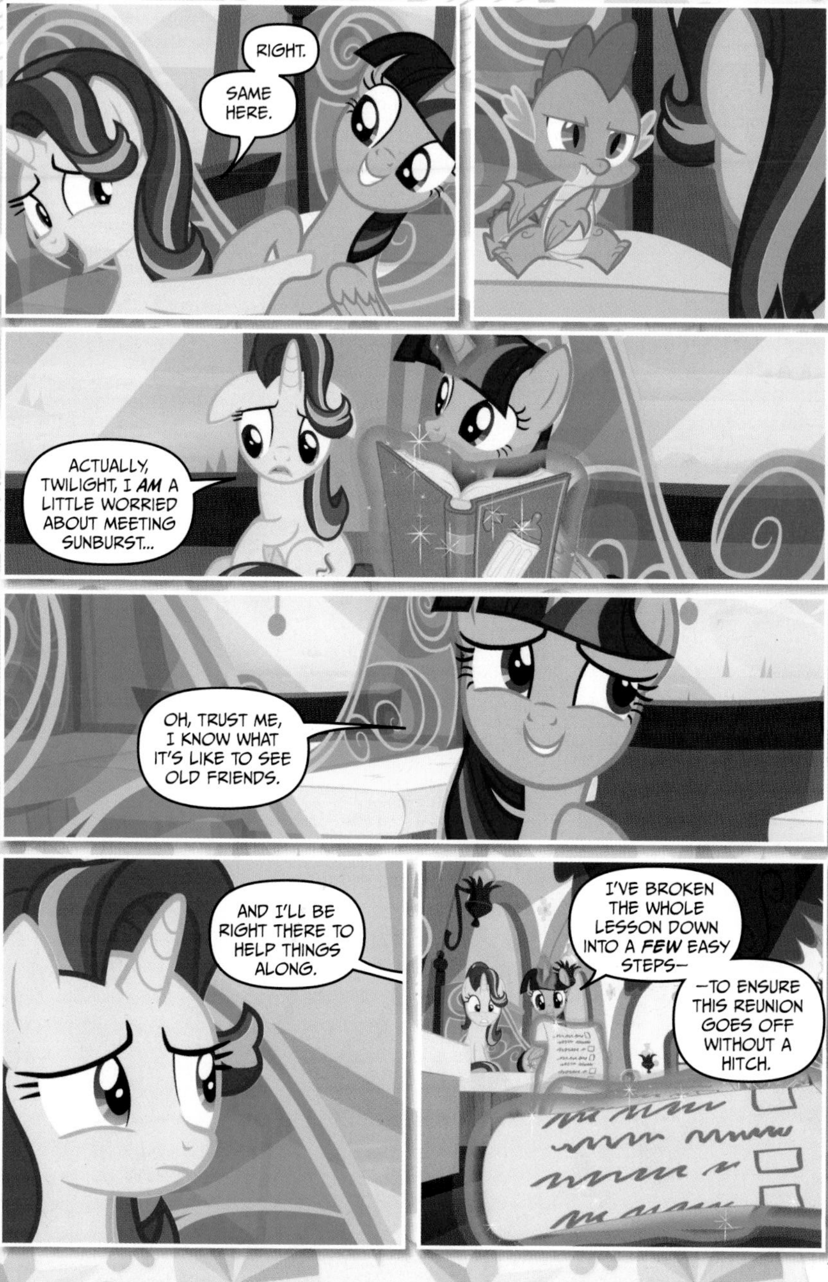
RIGHT.
SAME HERE.
ACTUALLY, TWILIGHT, I *AM* A LITTLE WORRIED ABOUT MEETING SUNBURST...
OH, TRUST ME, I KNOW WHAT IT'S LIKE TO SEE OLD FRIENDS.
AND I'LL BE RIGHT THERE TO HELP THINGS ALONG.
I'VE BROKEN THE WHOLE LESSON DOWN INTO A *FEW* EASY STEPS—
—TO ENSURE THIS REUNION GOES OFF WITHOUT A HITCH.

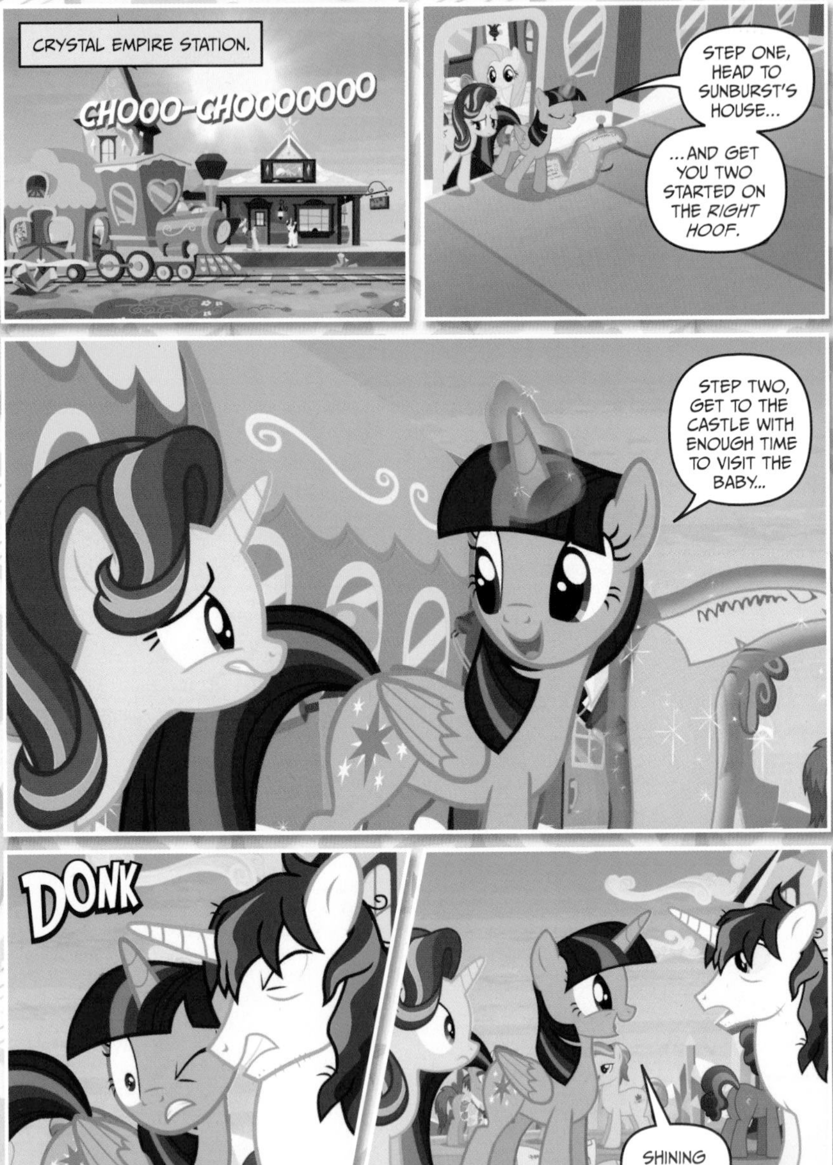
CRYSTAL EMPIRE STATION.
CHOOO-CHOOOOOOO
STEP ONE, HEAD TO SUNBURST'S HOUSE...
...AND GET YOU TWO STARTED ON THE *RIGHT HOOF*.
STEP TWO, GET TO THE CASTLE WITH ENOUGH TIME TO VISIT THE BABY...
DONK
SHINING ARMOR!

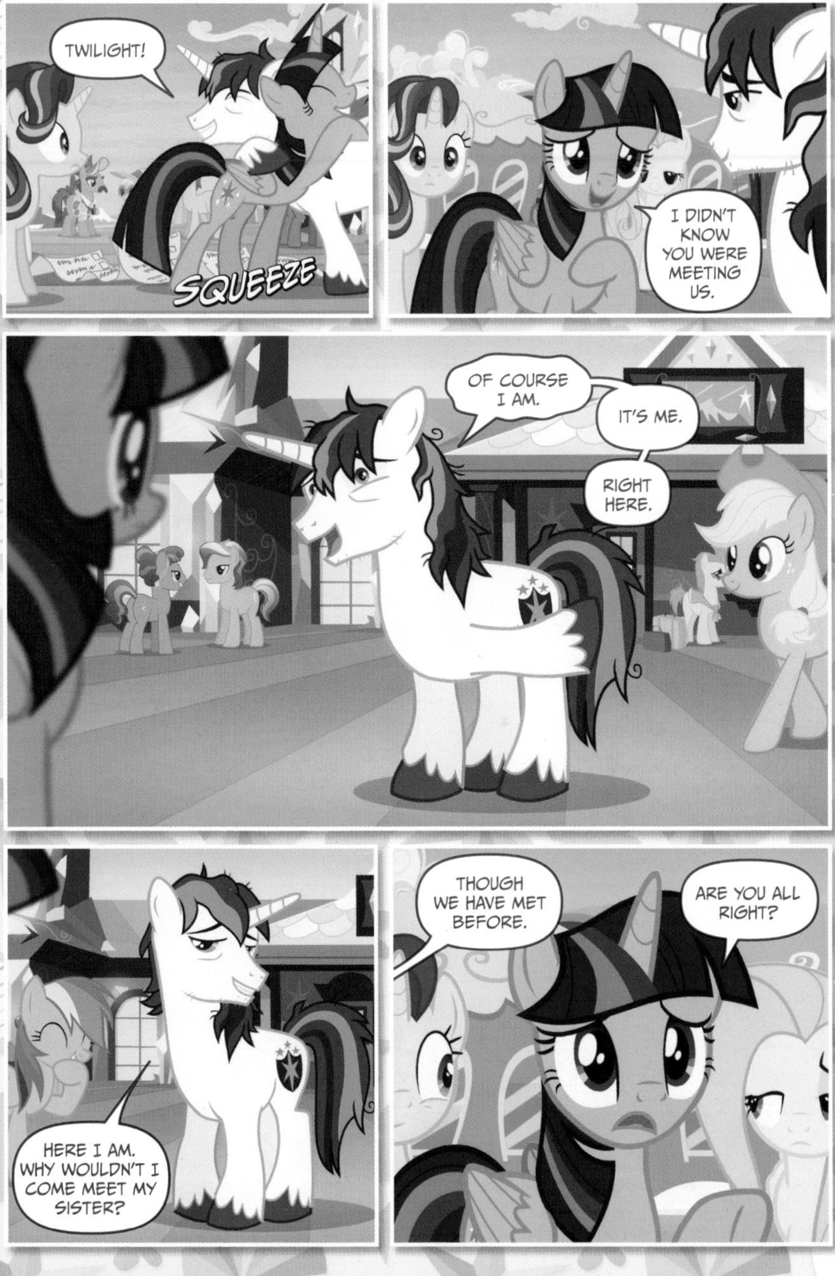
TWILIGHT!
SQUEEZE
I DIDN'T KNOW YOU WERE MEETING US.
OF COURSE I AM.
IT'S ME.
RIGHT HERE.
HERE I AM. WHY WOULDN'T I COME MEET MY SISTER?
THOUGH WE HAVE MET BEFORE.
ARE YOU ALL RIGHT?

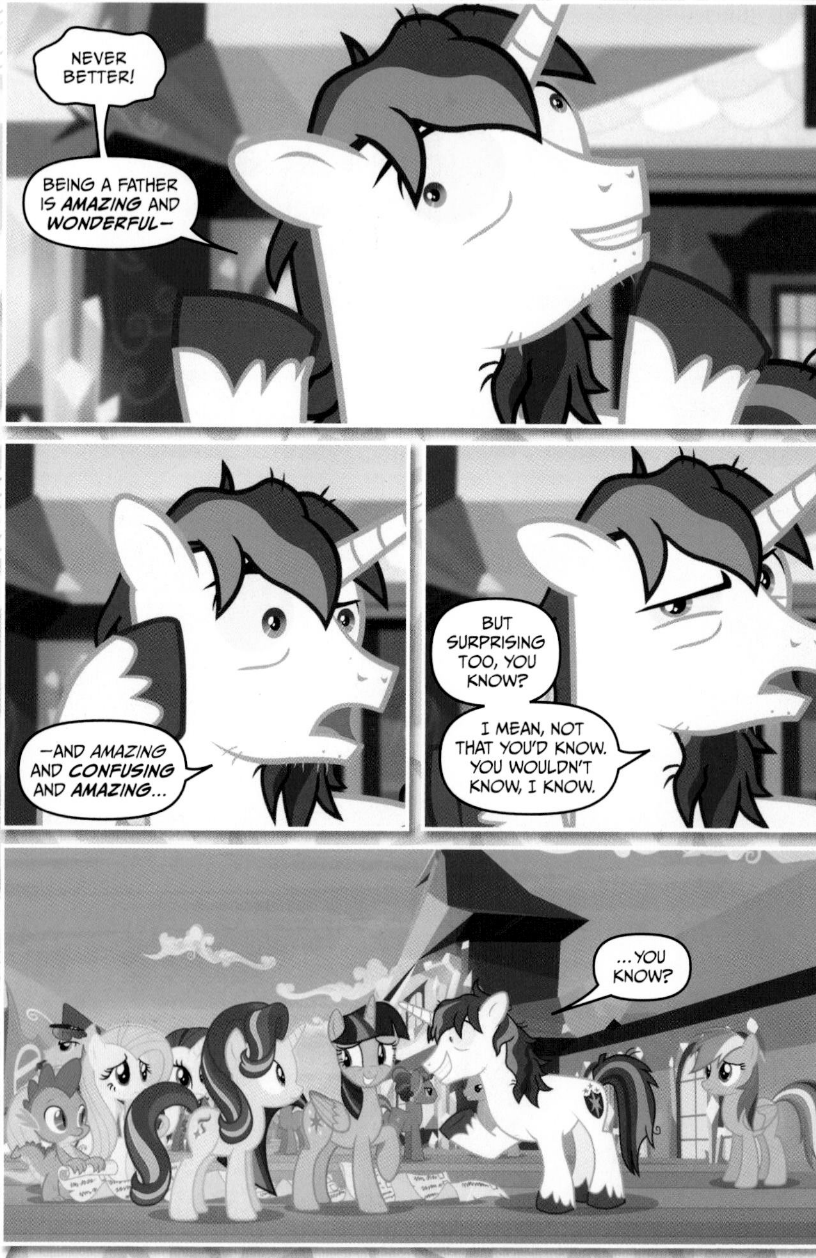
NEVER BETTER!
BEING A FATHER IS AMAZING AND WONDERFUL—
—AND AMAZING AND CONFUSING AND AMAZING...
BUT SURPRISING TOO, YOU KNOW?
I MEAN, NOT THAT YOU'D KNOW. YOU WOULDN'T KNOW, I KNOW.
...YOU KNOW?

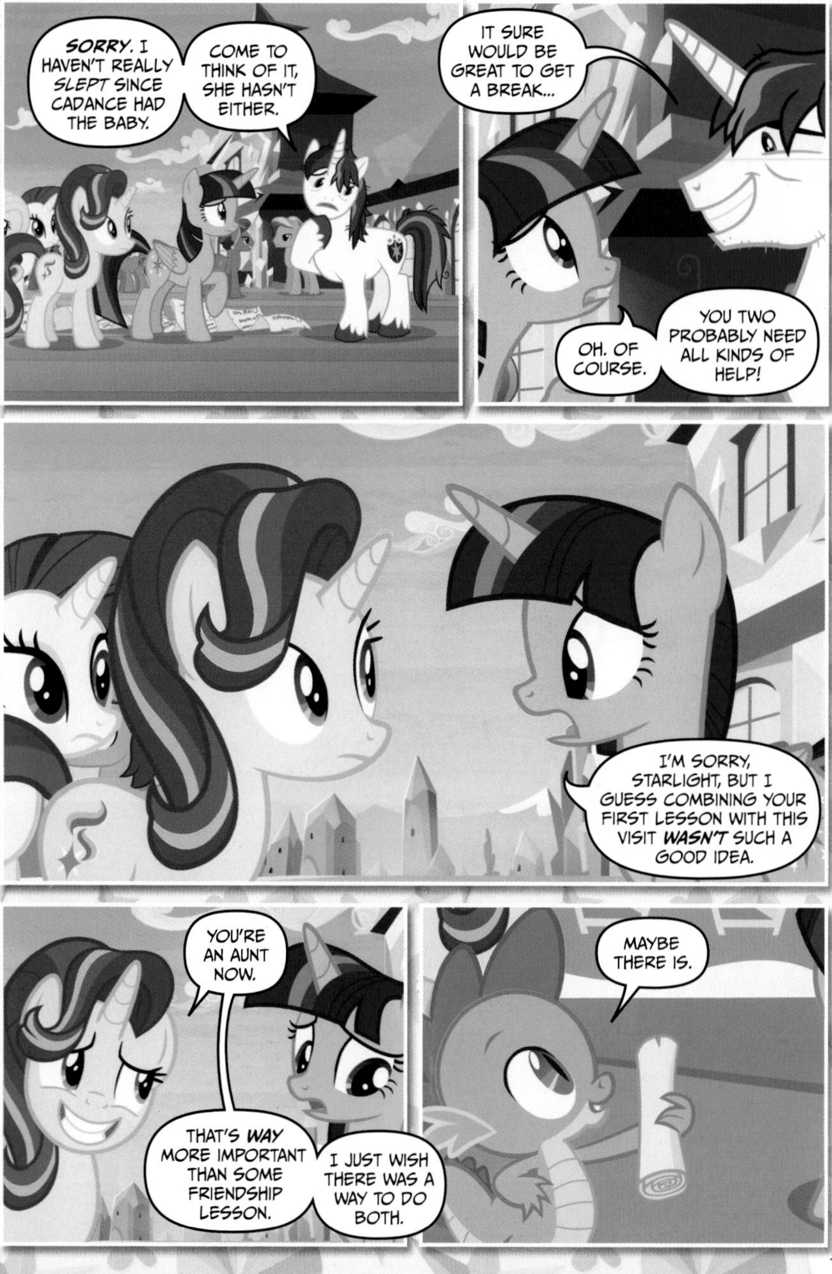
SORRY. I HAVEN'T REALLY SLEPT SINCE CADANCE HAD THE BABY.
COME TO THINK OF IT, SHE HASN'T EITHER.
IT SURE WOULD BE GREAT TO GET A BREAK...
OH. OF COURSE.
YOU TWO PROBABLY NEED ALL KINDS OF HELP!
I'M SORRY, STARLIGHT, BUT I GUESS COMBINING YOUR FIRST LESSON WITH THIS VISIT WASN'T SUCH A GOOD IDEA.
YOU'RE AN AUNT NOW.
THAT'S WAY MORE IMPORTANT THAN SOME FRIENDSHIP LESSON.
I JUST WISH THERE WAS A WAY TO DO BOTH.
MAYBE THERE IS.

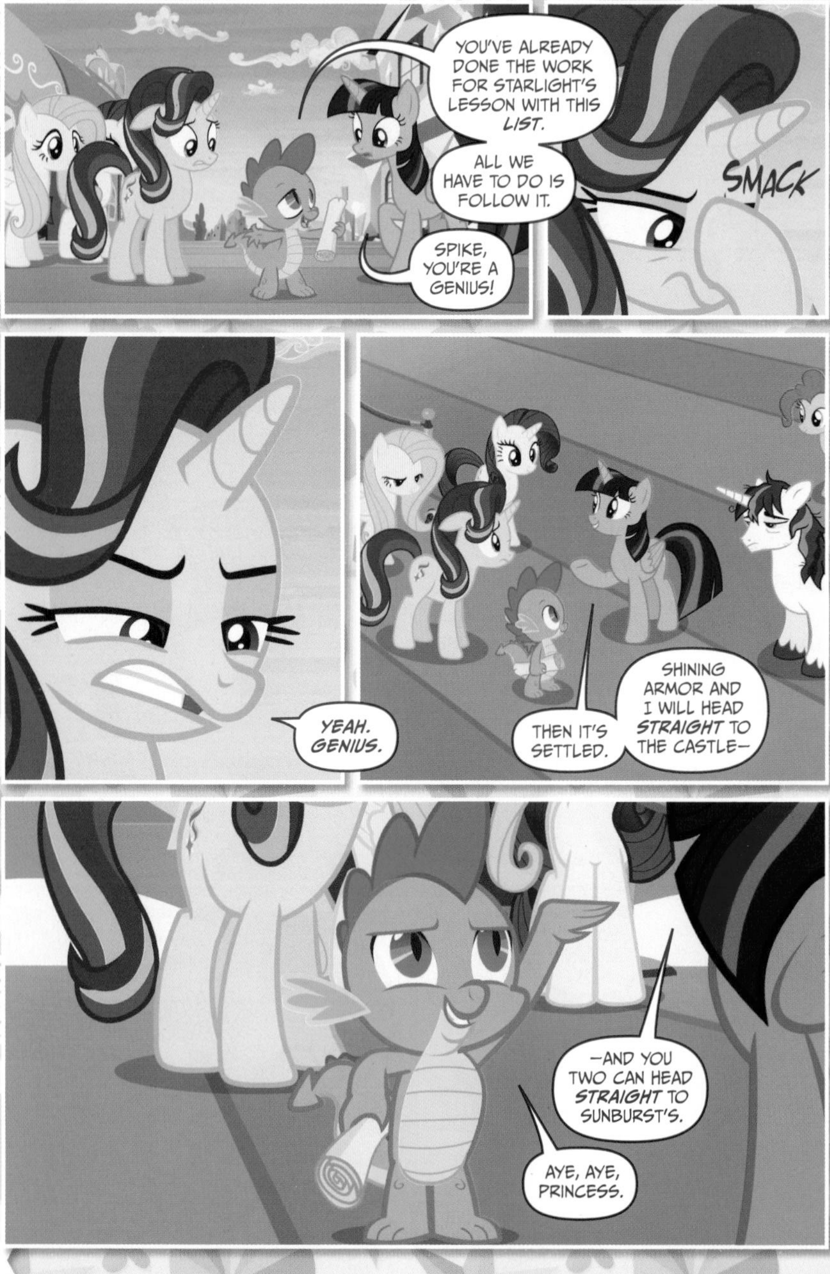
YOU'VE ALREADY DONE THE WORK FOR STARLIGHT'S LESSON WITH THIS LIST.
ALL WE HAVE TO DO IS FOLLOW IT.
SPIKE, YOU'RE A GENIUS!
SMACK
YEAH. GENIUS.
THEN IT'S SETTLED.
SHINING ARMOR AND I WILL HEAD STRAIGHT TO THE CASTLE—
—AND YOU TWO CAN HEAD STRAIGHT TO SUNBURST'S.
AYE, AYE, PRINCESS.

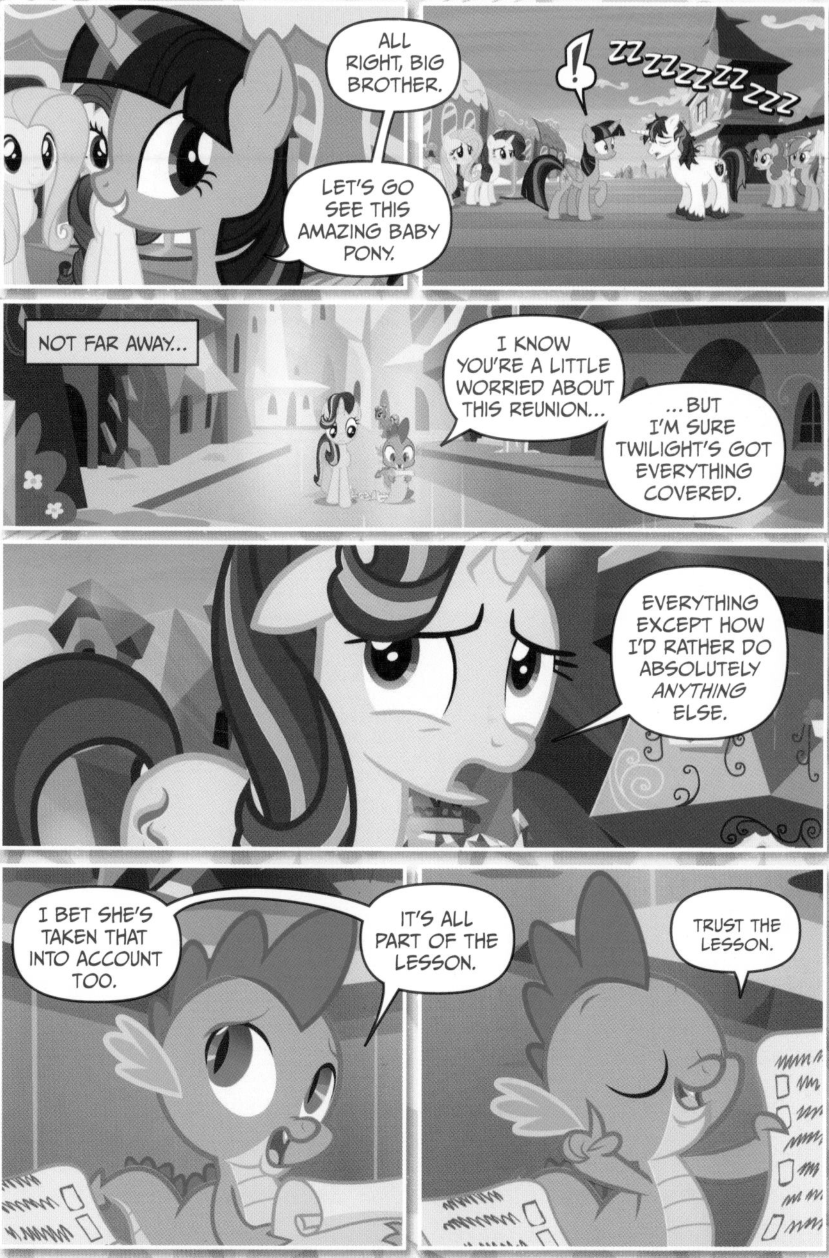
ALL RIGHT, BIG BROTHER.
LET'S GO SEE THIS AMAZING BABY PONY.
!
ZZZZZZZZZZZ
NOT FAR AWAY...
I KNOW YOU'RE A LITTLE WORRIED ABOUT THIS REUNION...
...BUT I'M SURE TWILIGHT'S GOT EVERYTHING COVERED.
EVERYTHING EXCEPT HOW I'D RATHER DO ABSOLUTELY *ANYTHING* ELSE.
I BET SHE'S TAKEN THAT INTO ACCOUNT TOO.
IT'S ALL PART OF THE LESSON.
TRUST THE LESSON.

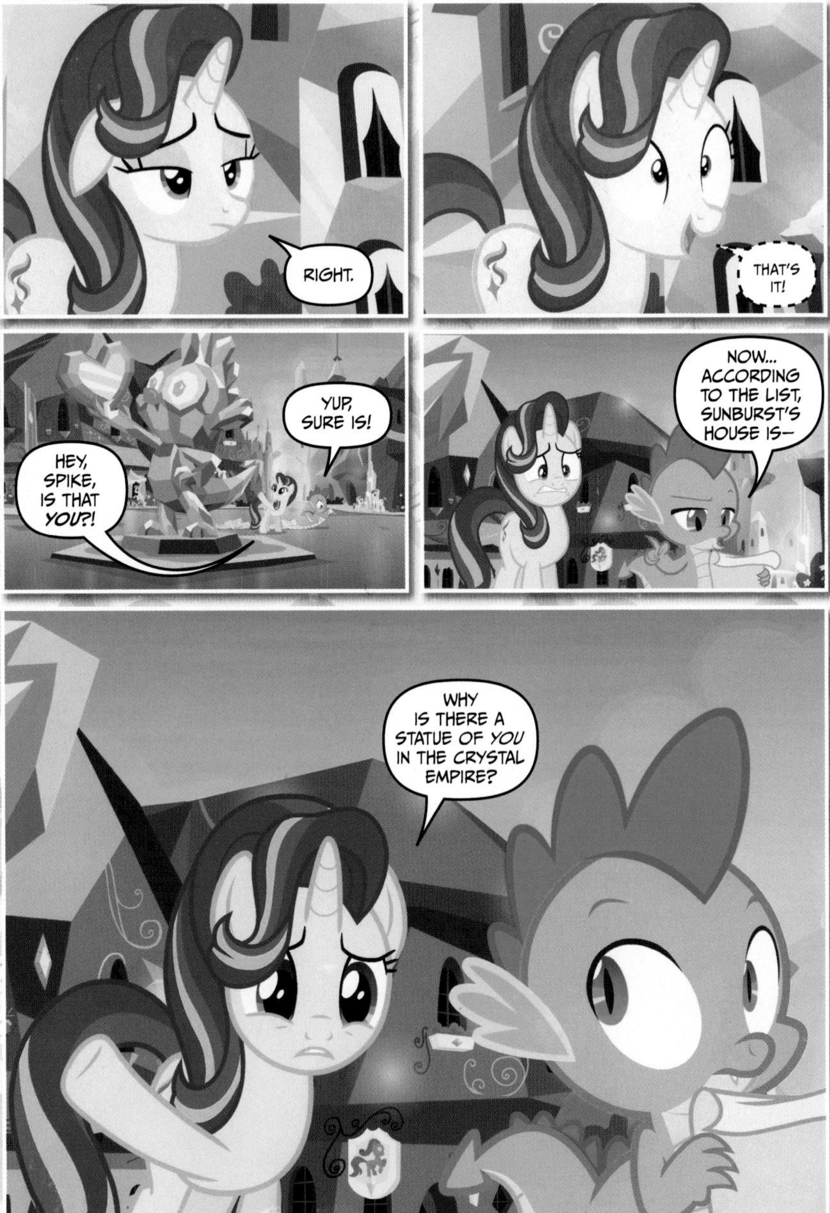
RIGHT.
THAT'S IT!
HEY, SPIKE, IS THAT *YOU*?!
YUP, SURE IS!
NOW... ACCORDING TO THE LIST, SUNBURST'S HOUSE IS—
WHY IS THERE A STATUE OF *YOU* IN THE CRYSTAL EMPIRE?

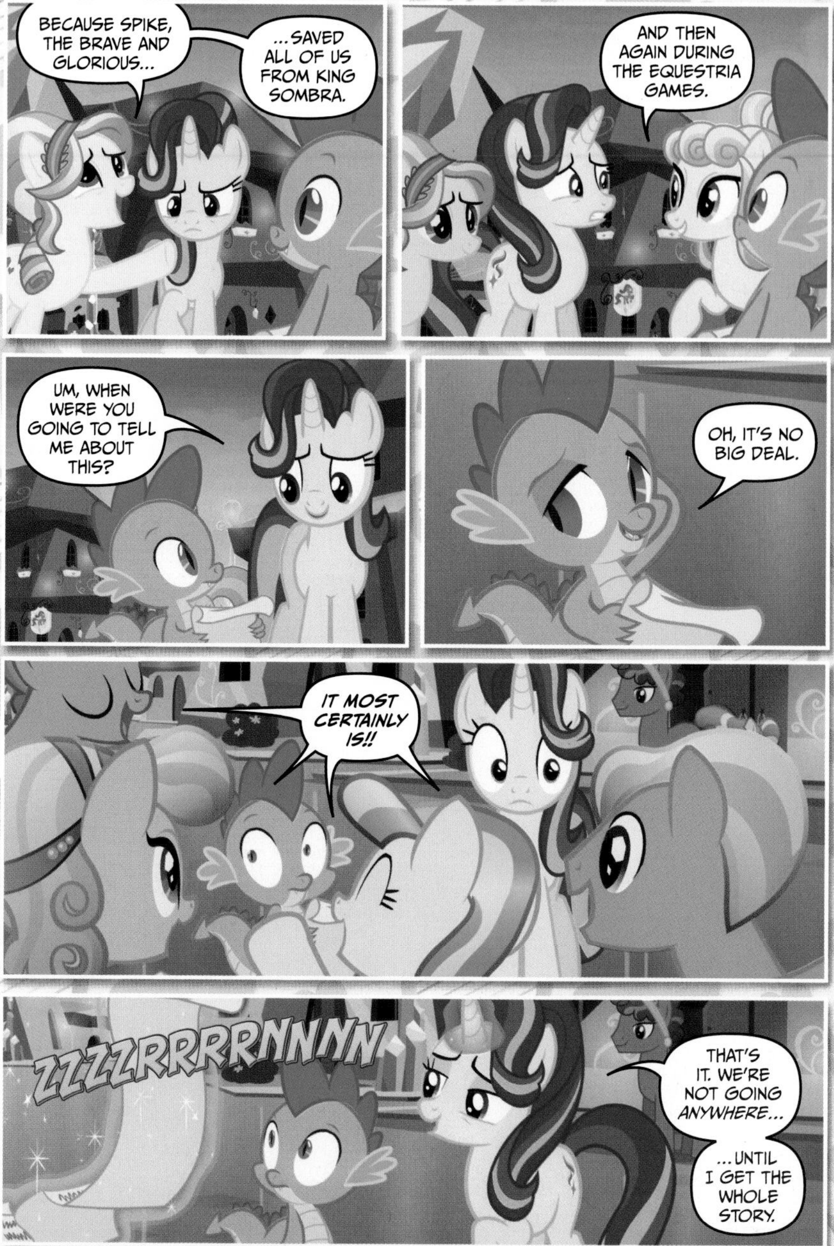
BECAUSE SPIKE, THE BRAVE AND GLORIOUS...
...SAVED ALL OF US FROM KING SOMBRA.
AND THEN AGAIN DURING THE EQUESTRIA GAMES.
UM, WHEN WERE YOU GOING TO TELL ME ABOUT THIS?
OH, IT'S NO BIG DEAL.
IT MOST CERTAINLY IS!!
ZZZZRRRRRNNNN
THAT'S IT. WE'RE NOT GOING *ANYWHERE*...
...UNTIL I GET THE WHOLE STORY.

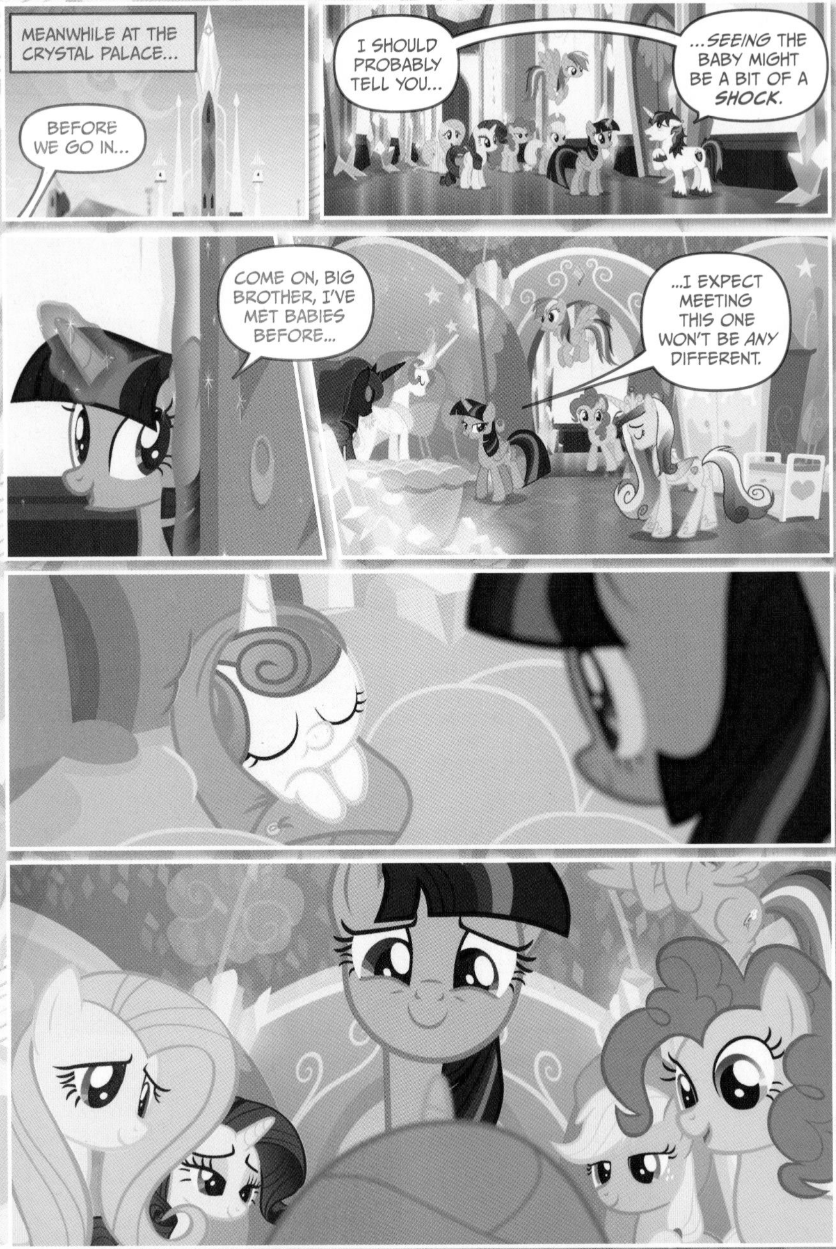
MEANWHILE AT THE CRYSTAL PALACE...
BEFORE WE GO IN...
I SHOULD PROBABLY TELL YOU...
...*SEEING* THE BABY MIGHT BE A BIT OF A ***SHOCK***.
COME ON, BIG BROTHER, I'VE MET BABIES BEFORE...
...I EXPECT MEETING THIS ONE WON'T BE *ANY* DIFFERENT.

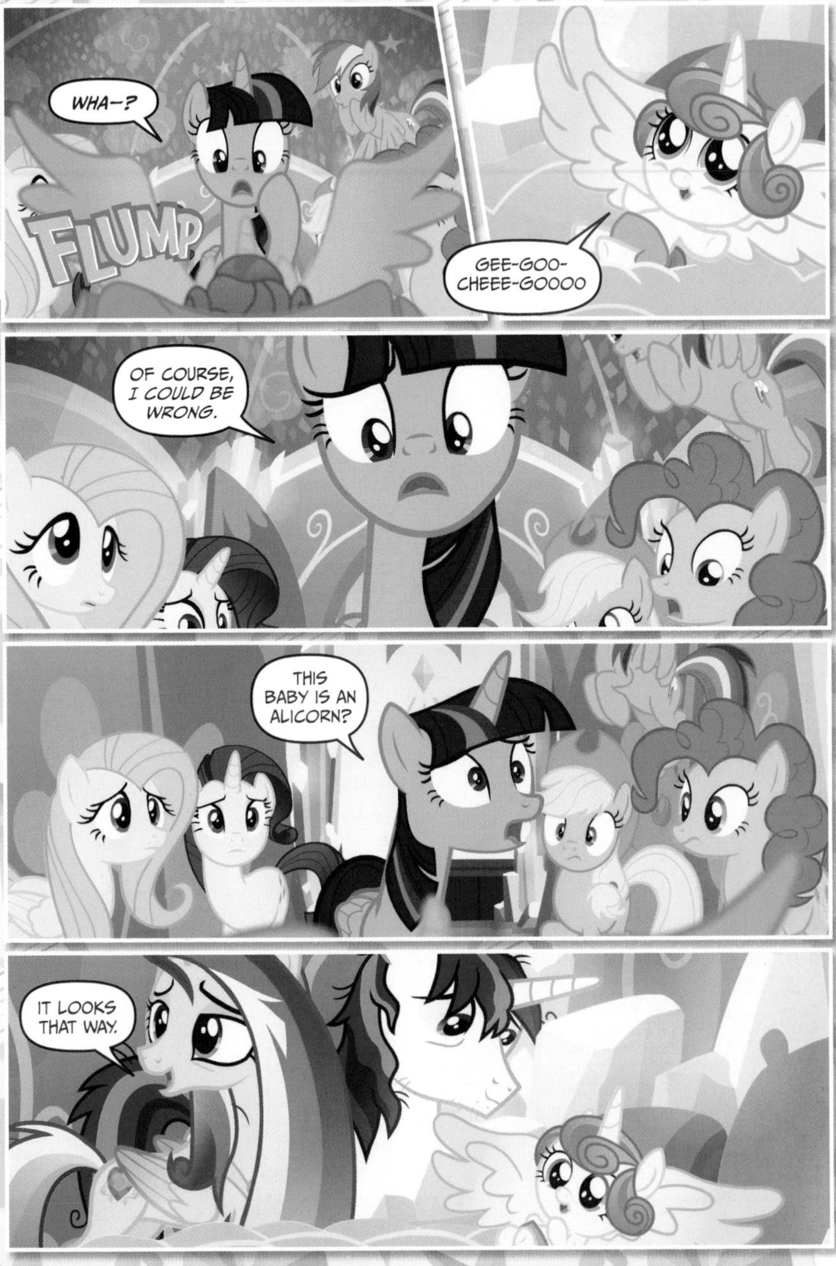
WHA–?
FLUMP
GEE-GOO-CHEEE-GOOOO
OF COURSE, I COULD BE WRONG.
THIS BABY IS AN ALICORN?
IT LOOKS THAT WAY.

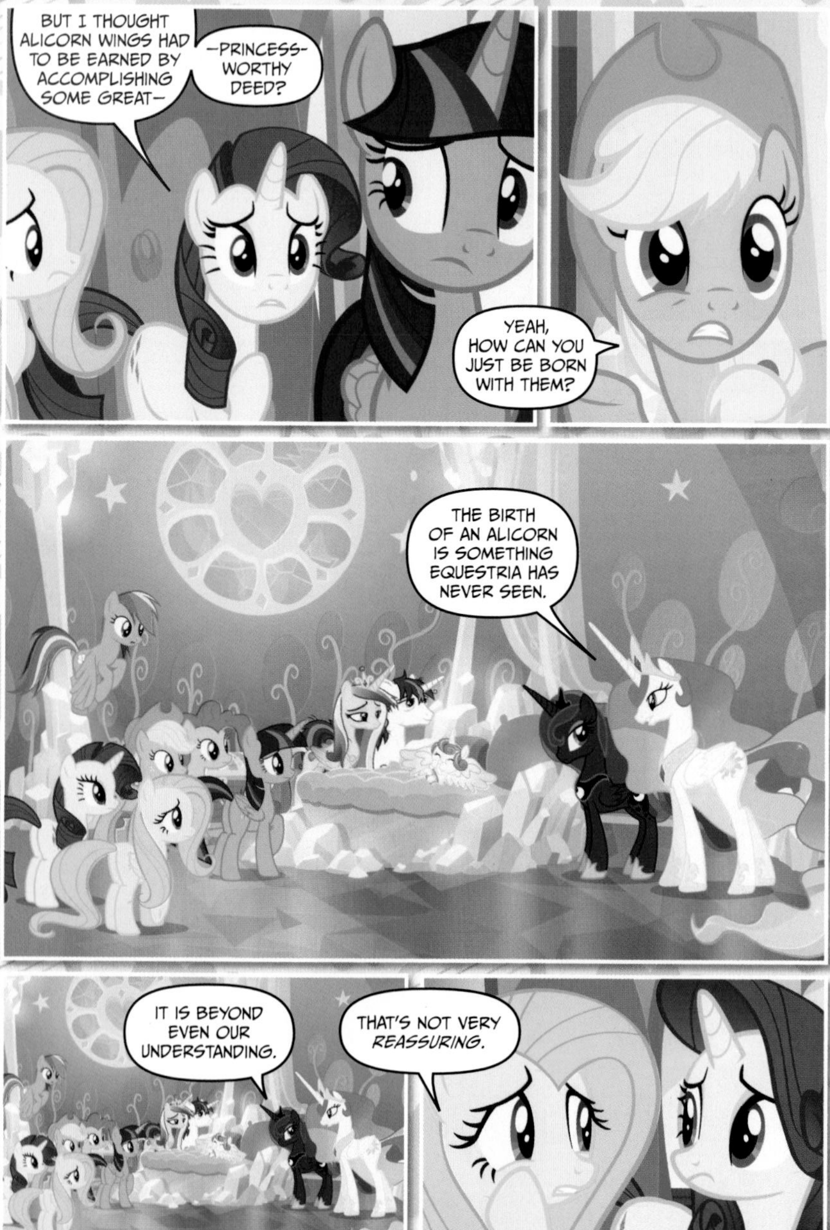

BUT I THOUGHT ALICORN WINGS HAD TO BE EARNED BY ACCOMPLISHING SOME GREAT—
—PRINCESS-WORTHY DEED?
YEAH, HOW CAN YOU JUST BE BORN WITH THEM?
THE BIRTH OF AN ALICORN IS SOMETHING EQUESTRIA HAS NEVER SEEN.
IT IS BEYOND EVEN OUR UNDERSTANDING.
THAT'S NOT VERY *REASSURING*.

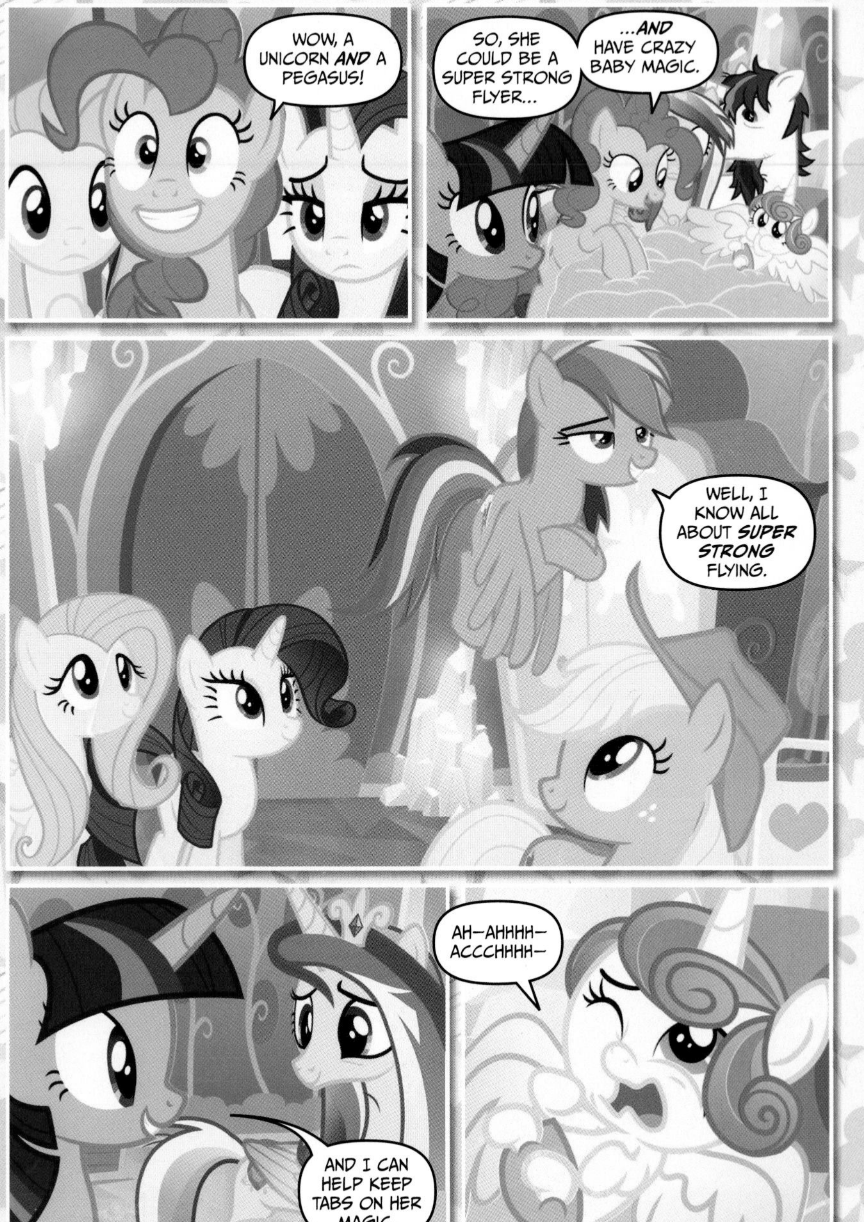
WOW, A UNICORN **AND** A PEGASUS!
SO, SHE COULD BE A SUPER STRONG FLYER...
...**AND** HAVE CRAZY BABY MAGIC.
WELL, I KNOW ALL ABOUT **SUPER STRONG** FLYING.
AND I CAN HELP KEEP TABS ON HER MAGIC.
AH—AHHHH— ACCCHHHH—

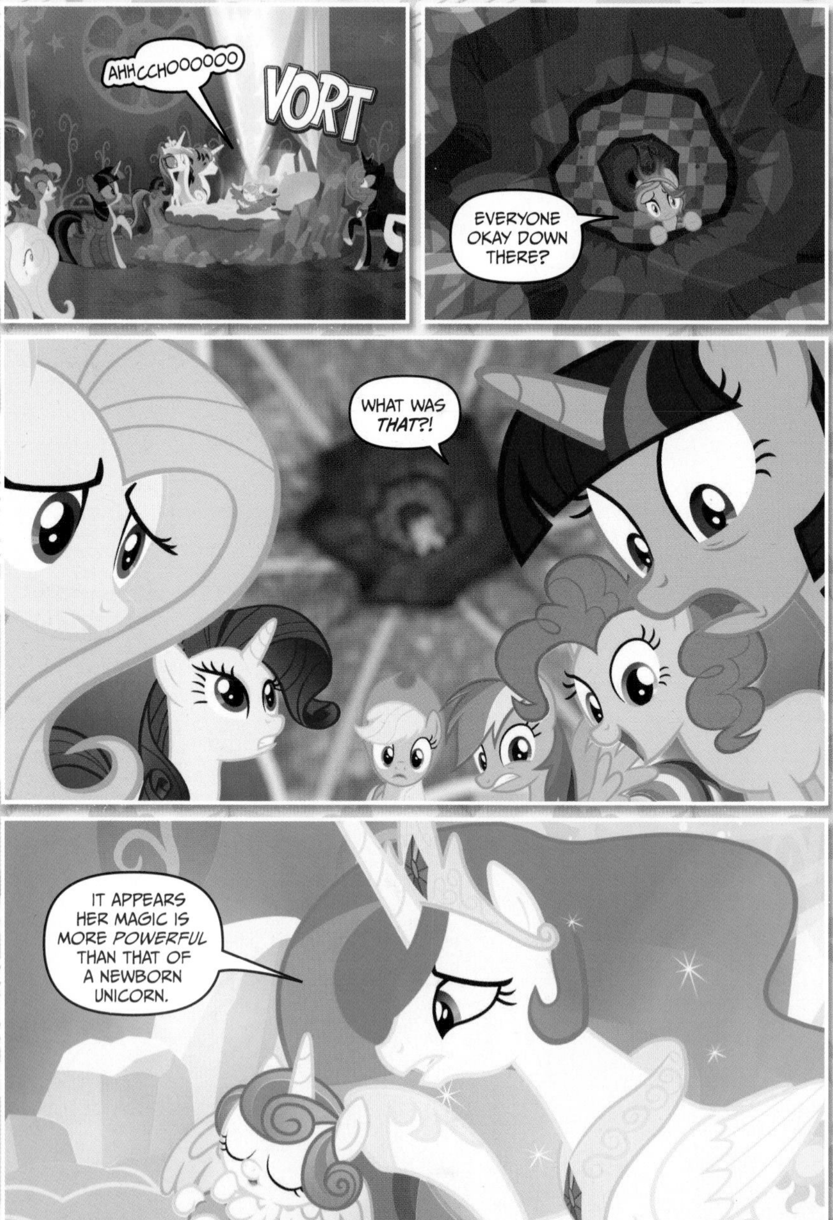
AHHCCHOOOOOOO
VORT
EVERYONE OKAY DOWN THERE?
WHAT WAS *THAT?!*
IT APPEARS HER MAGIC IS MORE *POWERFUL* THAN THAT OF A NEWBORN UNICORN.

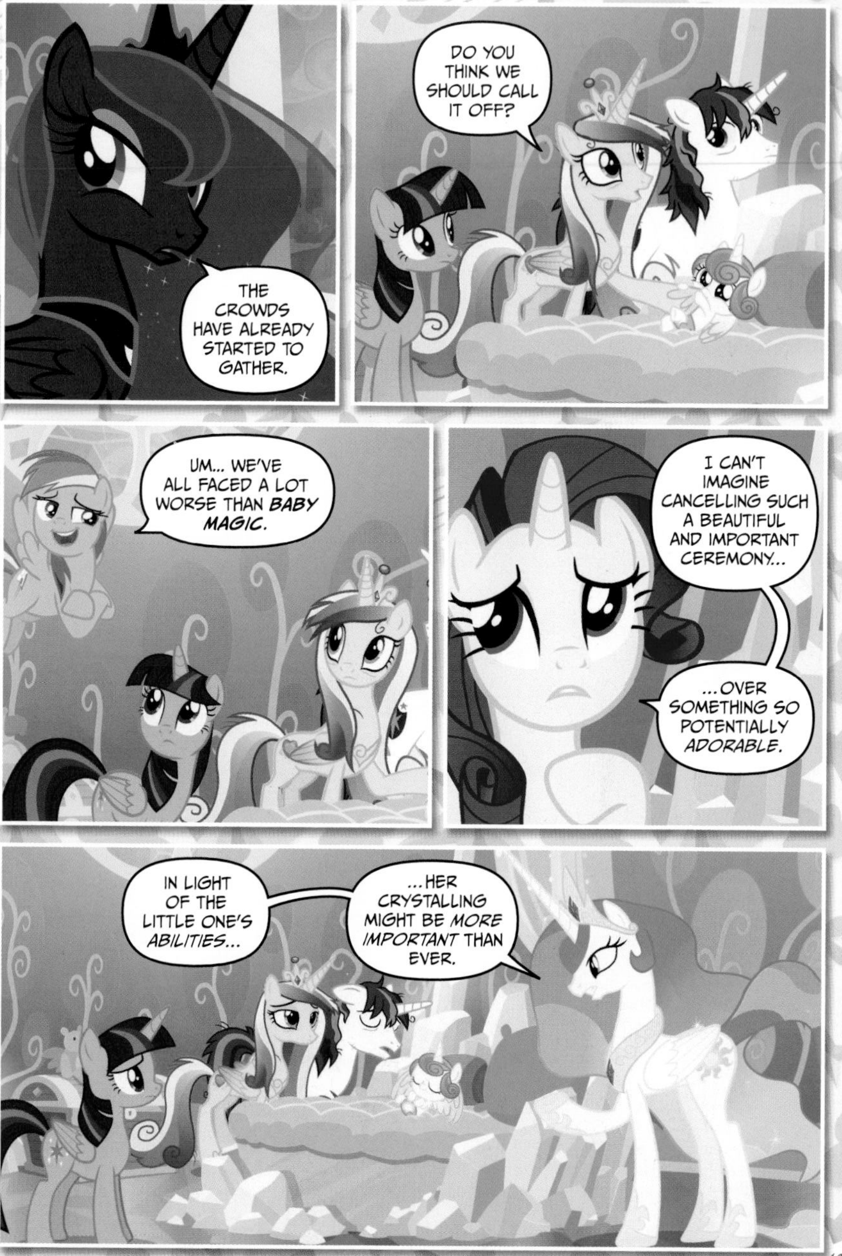
THE CROWDS HAVE ALREADY STARTED TO GATHER.
DO YOU THINK WE SHOULD CALL IT OFF?
UM... WE'VE ALL FACED A LOT WORSE THAN *BABY MAGIC*.
I CAN'T IMAGINE CANCELLING SUCH A BEAUTIFUL AND IMPORTANT CEREMONY...
...OVER SOMETHING SO POTENTIALLY *ADORABLE*.
IN LIGHT OF THE LITTLE ONE'S *ABILITIES*...
...HER CRYSTALLING MIGHT BE *MORE IMPORTANT* THAN EVER.

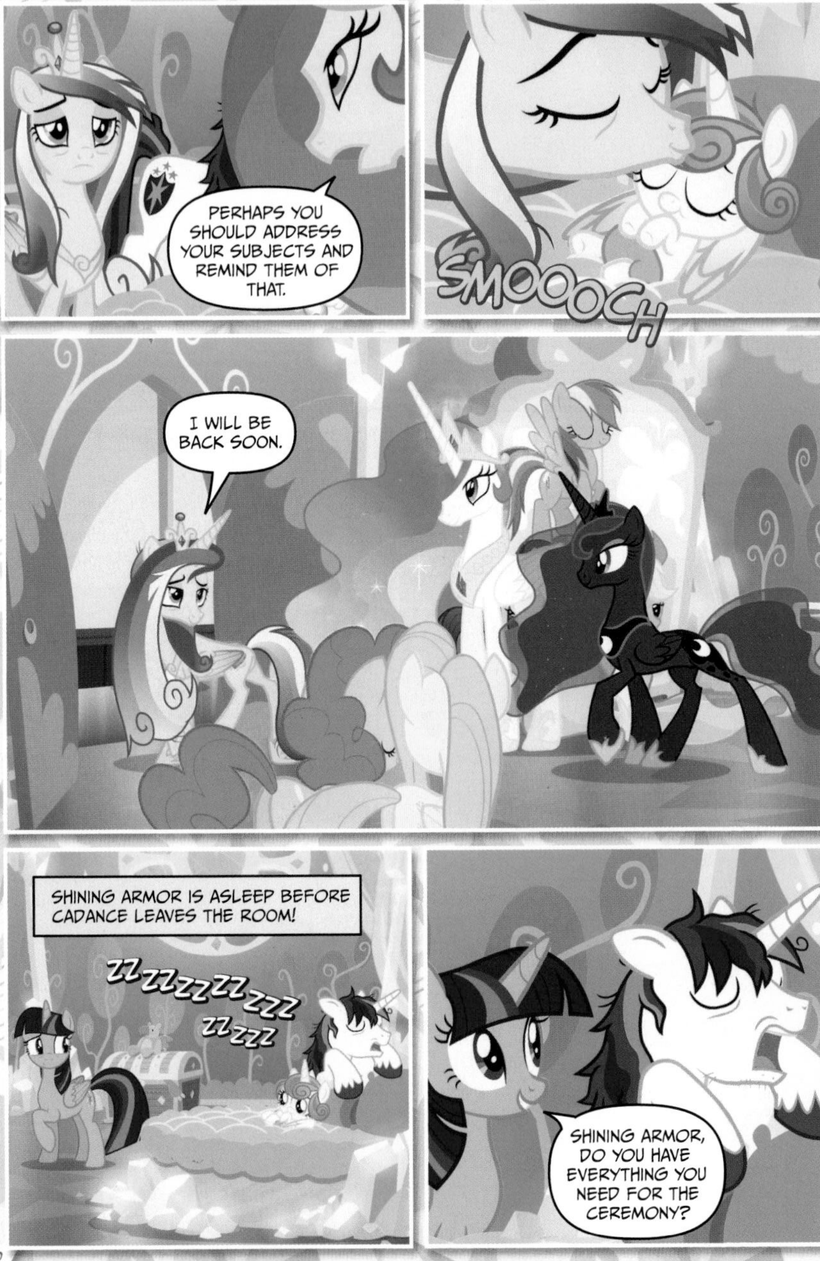
PERHAPS YOU SHOULD ADDRESS YOUR SUBJECTS AND REMIND THEM OF THAT.
SMOOOCH
I WILL BE BACK SOON.
SHINING ARMOR IS ASLEEP BEFORE CADANCE LEAVES THE ROOM!
ZZZZZZZZZZZ
ZZZZZ
SHINING ARMOR, DO YOU HAVE EVERYTHING YOU NEED FOR THE CEREMONY?

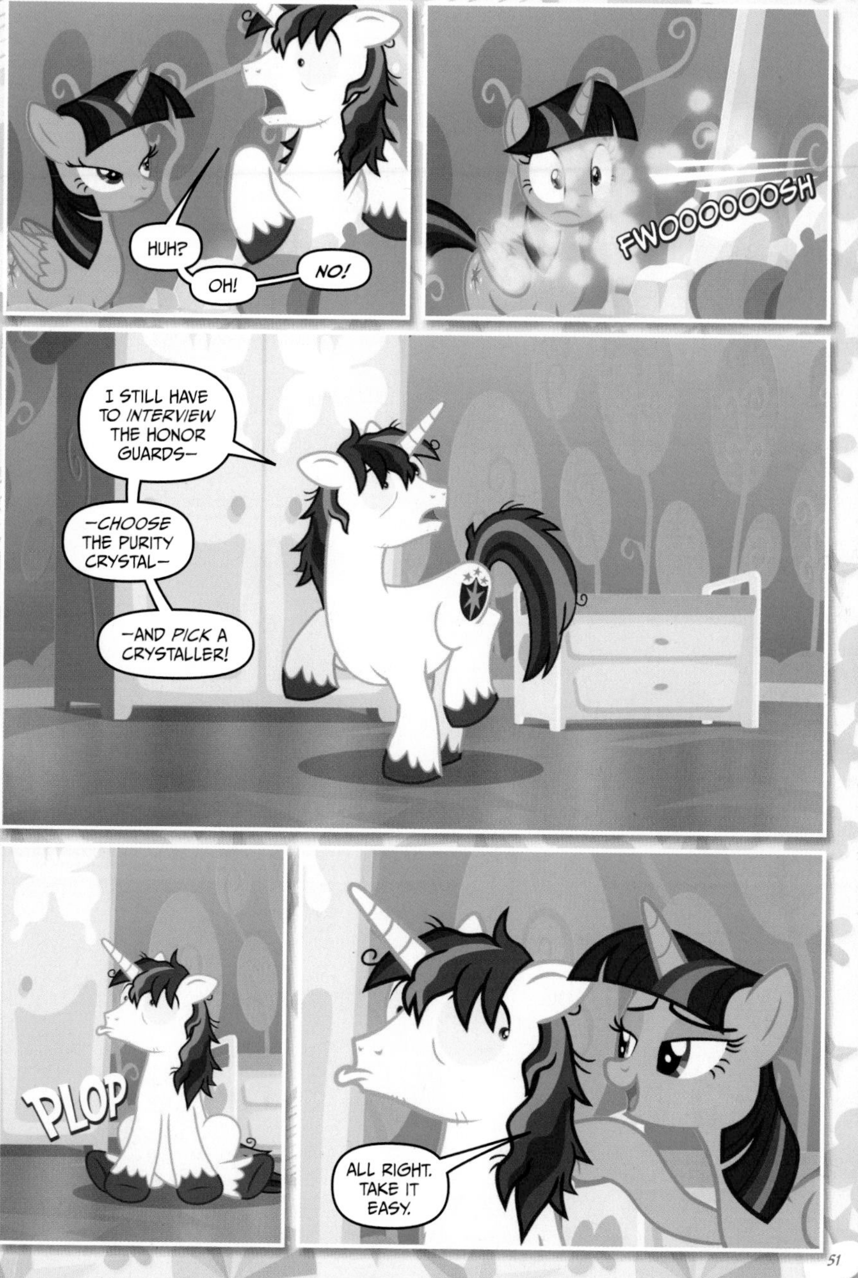
HUH?
OH!
NO!
FWOOOOOOOSH
I STILL HAVE TO *INTERVIEW* THE HONOR GUARDS—
—*CHOOSE* THE PURITY CRYSTAL—
—AND *PICK* A CRYSTALLER!
PLOP
ALL RIGHT. TAKE IT EASY.

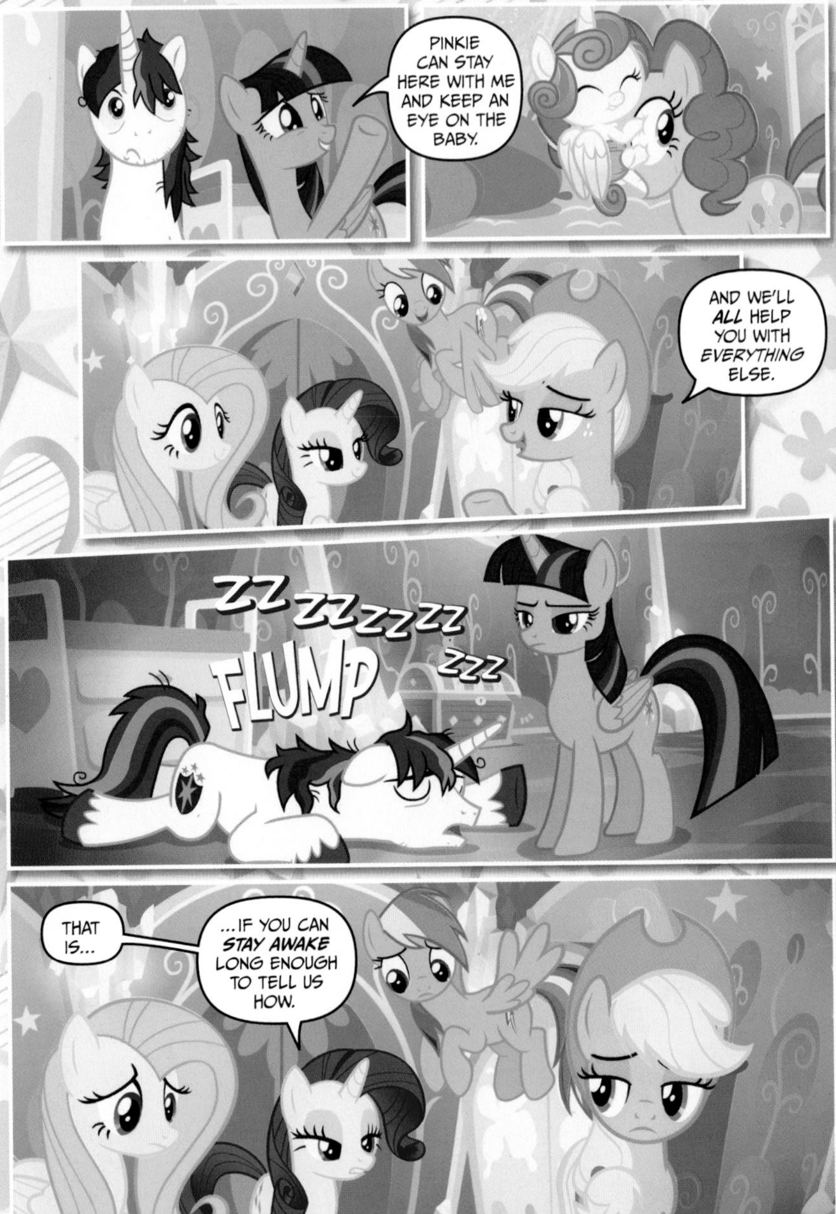
PINKIE CAN STAY HERE WITH ME AND KEEP AN EYE ON THE BABY.
AND WE'LL ALL HELP YOU WITH EVERYTHING ELSE.
ZZ ZZZZZZ
FLUMP
ZZZ
THAT IS...
...IF YOU CAN STAY AWAKE LONG ENOUGH TO TELL US HOW.

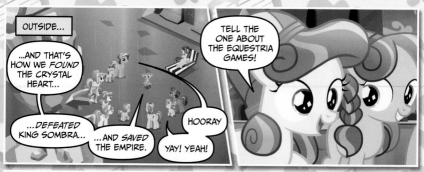

OUTSIDE...

...AND THAT'S HOW WE *FOUND* THE CRYSTAL HEART...

...DEFEATED KING SOMBRA...

...AND *SAVED* THE EMPIRE.

HOORAY

YAY! YEAH!

TELL THE ONE ABOUT THE EQUESTRIA GAMES!

WELL, AS MUCH AS I LOVE RELIVING MY HEROIC DEEDS...

CHOMP CHOMP

...STARLIGHT AND I HAVE AN IMPORTANT LESSON TO FINISH...

...BY ORDER OF THE PRINCESS OF FRIENDSHIP.

AWWWW!

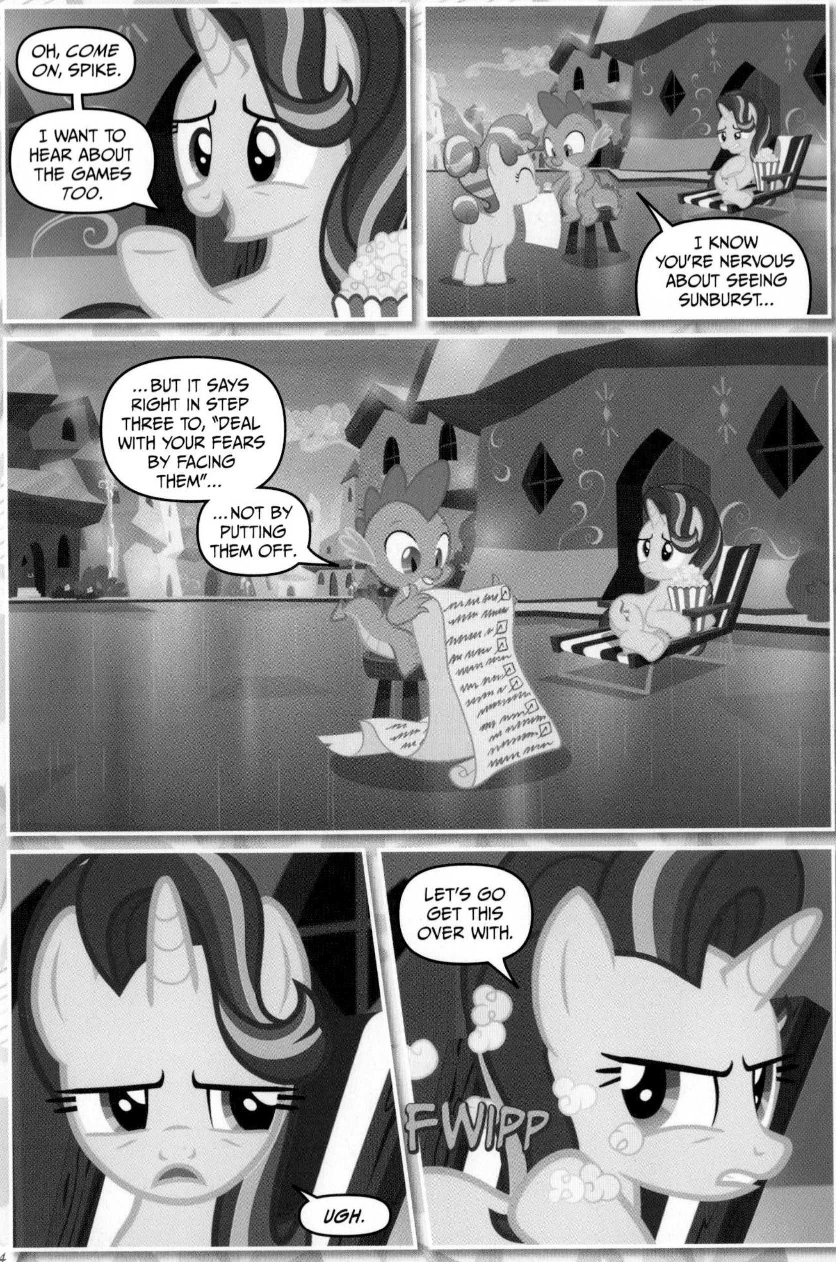
OH, COME ON, SPIKE.
I WANT TO HEAR ABOUT THE GAMES TOO.
I KNOW YOU'RE NERVOUS ABOUT SEEING SUNBURST...
...BUT IT SAYS RIGHT IN STEP THREE TO, "DEAL WITH YOUR FEARS BY FACING THEM"...
...NOT BY PUTTING THEM OFF.
UGH.
LET'S GO GET THIS OVER WITH.
FWIPP

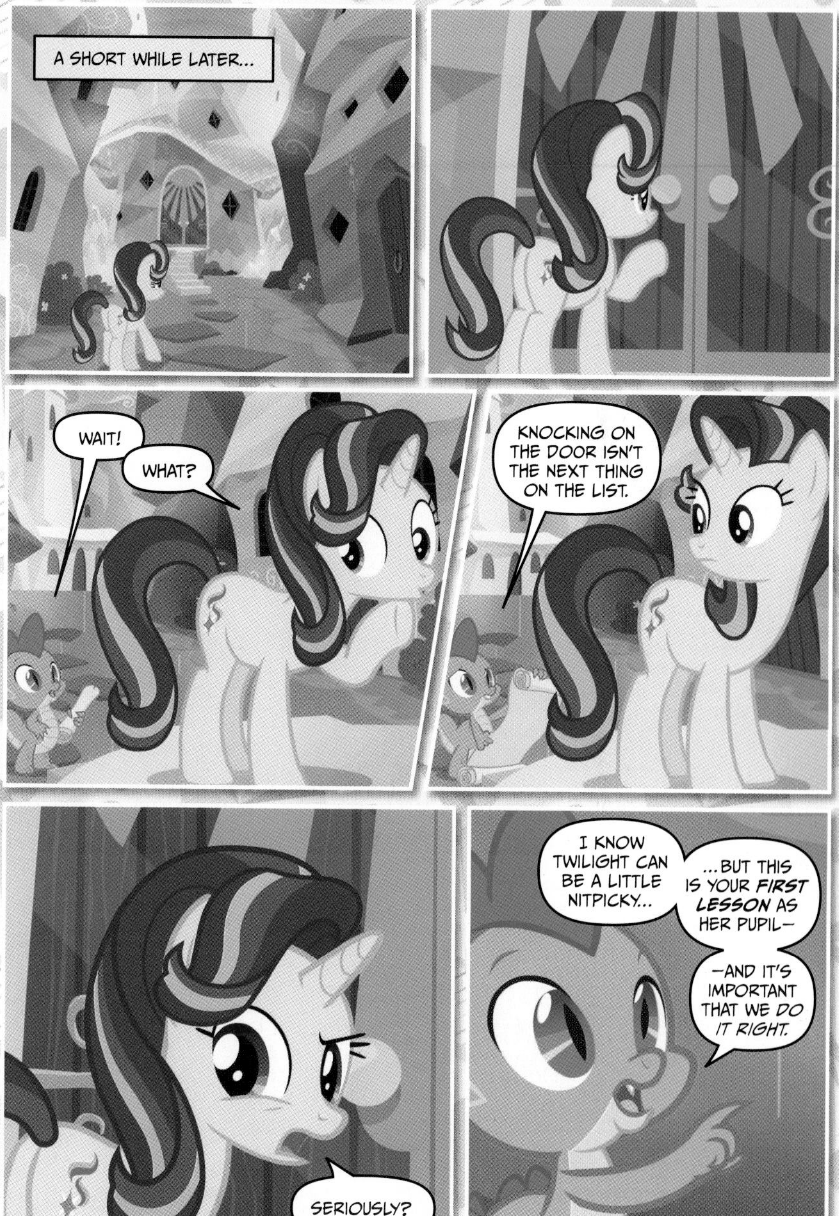
A SHORT WHILE LATER...
WAIT!
WHAT?
KNOCKING ON THE DOOR ISN'T THE NEXT THING ON THE LIST.
SERIOUSLY?
I KNOW TWILIGHT CAN BE A LITTLE NITPICKY...
...BUT THIS IS YOUR *FIRST LESSON* AS HER PUPIL—
—AND IT'S IMPORTANT THAT WE *DO IT RIGHT.*

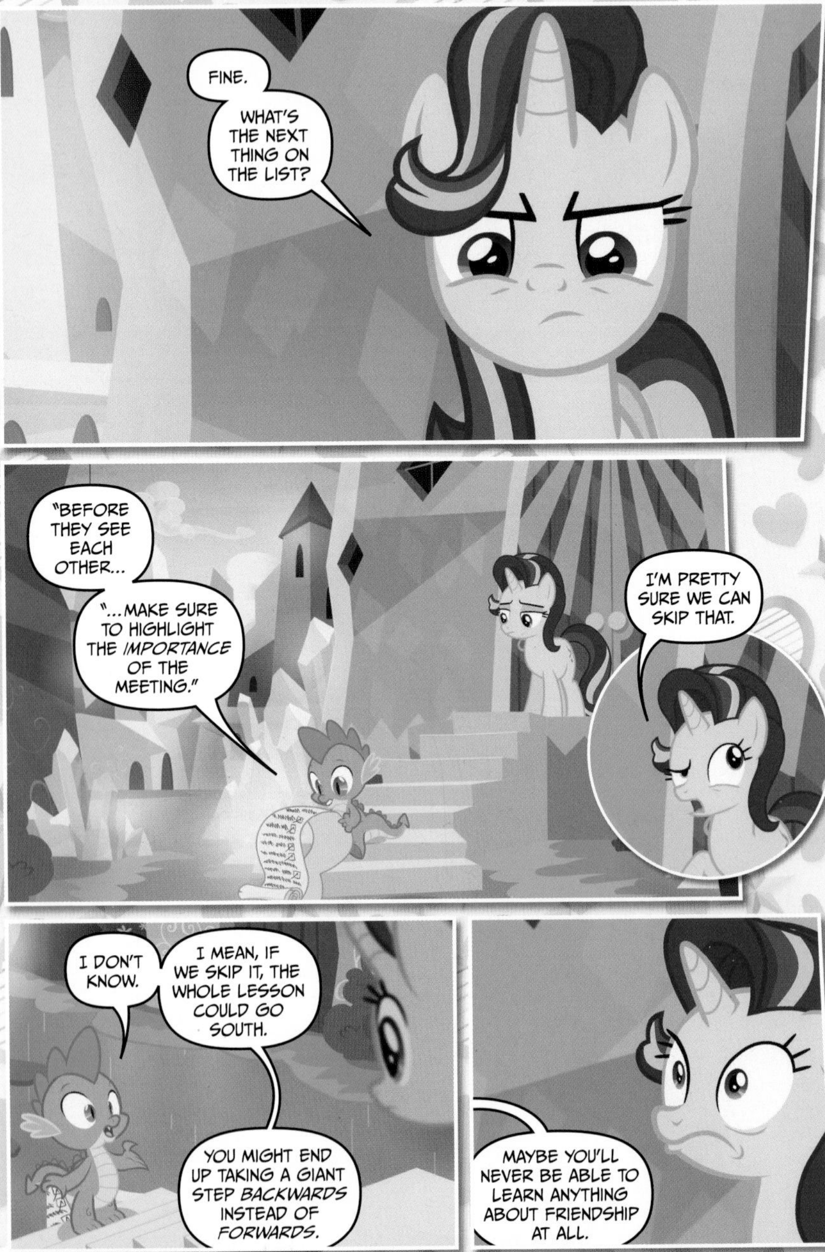
FINE.
WHAT'S THE NEXT THING ON THE LIST?
"BEFORE THEY SEE EACH OTHER...
"...MAKE SURE TO HIGHLIGHT THE *IMPORTANCE* OF THE MEETING."
I'M PRETTY SURE WE CAN SKIP THAT.
I DON'T KNOW.
I MEAN, IF WE SKIP IT, THE WHOLE LESSON COULD GO SOUTH.
YOU MIGHT END UP TAKING A GIANT STEP *BACKWARDS* INSTEAD OF *FORWARDS*.
MAYBE YOU'LL NEVER BE ABLE TO LEARN ANYTHING ABOUT FRIENDSHIP AT ALL.

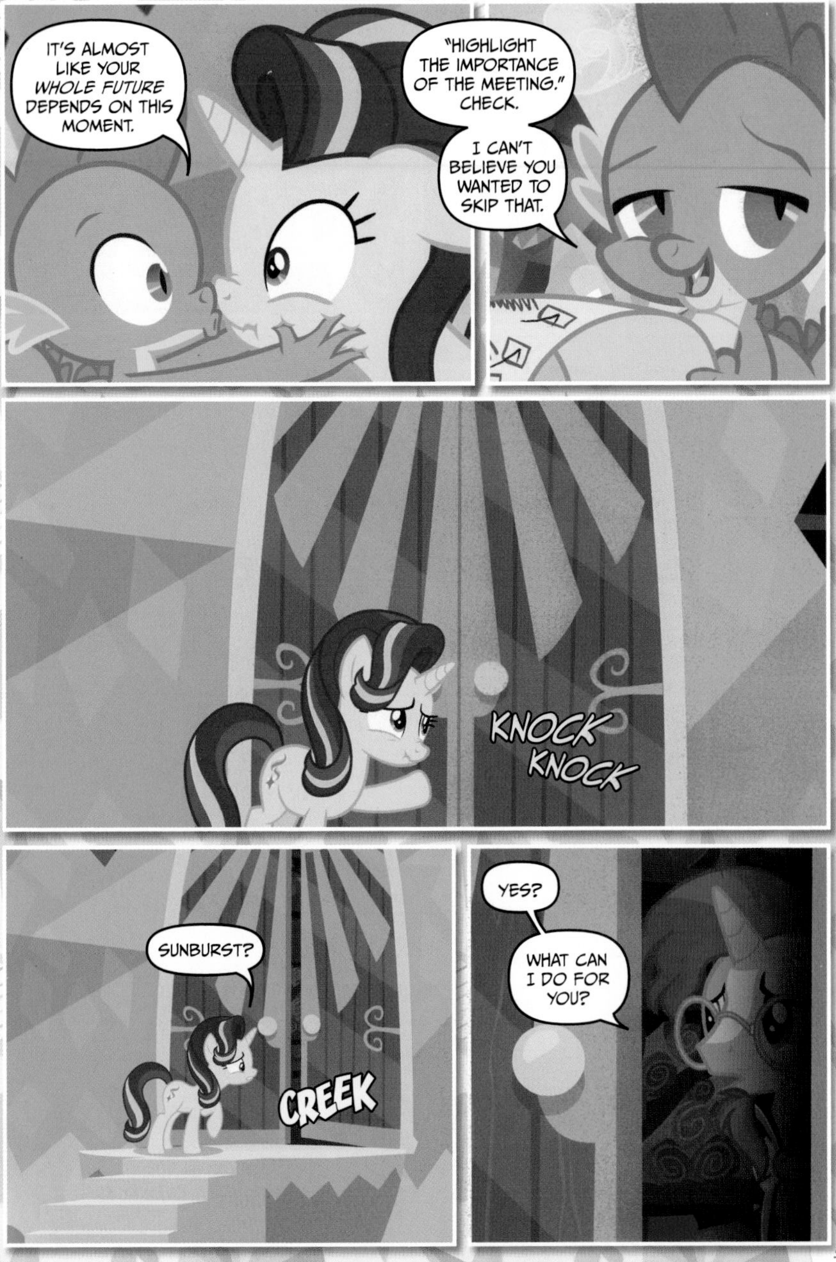
IT'S ALMOST LIKE YOUR *WHOLE FUTURE* DEPENDS ON THIS MOMENT.
"HIGHLIGHT THE IMPORTANCE OF THE MEETING." CHECK.
I CAN'T BELIEVE YOU WANTED TO SKIP THAT.
KNOCK KNOCK
SUNBURST?
CREEK
YES?
WHAT CAN I DO FOR YOU?

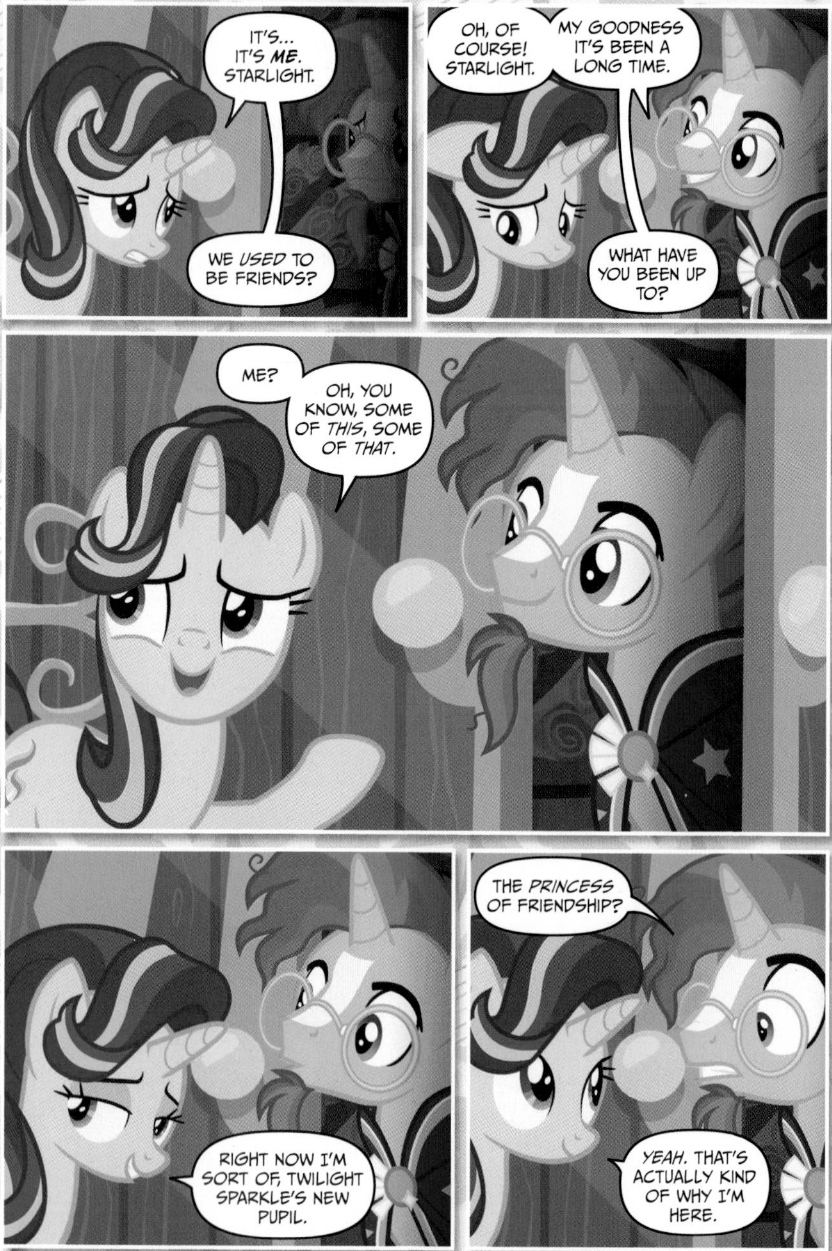
IT'S... IT'S **ME**. STARLIGHT.
WE *USED* TO BE FRIENDS?
OH, OF COURSE! STARLIGHT.
MY GOODNESS IT'S BEEN A LONG TIME.
WHAT HAVE YOU BEEN UP TO?
ME?
OH, YOU KNOW, SOME OF *THIS*, SOME OF *THAT*.
RIGHT NOW I'M SORT OF, TWILIGHT SPARKLE'S NEW PUPIL.
THE *PRINCESS* OF FRIENDSHIP?
YEAH. THAT'S ACTUALLY KIND OF WHY I'M HERE.

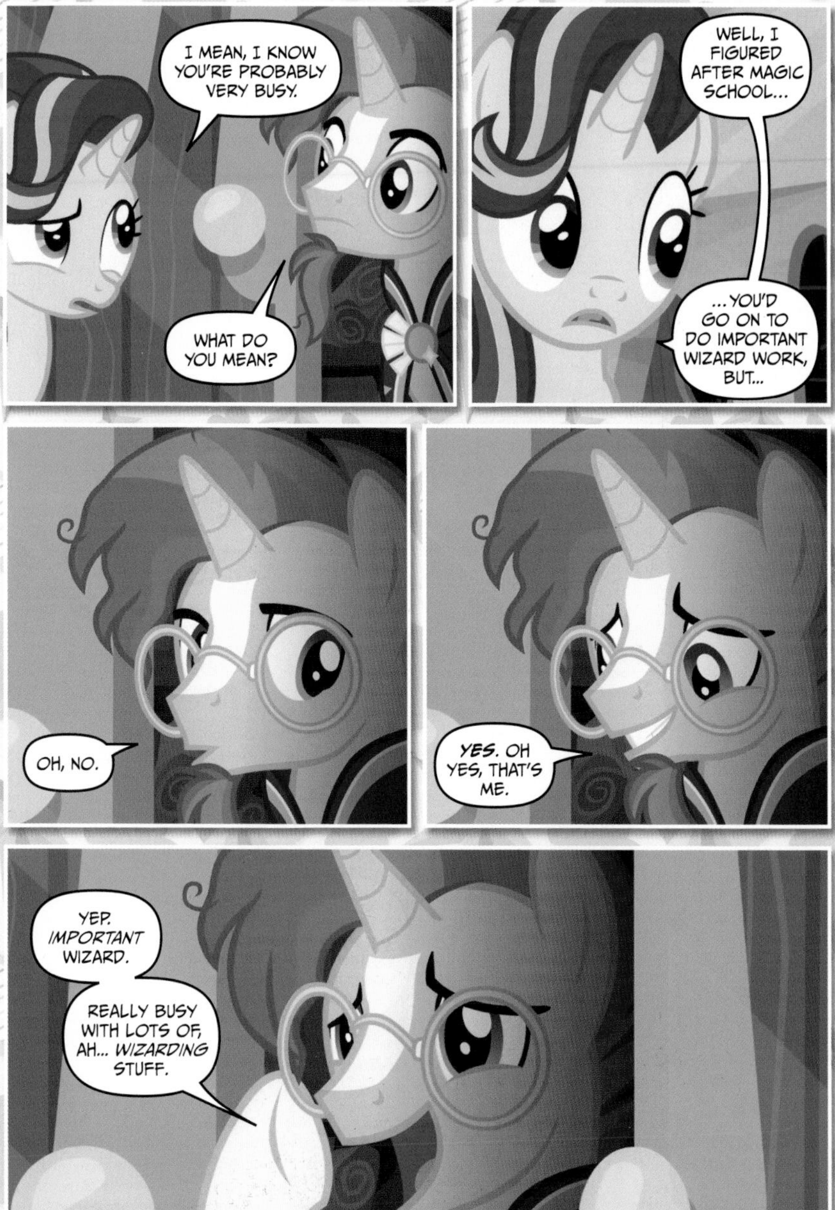
I MEAN, I KNOW YOU'RE PROBABLY VERY BUSY.
WHAT DO YOU MEAN?
WELL, I FIGURED AFTER MAGIC SCHOOL...
...YOU'D GO ON TO DO IMPORTANT WIZARD WORK, BUT...
OH, NO.
YES. OH YES, THAT'S ME.
YEP. *IMPORTANT* WIZARD.
REALLY BUSY WITH LOTS OF, AH... *WIZARDING* STUFF.

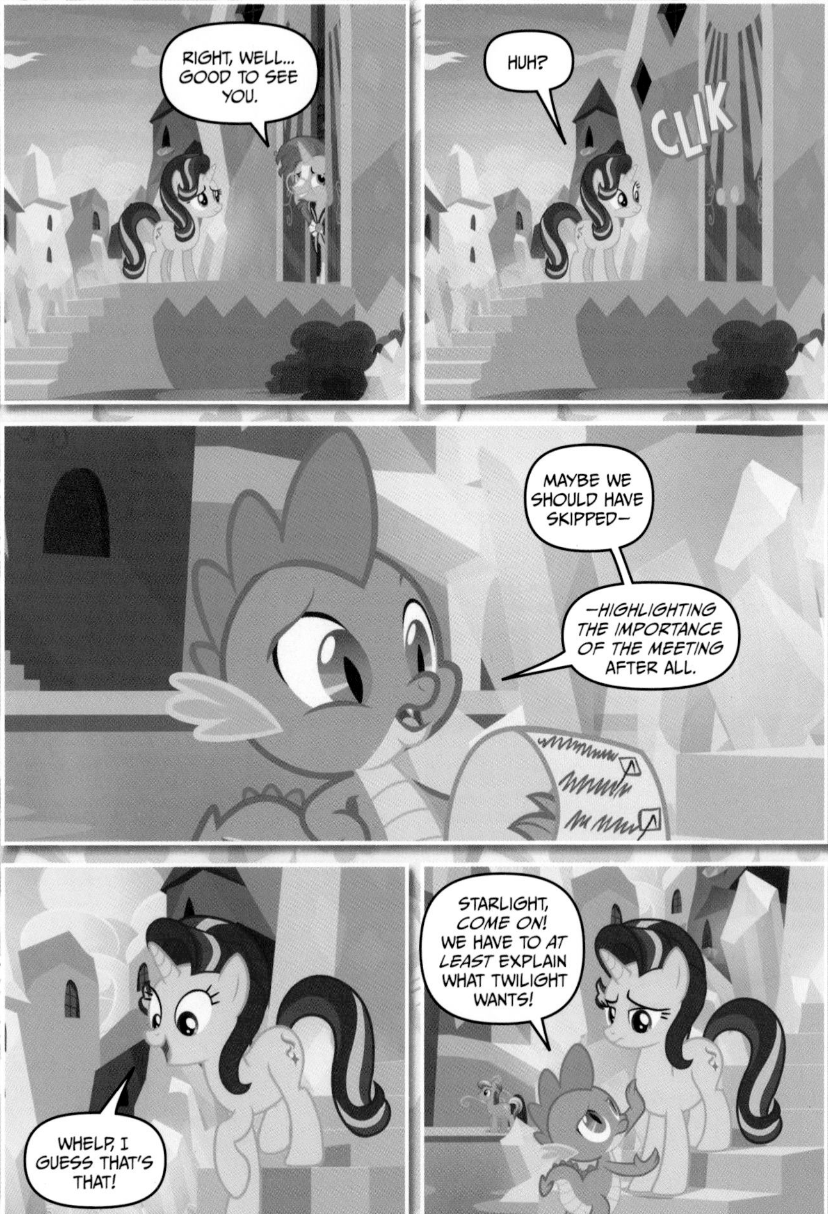
RIGHT, WELL... GOOD TO SEE YOU.
HUH?
CLIK
MAYBE WE SHOULD HAVE SKIPPED—
—HIGHLIGHTING THE IMPORTANCE OF THE MEETING AFTER ALL.
WHELP, I GUESS THAT'S THAT!
STARLIGHT, *COME ON!* WE HAVE TO AT *LEAST* EXPLAIN WHAT TWILIGHT WANTS!

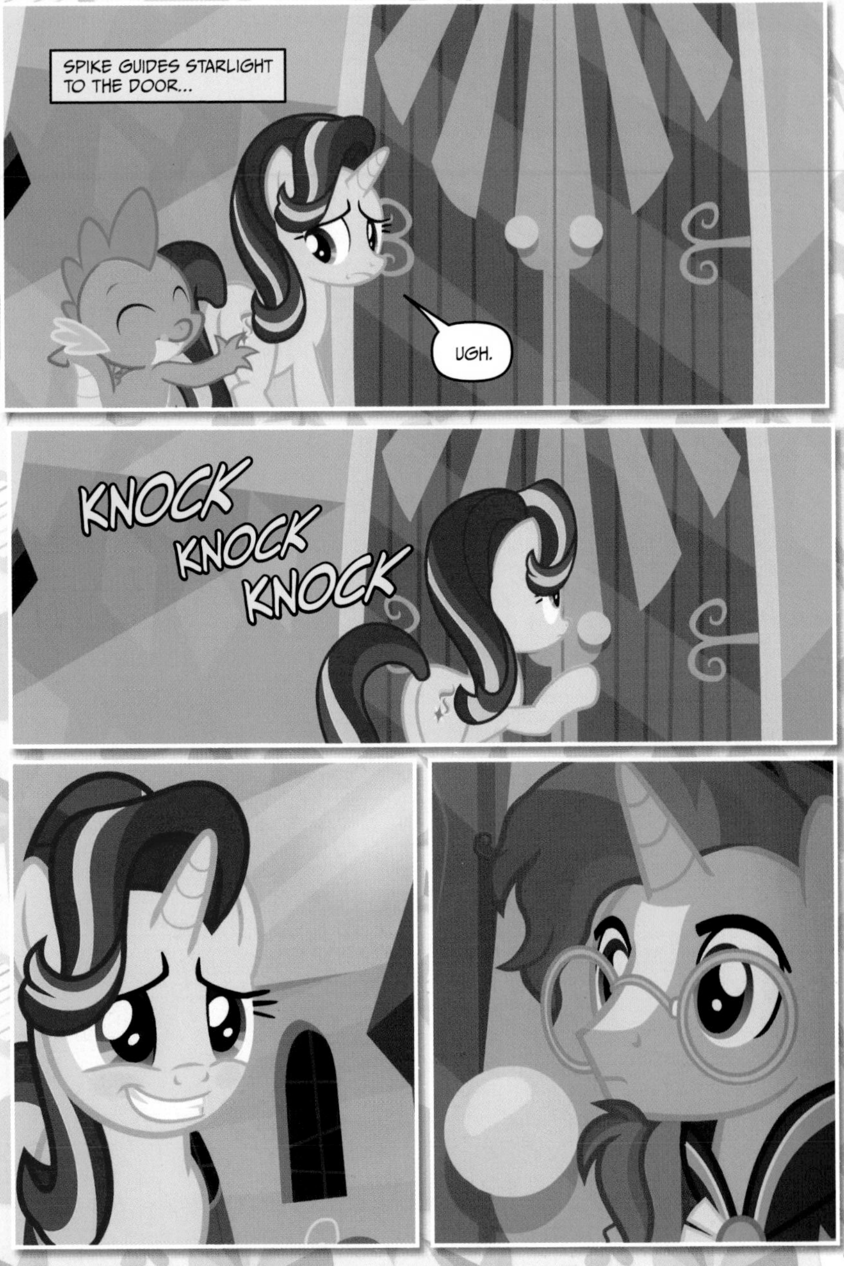
SPIKE GUIDES STARLIGHT TO THE DOOR...
UGH.
KNOCK
KNOCK
KNOCK

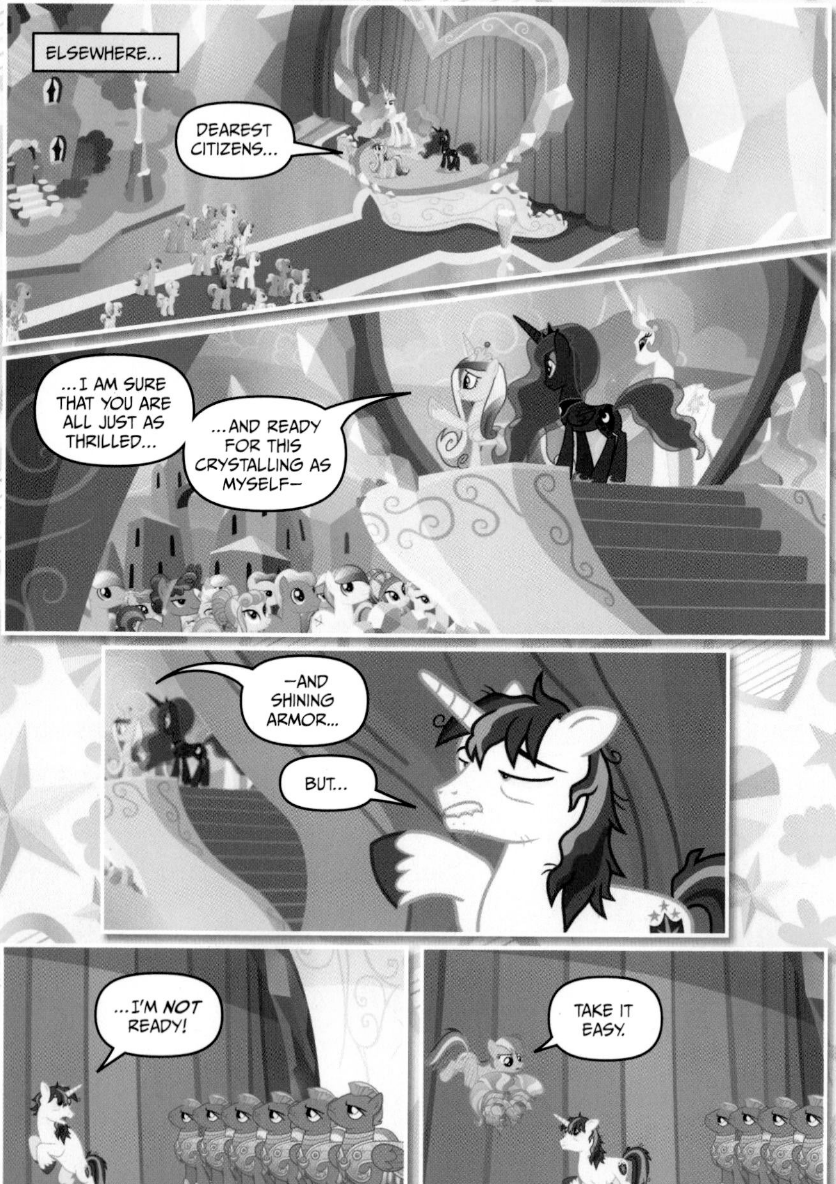
ELSEWHERE...
DEAREST CITIZENS...
...I AM SURE THAT YOU ARE ALL JUST AS THRILLED...
...AND READY FOR THIS CRYSTALLING AS MYSELF—
—AND SHINING ARMOR...
BUT...
...I'M *NOT* READY!
TAKE IT EASY.

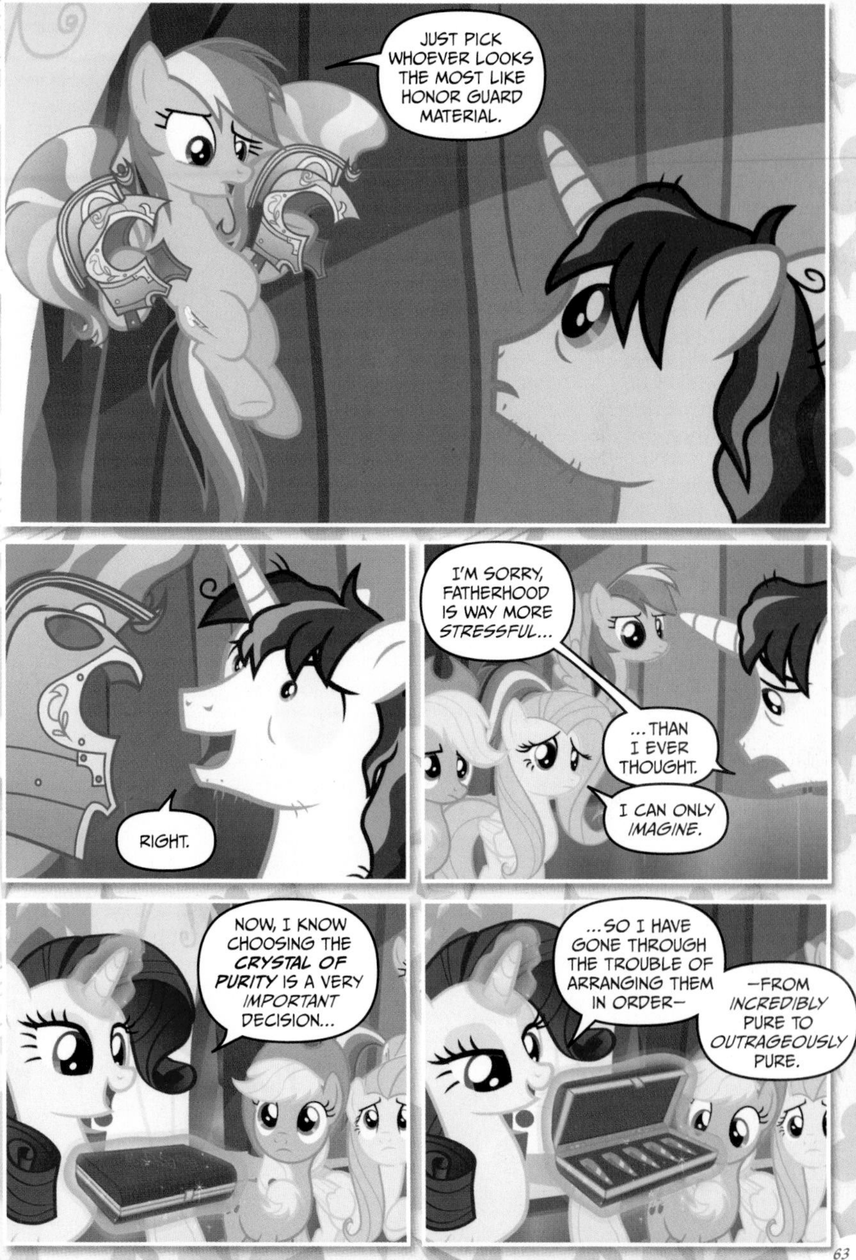
JUST PICK WHOEVER LOOKS THE MOST LIKE HONOR GUARD MATERIAL.
RIGHT.
I'M SORRY, FATHERHOOD IS WAY MORE *STRESSFUL*...
...THAN I EVER THOUGHT.
I CAN ONLY *IMAGINE*.
NOW, I KNOW CHOOSING THE ***CRYSTAL OF PURITY*** IS A VERY *IMPORTANT* DECISION...
...SO I HAVE GONE THROUGH THE TROUBLE OF ARRANGING THEM IN ORDER—
—FROM *INCREDIBLY* PURE TO *OUTRAGEOUSLY* PURE.

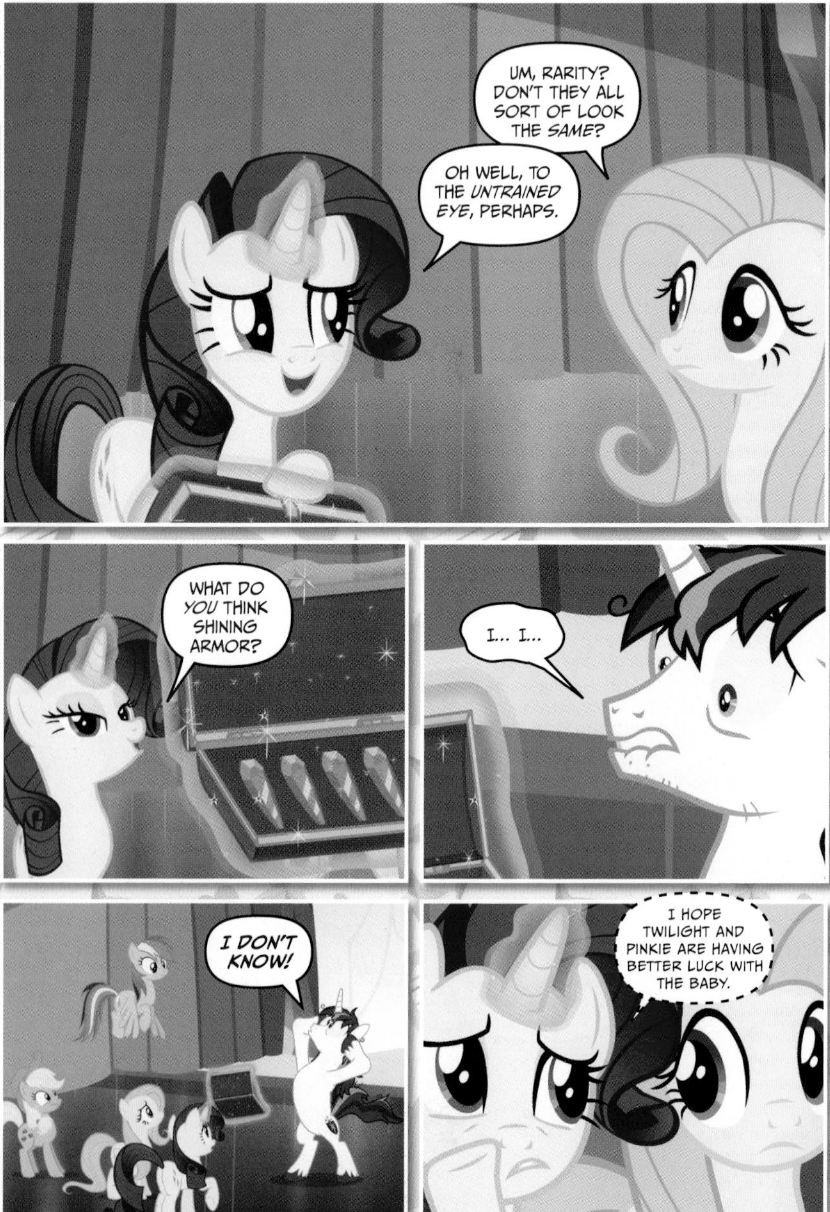
UM, RARITY? DON'T THEY ALL SORT OF LOOK THE *SAME*?
OH WELL, TO THE *UNTRAINED* EYE, PERHAPS.
WHAT DO *YOU* THINK SHINING ARMOR?
I... I...
I DON'T KNOW!
I HOPE TWILIGHT AND PINKIE ARE HAVING BETTER LUCK WITH THE BABY.

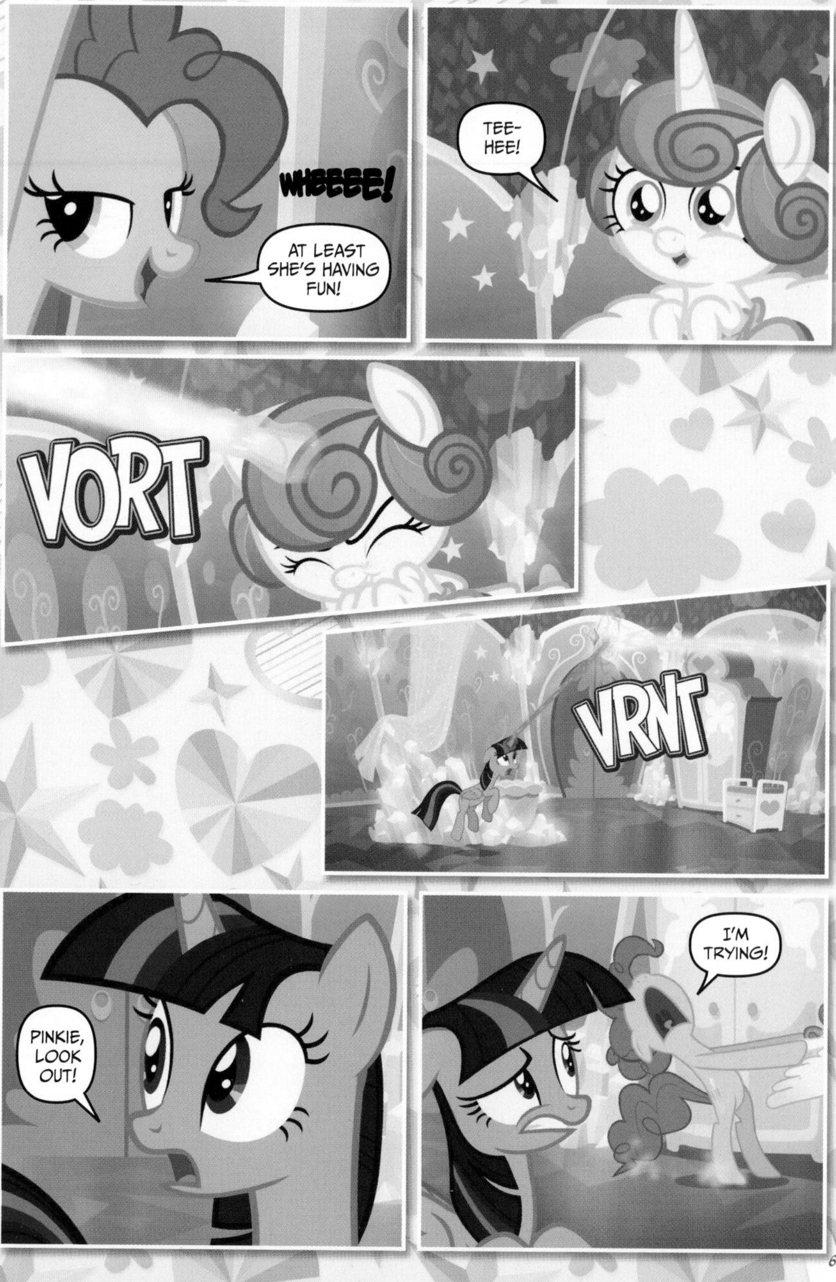
WHBEEEE!
AT LEAST SHE'S HAVING FUN!
TEE-HEE!
VORT
VRNT
PINKIE, LOOK OUT!
I'M TRYING!

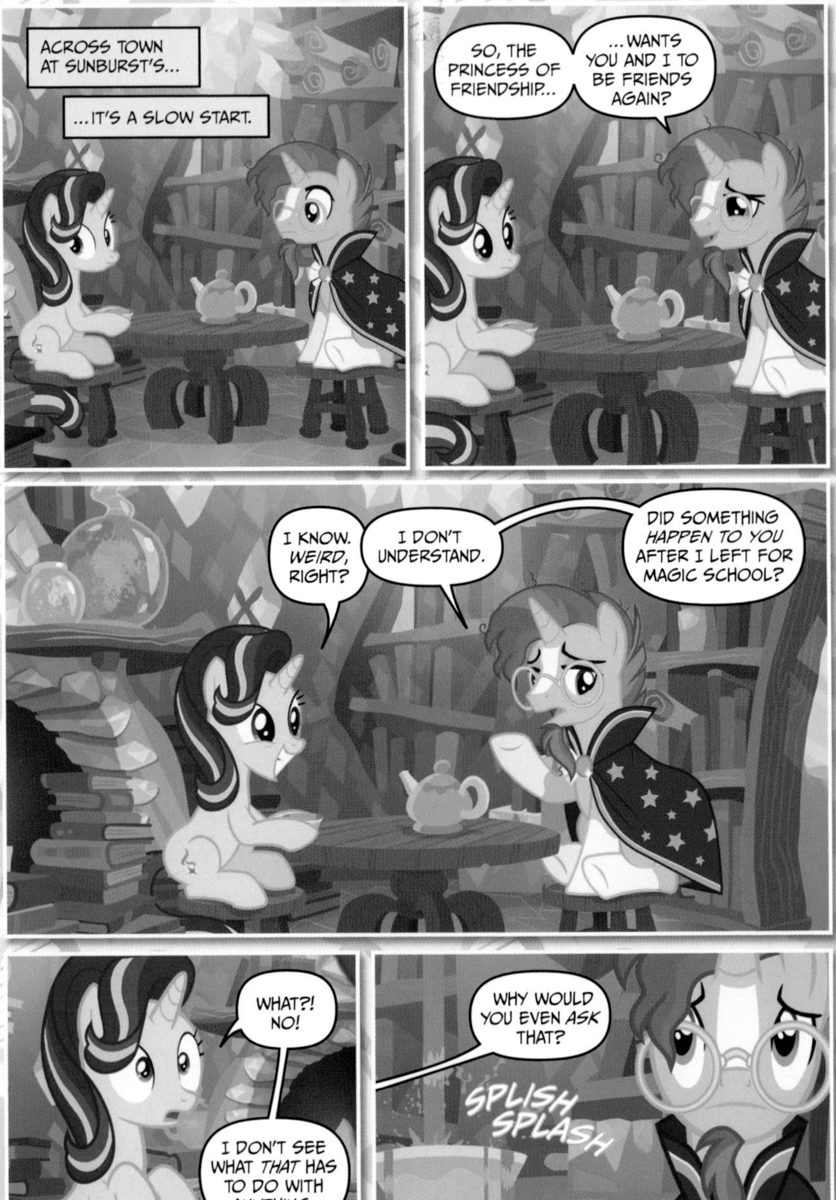
ACROSS TOWN AT SUNBURST'S...
...IT'S A SLOW START.
SO, THE PRINCESS OF FRIENDSHIP...
...WANTS YOU AND I TO BE FRIENDS AGAIN?
I KNOW. *WEIRD,* RIGHT?
I DON'T UNDERSTAND.
DID SOMETHING *HAPPEN TO YOU* AFTER I LEFT FOR MAGIC SCHOOL?
WHAT?! NO!
I DON'T SEE WHAT *THAT* HAS TO DO WITH ANYTHING.
WHY WOULD YOU EVEN *ASK* THAT?
SPLISH SPLASH

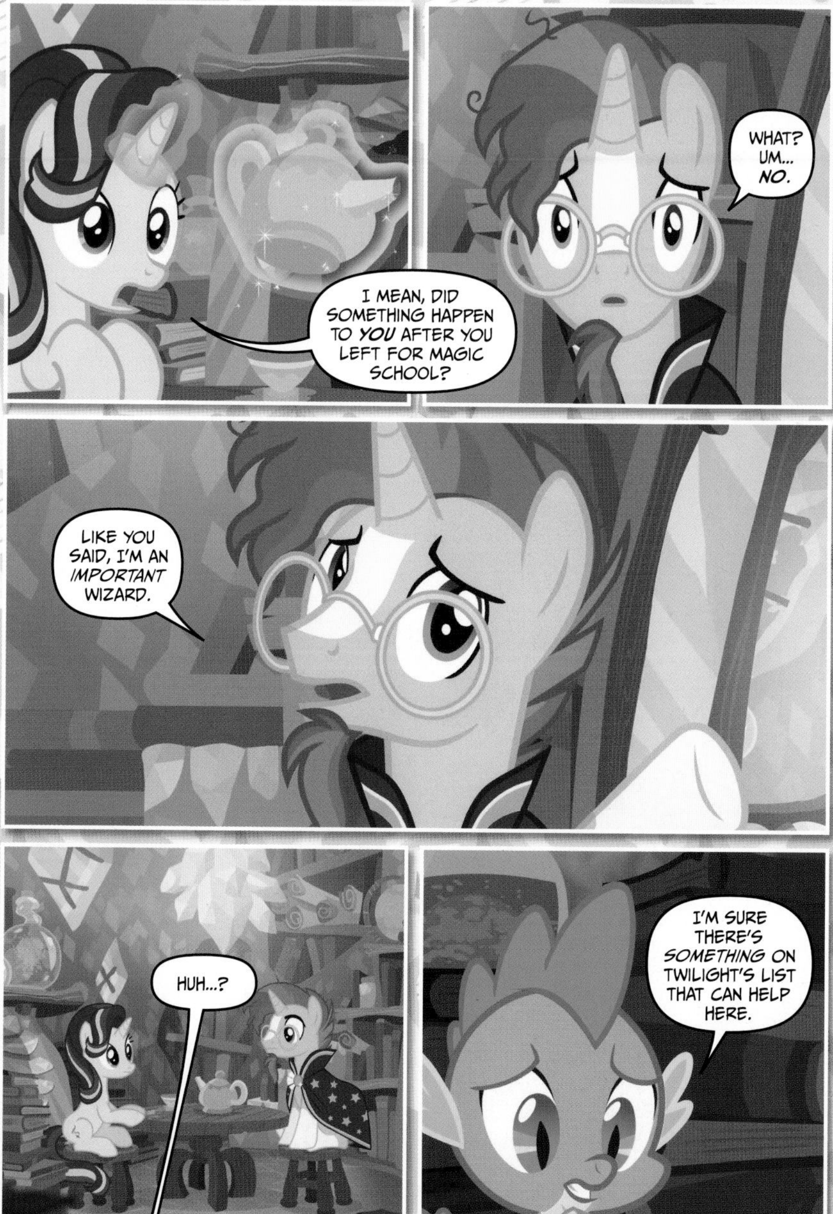
I MEAN, DID SOMETHING HAPPEN TO *YOU* AFTER YOU LEFT FOR MAGIC SCHOOL?
WHAT? UM... *NO.*
LIKE YOU SAID, I'M AN *IMPORTANT* WIZARD.
HUH...?
I'M SURE THERE'S *SOMETHING* ON TWILIGHT'S LIST THAT CAN HELP HERE.

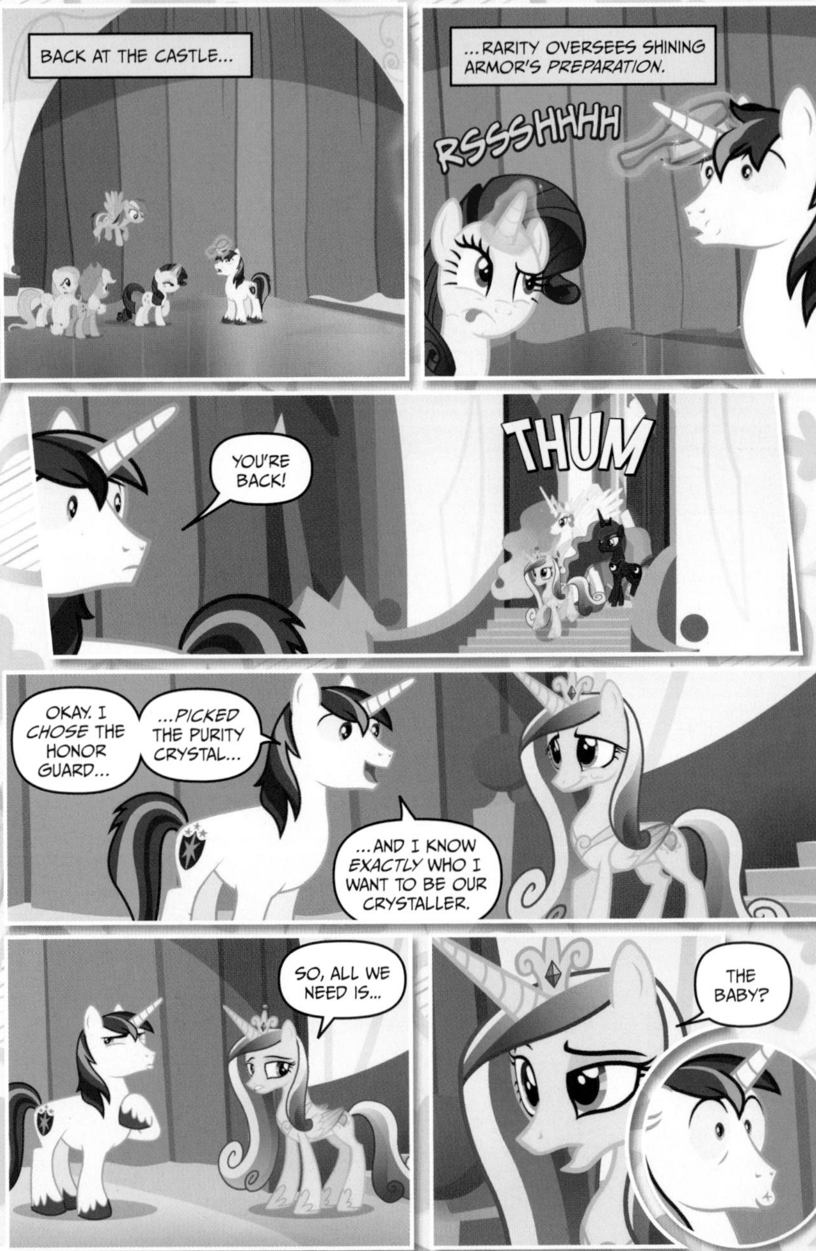
BACK AT THE CASTLE...
...RARITY OVERSEES SHINING ARMOR'S *PREPARATION*.
RSSSHHHH
YOU'RE BACK!
THUM
OKAY. I *CHOSE* THE HONOR GUARD...
...*PICKED* THE PURITY CRYSTAL...
...AND I KNOW *EXACTLY* WHO I WANT TO BE OUR CRYSTALLER.
SO, ALL WE NEED IS...
THE BABY?

WE'RE HERE!

SHE'S A *REALLY* STRONG FLYER!

VVVRRRRRMMMMM

VVRRRRRNNN

VVRRRRRNNN

PRINCESS CADANCE TAKES CONTROL WITH HER MAGIC...

BUT LITTLE BABY LIKES BEING WITH PINKIE PIE!

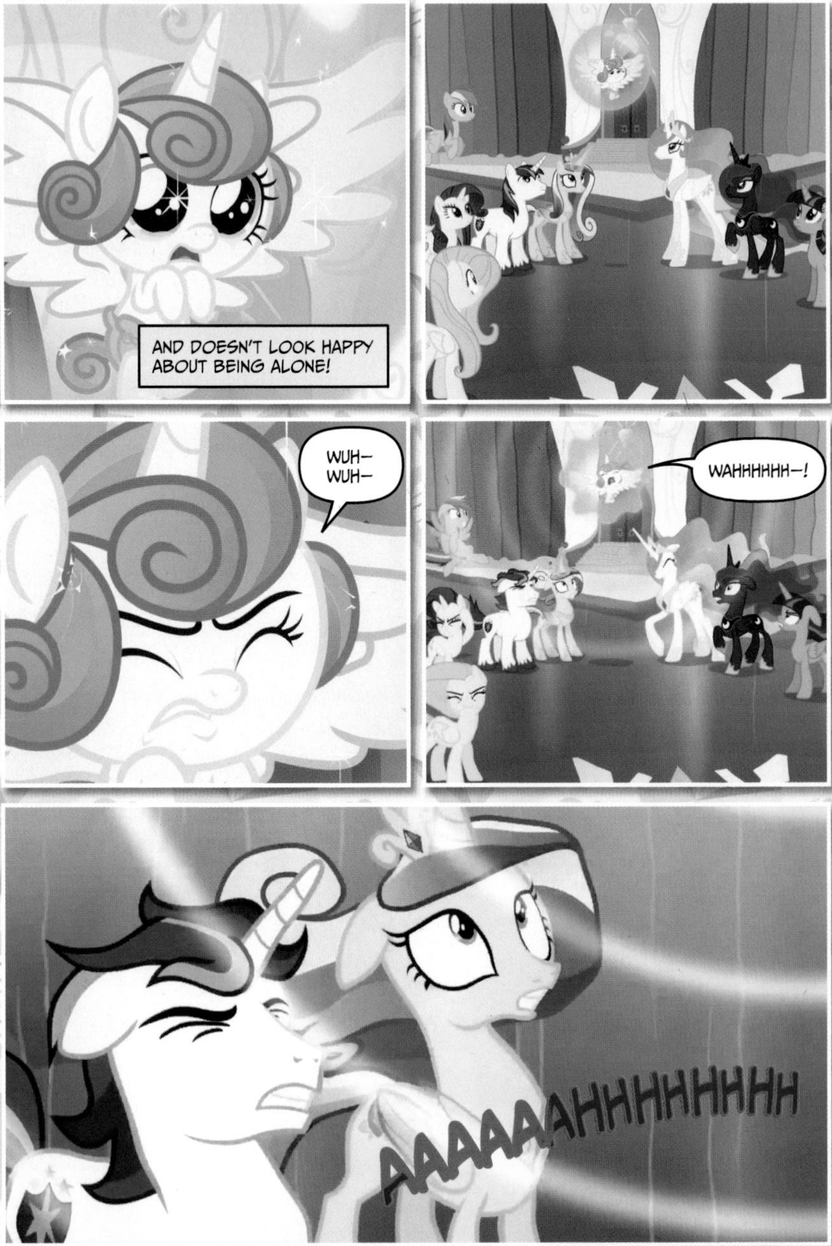
AND DOESN'T LOOK HAPPY ABOUT BEING ALONE!
WUH- WUH-
WAHHHHHH-!
AAAAAAHHHHHHHHH

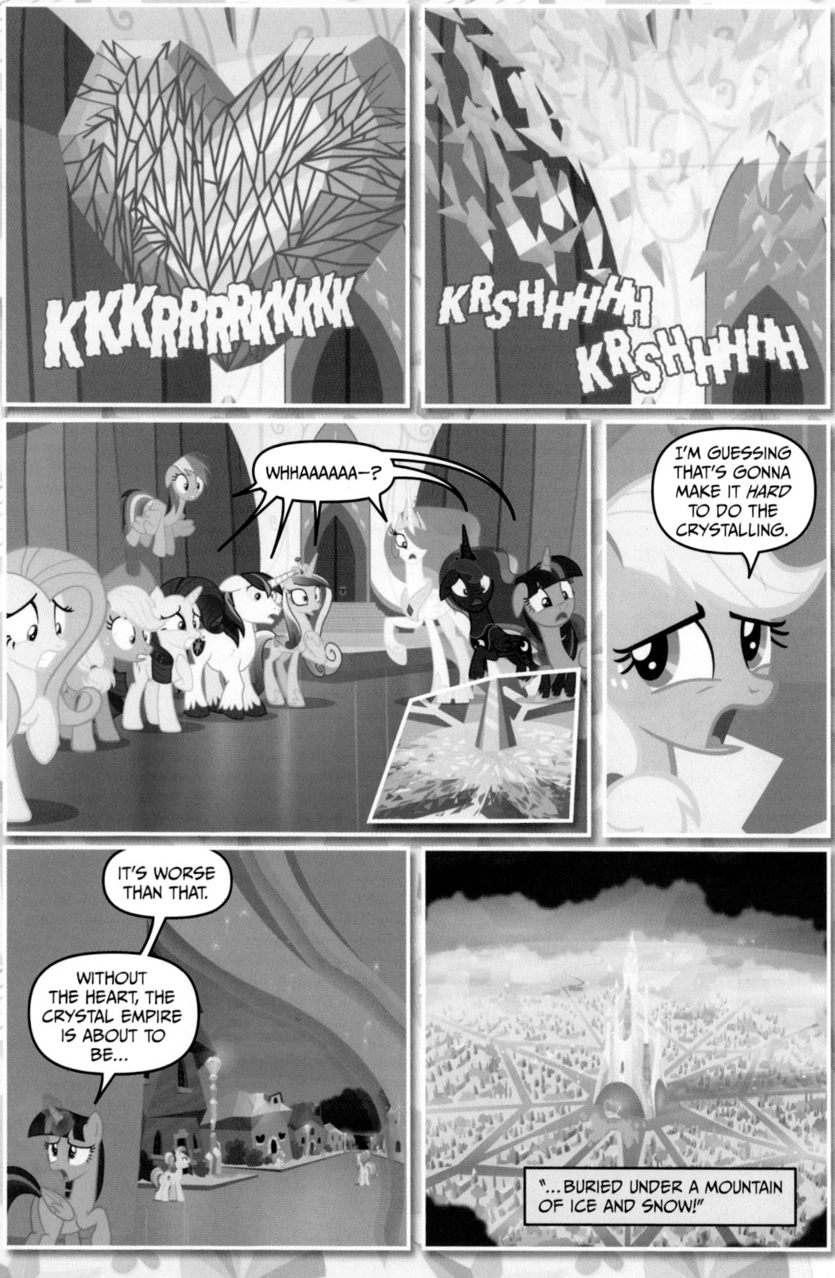
KKKRRRRKKKK
KRSHHHHH
KRSHHHHH
WHHAAAAAA–?
I'M GUESSING THAT'S GONNA MAKE IT *HARD* TO DO THE CRYSTALLING.
IT'S WORSE THAN THAT.
WITHOUT THE HEART, THE CRYSTAL EMPIRE IS ABOUT TO BE...
"...BURIED UNDER A MOUNTAIN OF ICE AND SNOW!"

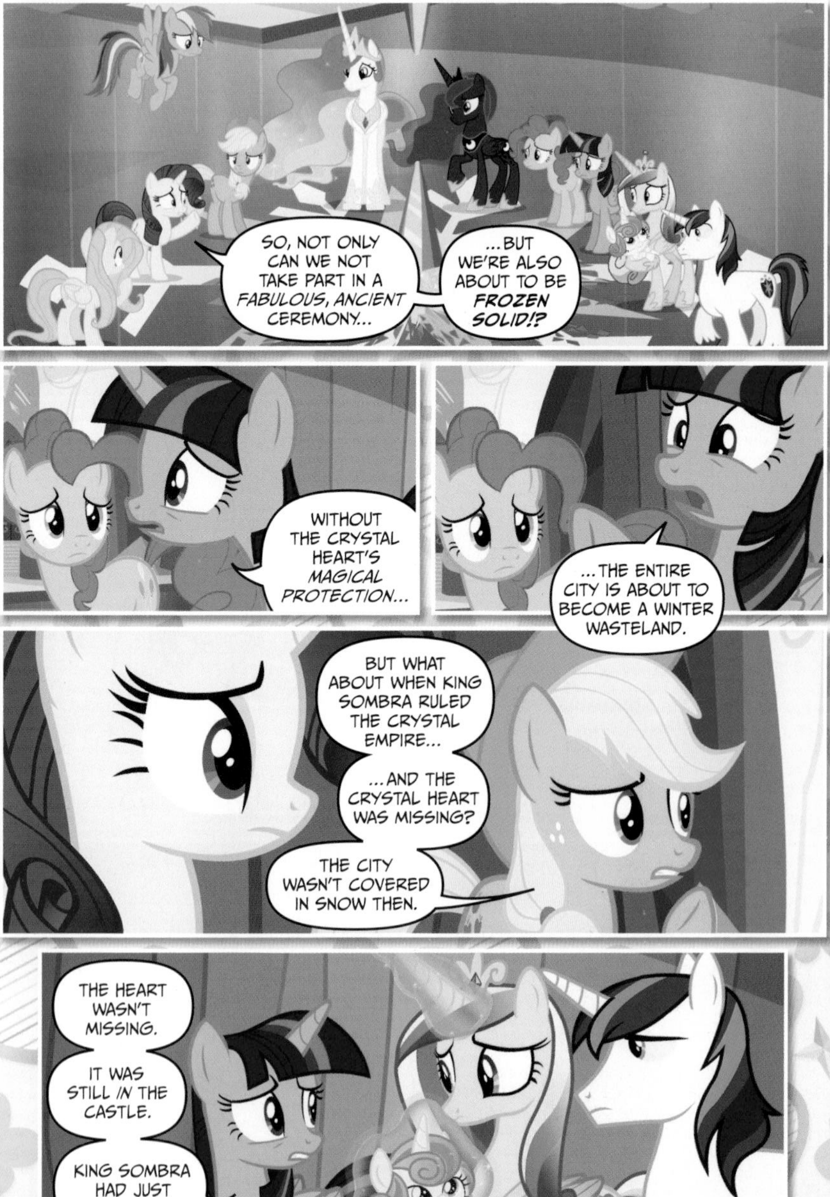
SO, NOT ONLY CAN WE NOT TAKE PART IN A *FABULOUS, ANCIENT* CEREMONY...
...BUT WE'RE ALSO ABOUT TO BE **FROZEN SOLID!?**
WITHOUT THE CRYSTAL HEART'S *MAGICAL PROTECTION*...
...THE ENTIRE CITY IS ABOUT TO BECOME A WINTER WASTELAND.
BUT WHAT ABOUT WHEN KING SOMBRA RULED THE CRYSTAL EMPIRE...
...AND THE CRYSTAL HEART WAS MISSING?
THE CITY WASN'T COVERED IN SNOW THEN.
THE HEART WASN'T MISSING.
IT WAS STILL *IN* THE CASTLE.
KING SOMBRA HAD JUST HIDDEN IT.

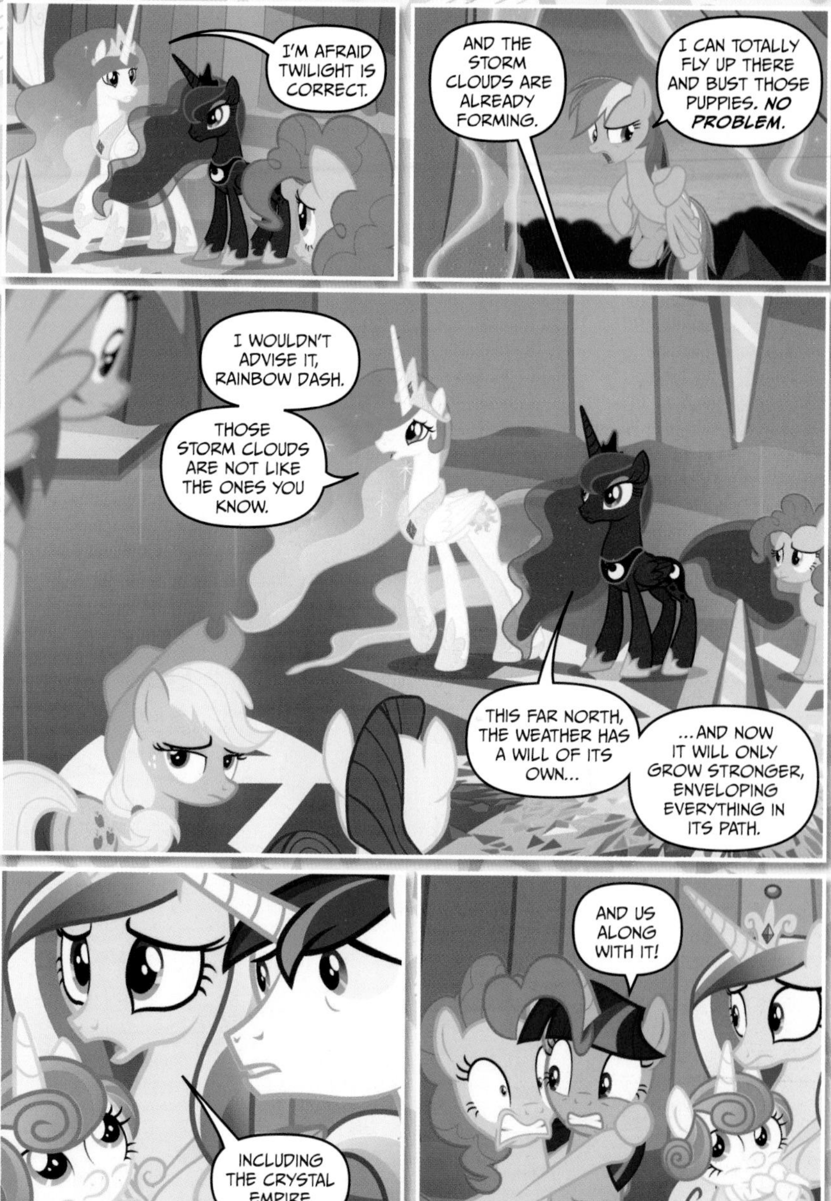
I'M AFRAID TWILIGHT IS CORRECT.
AND THE STORM CLOUDS ARE ALREADY FORMING.
I CAN TOTALLY FLY UP THERE AND BUST THOSE PUPPIES. **NO PROBLEM.**
I WOULDN'T ADVISE IT, RAINBOW DASH.
THOSE STORM CLOUDS ARE NOT LIKE THE ONES YOU KNOW.
THIS FAR NORTH, THE WEATHER HAS A WILL OF ITS OWN...
...AND NOW IT WILL ONLY GROW STRONGER, ENVELOPING EVERYTHING IN ITS PATH.
INCLUDING THE CRYSTAL EMPIRE.
AND US ALONG WITH IT!

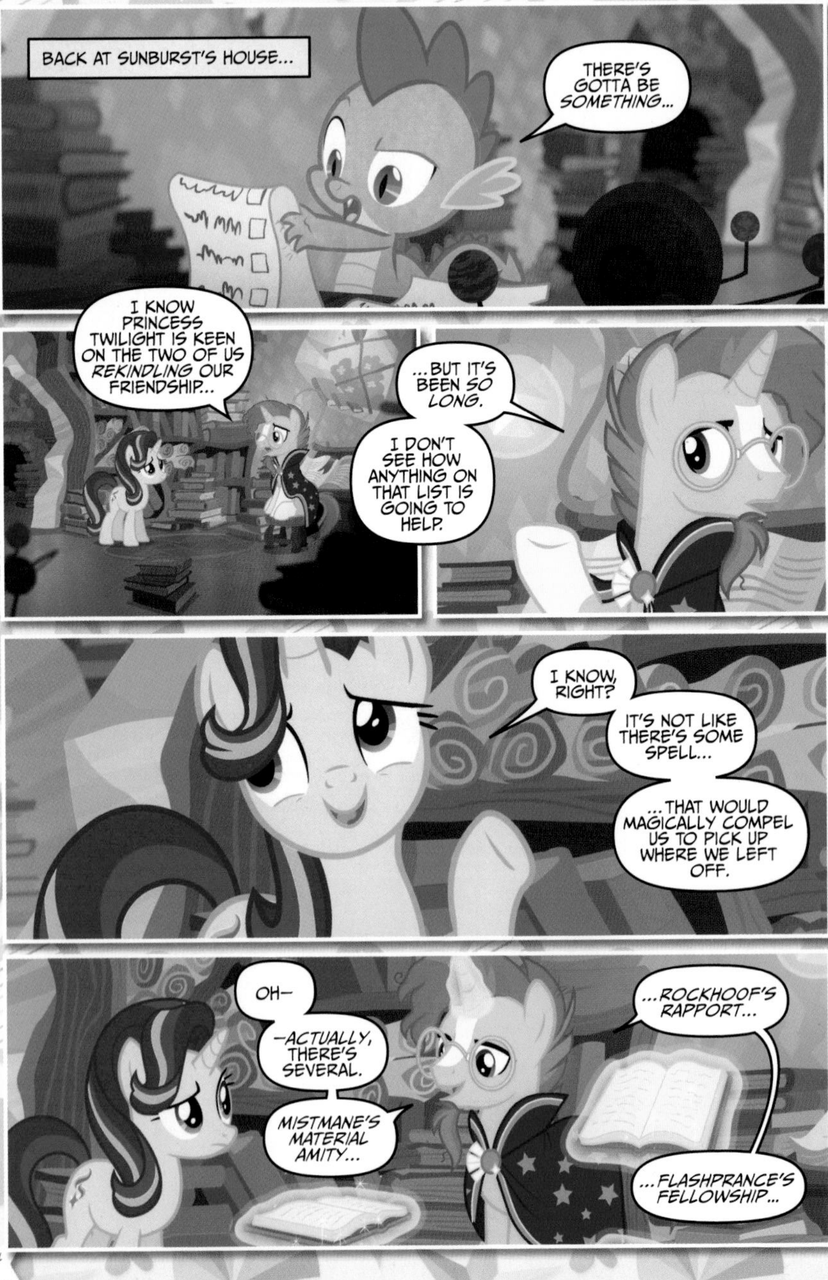
BACK AT SUNBURST'S HOUSE...
THERE'S GOTTA BE SOMETHING...
I KNOW PRINCESS TWILIGHT IS KEEN ON THE TWO OF US REKINDLING OUR FRIENDSHIP...
...BUT IT'S BEEN SO LONG.
I DON'T SEE HOW ANYTHING ON THAT LIST IS GOING TO HELP.
I KNOW, RIGHT?
IT'S NOT LIKE THERE'S SOME SPELL...
...THAT WOULD MAGICALLY COMPEL US TO PICK UP WHERE WE LEFT OFF.
OH—
—ACTUALLY, THERE'S SEVERAL.
MISTMANE'S MATERIAL AMITY...
...ROCKHOOF'S RAPPORT...
...FLASHPRANCE'S FELLOWSHIP...

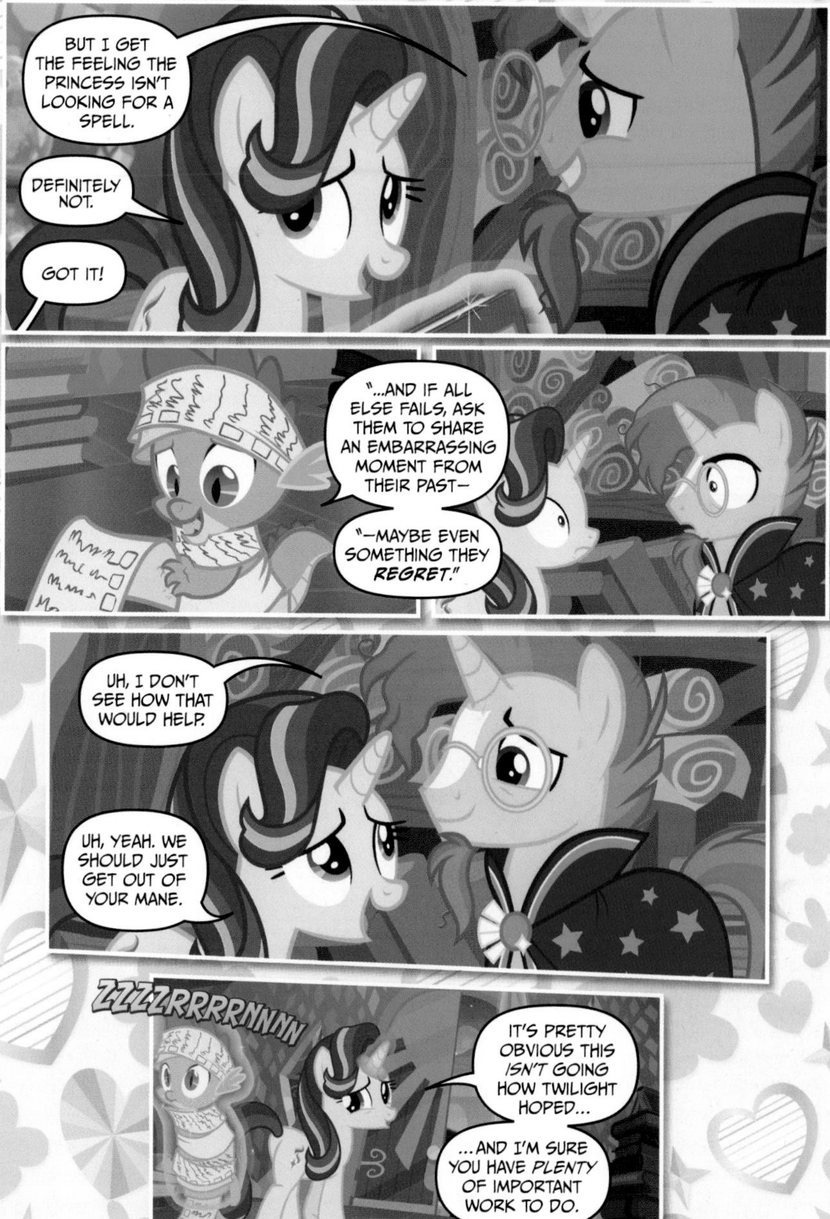
BUT I GET THE FEELING THE PRINCESS ISN'T LOOKING FOR A SPELL.
DEFINITELY NOT.
GOT IT!
"...AND IF ALL ELSE FAILS, ASK THEM TO SHARE AN EMBARRASSING MOMENT FROM THEIR PAST—
"—MAYBE EVEN SOMETHING THEY *REGRET*."
UH, I DON'T SEE HOW THAT WOULD HELP.
UH, YEAH. WE SHOULD JUST GET OUT OF YOUR MANE.
ZZZZRRRRNNNN
IT'S PRETTY OBVIOUS THIS *ISN'T* GOING HOW TWILIGHT HOPED...
...AND I'M SURE YOU HAVE *PLENTY* OF IMPORTANT WORK TO DO.

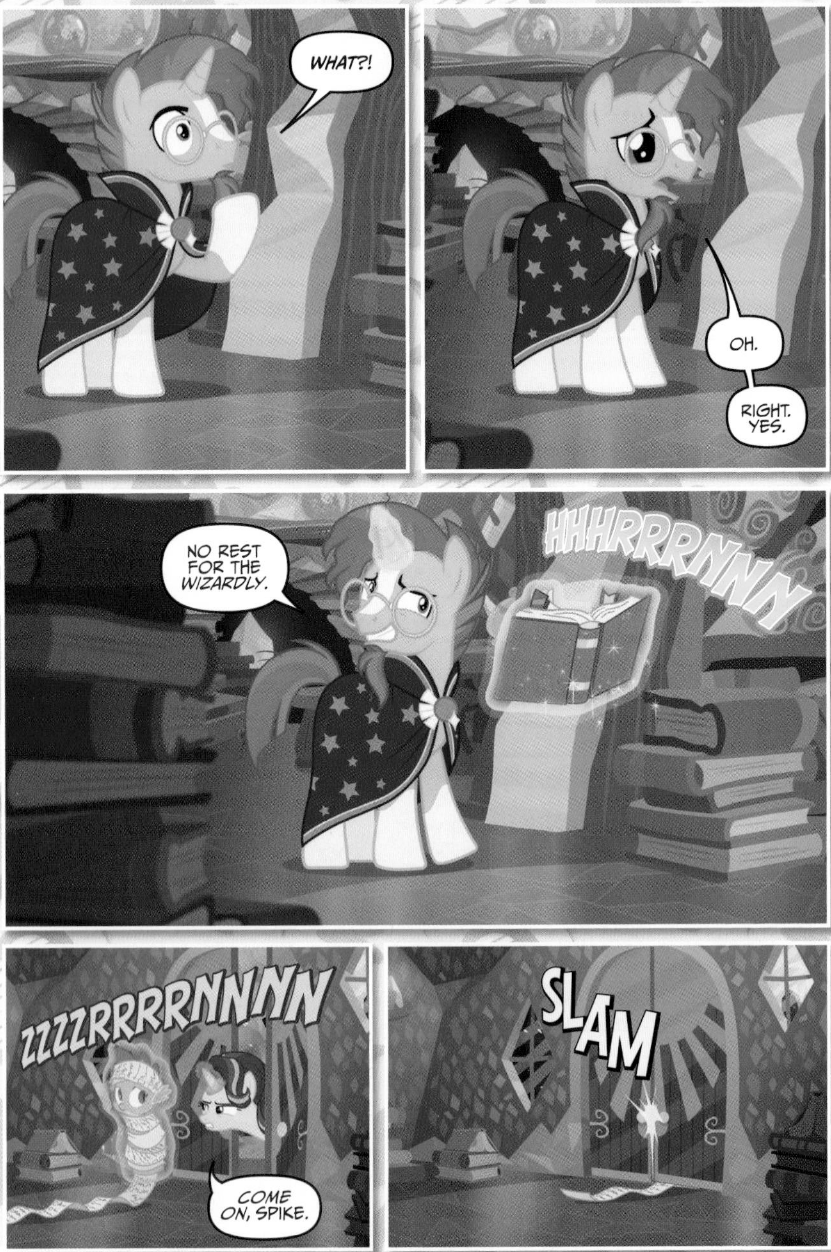
WHAT?!
OH.
RIGHT. YES.
NO REST FOR THE WIZARDLY.
HHHRRRRNNN
ZZZZRRRRNNNN
COME ON, SPIKE.
SLAM

THE STORM CLOSES IN ON THE CRYSTAL EMPIRE.

FFFWWWWWWWOOOOOOOSSSSSHHHH

THERE *MUST* BE A SPELL THAT CAN RESTORE THE CRYSTAL HEART.

PERHAPS.

BUT IT ISN'T SOMETHING EITHER OF US KNOW.

THE LIBRARY HERE AT THE CASTLE...

...IS *NEARLY* AS EXTENSIVE AS THE ONE IN CANTERLOT.

THERE'S A GOOD CHANCE WE CAN FIND SOMETHING THERE.

CAN YOU HOLD OFF THE STORM?

YES, FOR A TIME...

...BUT EVEN OUR MAGIC WILL EVENTUALLY SUCCUMB TO THE POWER OF THE FROZEN NORTH.

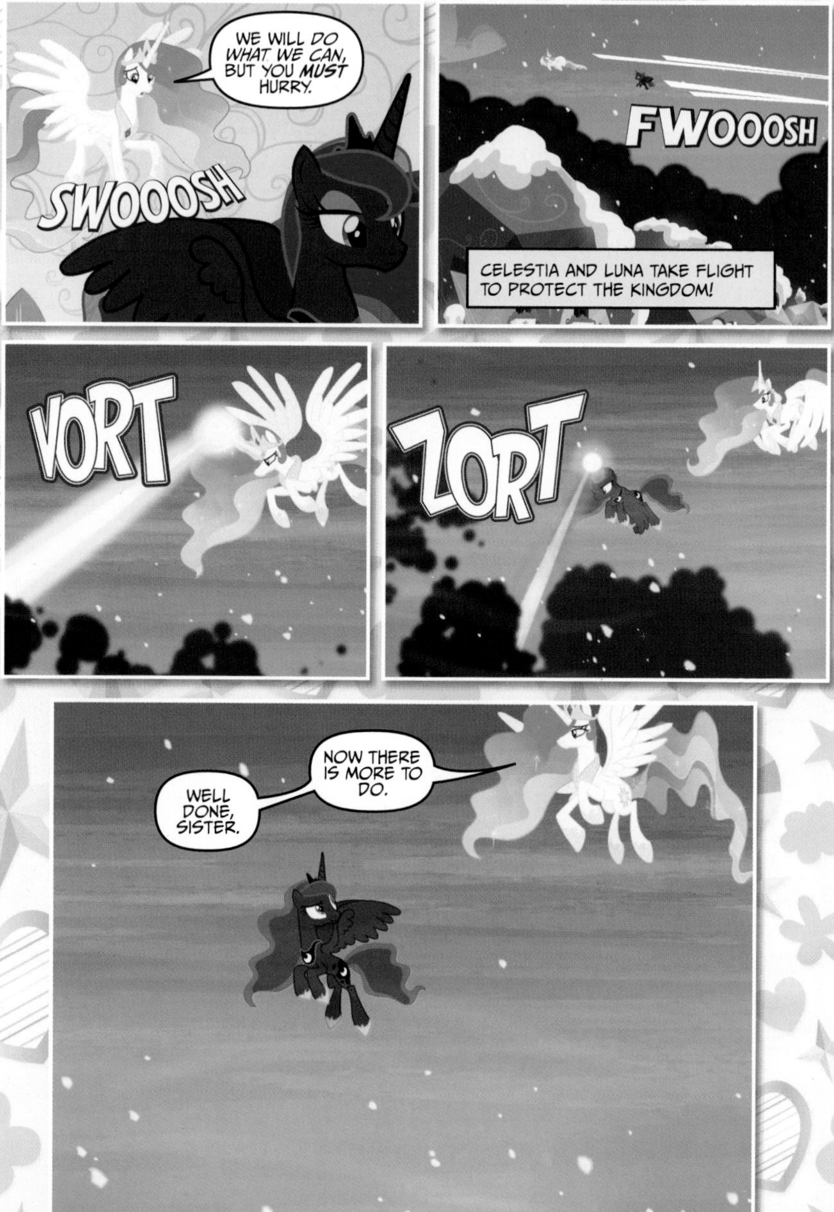
WE WILL DO WHAT WE CAN, BUT YOU MUST HURRY.
SWOOOSH
FWOOOSH
CELESTIA AND LUNA TAKE FLIGHT TO PROTECT THE KINGDOM!
VORT
ZORT
WELL DONE, SISTER.
NOW THERE IS MORE TO DO.

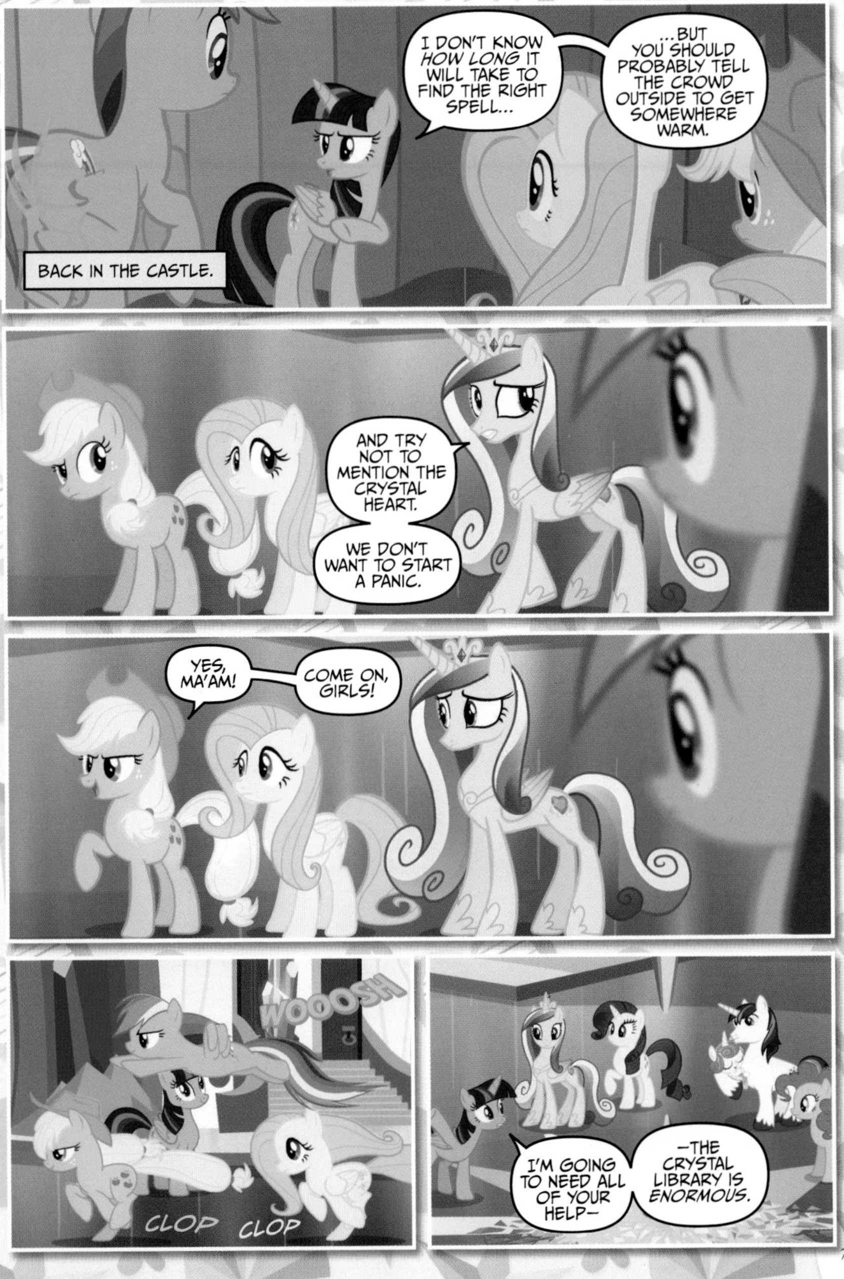
BACK IN THE CASTLE.
I DON'T KNOW *HOW LONG* IT WILL TAKE TO FIND THE RIGHT SPELL...
...BUT YOU SHOULD PROBABLY TELL THE CROWD OUTSIDE TO GET SOMEWHERE WARM.
AND TRY NOT TO MENTION THE CRYSTAL HEART.
WE DON'T WANT TO START A PANIC.
YES, MA'AM!
COME ON, GIRLS!
WOOOSH
CLOP CLOP
I'M GOING TO NEED ALL OF YOUR HELP—
—THE CRYSTAL LIBRARY IS *ENORMOUS*.

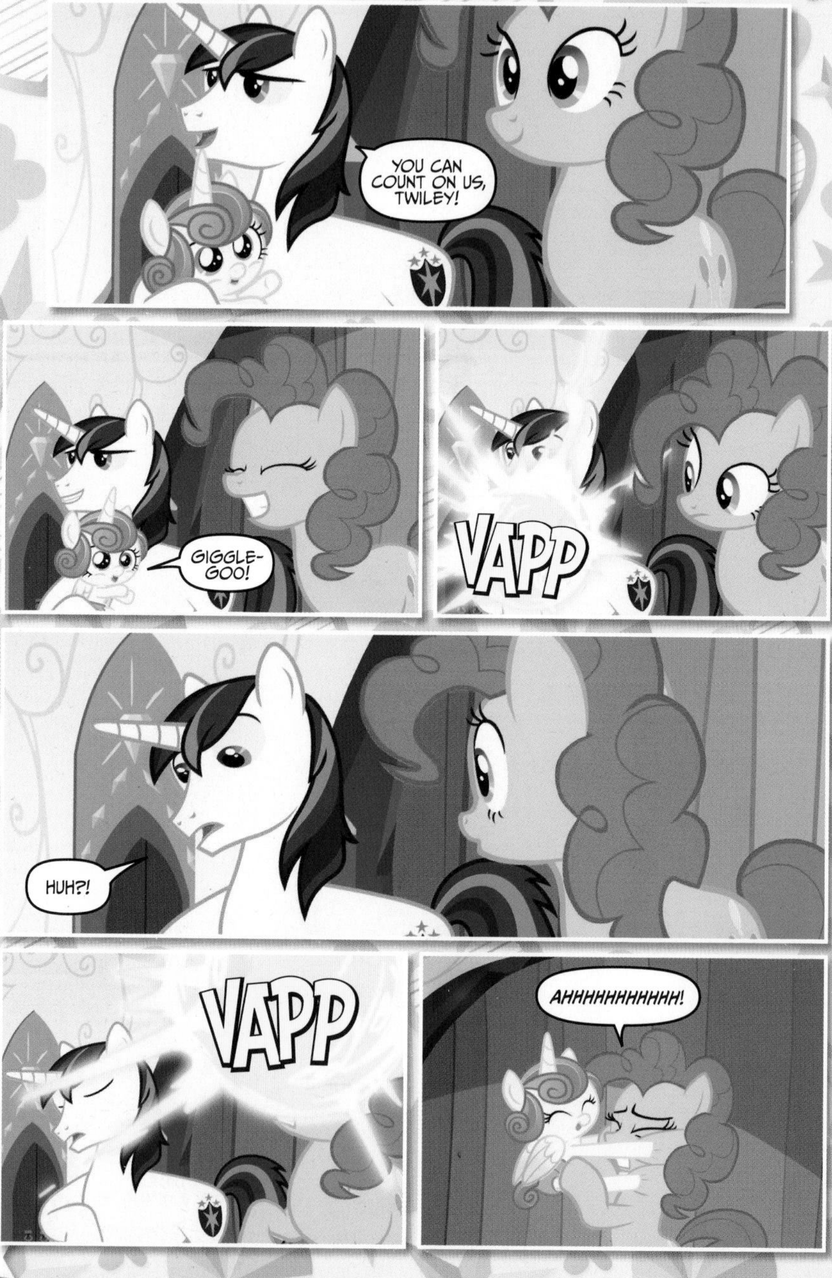
YOU CAN COUNT ON US, TWILEY!
GIGGLE-GOO!
VAPP
HUH?!
VAPP
AHHHHHHHHHHHH!

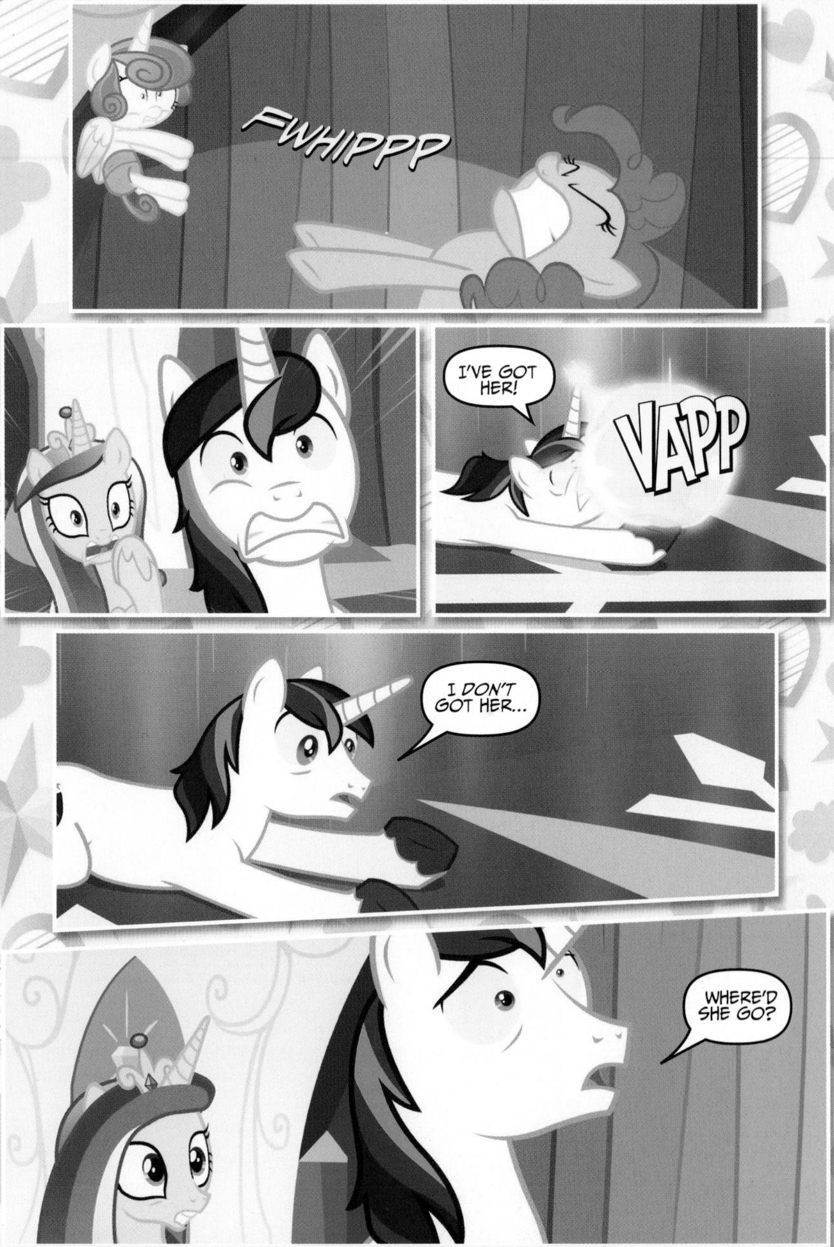
FWHIPPP
I'VE GOT HER!
VAPP
I DON'T GOT HER...
WHERE'D SHE GO?

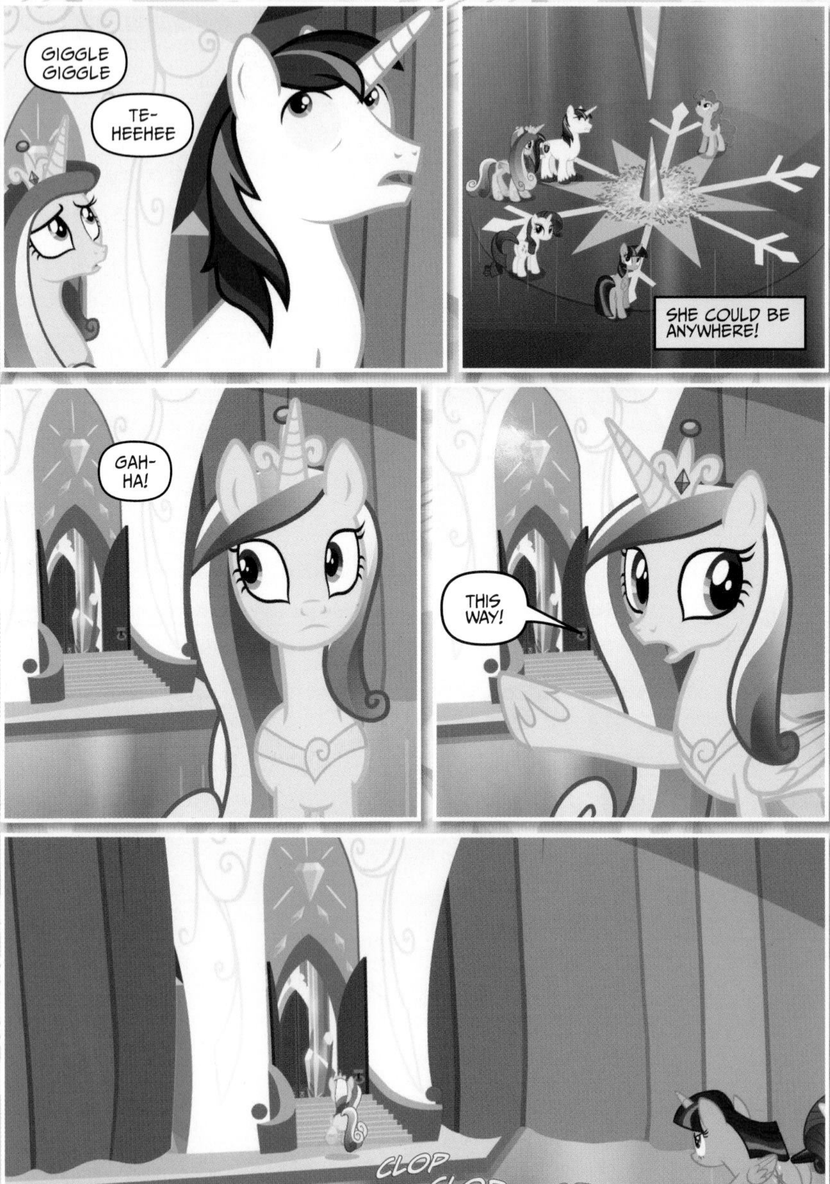
GIGGLE GIGGLE
TE-HEEHEE
SHE COULD BE ANYWHERE!
GAH-HA!
THIS WAY!
CLOP CLOP CLOP

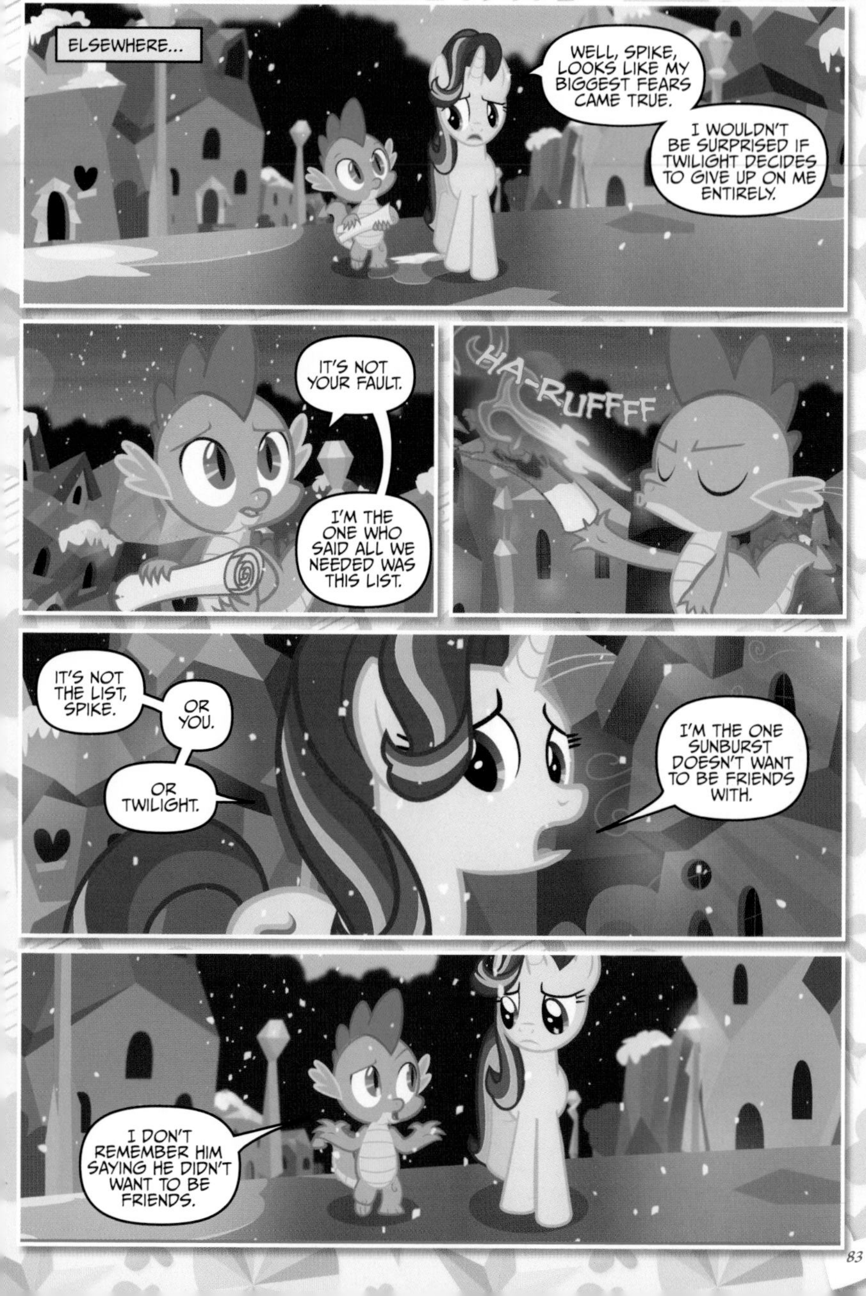
ELSEWHERE...
WELL, SPIKE, LOOKS LIKE MY BIGGEST FEARS CAME TRUE.
I WOULDN'T BE SURPRISED IF TWILIGHT DECIDES TO GIVE UP ON ME ENTIRELY.
IT'S NOT YOUR FAULT.
I'M THE ONE WHO SAID ALL WE NEEDED WAS THIS LIST.
HA-RUFFFF
IT'S NOT THE LIST, SPIKE.
OR YOU.
OR TWILIGHT.
I'M THE ONE SUNBURST DOESN'T WANT TO BE FRIENDS WITH.
I DON'T REMEMBER HIM SAYING HE DIDN'T WANT TO BE FRIENDS.

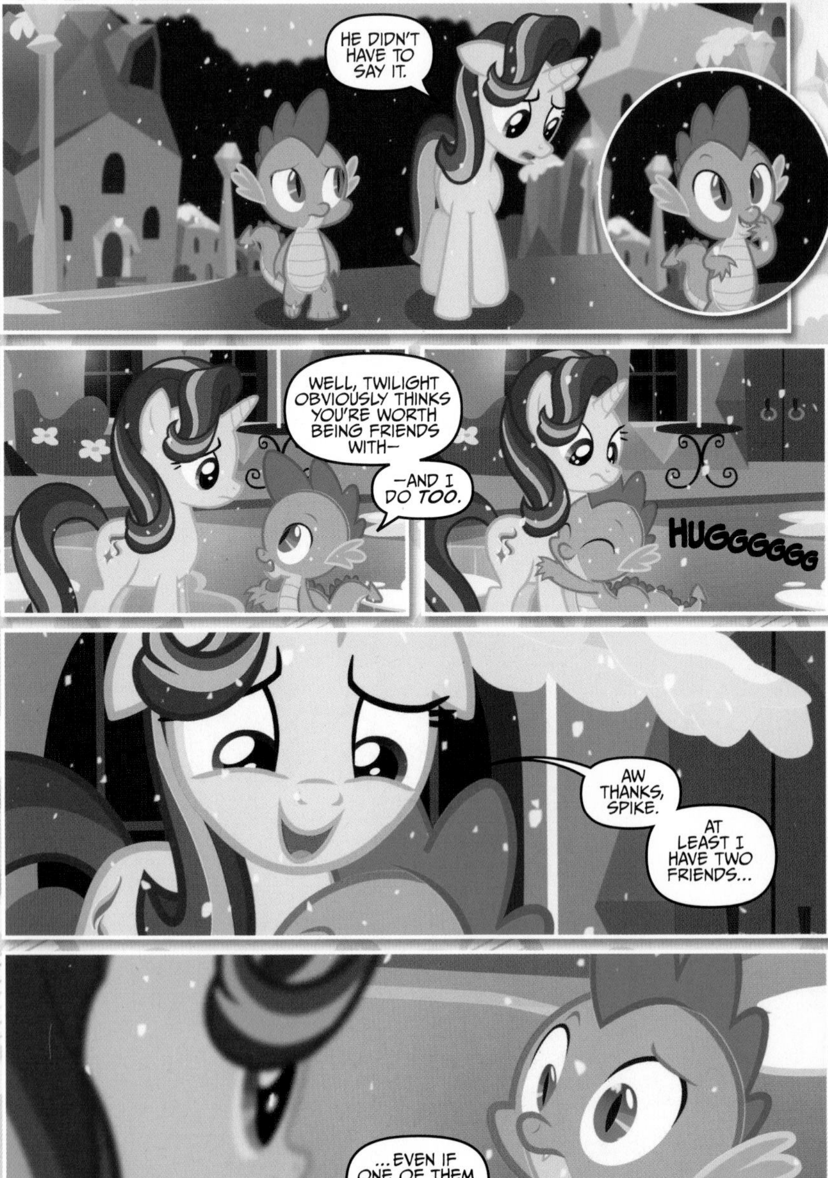
HE DIDN'T HAVE TO SAY IT.
WELL, TWILIGHT OBVIOUSLY THINKS YOU'RE WORTH BEING FRIENDS WITH—
—AND I DO *TOO*.
HUGGGGGGG
AW THANKS, SPIKE.
AT LEAST I HAVE TWO FRIENDS...
...EVEN IF ONE OF THEM HAS DRAGON BREATH.

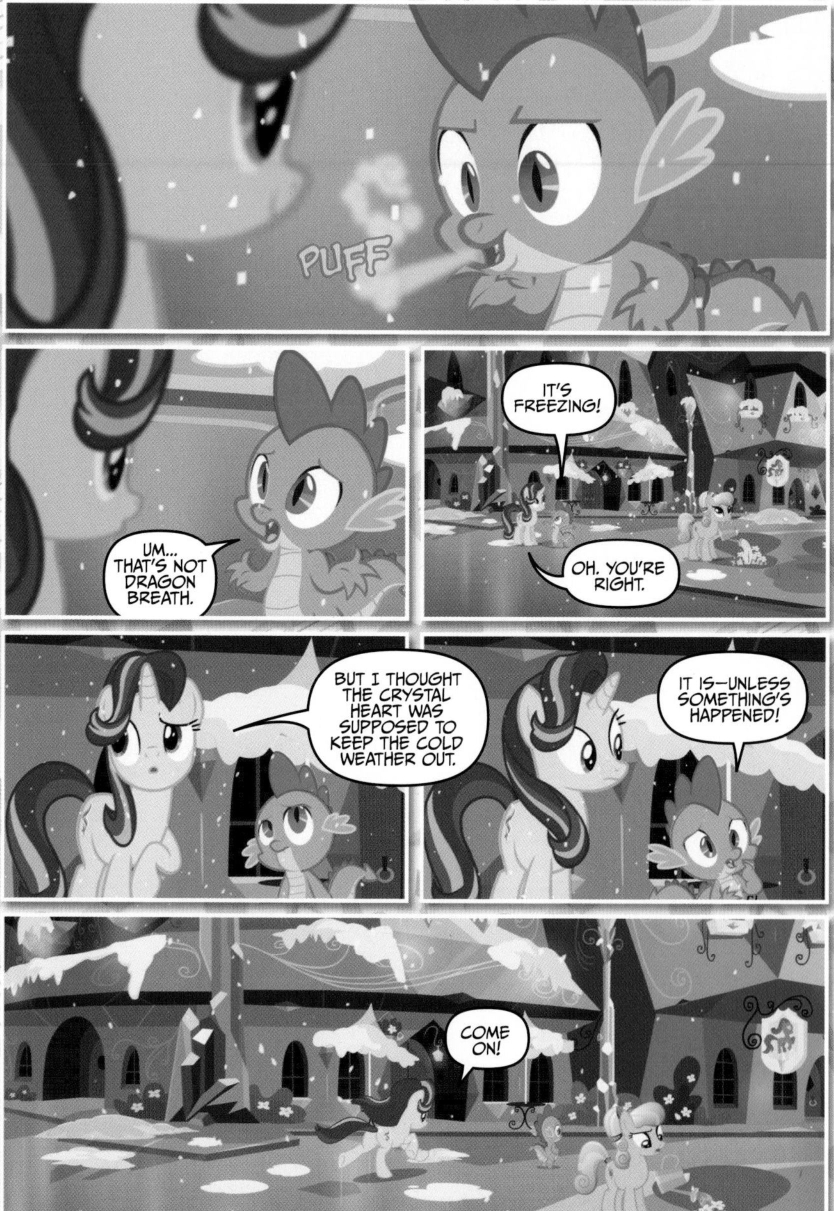
PUFF
UM... THAT'S NOT DRAGON BREATH.
IT'S FREEZING!
OH. YOU'RE RIGHT.
BUT I THOUGHT THE CRYSTAL HEART WAS SUPPOSED TO KEEP THE COLD WEATHER OUT.
IT IS—UNLESS SOMETHING'S HAPPENED!
COME ON!

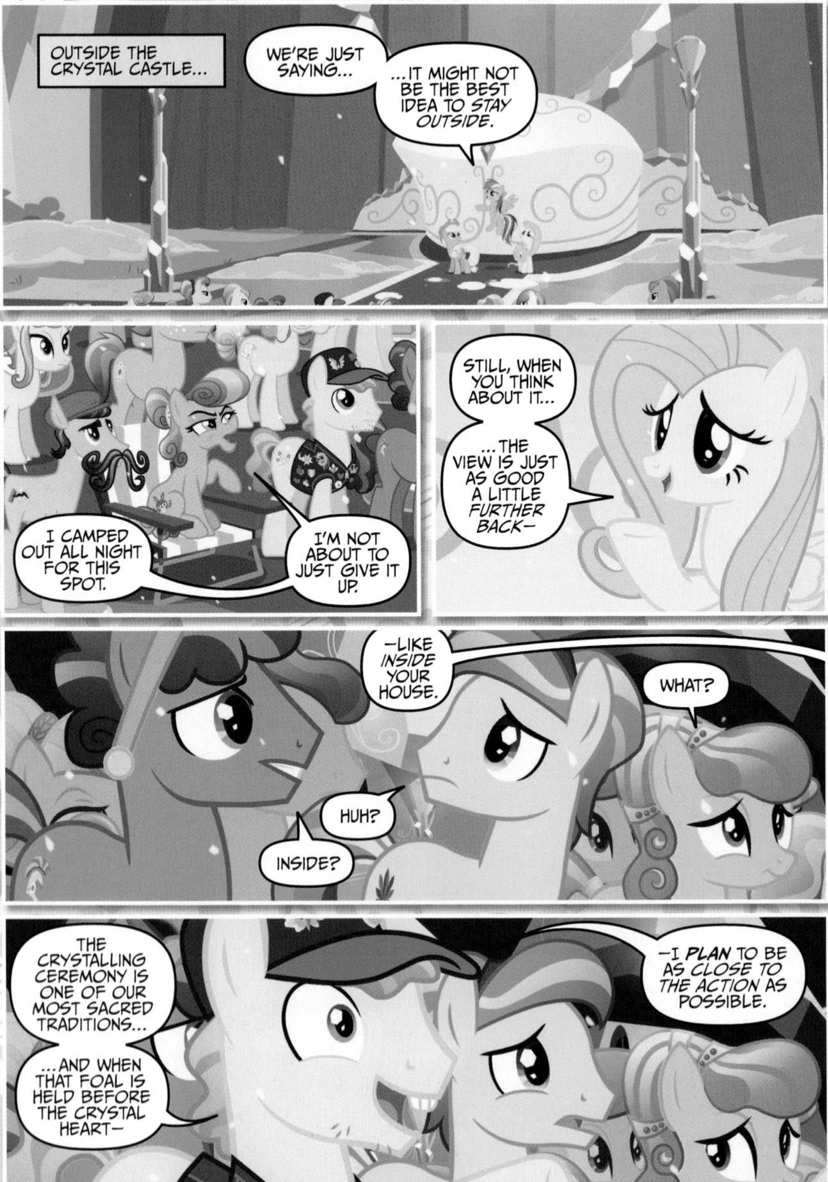
OUTSIDE THE CRYSTAL CASTLE...
WE'RE JUST SAYING...
...IT MIGHT NOT BE THE BEST IDEA TO *STAY OUTSIDE*.
I CAMPED OUT ALL NIGHT FOR THIS SPOT.
I'M NOT ABOUT TO JUST GIVE IT UP.
STILL, WHEN YOU THINK ABOUT IT...
...THE VIEW IS JUST AS GOOD A LITTLE *FURTHER BACK*—
—LIKE *INSIDE* YOUR HOUSE.
WHAT?
HUH?
INSIDE?
THE CRYSTALLING CEREMONY IS ONE OF OUR MOST SACRED TRADITIONS...
...AND WHEN THAT FOAL IS HELD BEFORE THE CRYSTAL HEART—
—I ***PLAN*** TO BE AS *CLOSE TO THE ACTION* AS POSSIBLE.

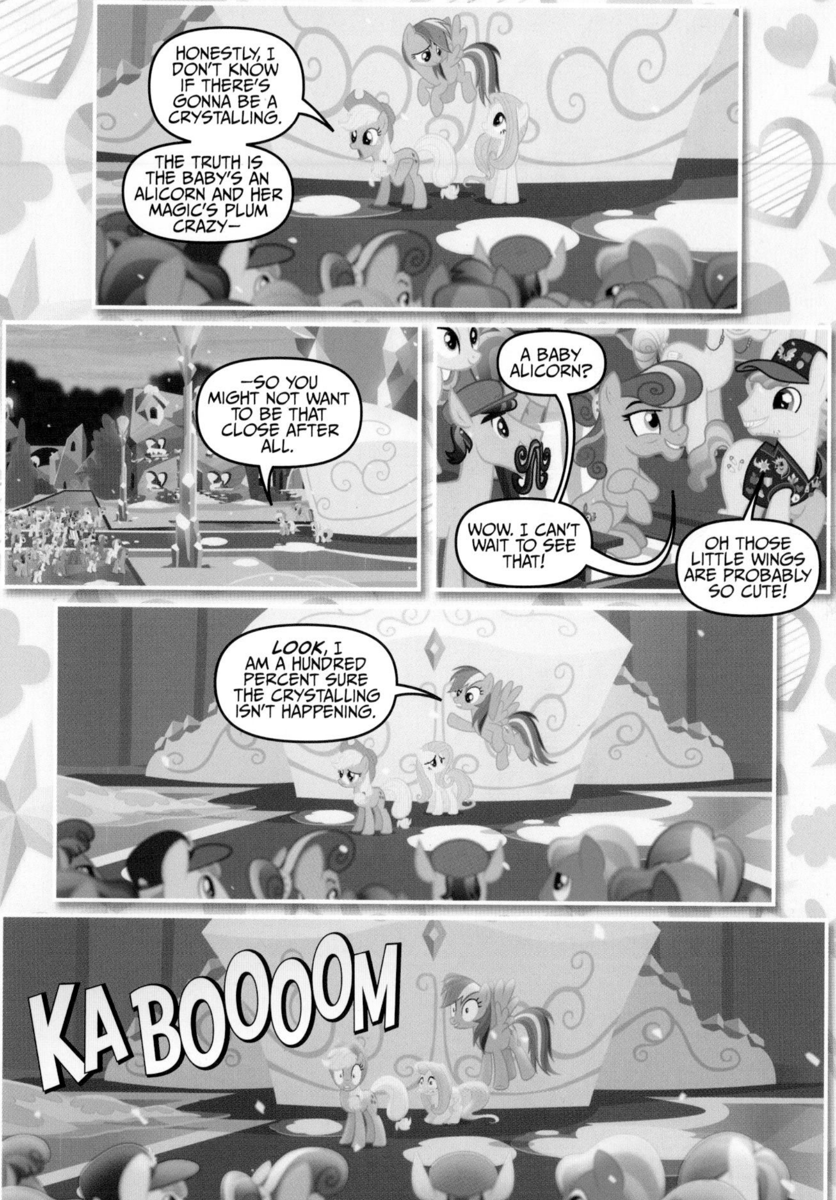
HONESTLY, I DON'T KNOW IF THERE'S GONNA BE A CRYSTALLING.
THE TRUTH IS THE BABY'S AN ALICORN AND HER MAGIC'S PLUM CRAZY—
—SO YOU MIGHT NOT WANT TO BE THAT CLOSE AFTER ALL.
A BABY ALICORN?
WOW. I CAN'T WAIT TO SEE THAT!
OH THOSE LITTLE WINGS ARE PROBABLY SO CUTE!
LOOK, I AM A HUNDRED PERCENT SURE THE CRYSTALLING ISN'T HAPPENING.
KA BOOOOOM

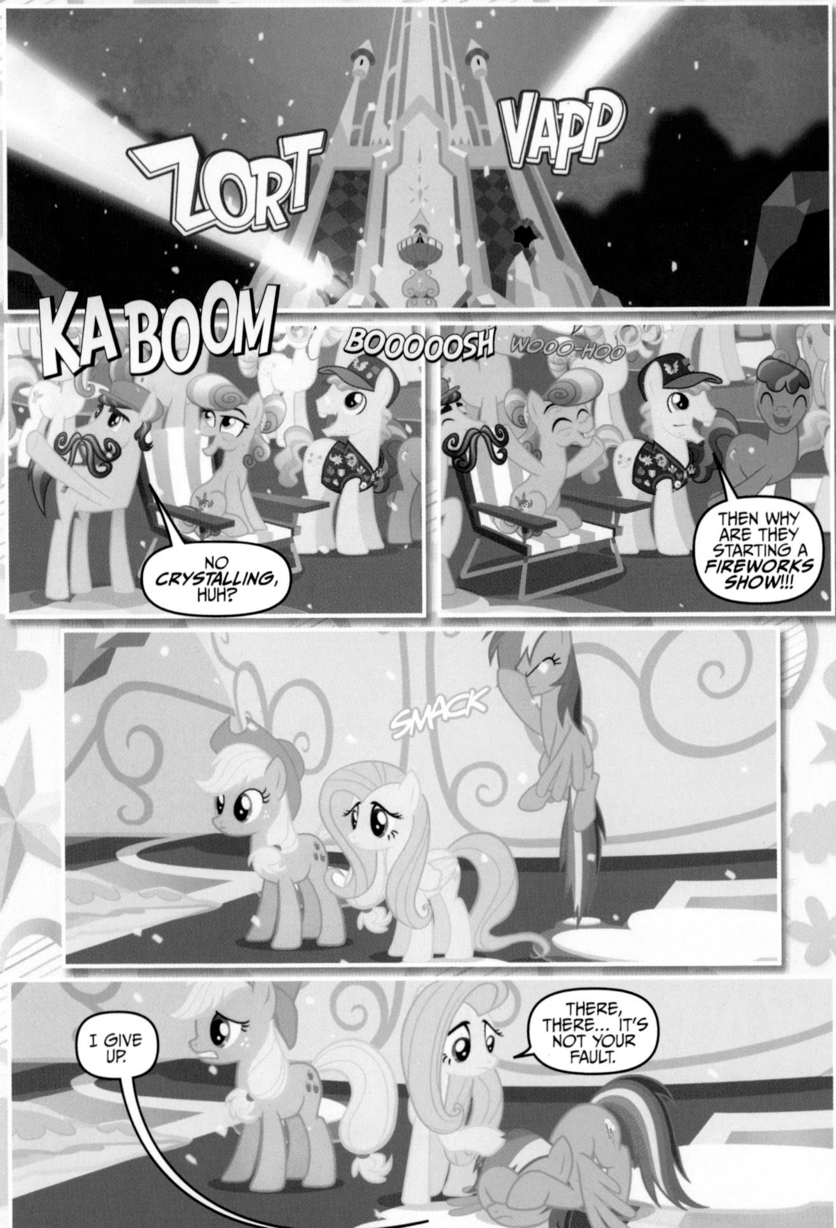
ZORT
VAPP
KA BOOM
BOOOOOSH
WOOO-HOO
NO CRYSTALLING, HUH?
THEN WHY ARE THEY STARTING A FIREWORKS SHOW!!!
SMACK
I GIVE UP.
THERE, THERE... IT'S NOT YOUR FAULT.

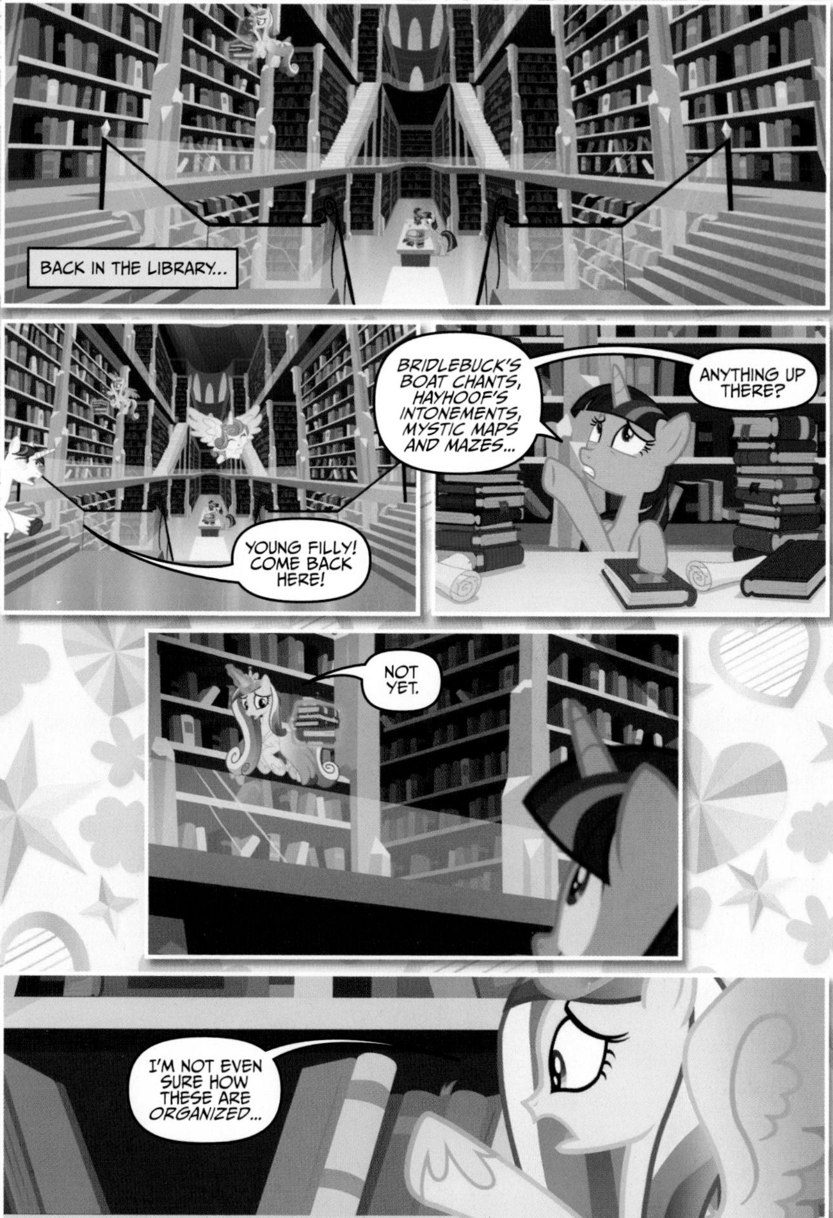
BACK IN THE LIBRARY...
YOUNG FILLY! COME BACK HERE!
BRIDLEBUCK'S BOAT CHANTS, HAYHOOF'S INTONEMENTS, MYSTIC MAPS AND MAZES...
ANYTHING UP THERE?
NOT YET.
I'M NOT EVEN SURE HOW THESE ARE ORGANIZED...

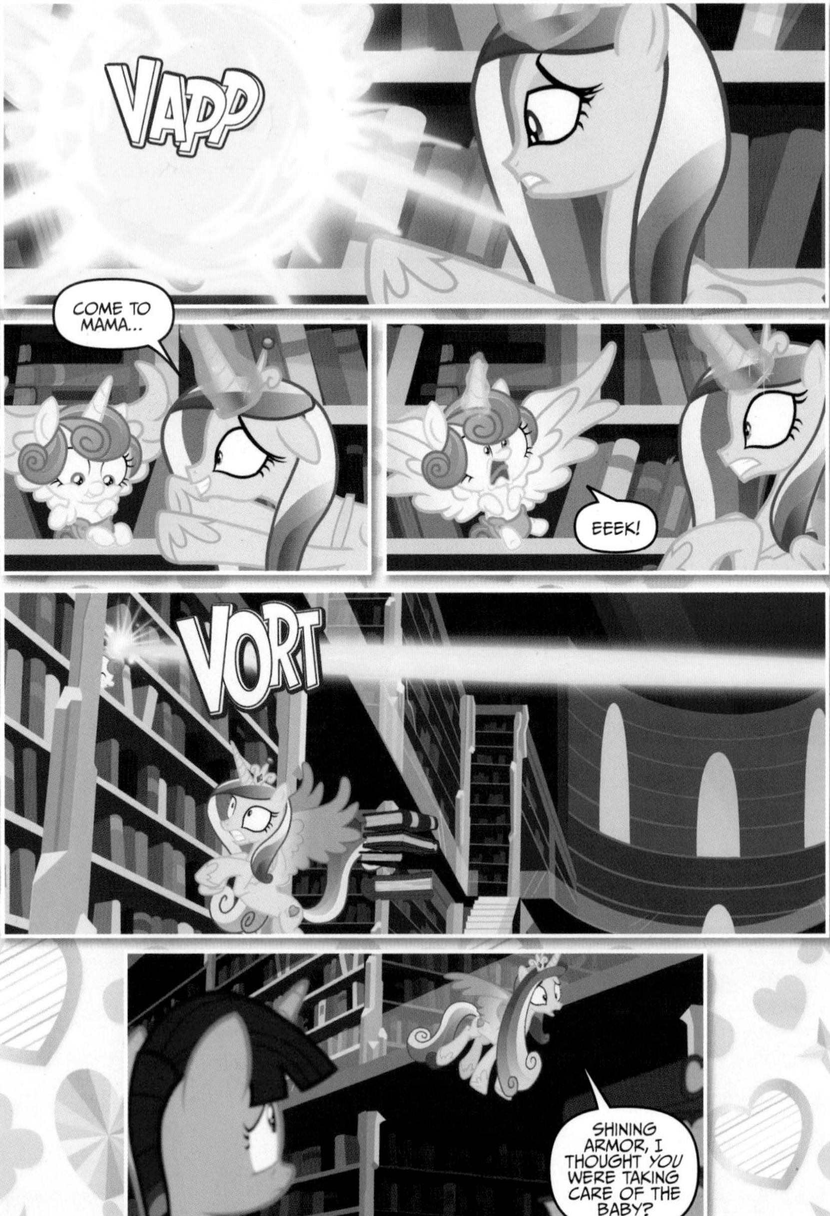
VAPP
COME TO MAMA...
EEEK!
VORT
SHINING ARMOR, I THOUGHT *YOU* WERE TAKING CARE OF THE BABY?

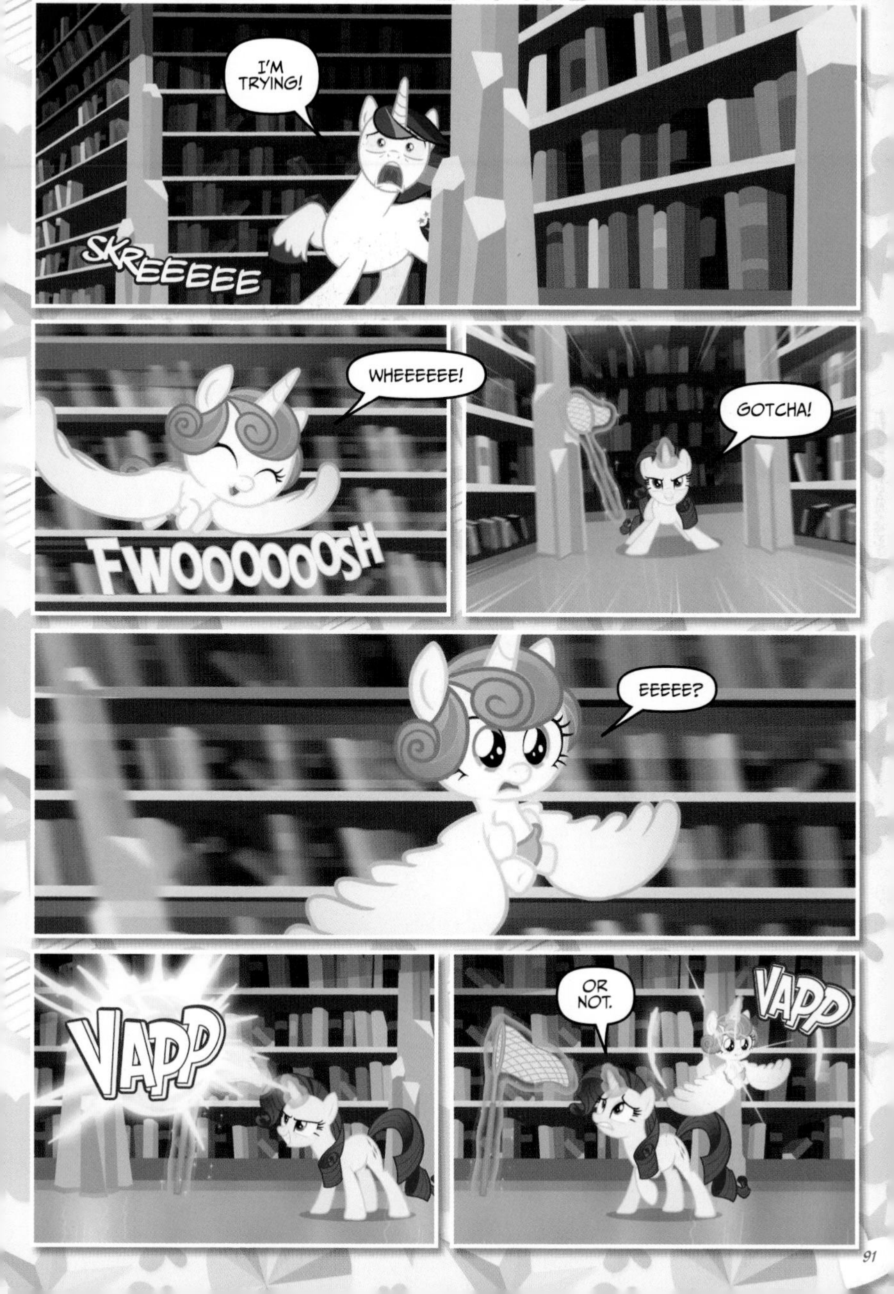
I'M TRYING!
SKREEEEEE
WHEEEEEEE!
FWOOOOOOSH
GOTCHA!
EEEEE?
VAPP
OR NOT.
VAPP

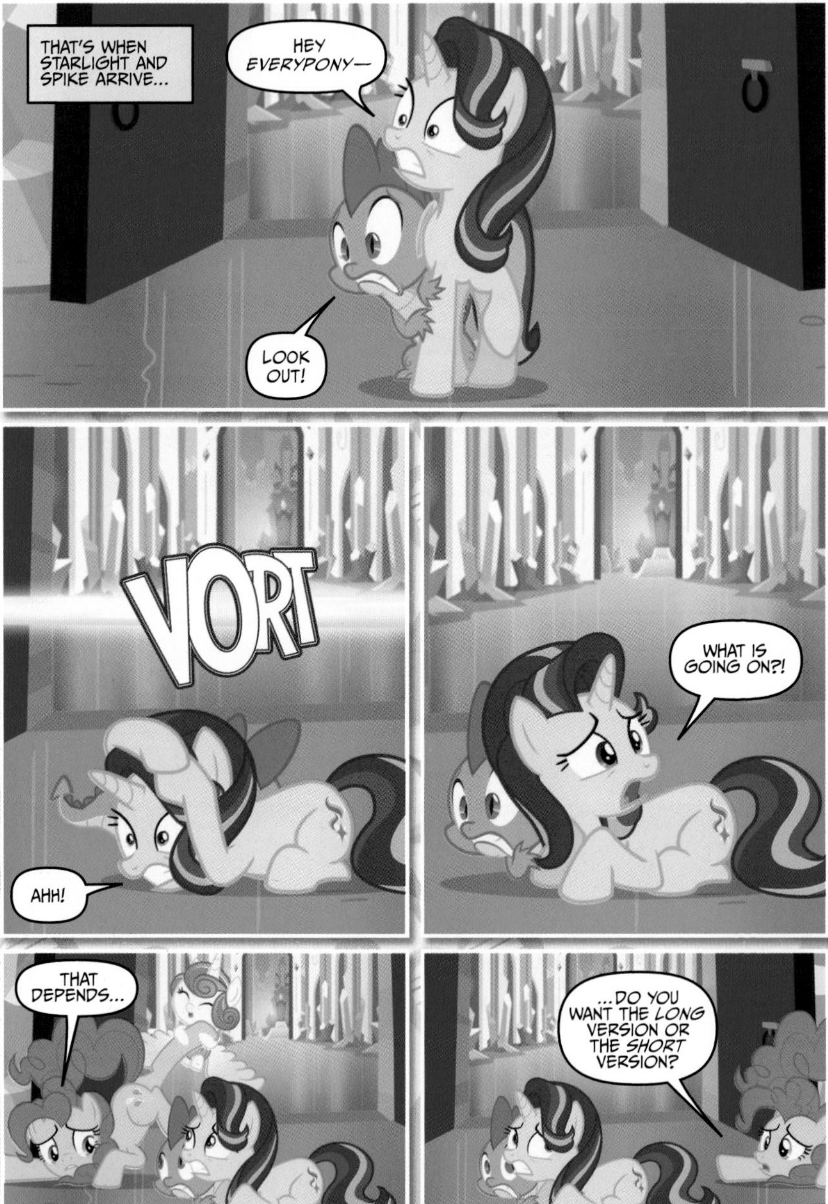
THAT'S WHEN STARLIGHT AND SPIKE ARRIVE...
HEY *EVERYPONY*—
LOOK OUT!
VORT
AHH!
WHAT IS GOING ON?!
THAT DEPENDS...
...DO YOU WANT THE *LONG* VERSION OR THE *SHORT* VERSION?

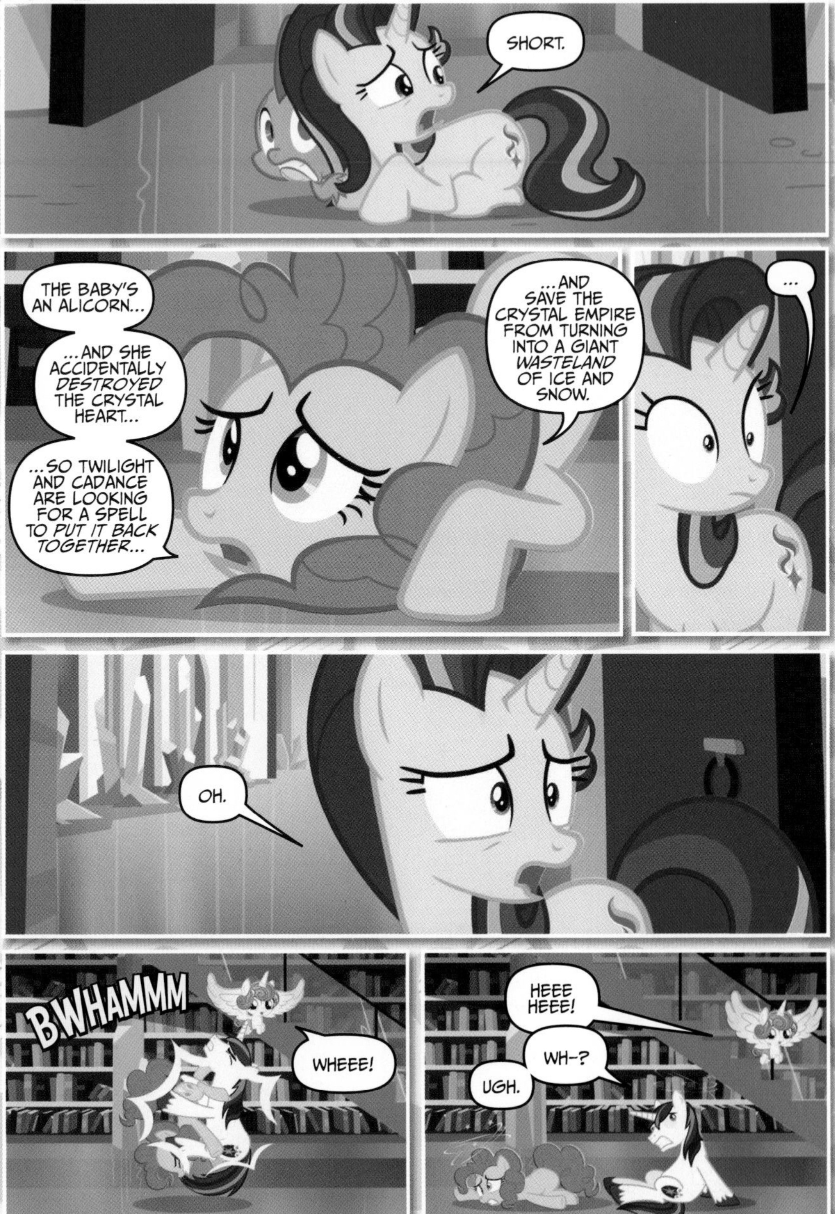
SHORT.
THE BABY'S AN ALICORN...
...AND SHE ACCIDENTALLY DESTROYED THE CRYSTAL HEART...
...SO TWILIGHT AND CADANCE ARE LOOKING FOR A SPELL TO PUT IT BACK TOGETHER...
...AND SAVE THE CRYSTAL EMPIRE FROM TURNING INTO A GIANT WASTELAND OF ICE AND SNOW.
...
OH.
BWHAMMM
WHEEE!
HEEE HEEE!
WH-?
UGH.

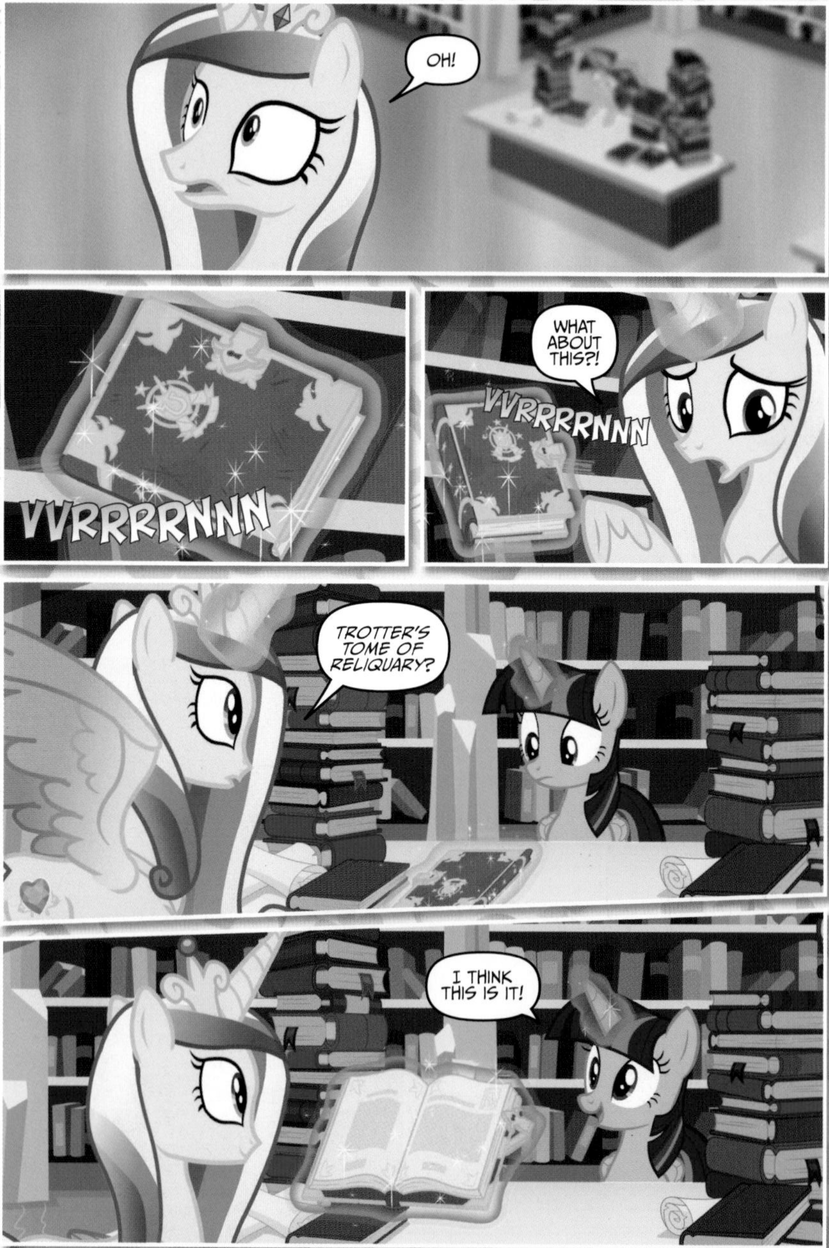
OH!
VVRRRRNNN
WHAT ABOUT THIS?!
VVRRRRNNN
TROTTER'S TOME OF RELIQUARY?
I THINK THIS IS IT!

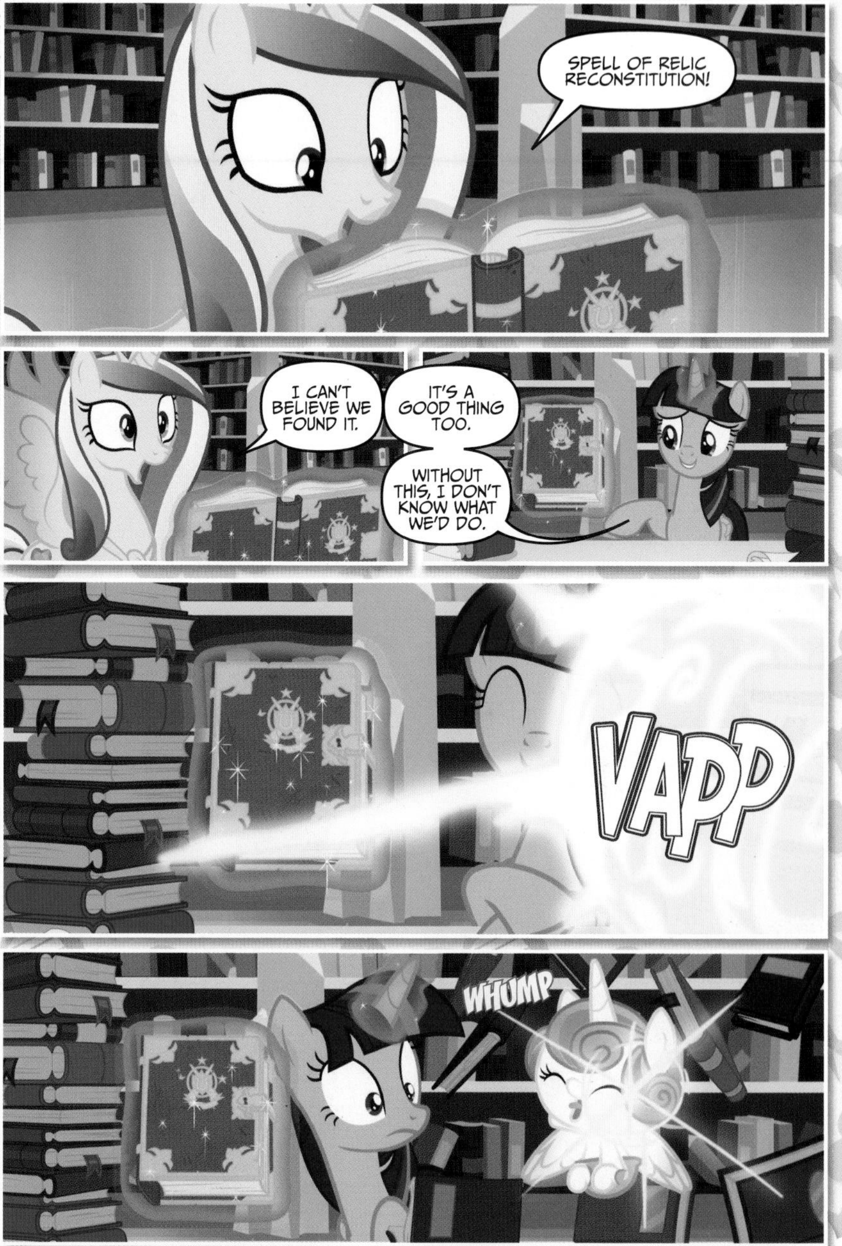
SPELL OF RELIC RECONSTITUTION!
I CAN'T BELIEVE WE FOUND IT.
IT'S A GOOD THING TOO.
WITHOUT THIS, I DON'T KNOW WHAT WE'D DO.
VAPP
WHUMP

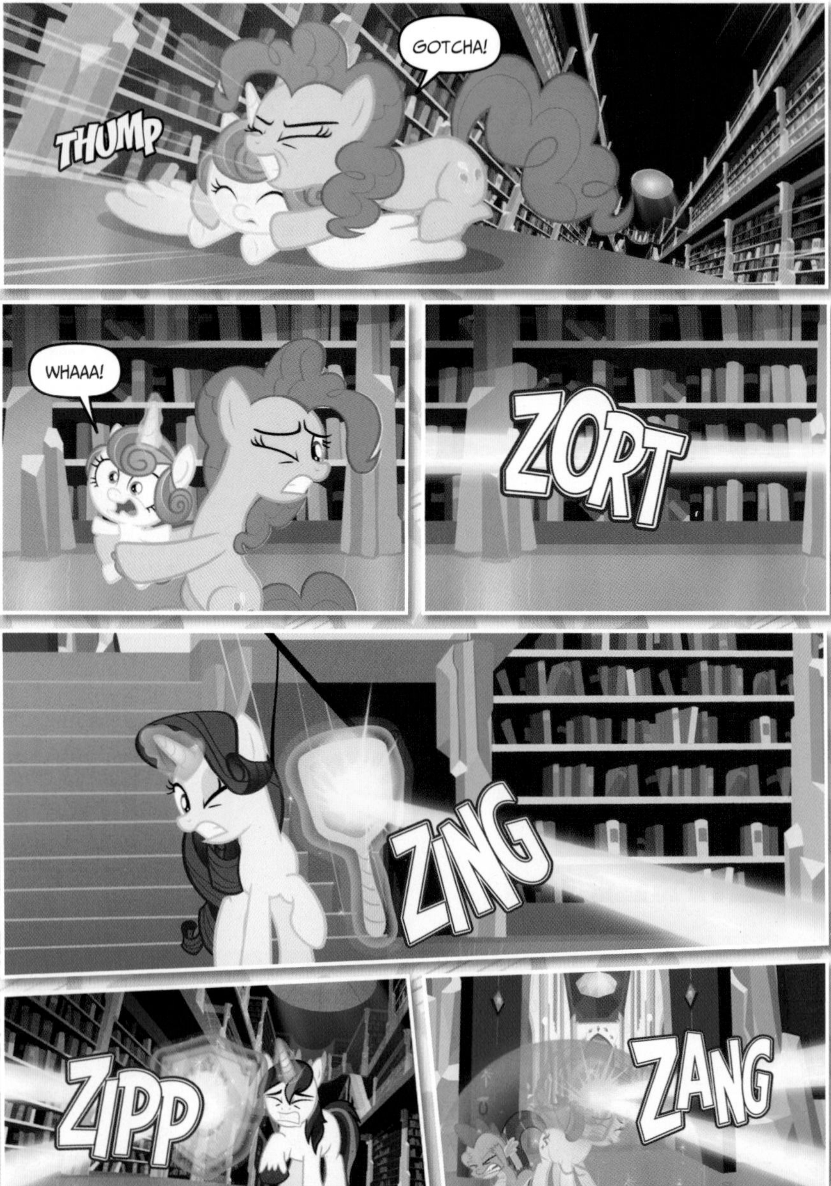
GOTCHA!
THUMP
WHAAA!
ZORT
ZING
ZIPP
ZANG

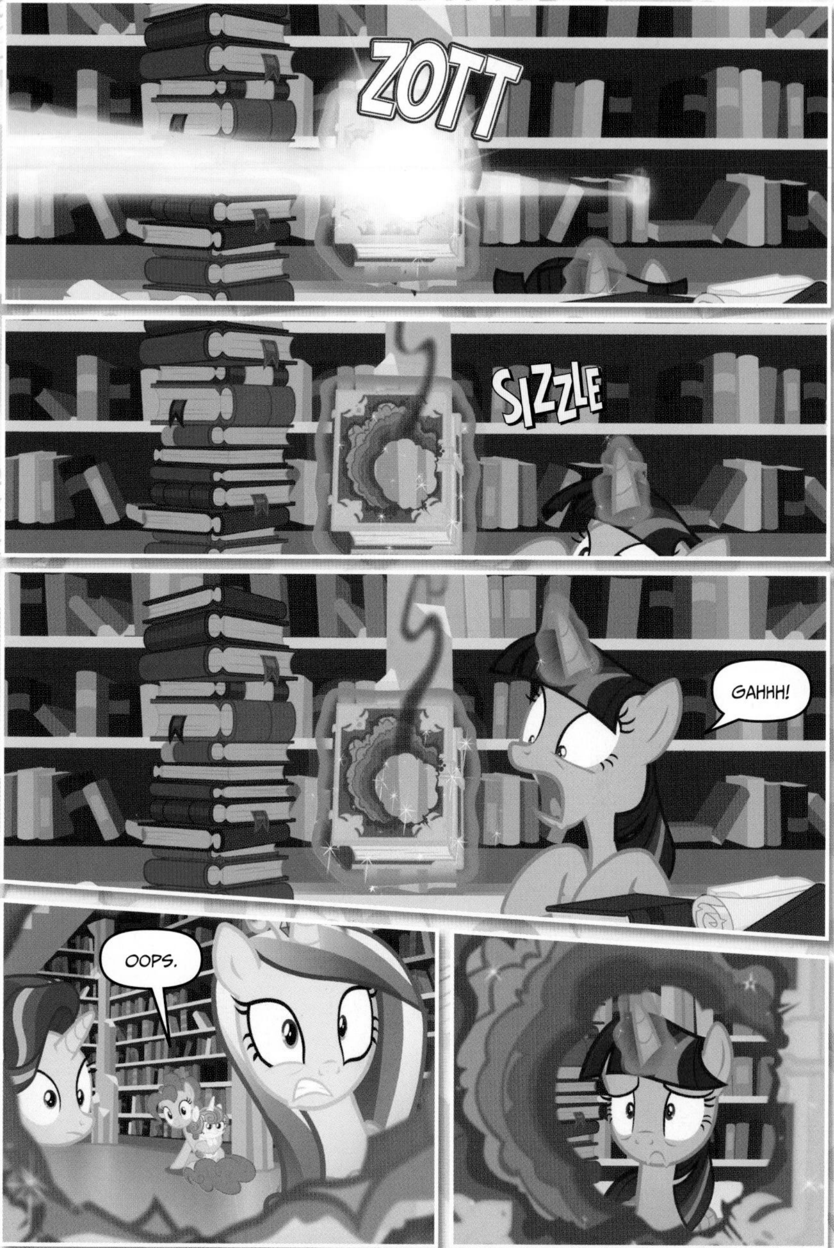
ZOTT
SIZZLE
GAHHH!
OOPS.

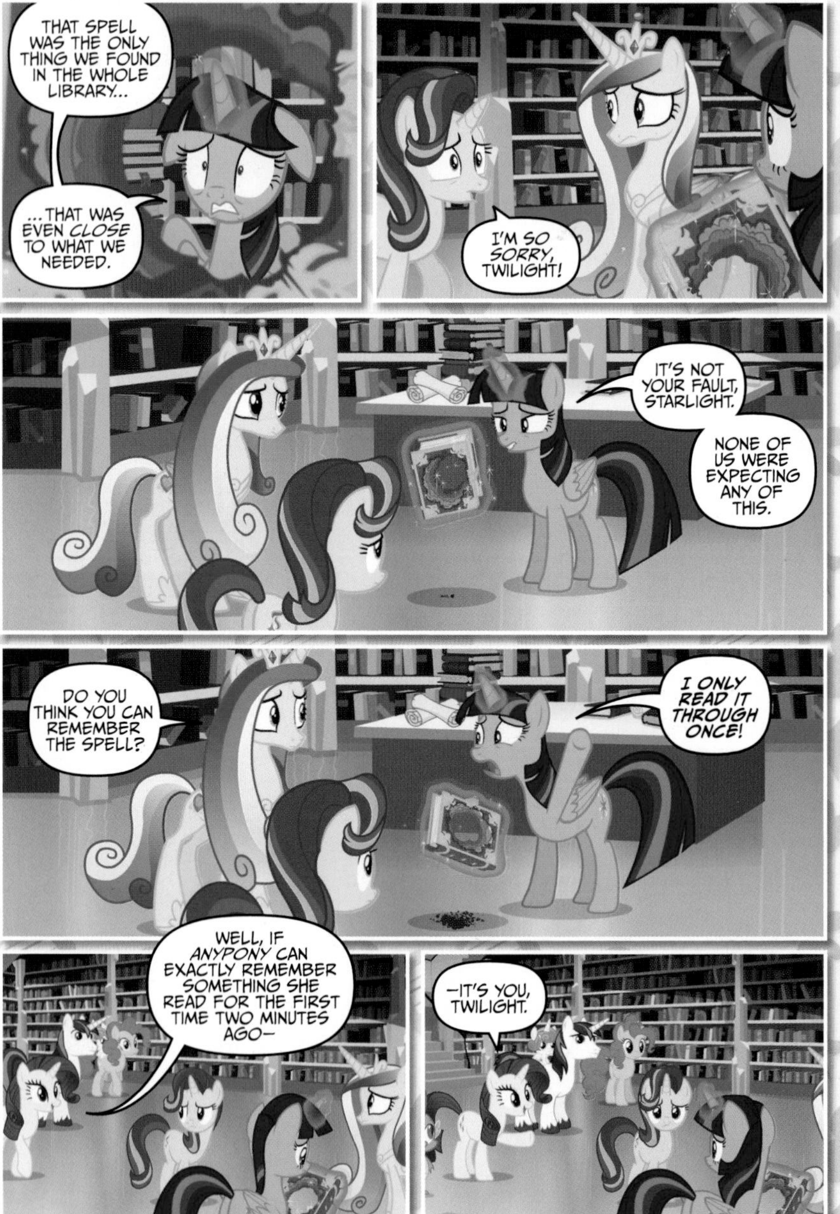
THAT SPELL WAS THE ONLY THING WE FOUND IN THE WHOLE LIBRARY...
...THAT WAS EVEN *CLOSE* TO WHAT WE NEEDED.
I'M SO *SORRY*, TWILIGHT!
IT'S NOT YOUR FAULT, STARLIGHT.
NONE OF US WERE EXPECTING ANY OF THIS.
DO YOU THINK YOU CAN REMEMBER THE SPELL?
I ONLY READ IT THROUGH ONCE!
WELL, IF *ANYPONY* CAN EXACTLY REMEMBER SOMETHING SHE READ FOR THE FIRST TIME TWO MINUTES AGO—
—IT'S YOU, TWILIGHT.

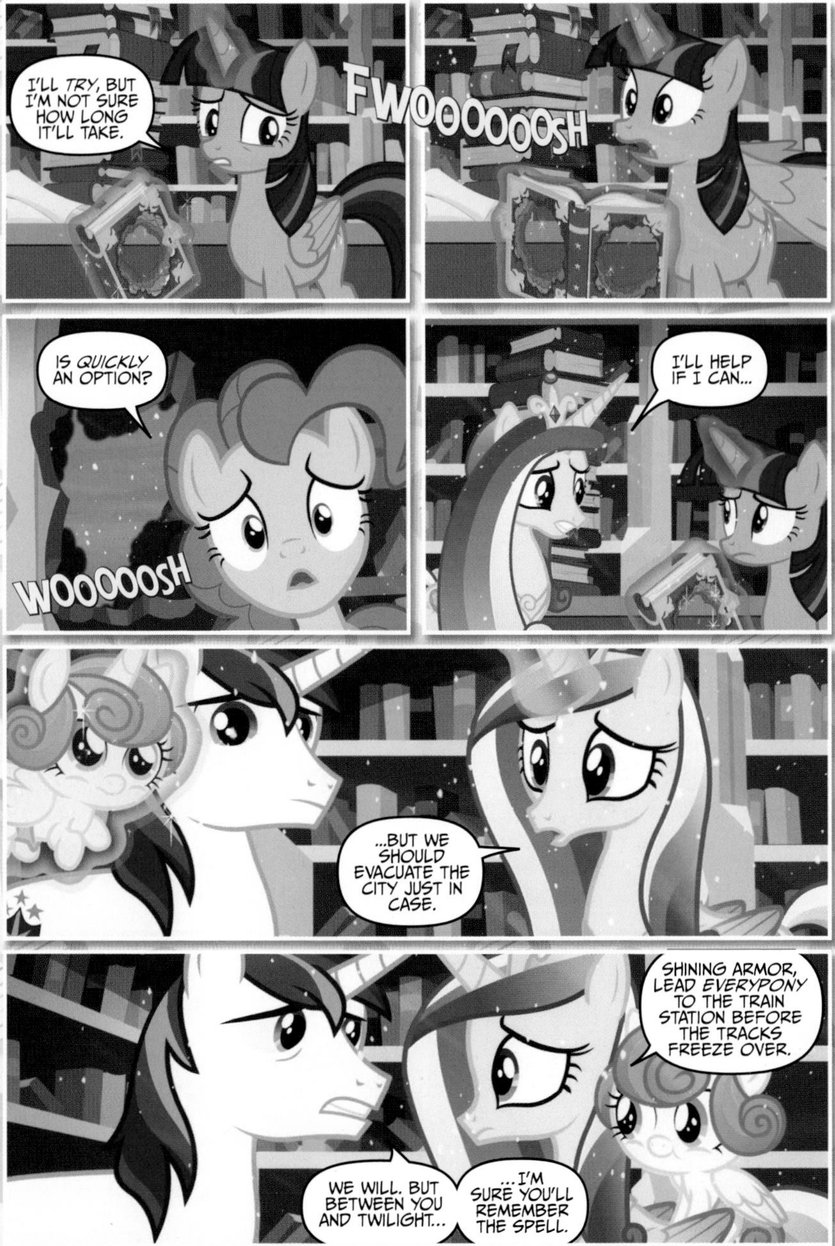
I'LL *TRY*, BUT I'M NOT SURE HOW LONG IT'LL TAKE.
FWOOOOOOSH
IS *QUICKLY* AN OPTION?
WOOOOOSH
I'LL HELP IF I CAN...
...BUT WE SHOULD EVACUATE THE CITY JUST IN CASE.
SHINING ARMOR, LEAD *EVERYPONY* TO THE TRAIN STATION BEFORE THE TRACKS FREEZE OVER.
WE WILL. BUT BETWEEN YOU AND TWILIGHT...
...I'M SURE YOU'LL REMEMBER THE SPELL.

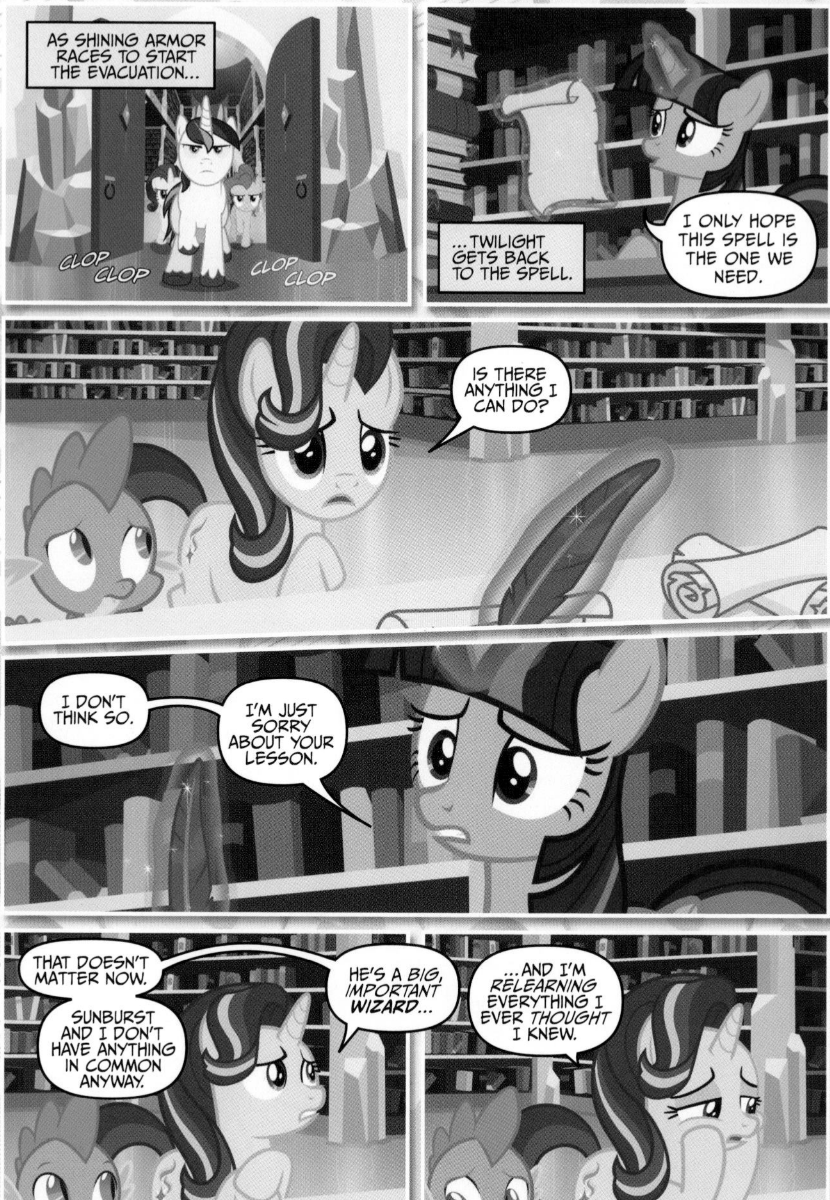

AS SHINING ARMOR RACES TO START THE EVACUATION...
CLOP CLOP
CLOP CLOP
...TWILIGHT GETS BACK TO THE SPELL.
I ONLY HOPE THIS SPELL IS THE ONE WE NEED.
IS THERE ANYTHING I CAN DO?
I DON'T THINK SO.
I'M JUST SORRY ABOUT YOUR LESSON.
THAT DOESN'T MATTER NOW.
SUNBURST AND I DON'T HAVE ANYTHING IN COMMON ANYWAY.
HE'S A *BIG, IMPORTANT* ***WIZARD***...
...AND I'M *RELEARNING* EVERYTHING I EVER *THOUGHT* I KNEW.

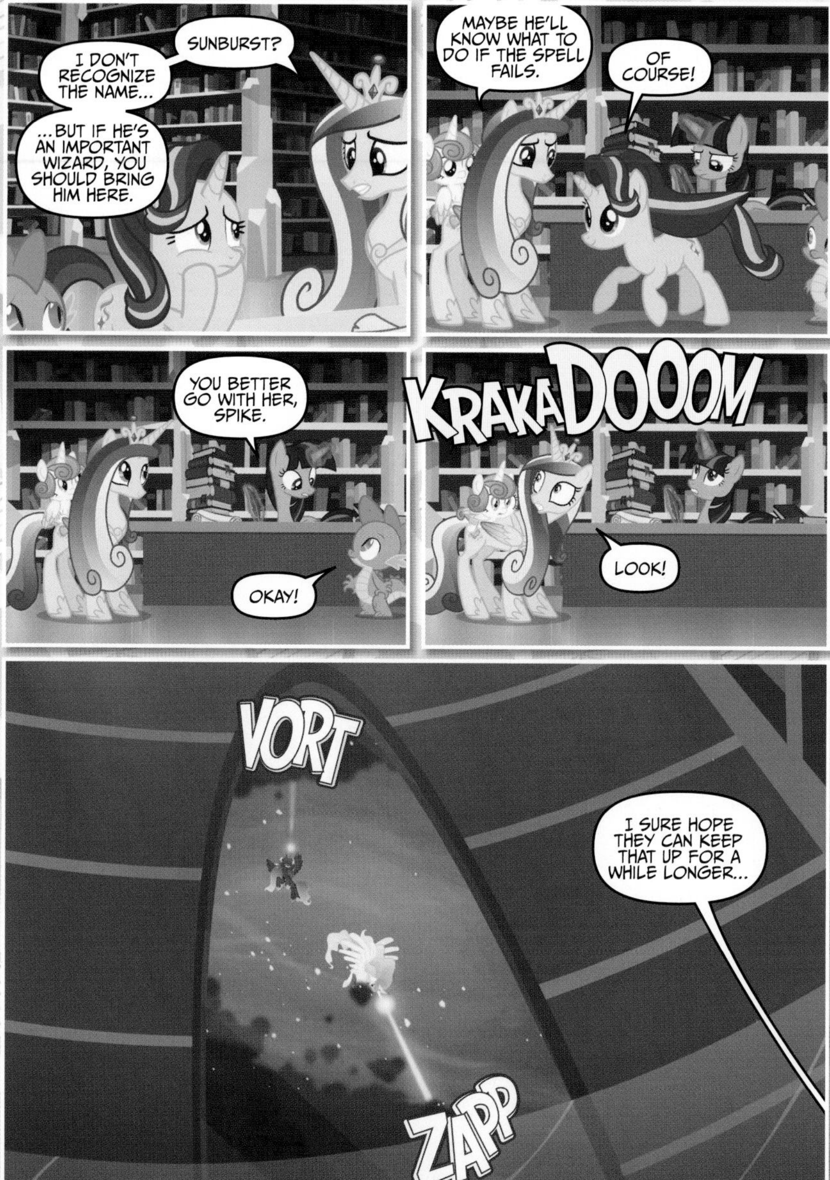
SUNBURST?
I DON'T RECOGNIZE THE NAME...
...BUT IF HE'S AN IMPORTANT WIZARD, YOU SHOULD BRING HIM HERE.
MAYBE HE'LL KNOW WHAT TO DO IF THE SPELL FAILS.
OF COURSE!
YOU BETTER GO WITH HER, SPIKE.
OKAY!
KRAKADOOOM
LOOK!
VORT
I SURE HOPE THEY CAN KEEP THAT UP FOR A WHILE LONGER...
ZAPP

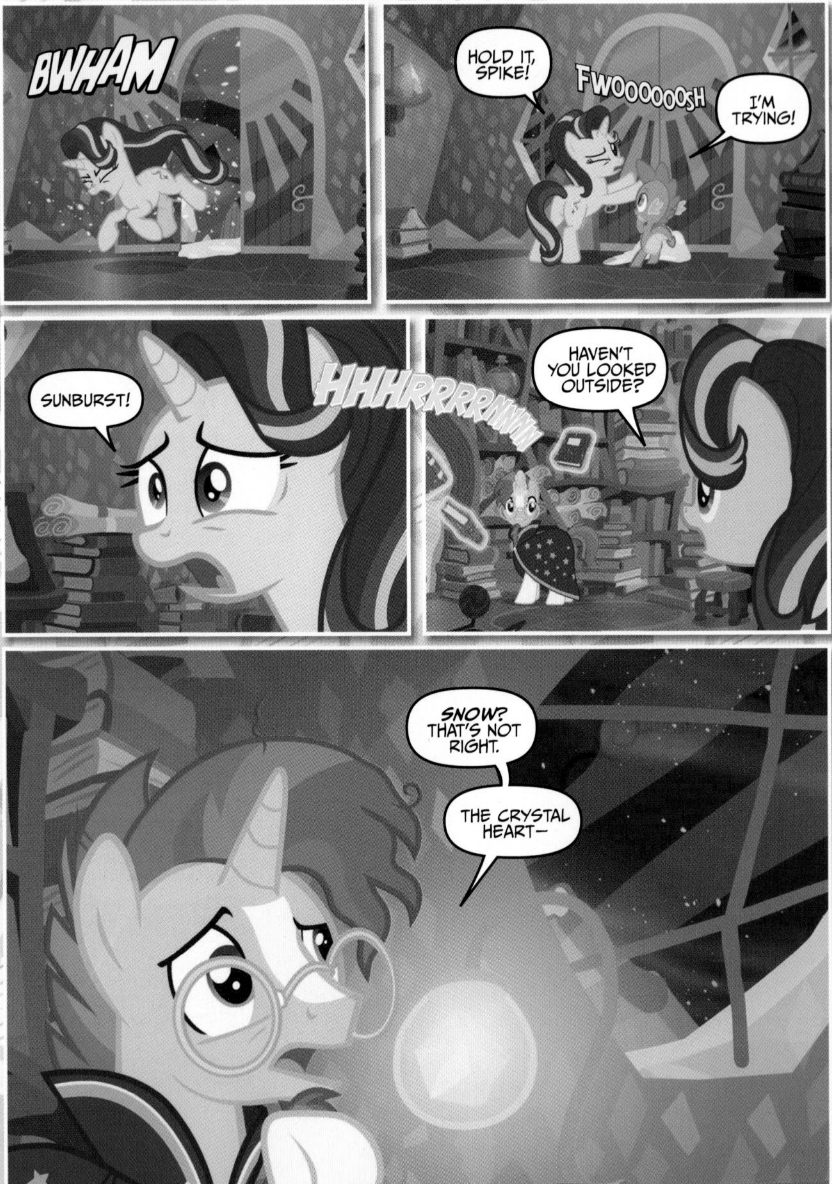
BWHAM
HOLD IT, SPIKE!
FWOOOOOOSH
I'M TRYING!
SUNBURST!
HHHRRRRRNNNN
HAVEN'T YOU LOOKED OUTSIDE?
SNOW? THAT'S NOT RIGHT.
THE CRYSTAL HEART—

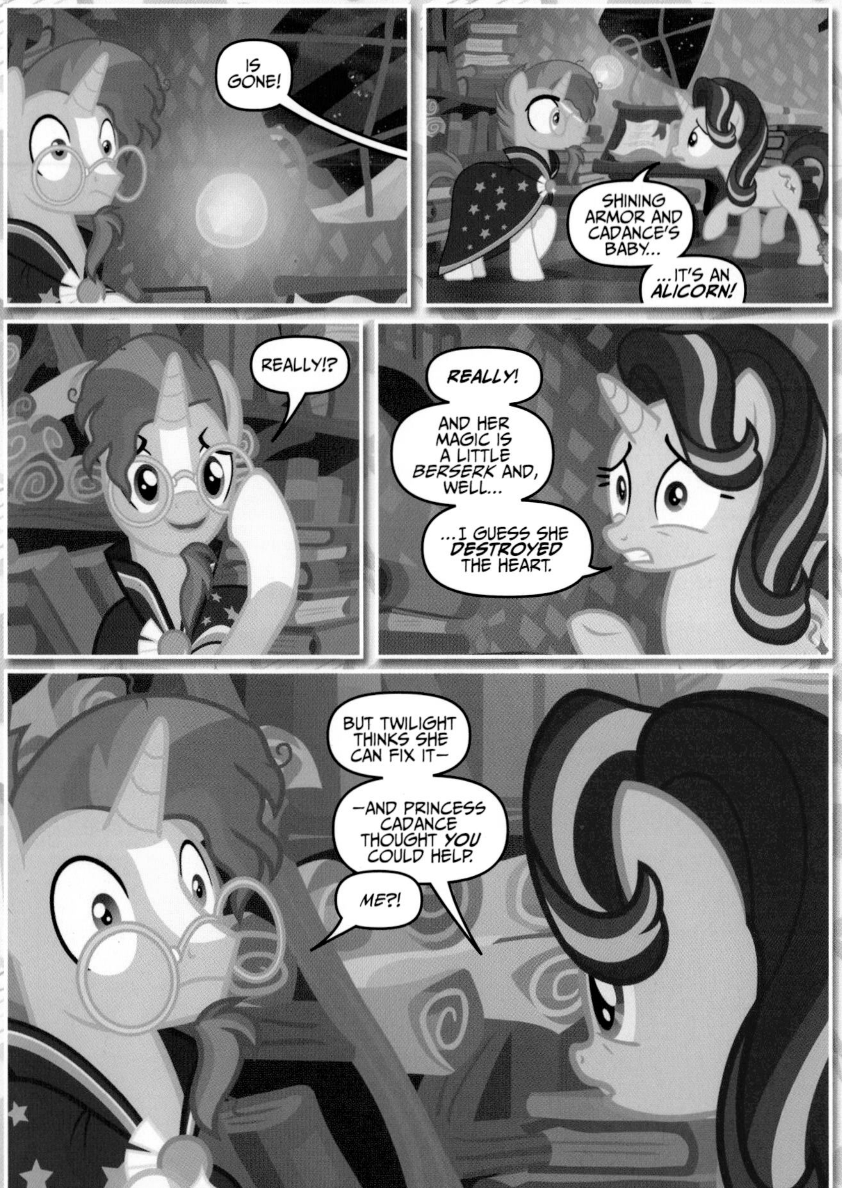

IS GONE!
SHINING ARMOR AND CADANCE'S BABY...
...IT'S AN *ALICORN!*
REALLY!?
REALLY!
AND HER MAGIC IS A LITTLE *BERSERK* AND, WELL...
...I GUESS SHE *DESTROYED* THE HEART.
BUT TWILIGHT THINKS SHE CAN FIX IT—
—AND PRINCESS CADANCE THOUGHT *YOU* COULD HELP.
ME?!

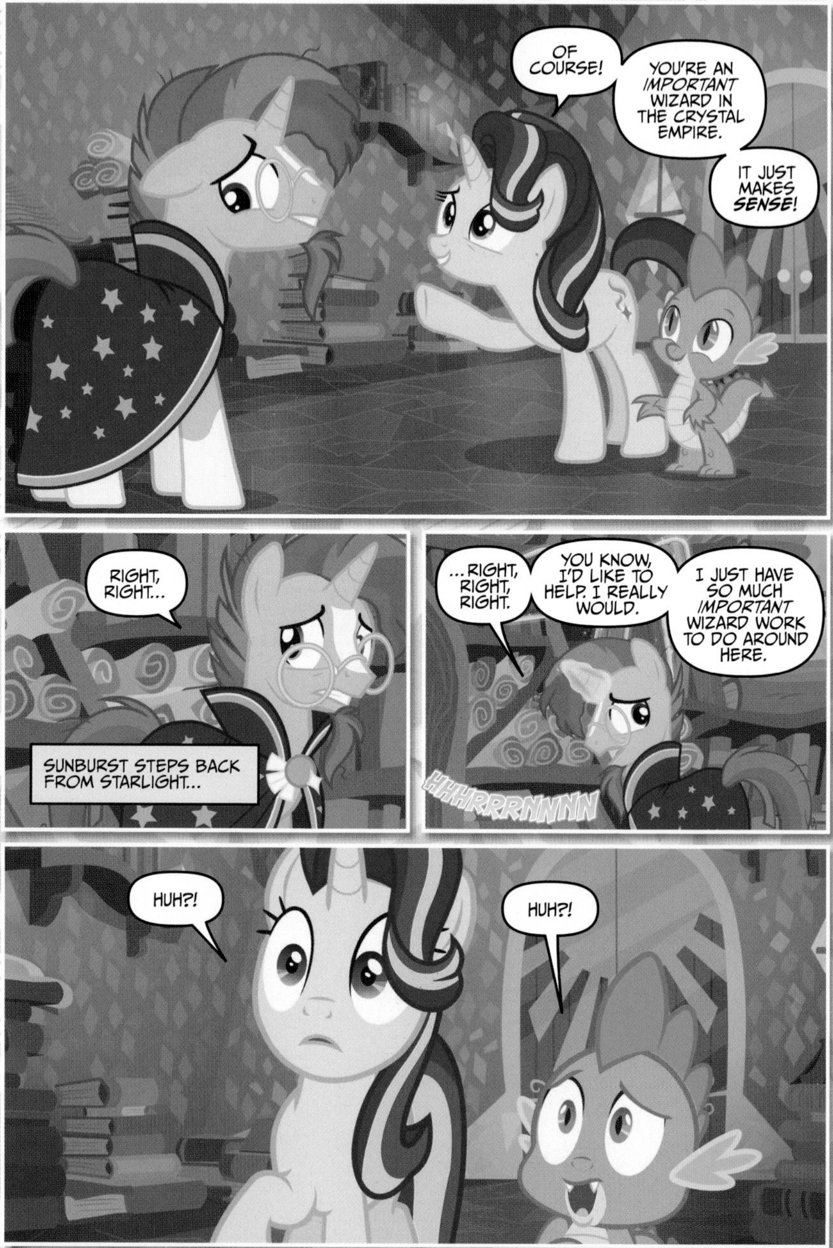

OF COURSE!
YOU'RE AN *IMPORTANT* WIZARD IN THE CRYSTAL EMPIRE.
IT JUST MAKES ***SENSE***!
RIGHT, RIGHT...
SUNBURST STEPS BACK FROM STARLIGHT...
...RIGHT, RIGHT, RIGHT.
YOU KNOW, I'D LIKE TO HELP. I REALLY WOULD.
I JUST HAVE SO MUCH *IMPORTANT* WIZARD WORK TO DO AROUND HERE.
HHHRRRNNNNN
HUH?!
HUH?!

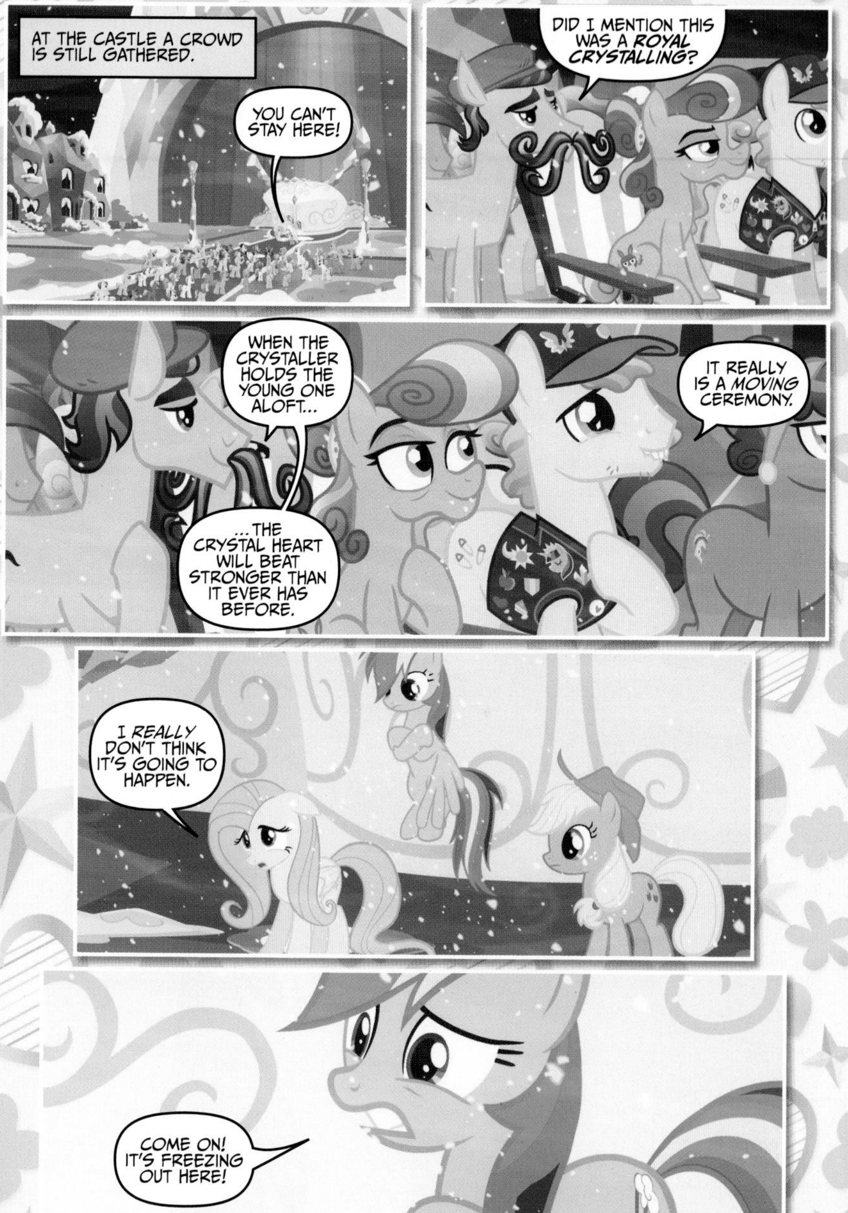
AT THE CASTLE A CROWD IS STILL GATHERED.
YOU CAN'T STAY HERE!
DID I MENTION THIS WAS A *ROYAL CRYSTALLING*?
WHEN THE CRYSTALLER HOLDS THE YOUNG ONE ALOFT...
...THE CRYSTAL HEART WILL BEAT STRONGER THAN IT EVER HAS BEFORE.
IT REALLY IS A *MOVING* CEREMONY.
I *REALLY* DON'T THINK IT'S GOING TO HAPPEN.
COME ON! IT'S FREEZING OUT HERE!

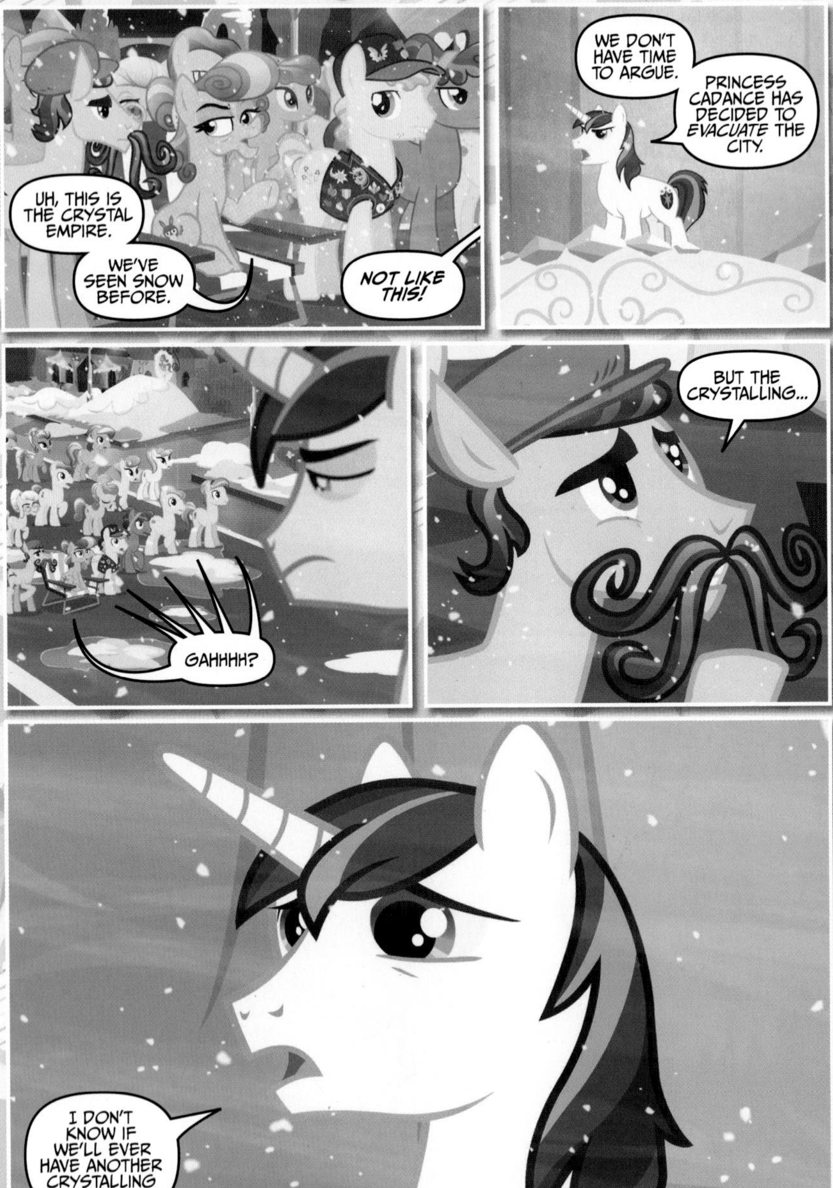
UH, THIS IS THE CRYSTAL EMPIRE.
WE'VE SEEN SNOW BEFORE.
NOT LIKE THIS!
WE DON'T HAVE TIME TO ARGUE.
PRINCESS CADANCE HAS DECIDED TO *EVACUATE* THE CITY.
GAHHHH?
BUT THE CRYSTALLING...
I DON'T KNOW IF WE'LL EVER HAVE ANOTHER CRYSTALLING AGAIN.

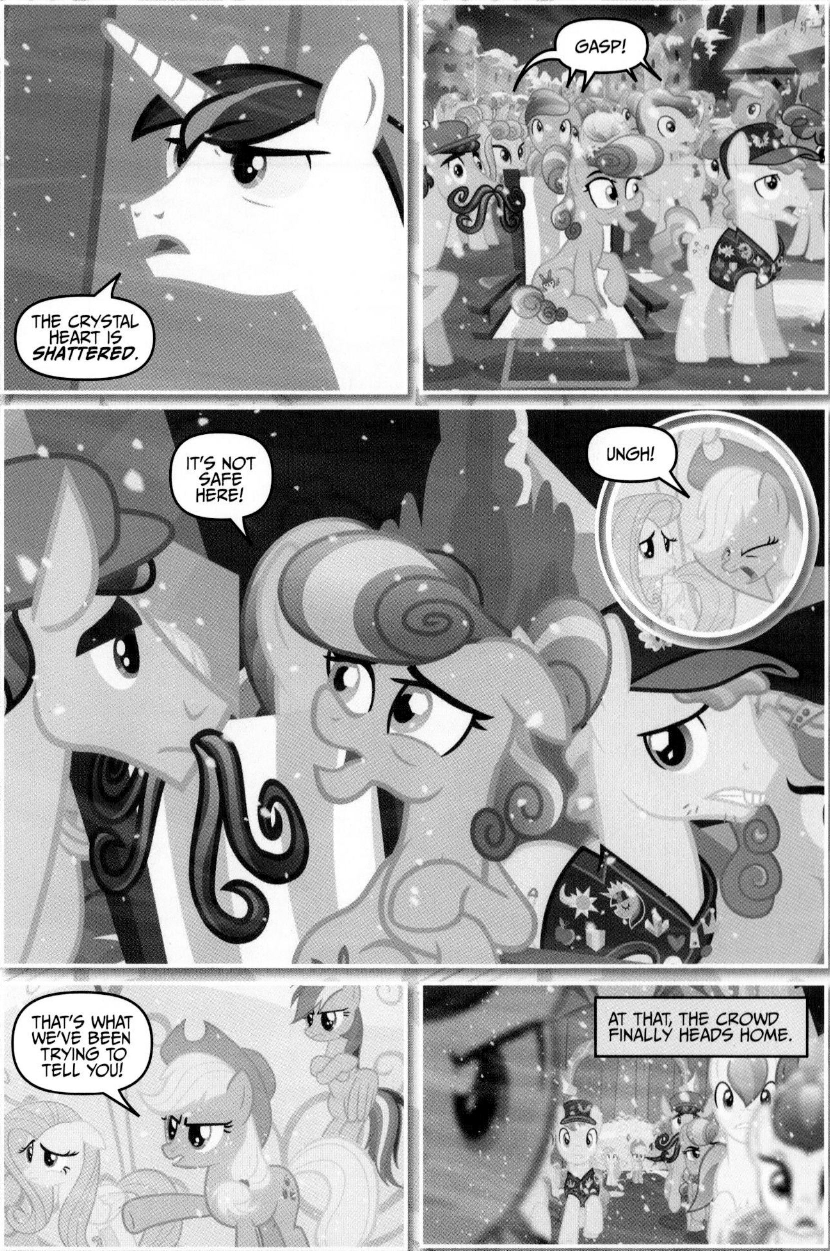
THE CRYSTAL HEART IS *SHATTERED*.
GASP!
IT'S NOT SAFE HERE!
UNGH!
THAT'S WHAT WE'VE BEEN TRYING TO TELL YOU!
AT THAT, THE CROWD FINALLY HEADS HOME.

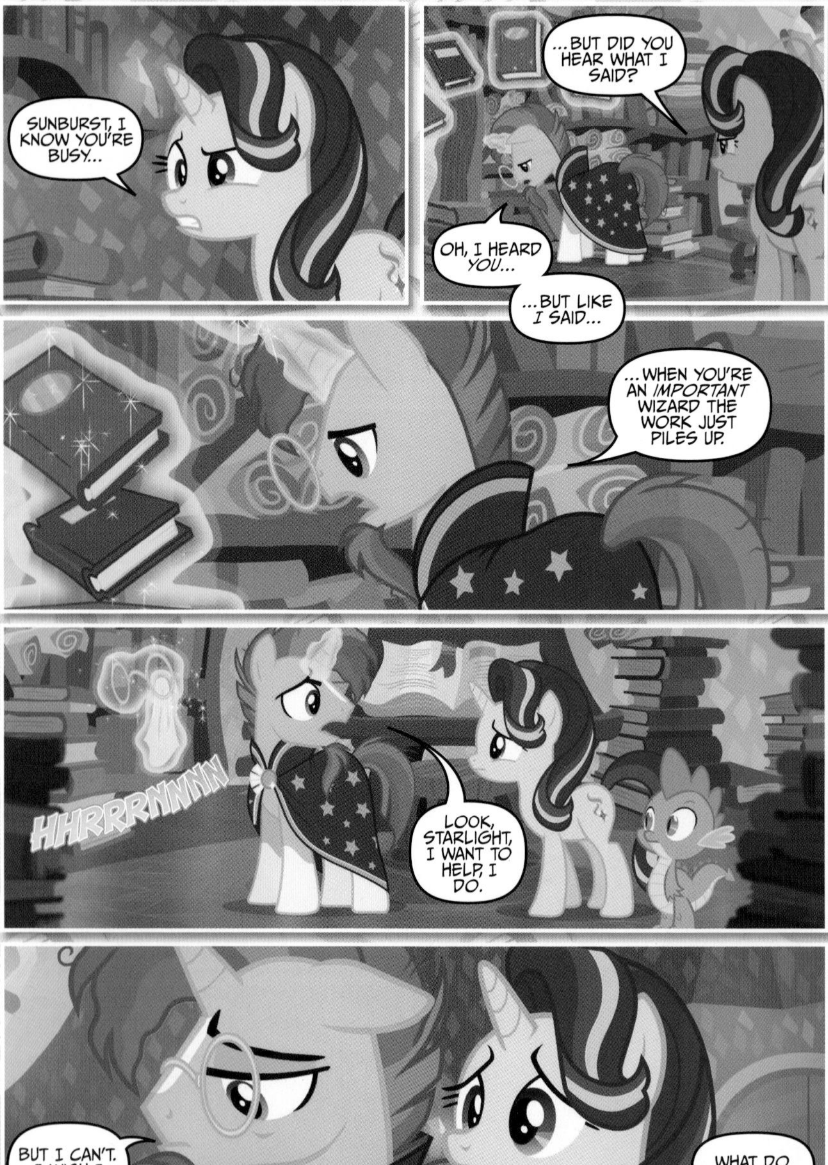
SUNBURST, I KNOW YOU'RE BUSY...
...BUT DID YOU HEAR WHAT I SAID?
OH, I HEARD *YOU*...
...BUT LIKE I SAID...
...WHEN YOU'RE AN *IMPORTANT* WIZARD THE WORK JUST PILES UP.
HHRRRNNNN
LOOK, STARLIGHT, I WANT TO HELP, I DO.
BUT I CAN'T. I WISH I COULD.
WHAT DO YOU MEAN?

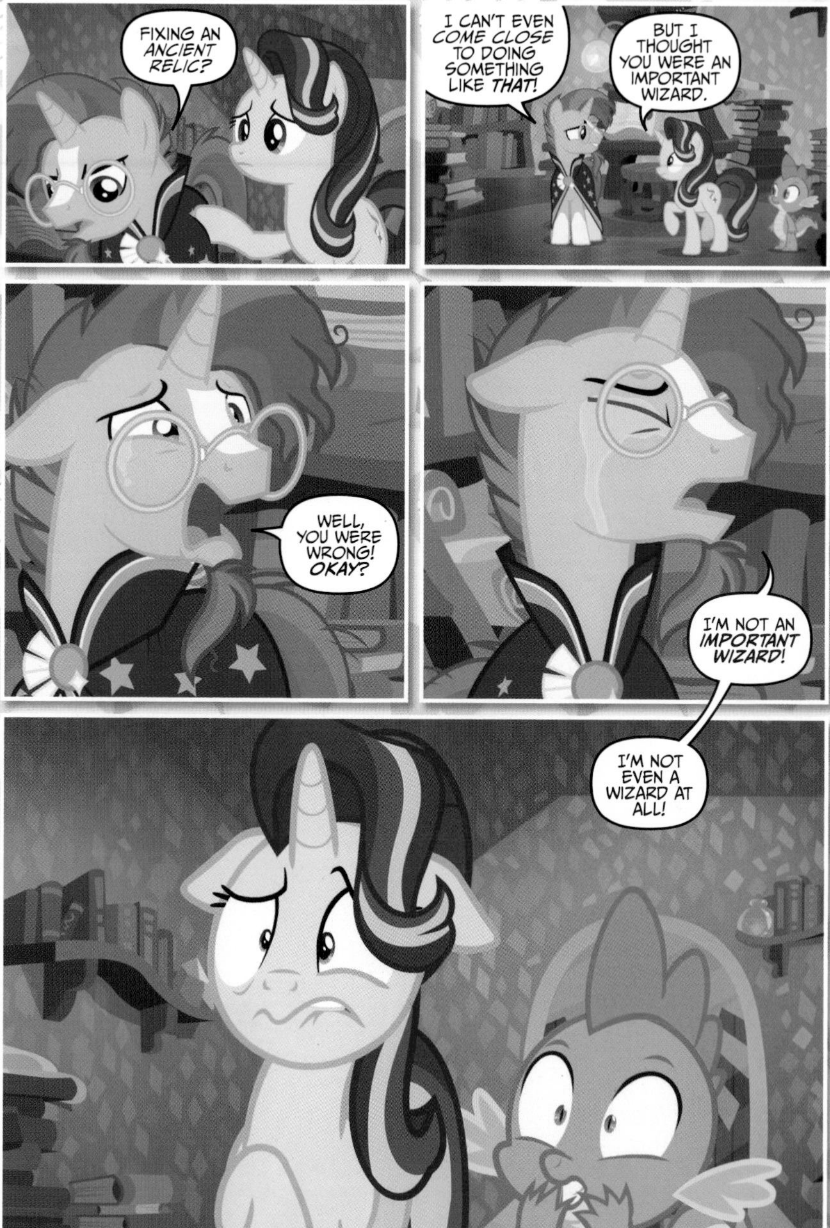
FIXING AN ANCIENT RELIC?
I CAN'T EVEN COME CLOSE TO DOING SOMETHING LIKE THAT!
BUT I THOUGHT YOU WERE AN IMPORTANT WIZARD.
WELL, YOU WERE WRONG! OKAY?
I'M NOT AN IMPORTANT WIZARD!
I'M NOT EVEN A WIZARD AT ALL!

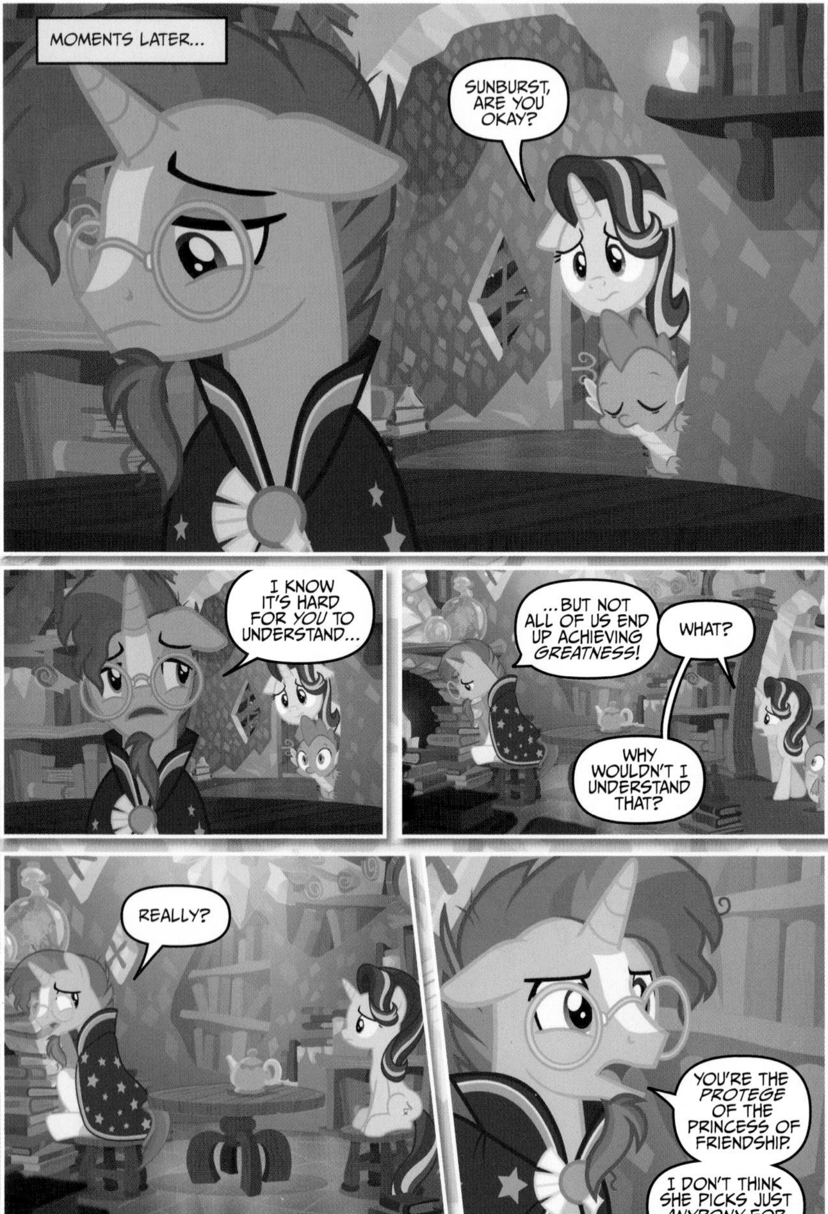
MOMENTS LATER...
SUNBURST, ARE YOU OKAY?
I KNOW IT'S HARD FOR *YOU* TO UNDERSTAND...
...BUT NOT ALL OF US END UP ACHIEVING *GREATNESS!*
WHAT?
WHY WOULDN'T I UNDERSTAND THAT?
REALLY?
YOU'RE THE *PROTEGE* OF THE PRINCESS OF FRIENDSHIP.
I DON'T THINK SHE PICKS JUST *ANYPONY* FOR THAT.

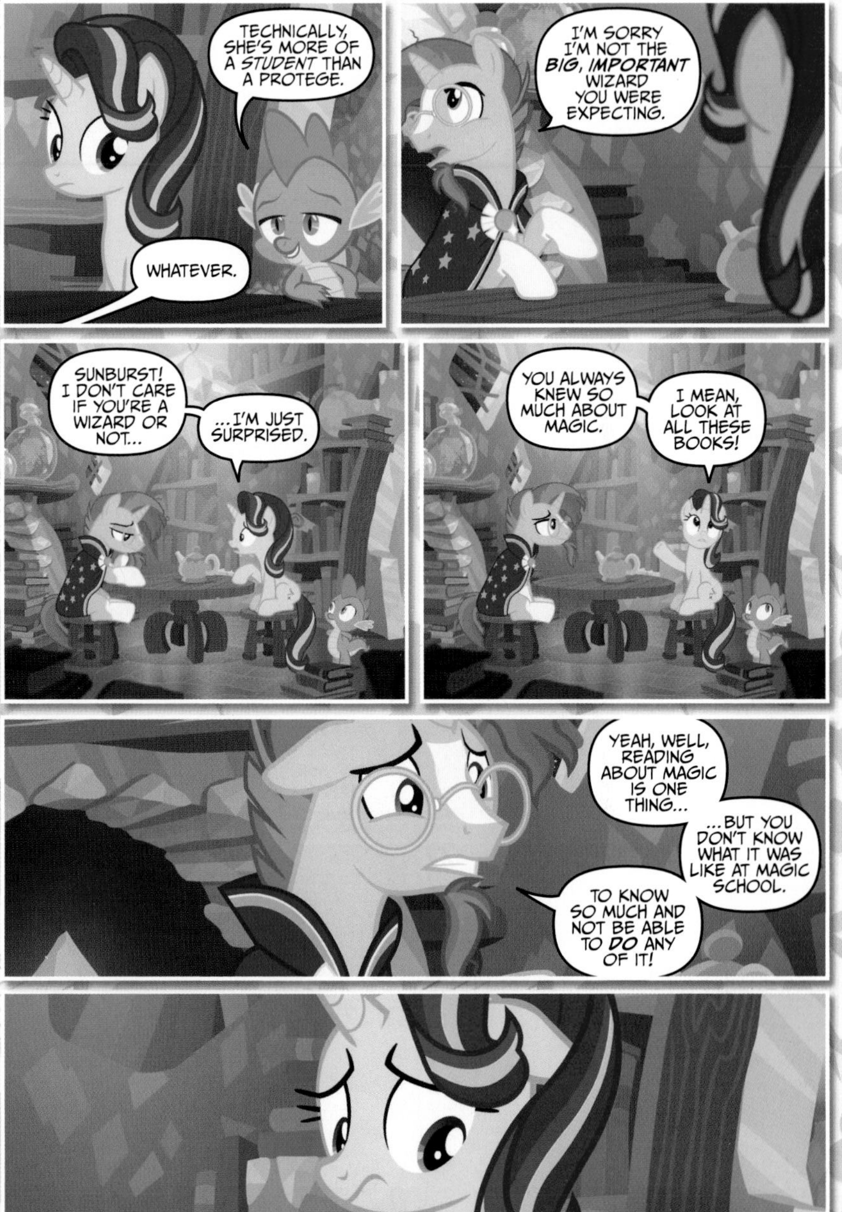
TECHNICALLY, SHE'S MORE OF A *STUDENT* THAN A PROTEGE.
WHATEVER.
I'M SORRY I'M NOT THE ***BIG, IMPORTANT*** WIZARD YOU WERE EXPECTING.
SUNBURST! I DON'T CARE IF YOU'RE A WIZARD OR NOT...
...I'M JUST SURPRISED.
YOU ALWAYS KNEW SO MUCH ABOUT MAGIC.
I MEAN, LOOK AT ALL THESE BOOKS!
YEAH, WELL, READING ABOUT MAGIC IS ONE THING...
...BUT YOU DON'T KNOW WHAT IT WAS LIKE AT MAGIC SCHOOL.
TO KNOW SO MUCH AND NOT BE ABLE TO ***DO*** ANY OF IT!

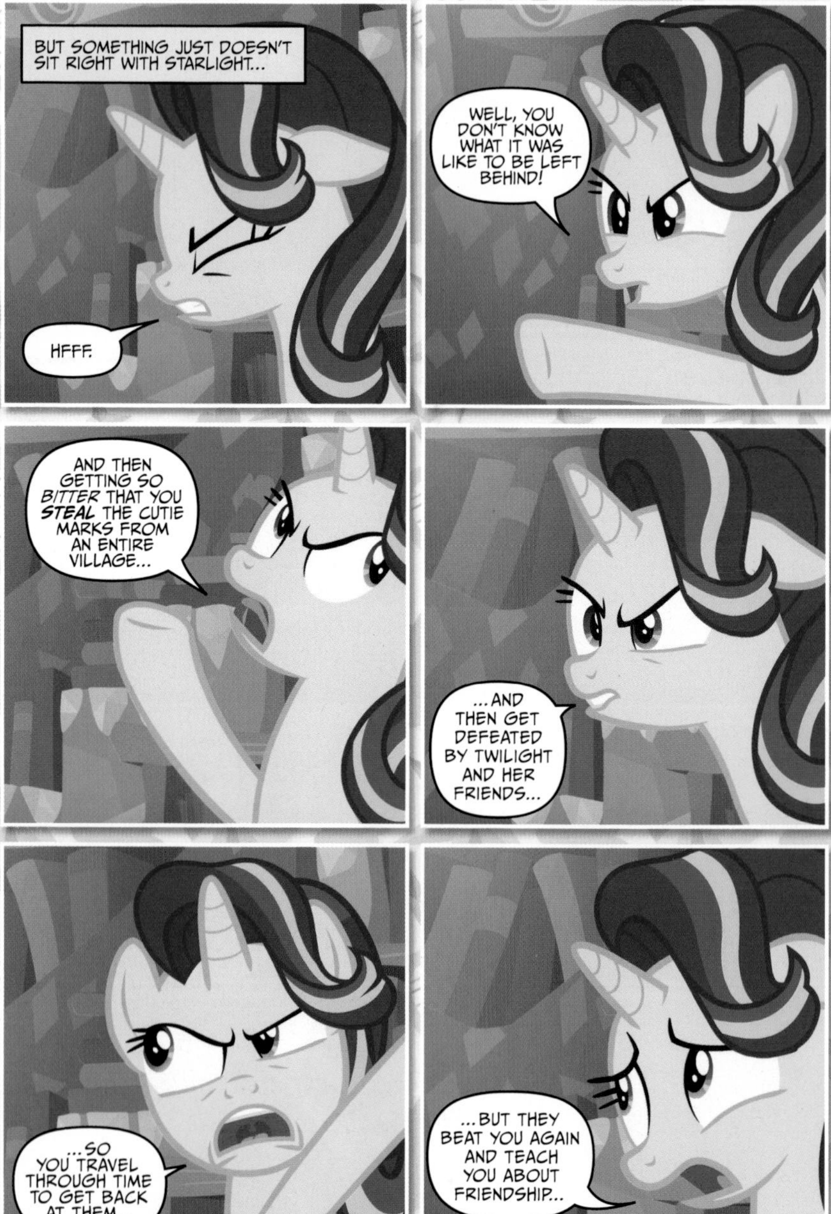

BUT SOMETHING JUST DOESN'T SIT RIGHT WITH STARLIGHT...
HFFF.
WELL, YOU DON'T KNOW WHAT IT WAS LIKE TO BE LEFT BEHIND!
AND THEN GETTING SO *BITTER* THAT YOU ***STEAL*** THE CUTIE MARKS FROM AN ENTIRE VILLAGE...
...AND THEN GET DEFEATED BY TWILIGHT AND HER FRIENDS...
...SO YOU TRAVEL THROUGH TIME TO GET BACK AT THEM...
...BUT THEY BEAT YOU AGAIN AND TEACH YOU ABOUT FRIENDSHIP...

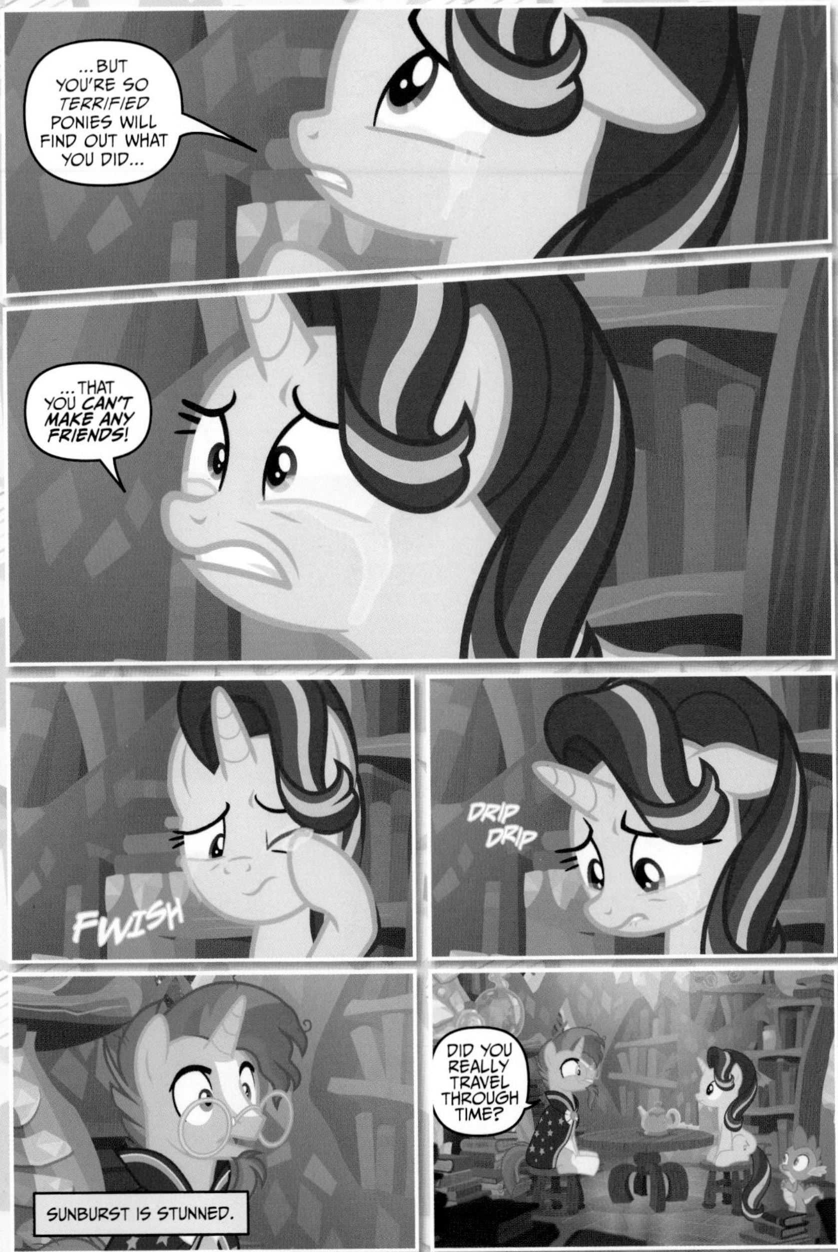
...BUT YOU'RE SO *TERRIFIED* PONIES WILL FIND OUT WHAT YOU DID...
...THAT YOU ***CAN'T MAKE ANY FRIENDS!***
FWISH
DRIP DRIP
SUNBURST IS STUNNED.
DID YOU REALLY TRAVEL THROUGH TIME?

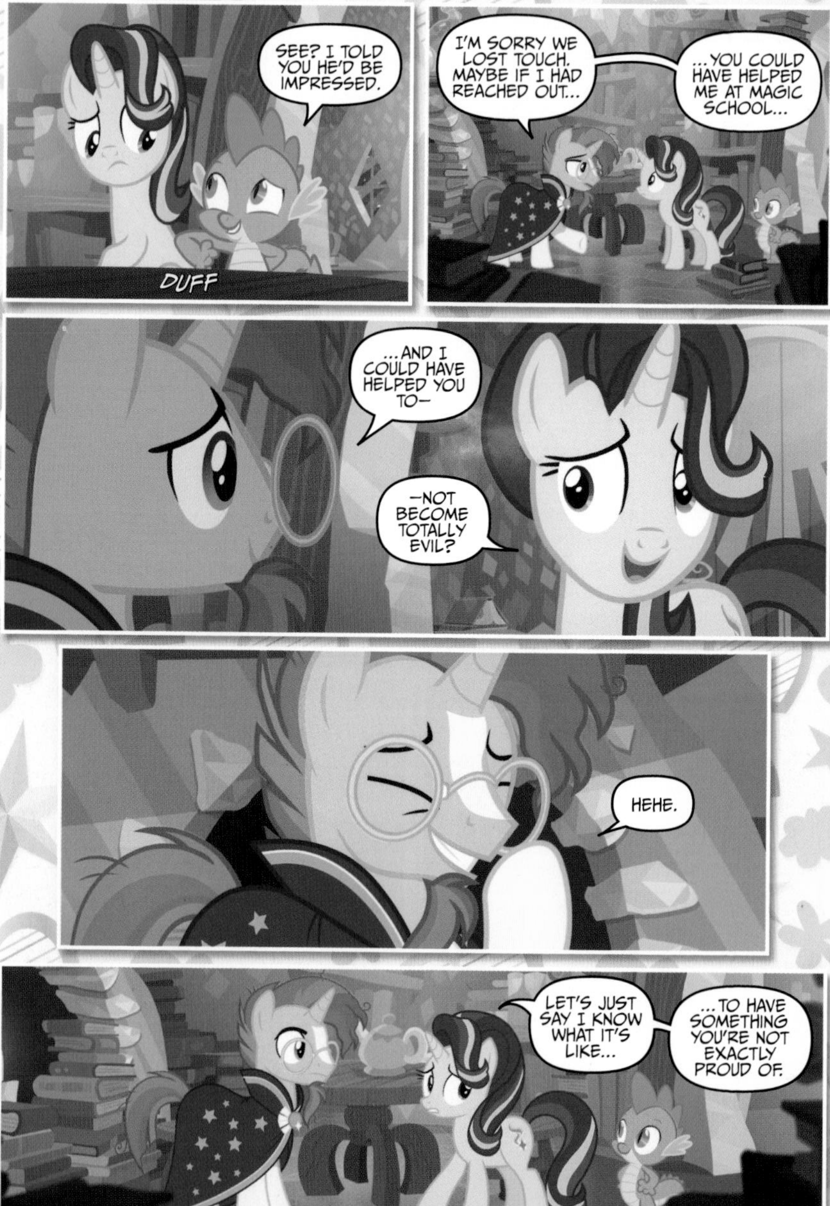
SEE? I TOLD YOU HE'D BE IMPRESSED.
DUFF
I'M SORRY WE LOST TOUCH. MAYBE IF I HAD REACHED OUT...
...YOU COULD HAVE HELPED ME AT MAGIC SCHOOL...
...AND I COULD HAVE HELPED YOU TO–
–NOT BECOME TOTALLY EVIL?
HEHE.
LET'S JUST SAY I KNOW WHAT IT'S LIKE...
...TO HAVE SOMETHING YOU'RE NOT EXACTLY PROUD OF.

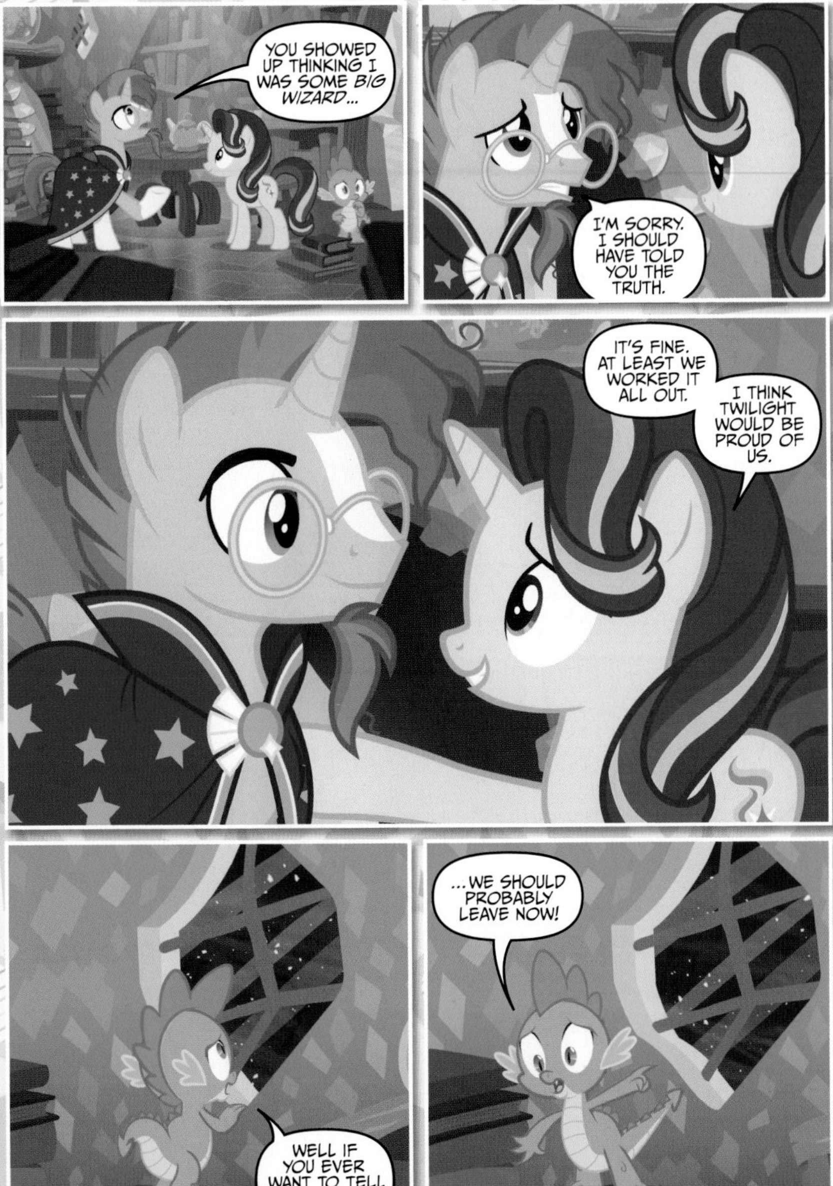

YOU SHOWED UP THINKING I WAS SOME BIG WIZARD...
I'M SORRY. I SHOULD HAVE TOLD YOU THE TRUTH.
IT'S FINE. AT LEAST WE WORKED IT ALL OUT.
I THINK TWILIGHT WOULD BE PROUD OF US.
WELL IF YOU EVER WANT TO TELL HER ABOUT IT...
...WE SHOULD PROBABLY LEAVE NOW!

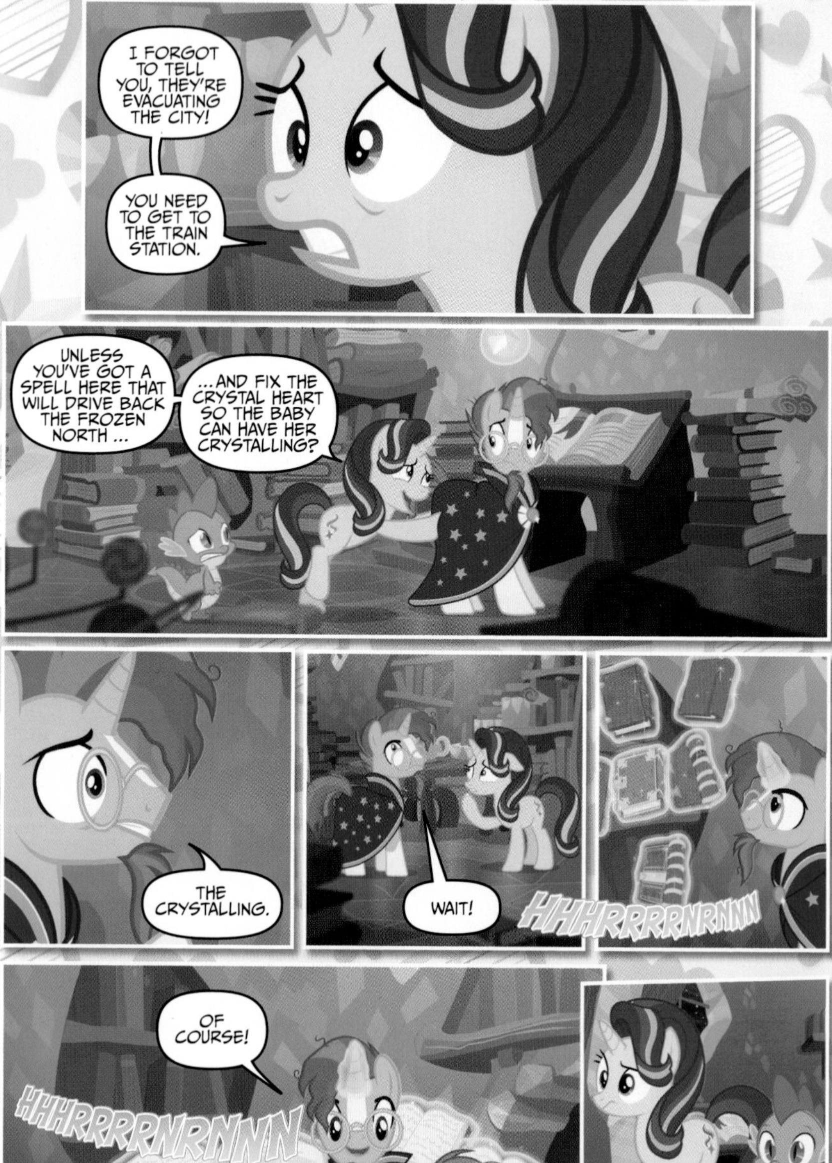
I FORGOT TO TELL YOU, THEY'RE EVACUATING THE CITY!
YOU NEED TO GET TO THE TRAIN STATION.
UNLESS YOU'VE GOT A SPELL HERE THAT WILL DRIVE BACK THE FROZEN NORTH ...
...AND FIX THE CRYSTAL HEART SO THE BABY CAN HAVE HER CRYSTALLING?
THE CRYSTALLING.
WAIT!
HHHRRRRNRNNN
OF COURSE!
HHHRRRRNRNNN

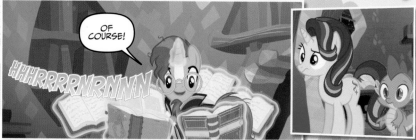

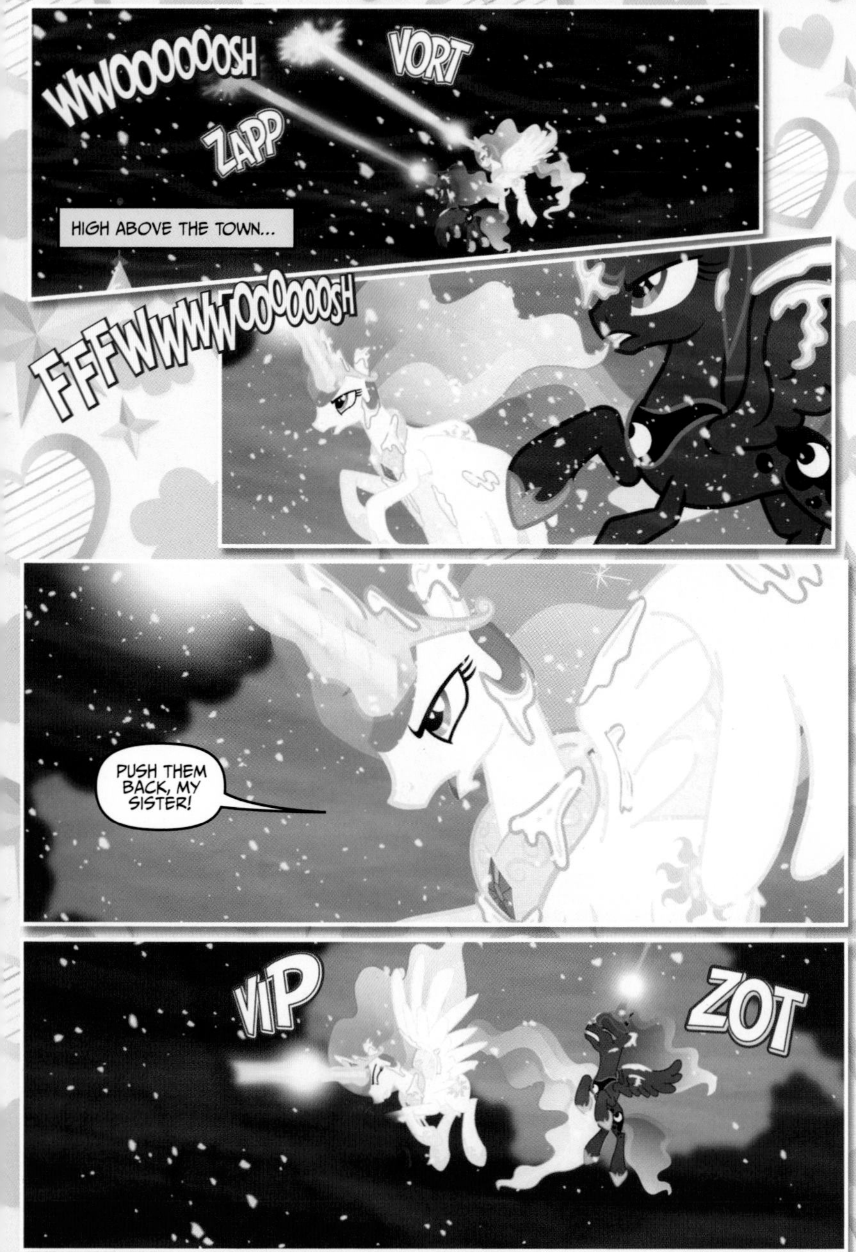
WWOOOOOOSH
VORT
ZAPP
HIGH ABOVE THE TOWN...
FFFWWWWOOOOOOSH
PUSH THEM BACK, MY SISTER!
VIP
ZOT

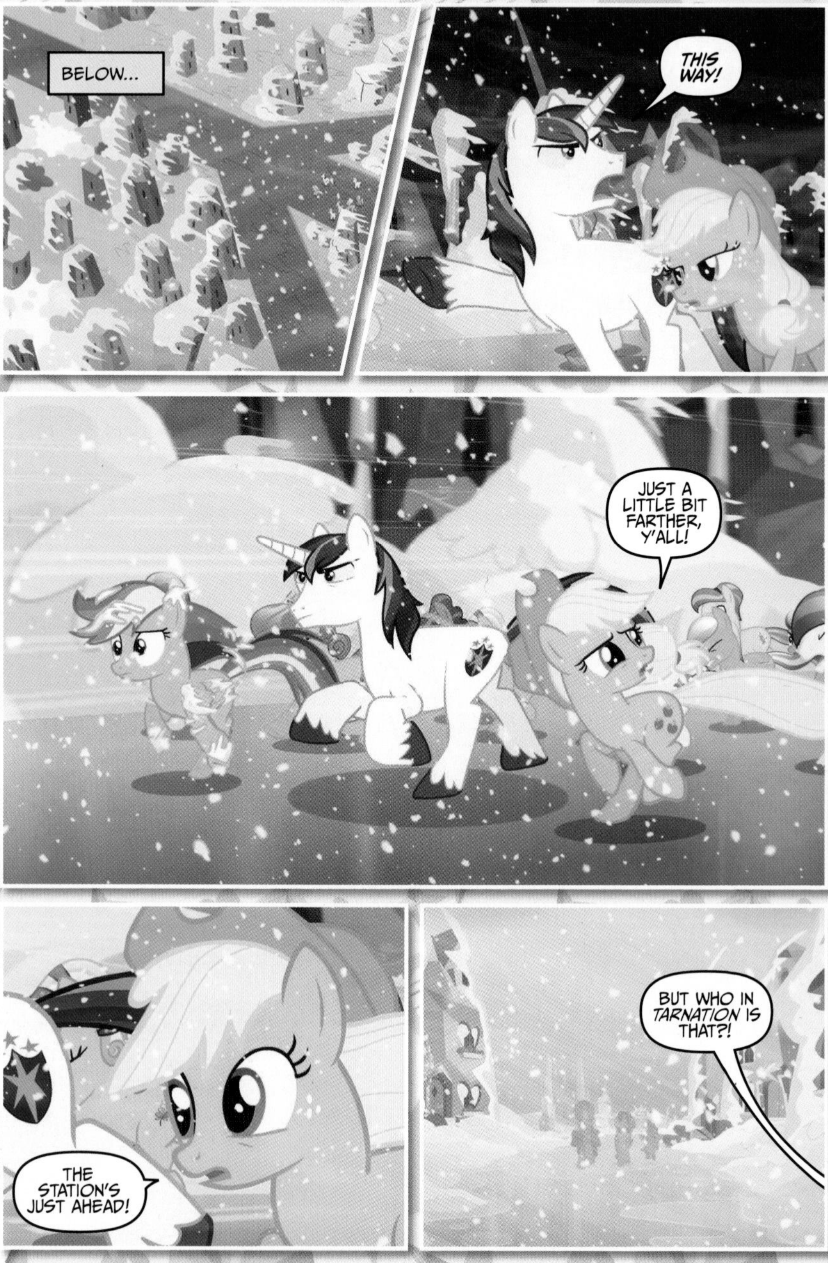

BELOW...
THIS WAY!
JUST A LITTLE BIT FARTHER, Y'ALL!
THE STATION'S JUST AHEAD!
BUT WHO IN *TARNATION* IS THAT?!

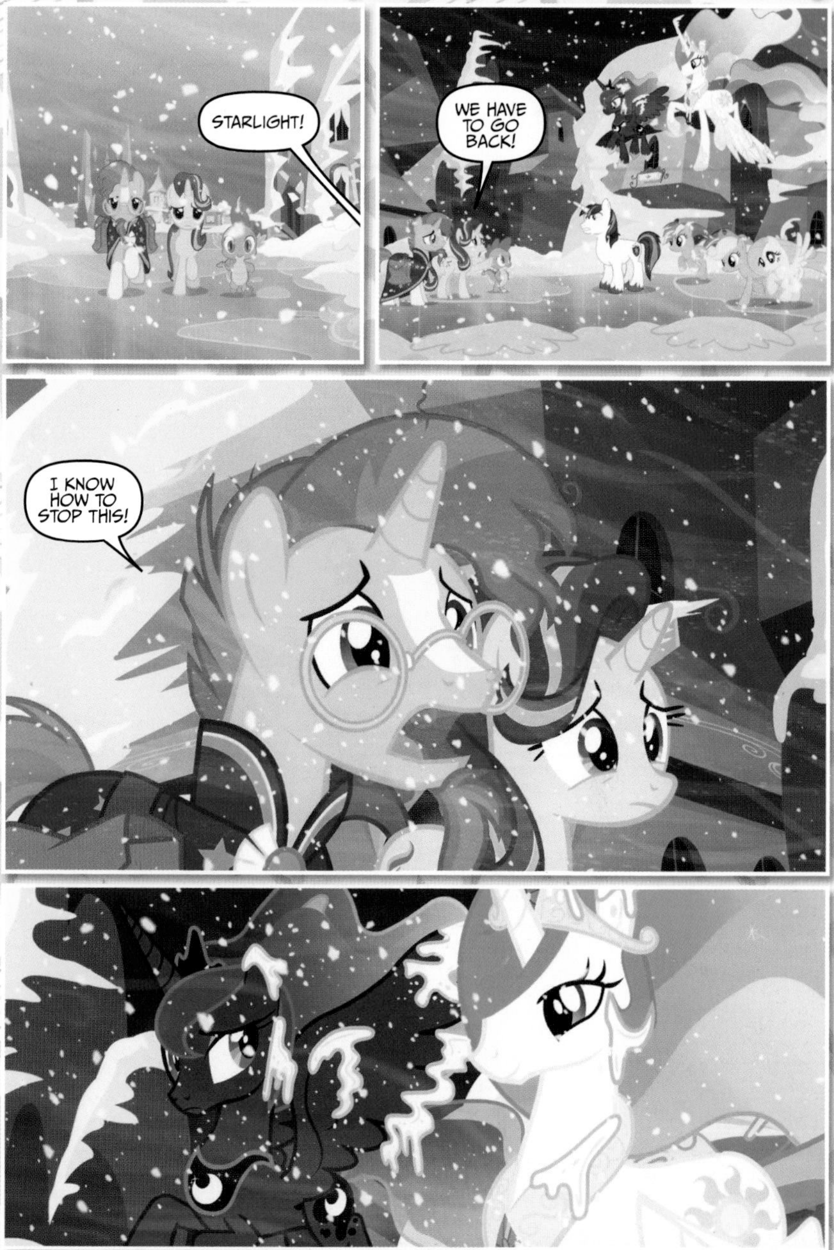

STARLIGHT!
WE HAVE TO GO BACK!
I KNOW HOW TO STOP THIS!

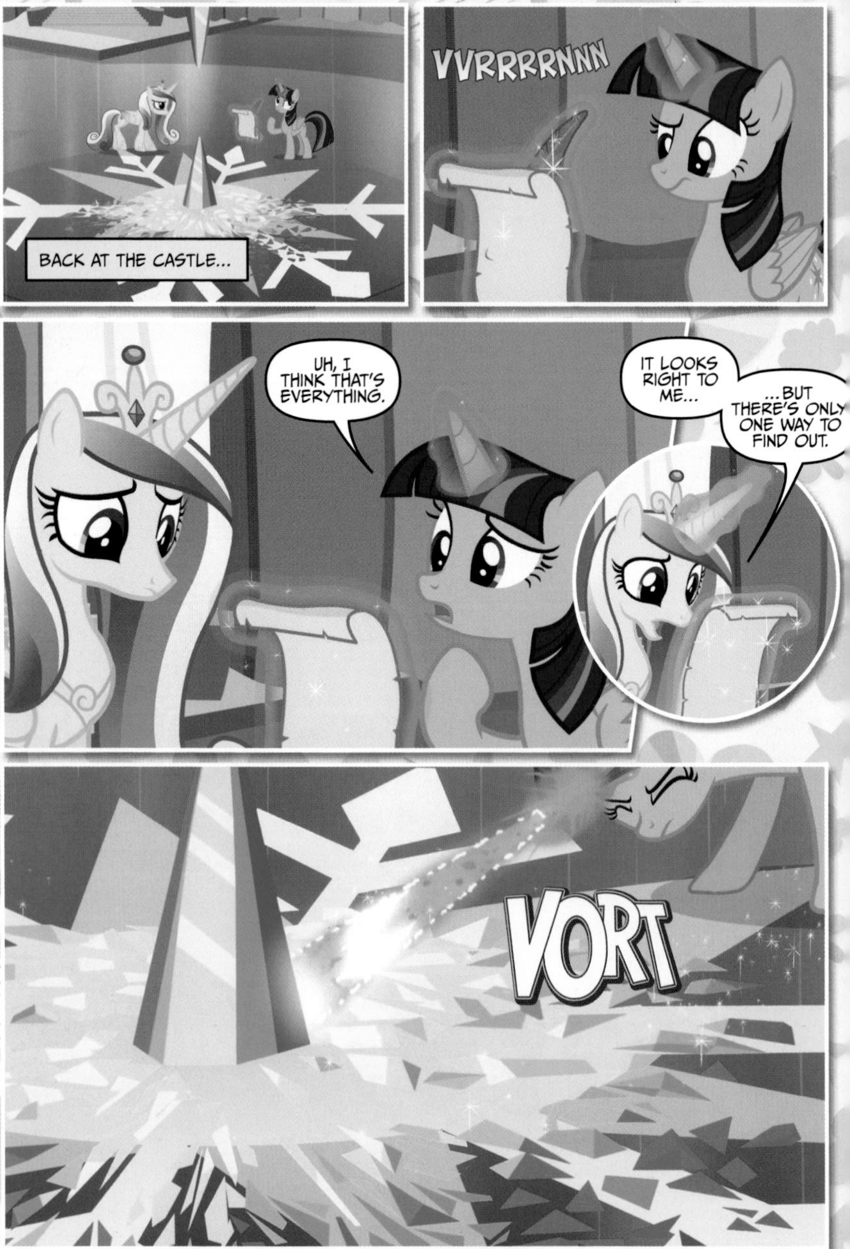

BACK AT THE CASTLE...
VVRRRRNNN
UH, I THINK THAT'S EVERYTHING.
IT LOOKS RIGHT TO ME...
...BUT THERE'S ONLY ONE WAY TO FIND OUT.
VORT

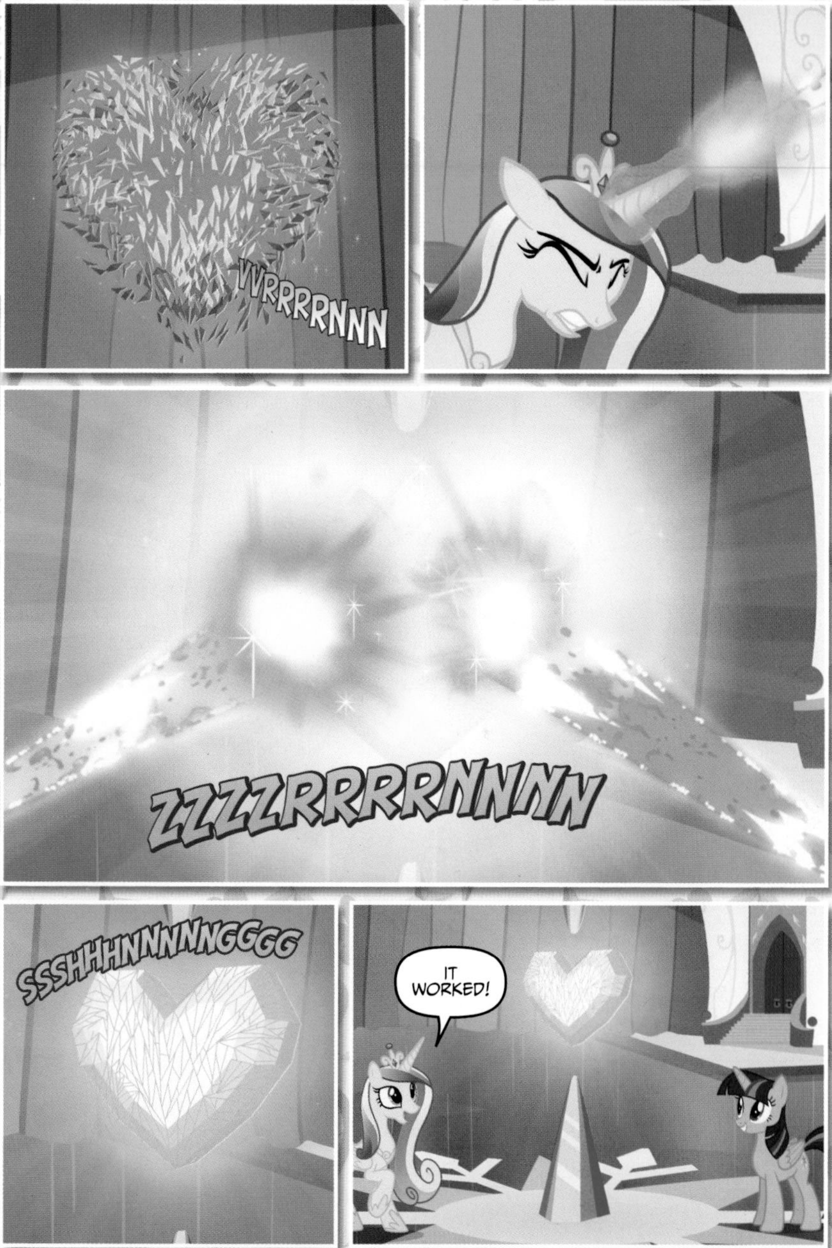
VVRRRRNNN
ZZZZRRRRRNNNN
SSSHHHNNNNNGGGG
IT WORKED!

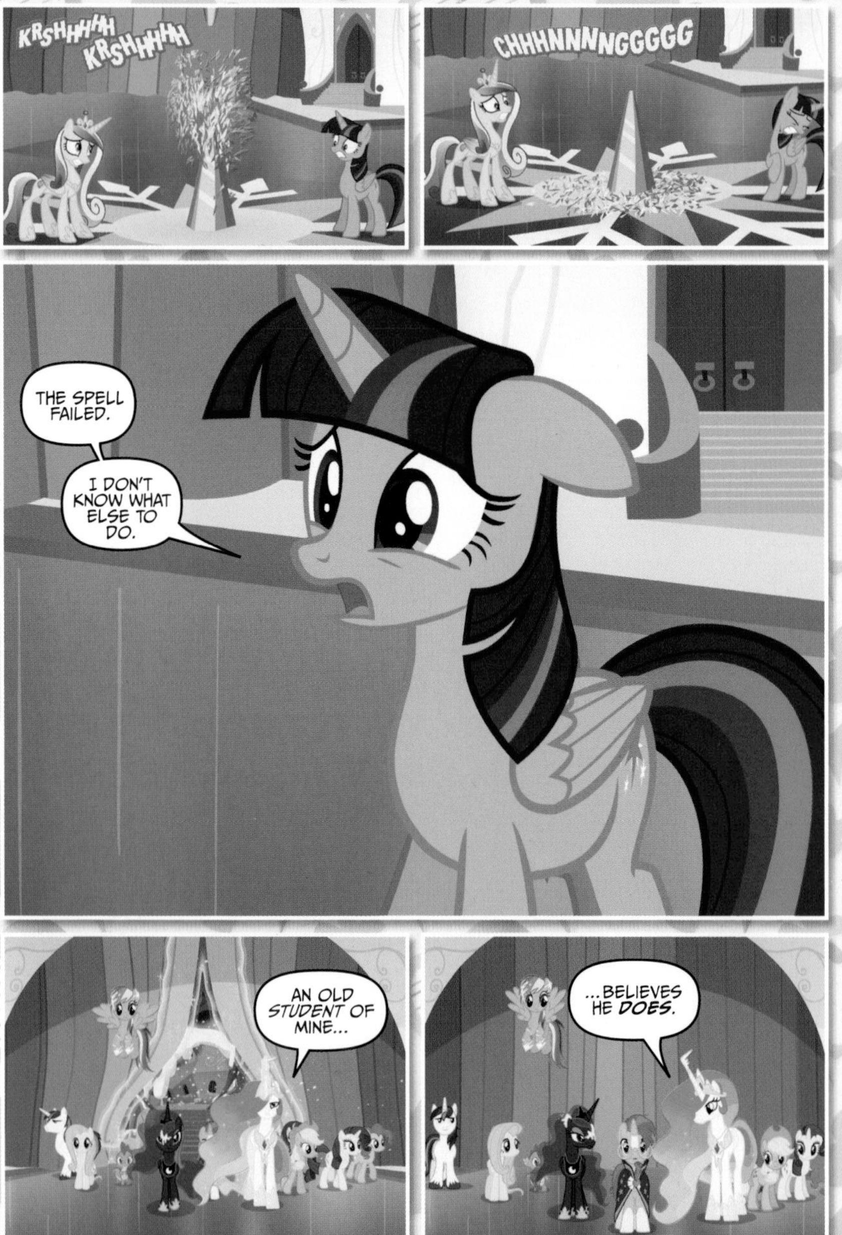
KRSHHHHH KRSHHHHH
CHHHNNNNGGGGG
THE SPELL FAILED.
I DON'T KNOW WHAT ELSE TO DO.
AN OLD STUDENT OF MINE...
...BELIEVES HE DOES.

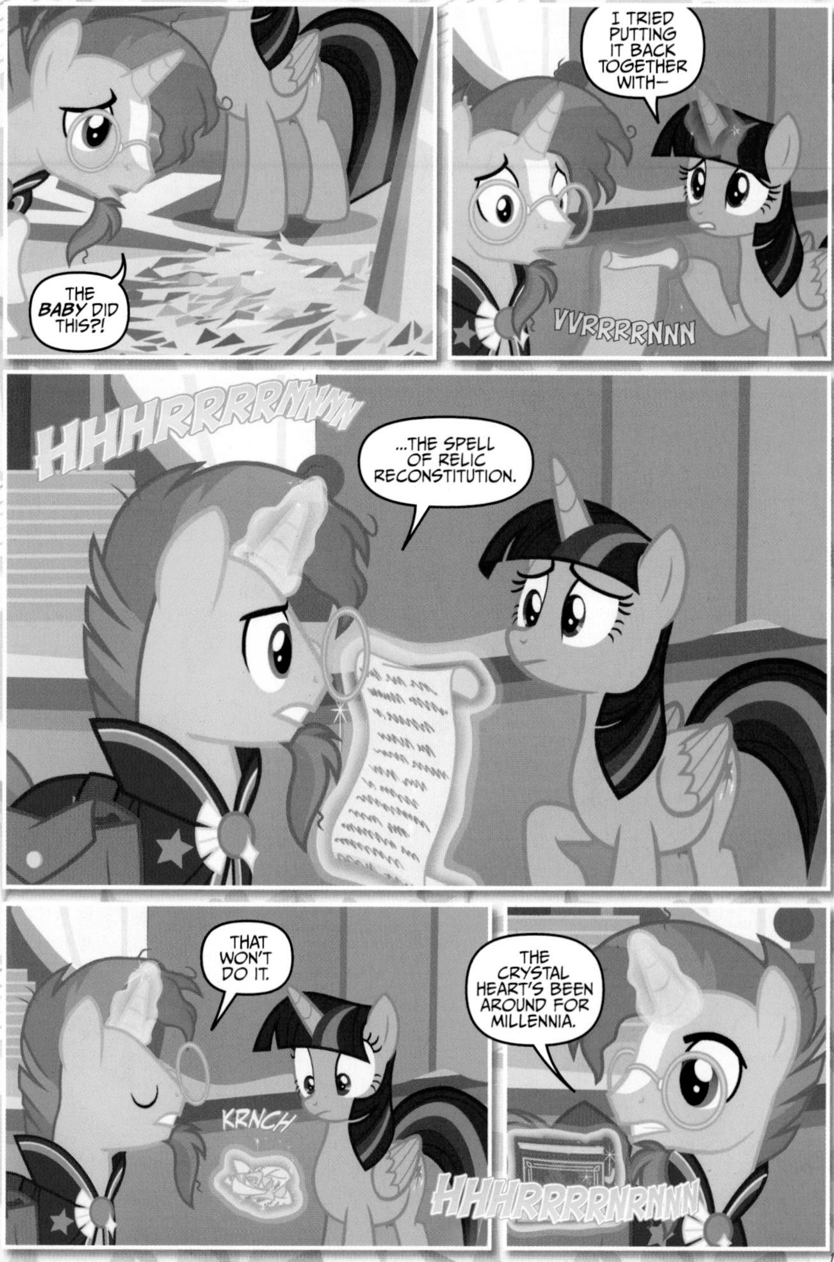

THE BABY DID THIS?!
I TRIED PUTTING IT BACK TOGETHER WITH—
VVRRRRNNN
HHHRRRRNNNN
...THE SPELL OF RELIC RECONSTITUTION.
THAT WON'T DO IT.
KRNCH
THE CRYSTAL HEART'S BEEN AROUND FOR MILLENNIA.
HHHRRRRNRNNN

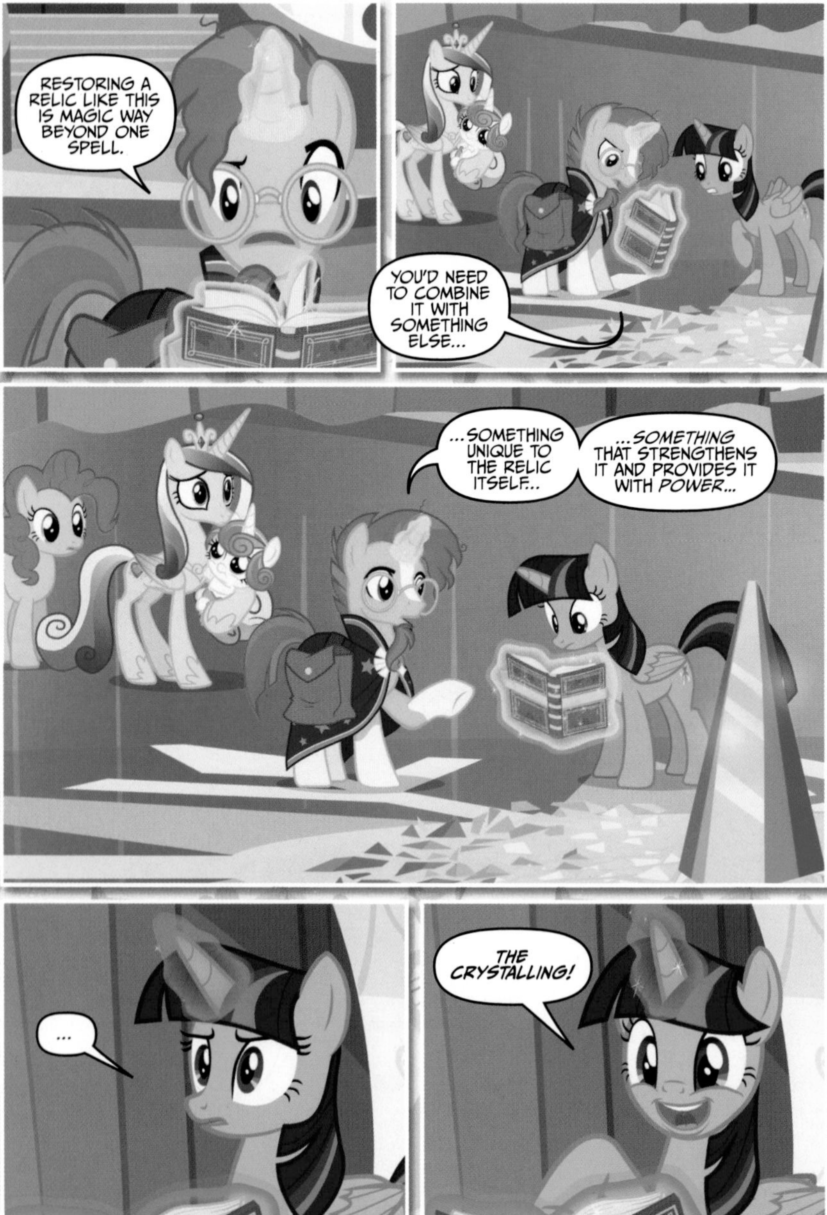
RESTORING A RELIC LIKE THIS IS MAGIC WAY BEYOND ONE SPELL.
YOU'D NEED TO COMBINE IT WITH SOMETHING ELSE...
...SOMETHING UNIQUE TO THE RELIC ITSELF...
...SOMETHING THAT STRENGTHENS IT AND PROVIDES IT WITH POWER...
...
THE CRYSTALLING!

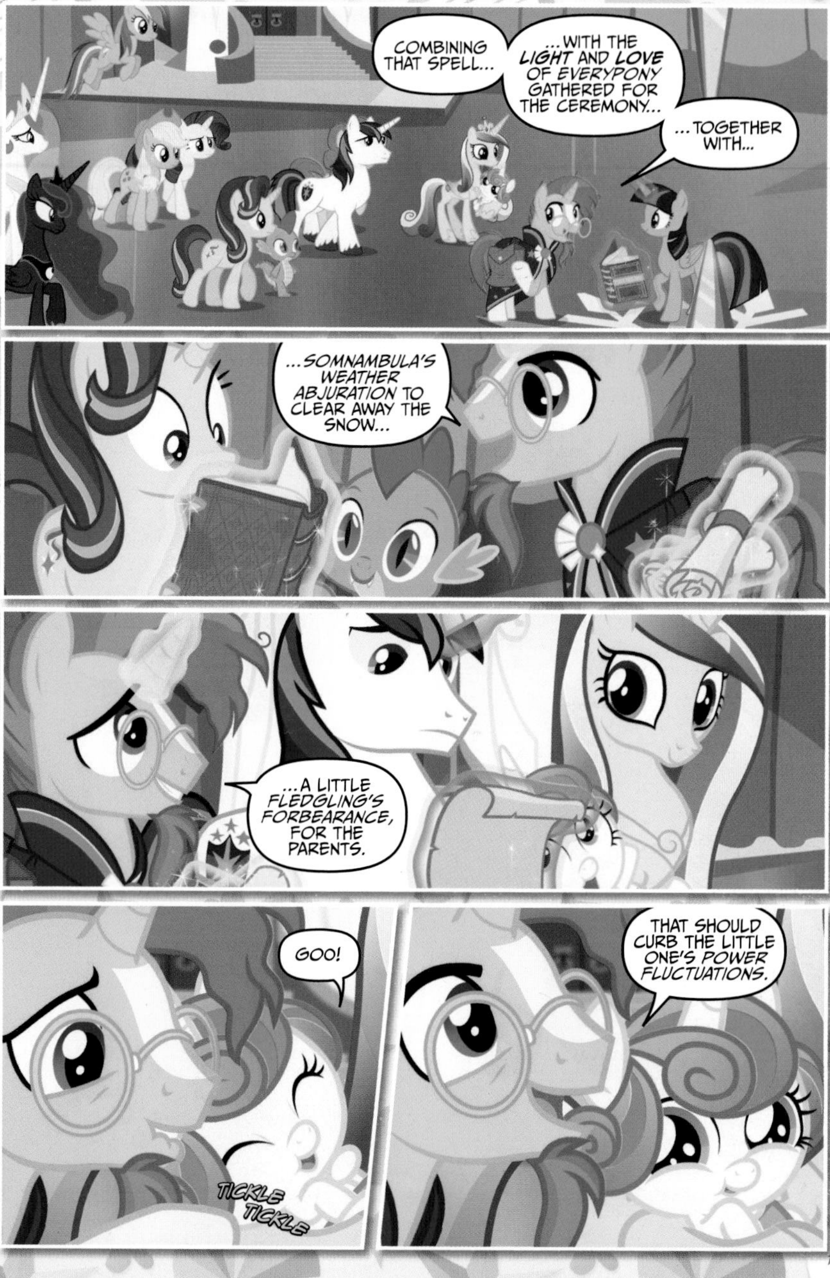
COMBINING THAT SPELL...
...WITH THE *LIGHT* AND *LOVE* OF *EVERYPONY* GATHERED FOR THE CEREMONY...
...TOGETHER WITH...
...SOMNAMBULA'S WEATHER ABJURATION TO CLEAR AWAY THE SNOW...
...A LITTLE FLEDGLING'S FORBEARANCE, FOR THE PARENTS.
GOO!
TICKLE TICKLE
THAT SHOULD CURB THE LITTLE ONE'S *POWER FLUCTUATIONS.*

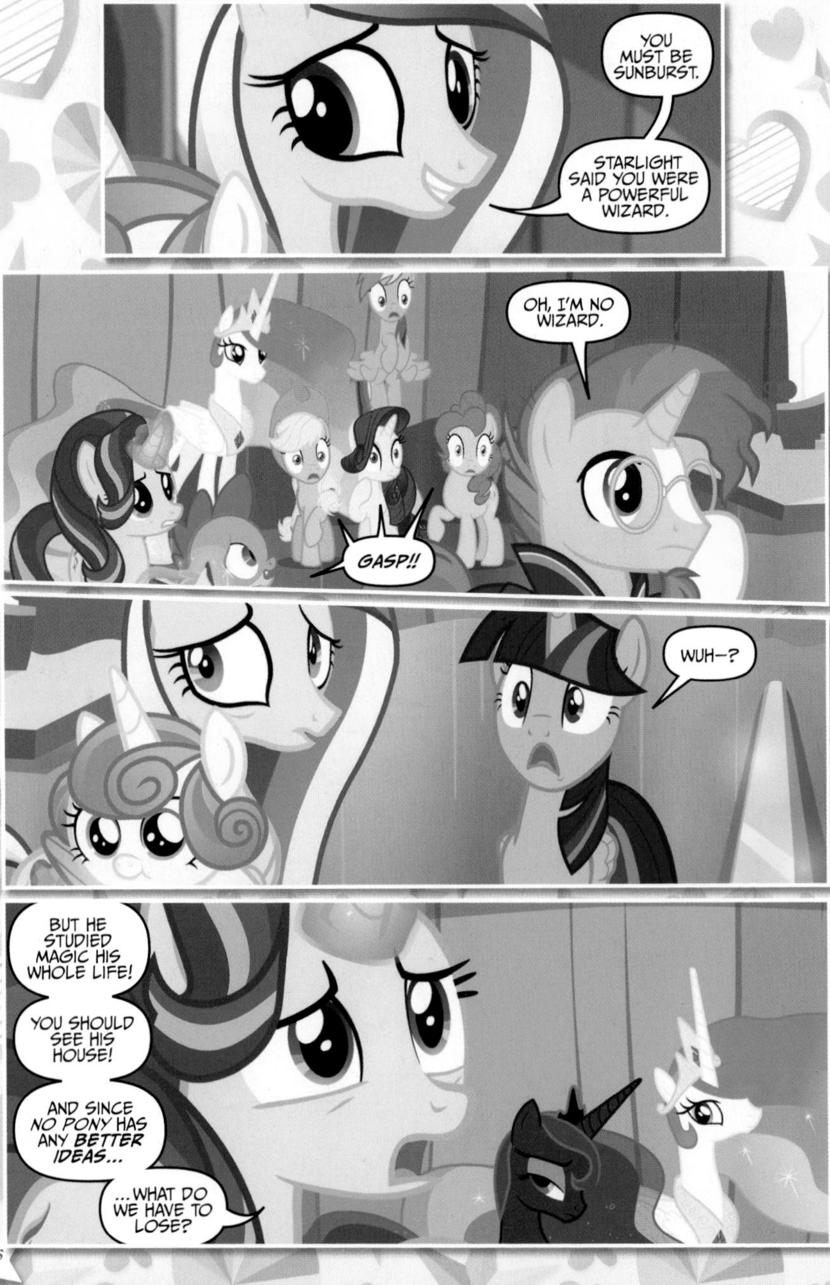
YOU MUST BE SUNBURST.
STARLIGHT SAID YOU WERE A POWERFUL WIZARD.
OH, I'M NO WIZARD.
GASP!!
WUH–?
BUT HE STUDIED MAGIC HIS WHOLE LIFE!
YOU SHOULD SEE HIS HOUSE!
AND SINCE *NO PONY* HAS ANY ***BETTER IDEAS...***
...WHAT DO WE HAVE TO LOSE?

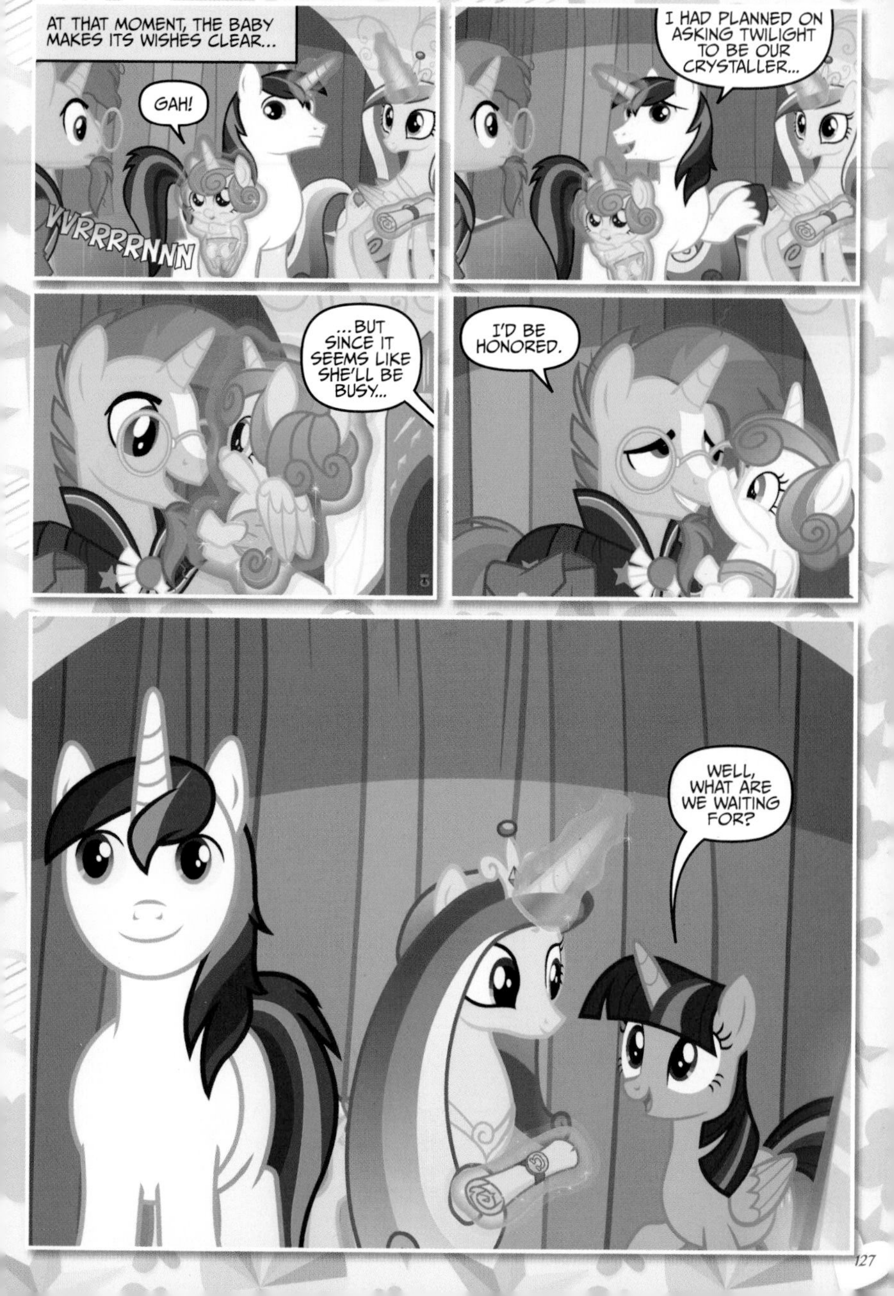
AT THAT MOMENT, THE BABY MAKES ITS WISHES CLEAR...
GAH!
VVRRRRRNNN
I HAD PLANNED ON ASKING TWILIGHT TO BE OUR CRYSTALLER...
...BUT SINCE IT SEEMS LIKE SHE'LL BE BUSY...
I'D BE HONORED.
WELL, WHAT ARE WE WAITING FOR?

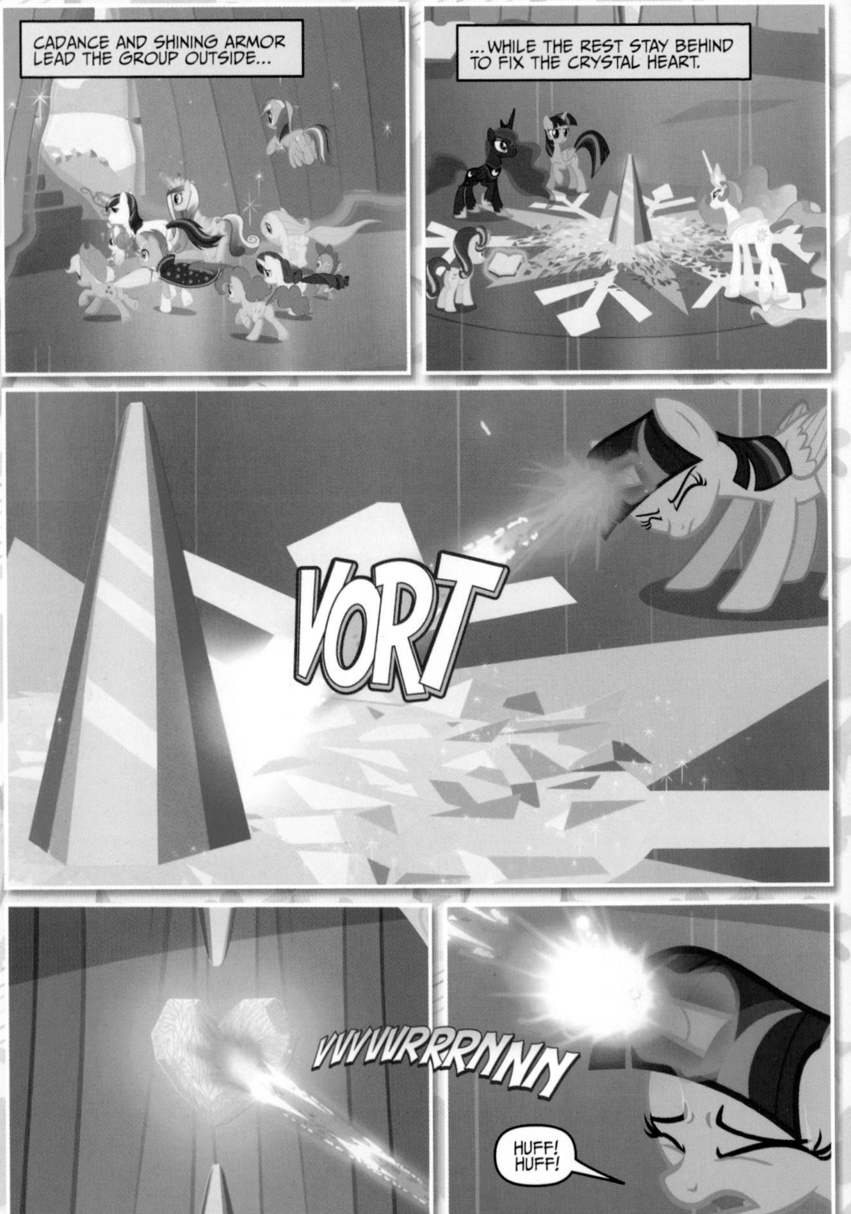
CADANCE AND SHINING ARMOR LEAD THE GROUP OUTSIDE...
...WHILE THE REST STAY BEHIND TO FIX THE CRYSTAL HEART.
VORT
VVVVVRRRRNNN
HUFF! HUFF!

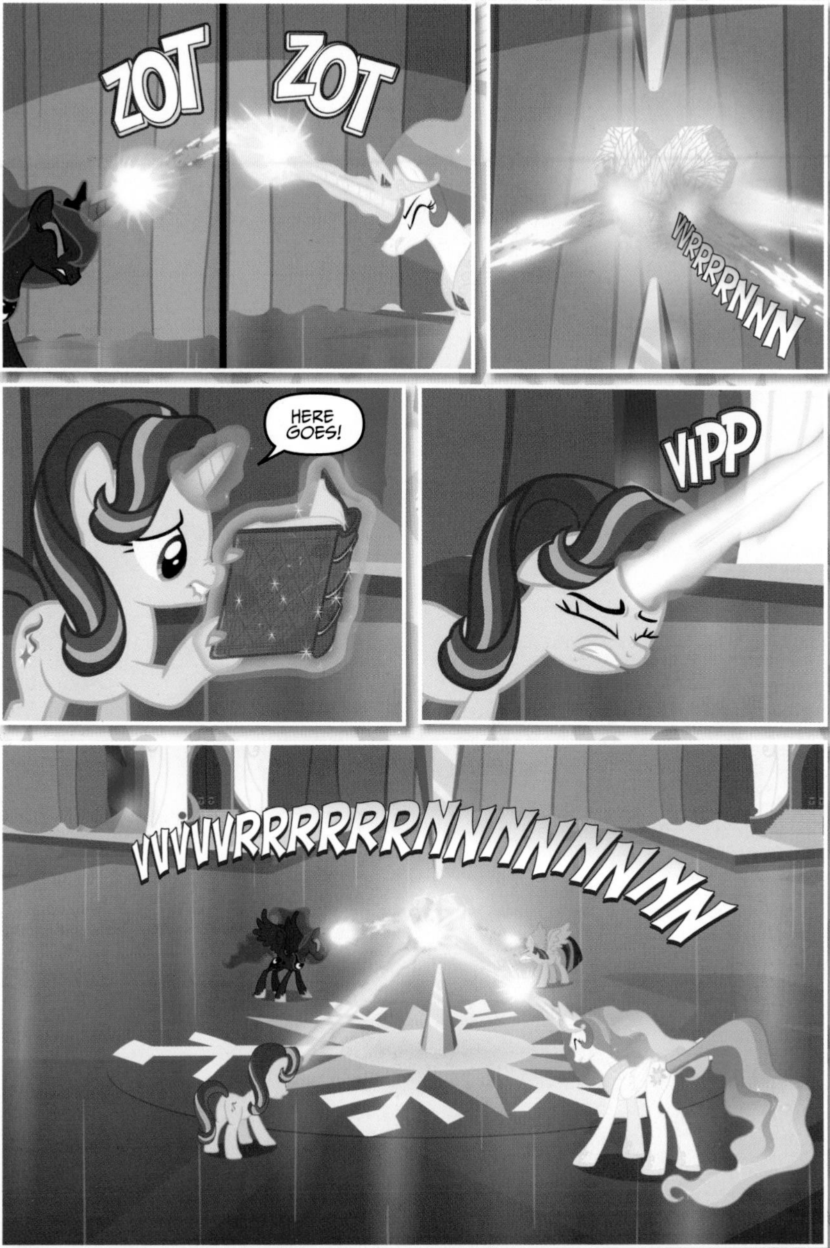
ZOT
ZOT
VVRRRRNNNN
HERE GOES!
VIPP
VVVVVRRRRRRRNNNNNNNNNN

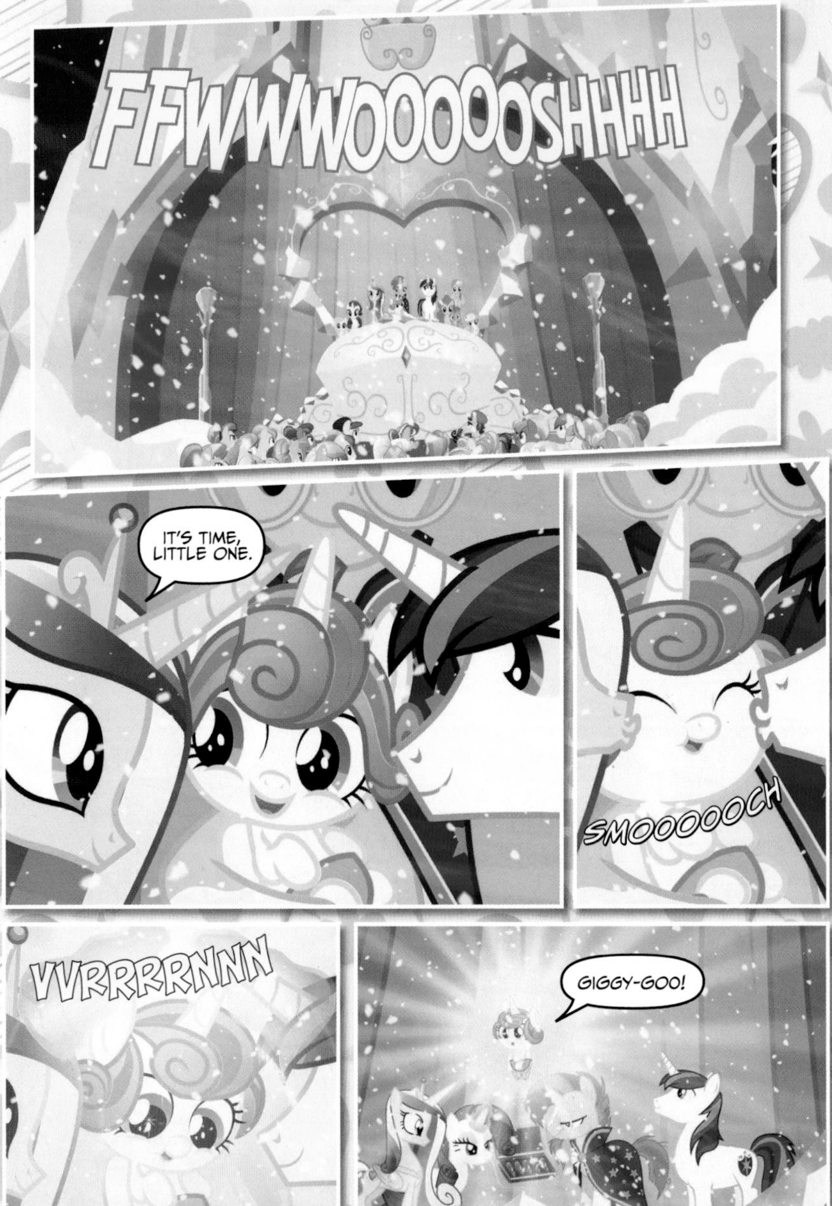
FFWWWOOOOOSHHHH
IT'S TIME, LITTLE ONE.
SMOOOOOOCH
VVRRRRNNN
GIGGY-GOO!

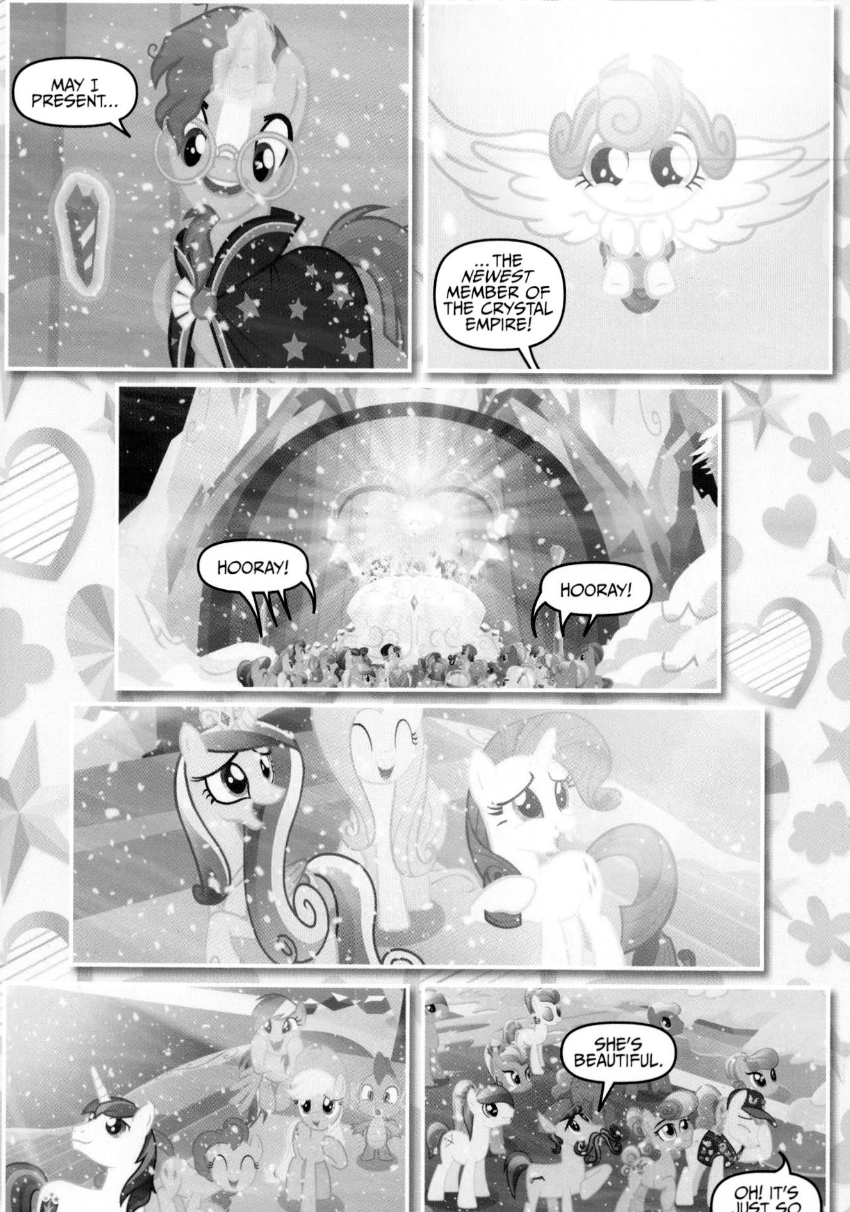
MAY I PRESENT...
...THE *NEWEST* MEMBER OF THE CRYSTAL EMPIRE!
HOORAY!
HOORAY!
SHE'S BEAUTIFUL.
OH! IT'S JUST SO MOVING.

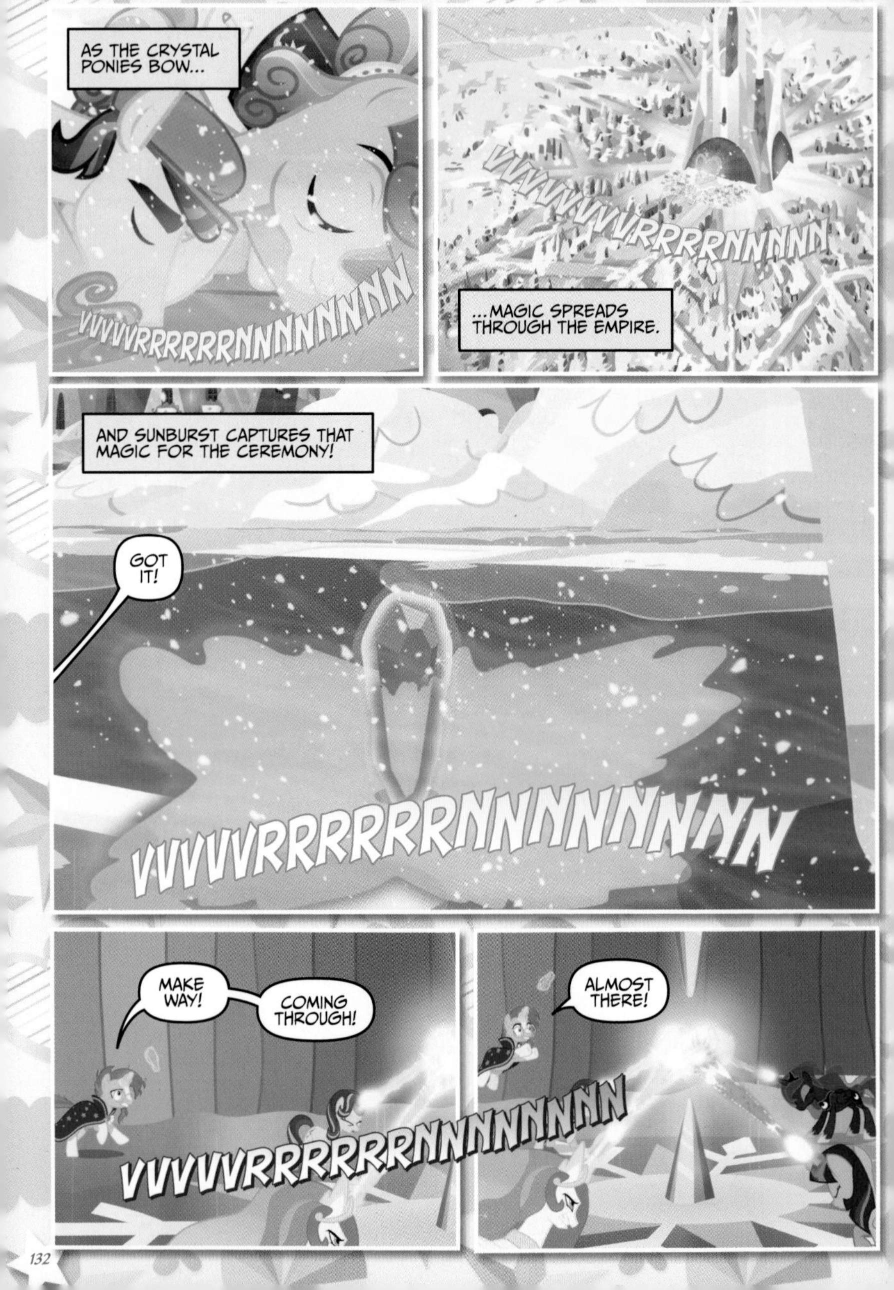
AS THE CRYSTAL PONIES BOW...
VVVVVRRRRRRNNNNNNNNN
VVVVVVVVVRRRRRNNNNNN
...MAGIC SPREADS THROUGH THE EMPIRE.
AND SUNBURST CAPTURES THAT MAGIC FOR THE CEREMONY!
GOT IT!
VVVVVRRRRRRNNNNNNNNN
MAKE WAY!
COMING THROUGH!
VVVVVRRRRRRNNNNNNNNN
ALMOST THERE!

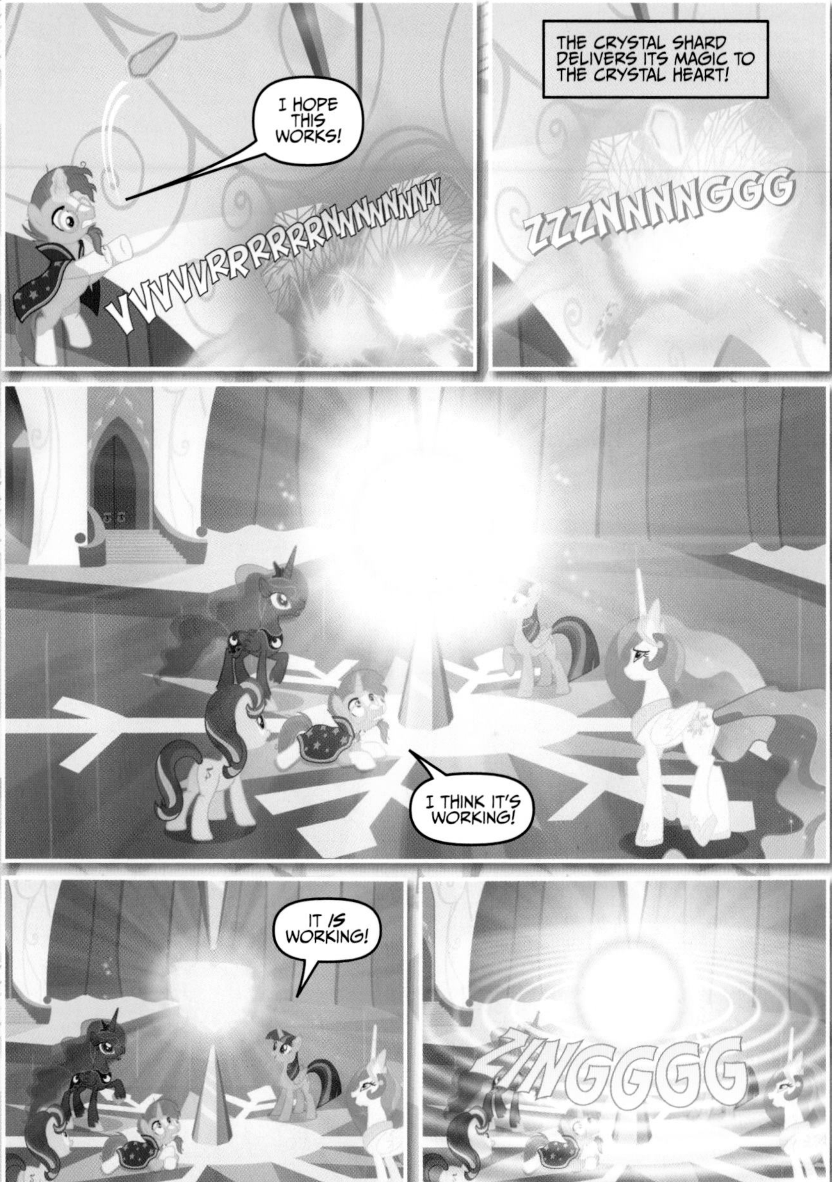
I HOPE THIS WORKS!
VVVVVRRRRRRNNNNNNN
THE CRYSTAL SHARD DELIVERS ITS MAGIC TO THE CRYSTAL HEART!
ZZZNNNNNGGG
I THINK IT'S WORKING!
IT *IS* WORKING!
ZINGGGG

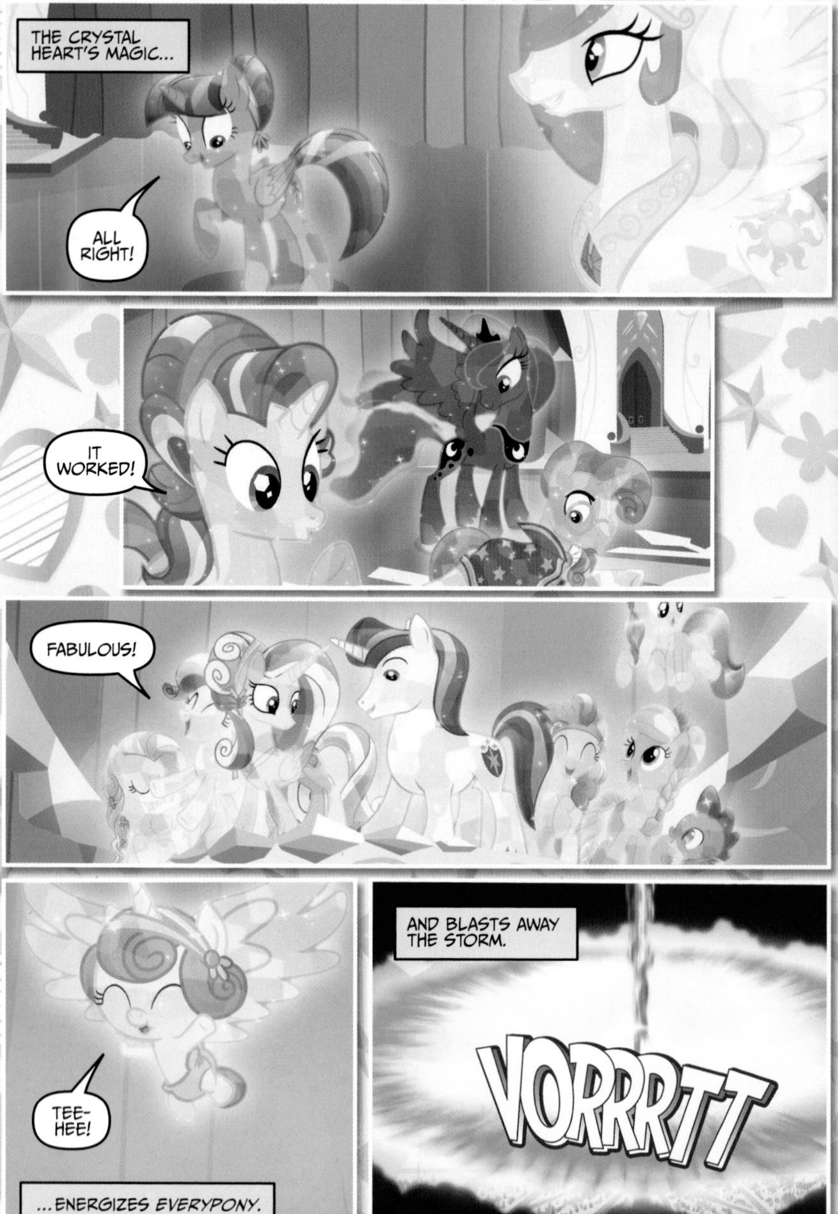
THE CRYSTAL HEART'S MAGIC...
ALL RIGHT!
IT WORKED!
FABULOUS!
TEE-HEE!
...ENERGIZES EVERYPONY.
AND BLASTS AWAY THE STORM.
VORRRRTT

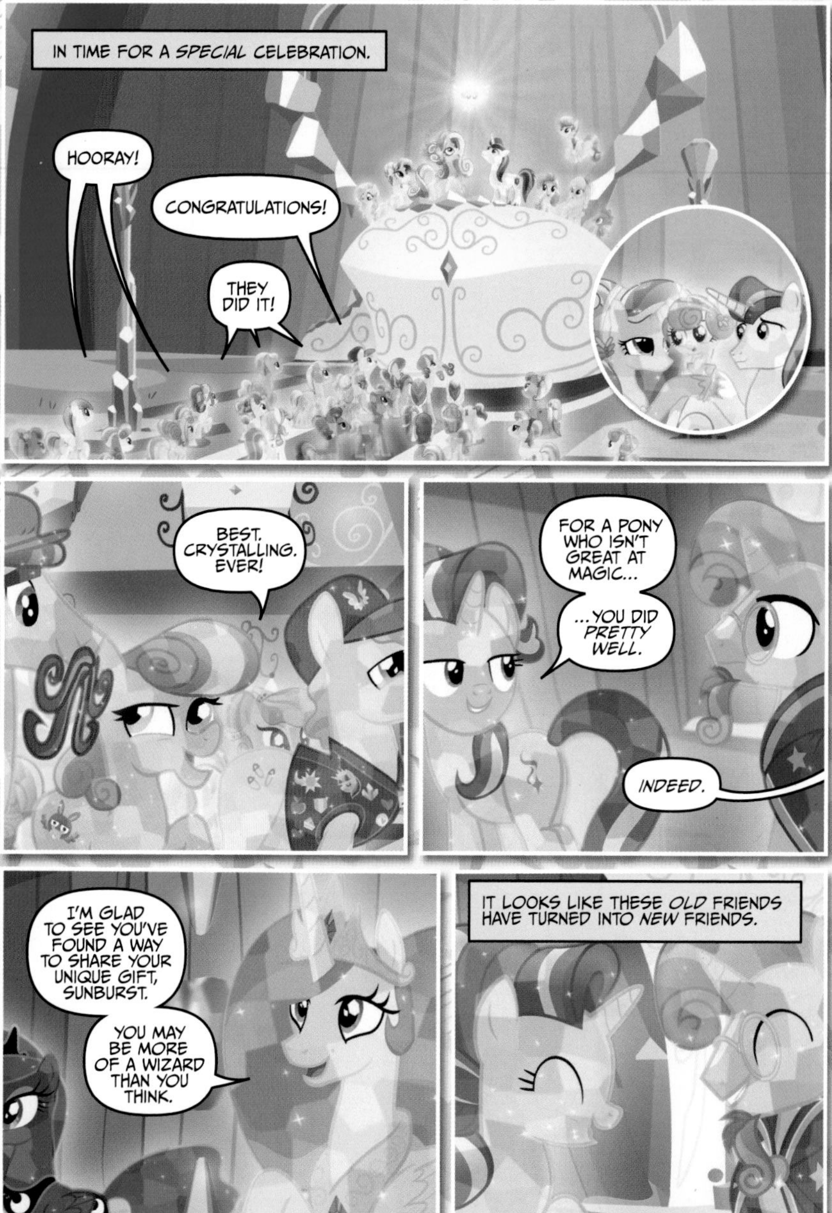

IN TIME FOR A SPECIAL CELEBRATION.
HOORAY!
CONGRATULATIONS!
THEY DID IT!
BEST. CRYSTALLING. EVER!
FOR A PONY WHO ISN'T GREAT AT MAGIC...
...YOU DID PRETTY WELL.
INDEED.
I'M GLAD TO SEE YOU'VE FOUND A WAY TO SHARE YOUR UNIQUE GIFT, SUNBURST.
YOU MAY BE MORE OF A WIZARD THAN YOU THINK.
IT LOOKS LIKE THESE OLD FRIENDS HAVE TURNED INTO NEW FRIENDS.

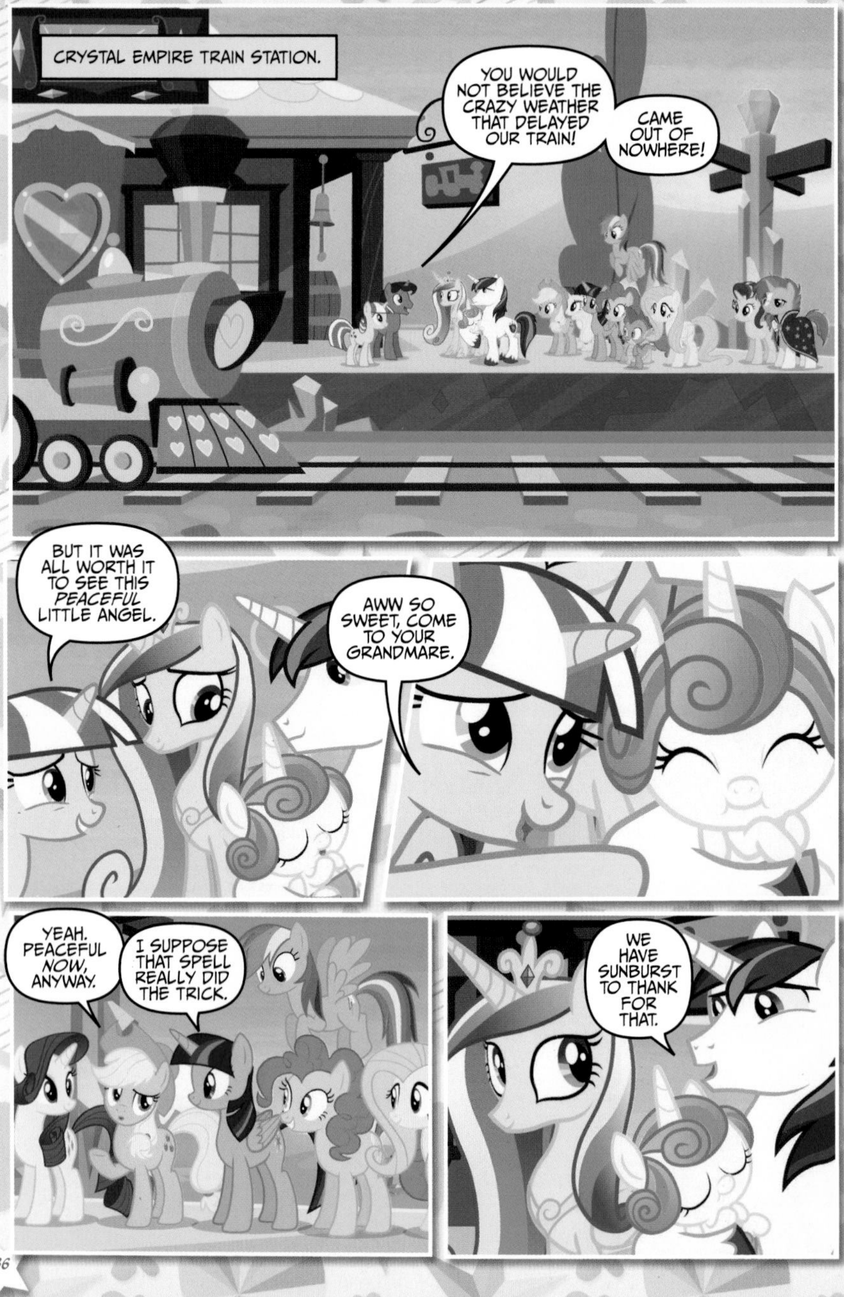
CRYSTAL EMPIRE TRAIN STATION.
YOU WOULD NOT BELIEVE THE CRAZY WEATHER THAT DELAYED OUR TRAIN!
CAME OUT OF NOWHERE!
BUT IT WAS ALL WORTH IT TO SEE THIS *PEACEFUL* LITTLE ANGEL.
AWW SO SWEET, COME TO YOUR GRANDMARE.
YEAH. PEACEFUL *NOW*, ANYWAY.
I SUPPOSE THAT SPELL REALLY DID THE TRICK.
WE HAVE SUNBURST TO THANK FOR THAT.

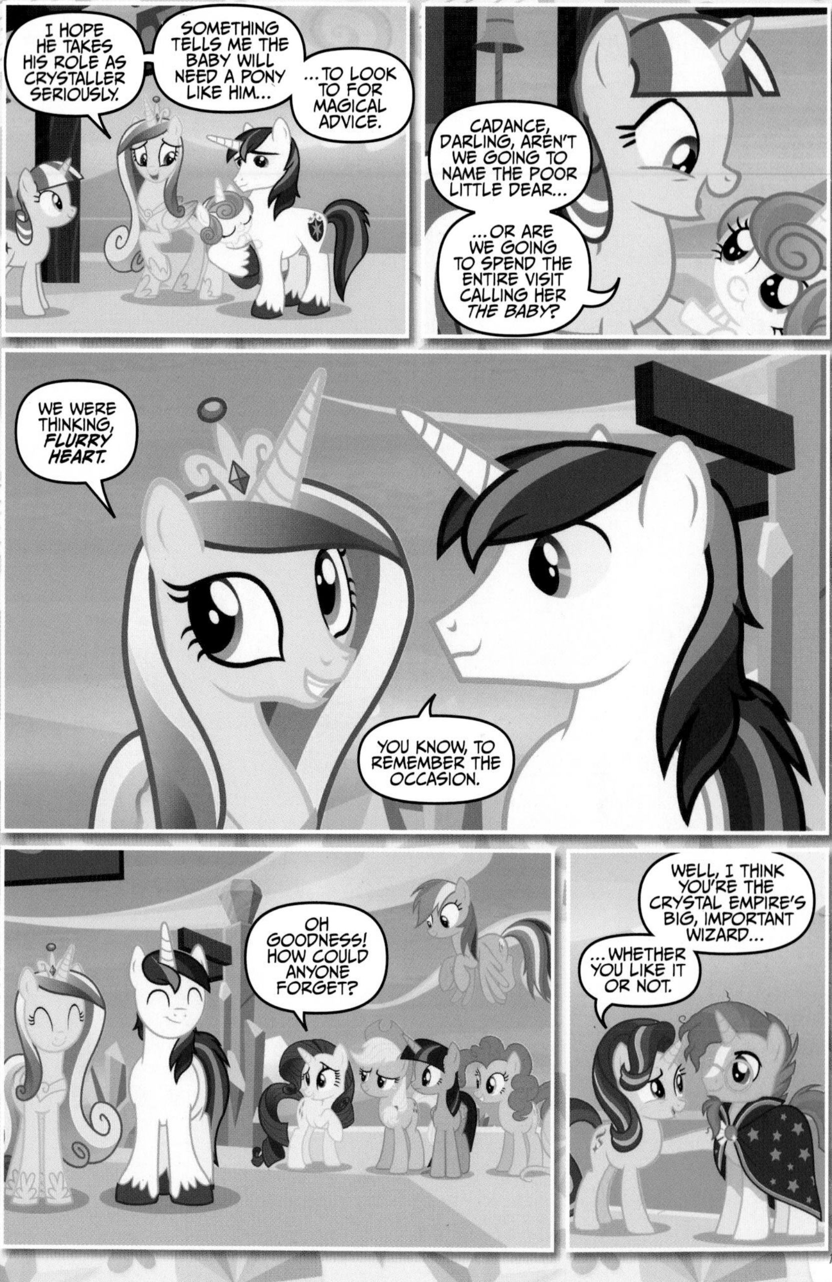
I HOPE HE TAKES HIS ROLE AS CRYSTALLER SERIOUSLY.
SOMETHING TELLS ME THE BABY WILL NEED A PONY LIKE HIM...
...TO LOOK TO FOR MAGICAL ADVICE.
CADANCE, DARLING, AREN'T WE GOING TO NAME THE POOR LITTLE DEAR...
...OR ARE WE GOING TO SPEND THE ENTIRE VISIT CALLING HER *THE BABY?*
WE WERE THINKING, ***FLURRY HEART.***
YOU KNOW, TO REMEMBER THE OCCASION.
OH GOODNESS! HOW COULD ANYONE FORGET?
WELL, I THINK YOU'RE THE CRYSTAL EMPIRE'S BIG, IMPORTANT WIZARD...
...WHETHER YOU LIKE IT OR NOT.

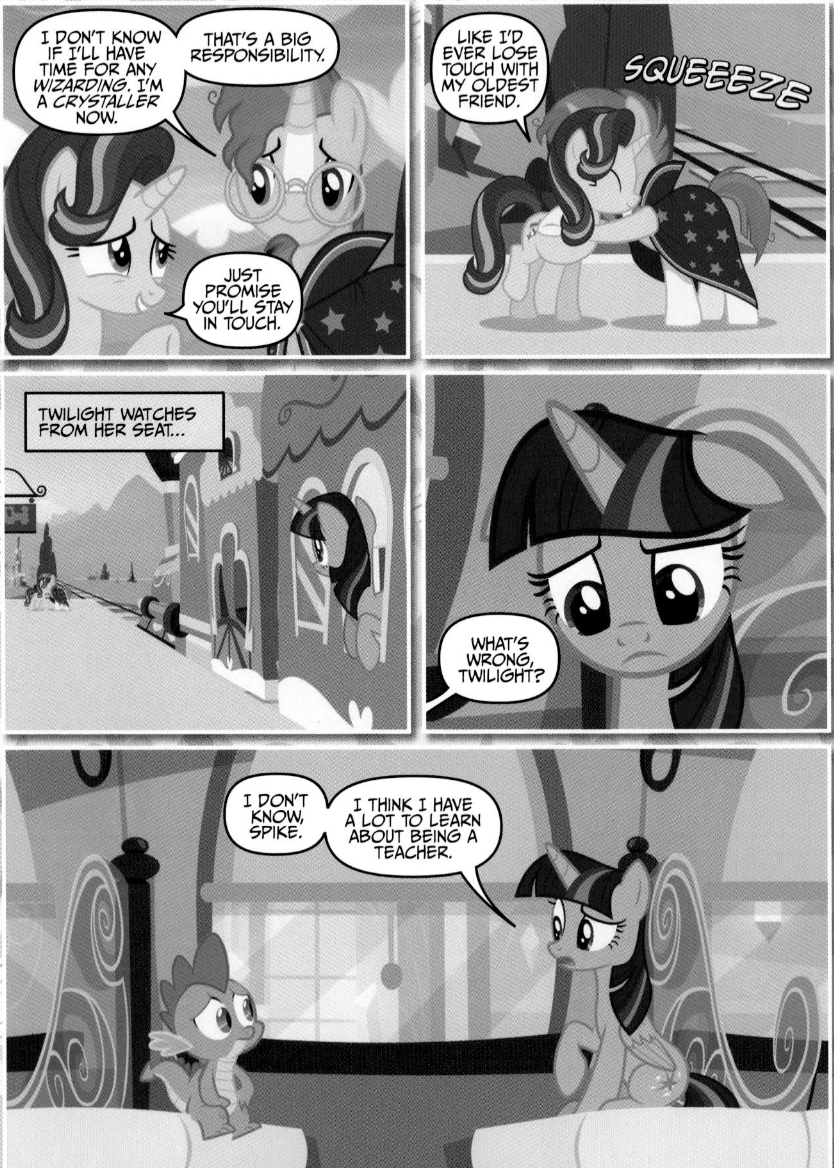
I DON'T KNOW IF I'LL HAVE TIME FOR ANY WIZARDING. I'M A CRYSTALLER NOW.
THAT'S A BIG RESPONSIBILITY.
JUST PROMISE YOU'LL STAY IN TOUCH.
LIKE I'D EVER LOSE TOUCH WITH MY OLDEST FRIEND.
SQUEEEEZE
TWILIGHT WATCHES FROM HER SEAT...
WHAT'S WRONG, TWILIGHT?
I DON'T KNOW, SPIKE.
I THINK I HAVE A LOT TO LEARN ABOUT BEING A TEACHER.

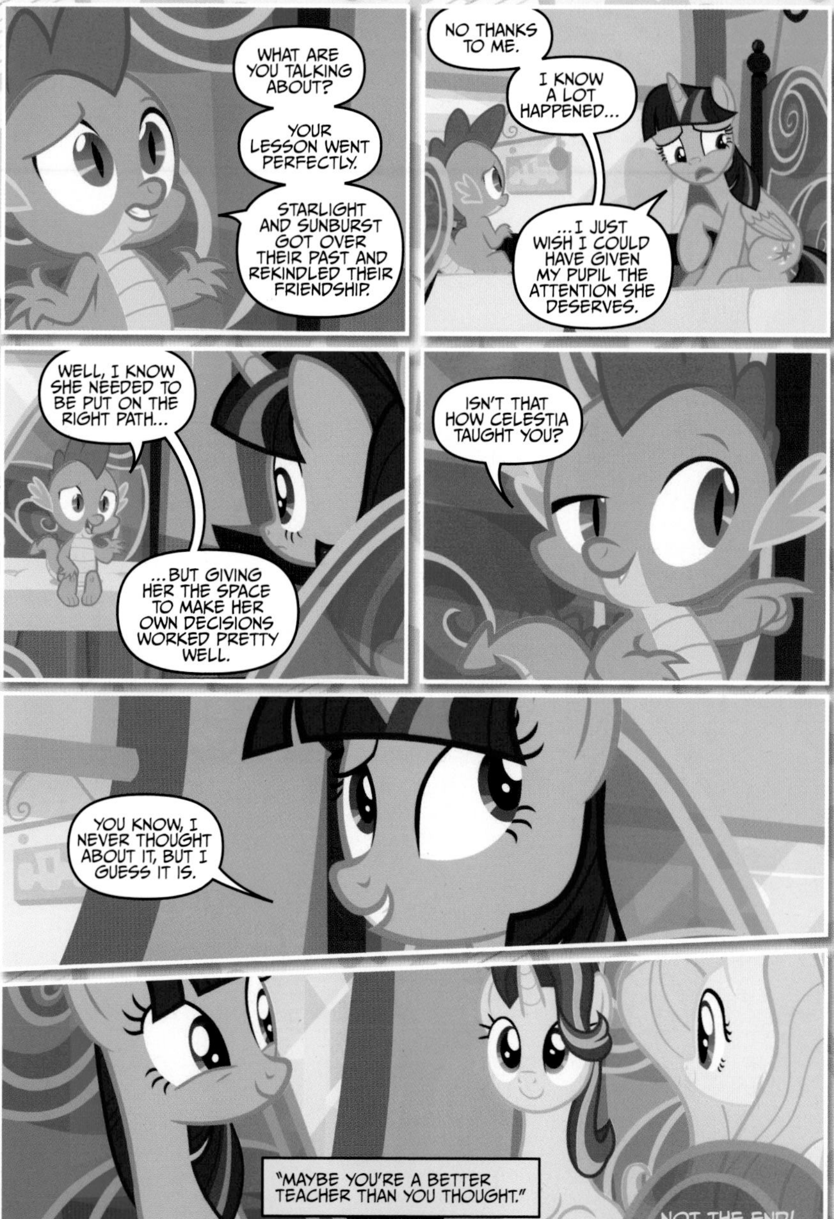
WHAT ARE YOU TALKING ABOUT?
YOUR LESSON WENT PERFECTLY.
STARLIGHT AND SUNBURST GOT OVER THEIR PAST AND REKINDLED THEIR FRIENDSHIP.
NO THANKS TO ME.
I KNOW A LOT HAPPENED...
...I JUST WISH I COULD HAVE GIVEN MY PUPIL THE ATTENTION SHE DESERVES.
WELL, I KNOW SHE NEEDED TO BE PUT ON THE RIGHT PATH...
...BUT GIVING HER THE SPACE TO MAKE HER OWN DECISIONS WORKED PRETTY WELL.
ISN'T THAT HOW CELESTIA TAUGHT YOU?
YOU KNOW, I NEVER THOUGHT ABOUT IT, BUT I GUESS IT IS.
"MAYBE YOU'RE A BETTER TEACHER THAN YOU THOUGHT."
NOT THE END!

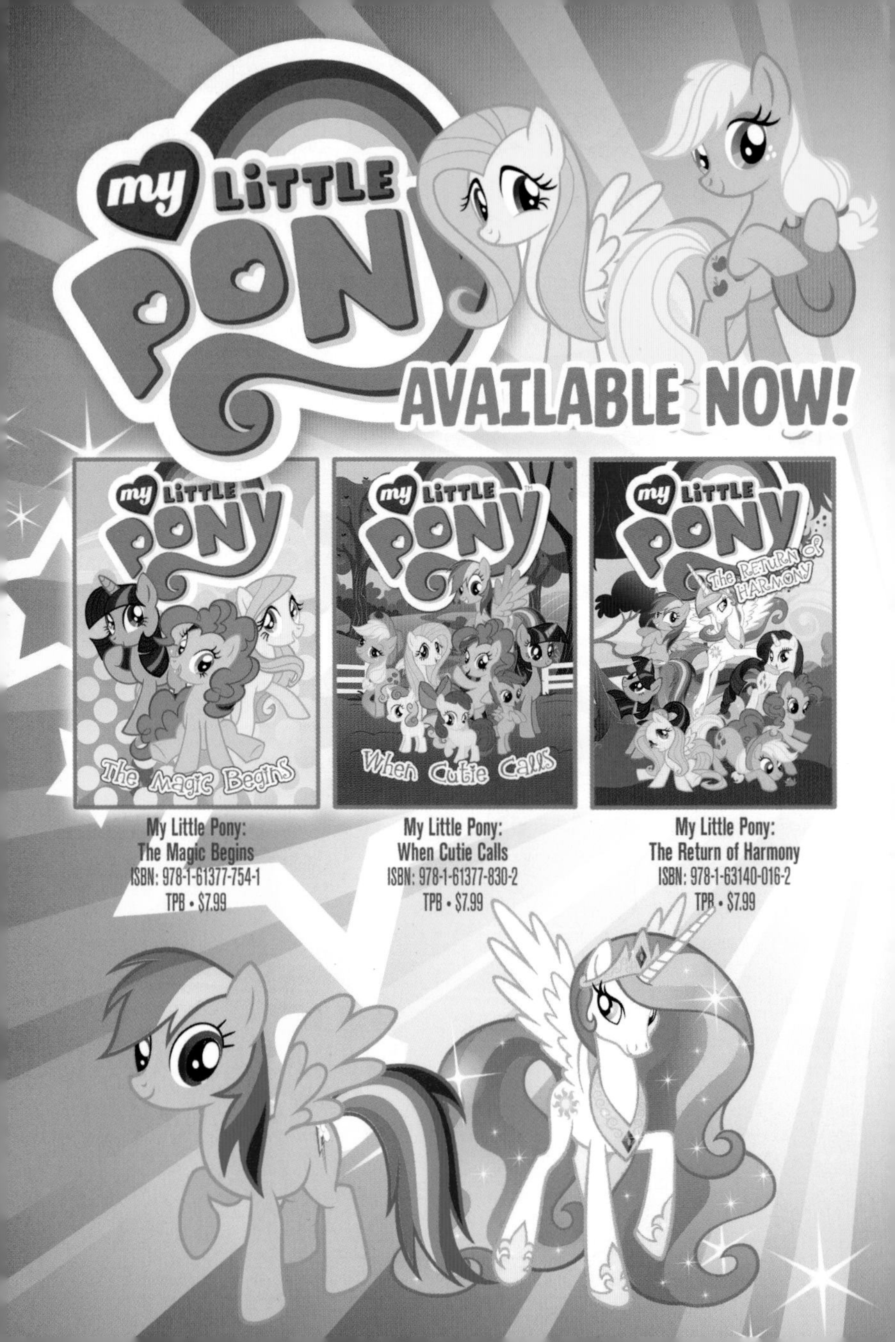
my LITTLE PONY
AVAILABLE NOW!
My Little Pony: The Magic Begins
ISBN: 978-1-61377-754-1
TPB • $7.99
My Little Pony: When Cutie Calls
ISBN: 978-1-61377-830-2
TPB • $7.99
My Little Pony: The Return of Harmony
ISBN: 978-1-63140-016-2
TPB • $7.99

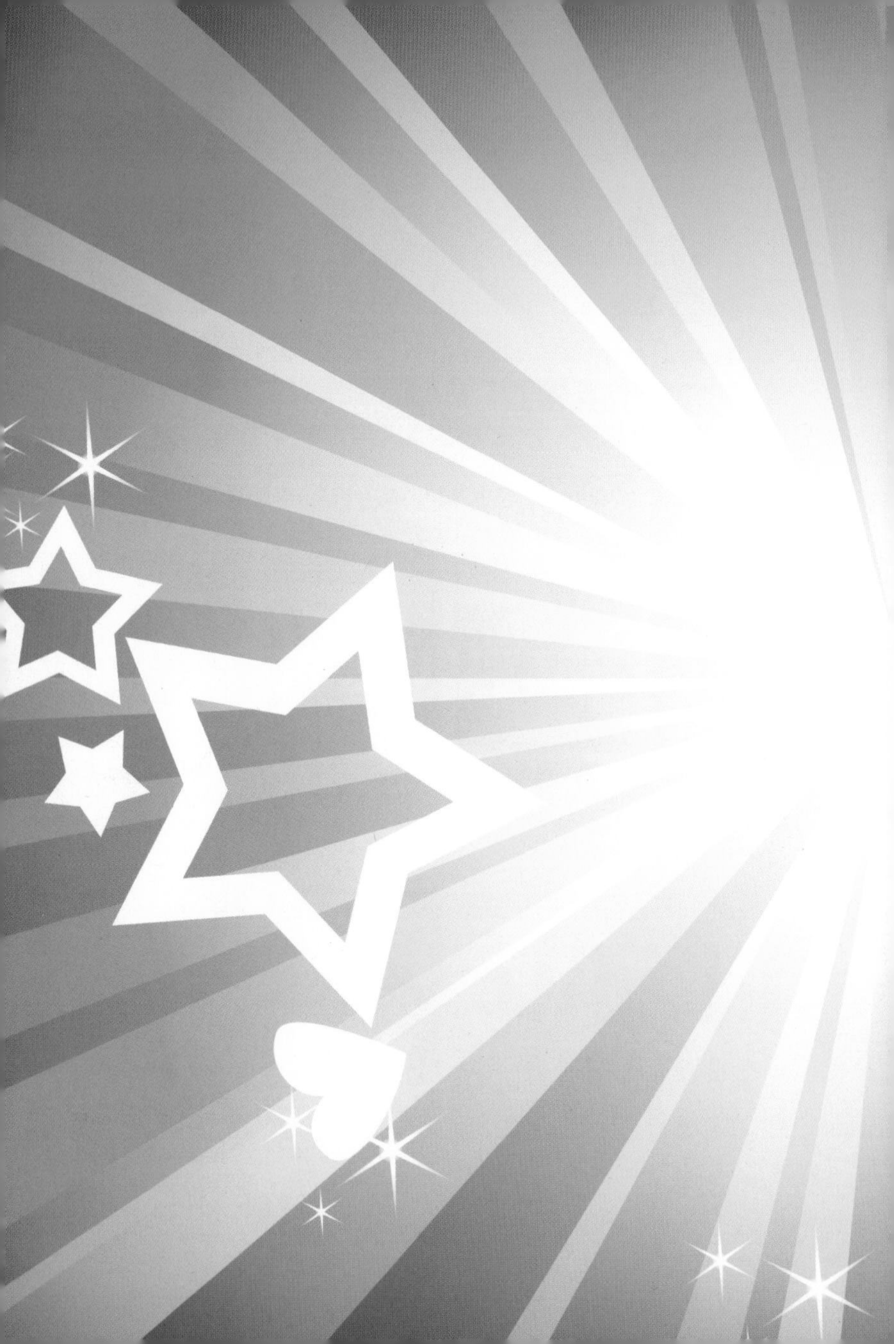

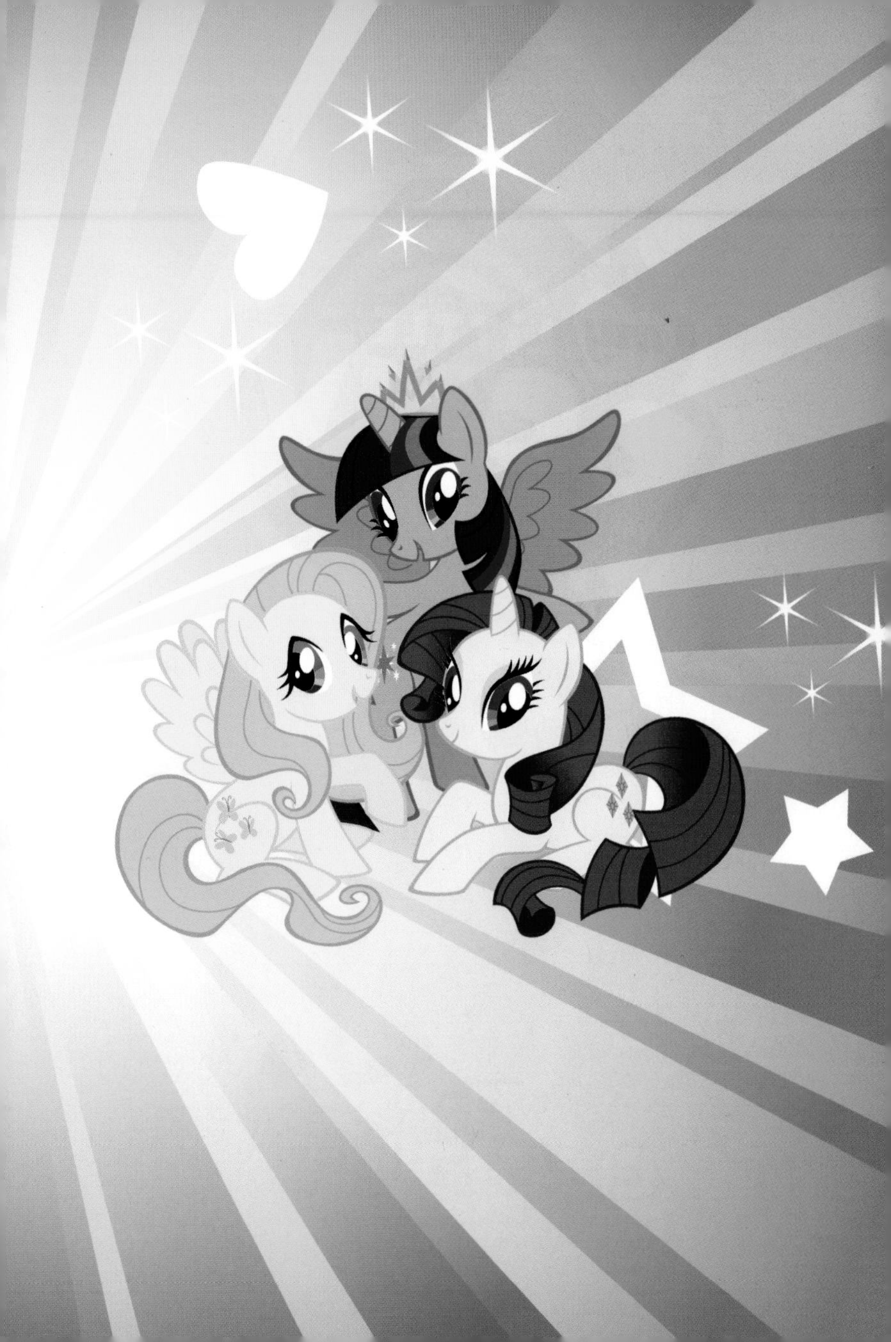

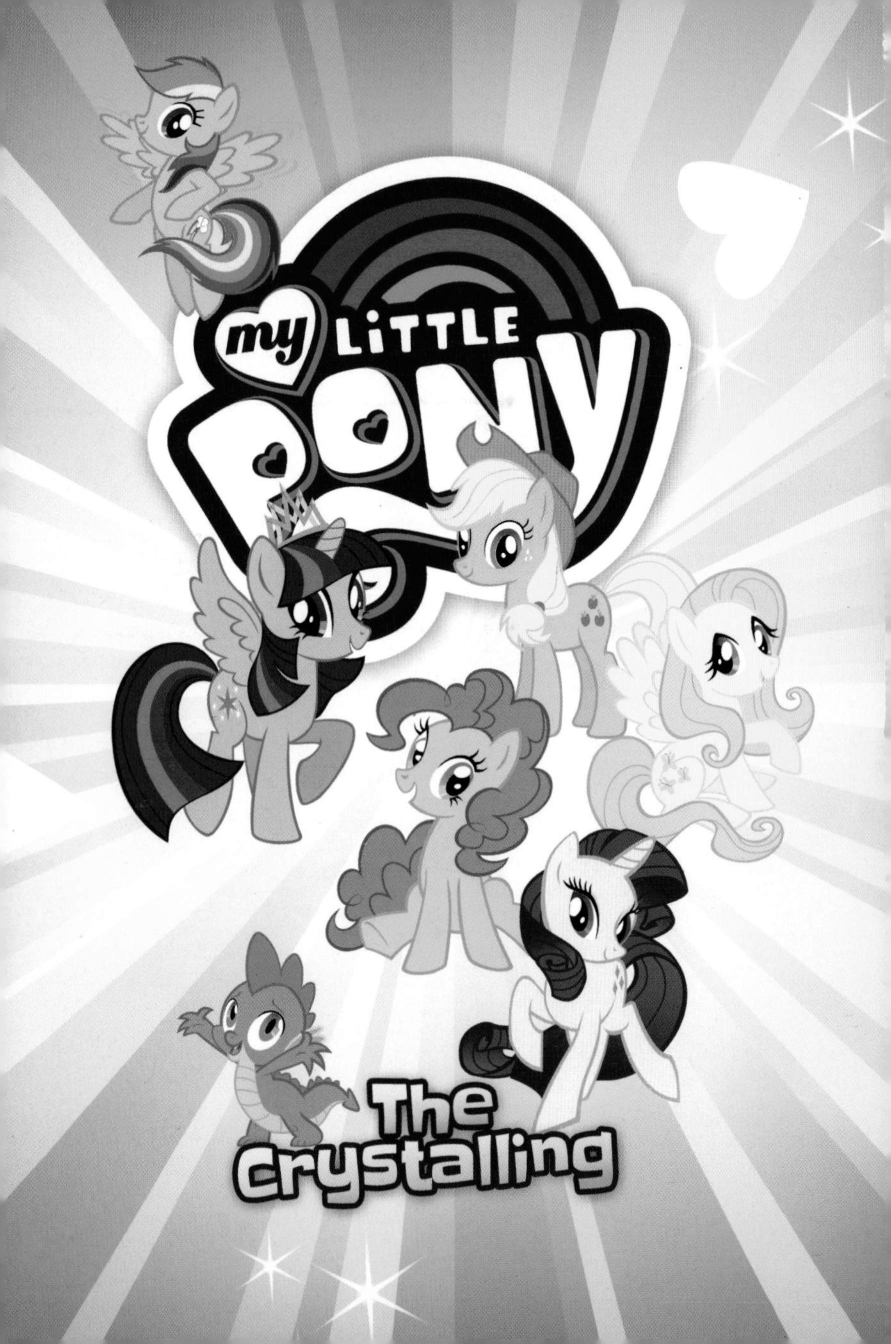
my LITTLE PONY
The Crystalling